Edward Thomson

Life of Edward Thomson, D.D., LL.D. : late a bishop of the Methodist Episcopal Church

Edward Thomson

Life of Edward Thomson, D.D., LL.D. : late a bishop of the Methodist Episcopal Church

ISBN/EAN: 9783337260903

Printed in Europe, USA, Canada, Australia, Japan

Cover: Foto ©Raphael Reischuk / pixelio.de

More available books at **www.hansebooks.com**

LIFE

OF

EDWARD THOMSON, D.D., LL.D.,

Late a Bishop of the Methodist Episcopal Church.

BY HIS SON

REV. EDWARD·THOMSON, M. A.

———————

CINCINNATI: CRANSTON & STOWE.
NEW YORK: PHILLIPS & HUNT.
1885.

PREFACE.

FOR over twelve years I waited for some competent person to write the life of my beloved father. Bishop Gilbert Haven, one of his greatest admirers, intended to do it, but his unexpected and premature death prevented the consummation. My step-mother undertook the work, but had gathered together only a few materials when the voice of the Master called her to heavenly employments.

Two years ago some friends suggested the propriety of my embalming the memory of Bishop Thomson. I acknowledged that the work ought to be done, yet I deemed myself incompetent for such an undertaking. All who consider the subject will see that it is a very delicate matter for a son to write "the life" of his father, even though he may be possessed of more facts worthy of record than any other living person; and after undertaking this work, I shrank from it time and again. What my heart wanted to utter I could not say, fearing it would be regarded as too eulogistic.

To prevent the raising of such an objection to the book, I have aimed to do three things:

First. To avoid extravagant panegyric, to hold my pen from rhetorical display, and to make a simple, brief, and clear statement of facts.

Secondly. I have made my estimates of Bishop Thomson's excellencies after having learned what others thought of him, and have advanced no opinion which has not been sanctioned by good authority, and in many instances I have quoted the language of those most competent to judge.

Thirdly. Instead of reporting my own belief only as to my father's sentiments on various questions, I have in most instances given his own words, as found in his published and unissued works.

I ought perhaps to have omitted from the letters which appear in this volume all reference to myself, but a friend, in whose judgment I have confidence, insisted that they should not be mutilated, since they exhibited so beautifully the father's love for his child. Therefore, I have omitted only the opening or closing of the letters to avoid too much repetition, and occasionally have left out a statement of purely personal character, which could be of no possible interest to the public.

I take pleasure in acknowledging my obligations to various persons who have assisted me in collecting materials for this work, whose names are mentioned in connection with the favors extended; but I must especially mention the great kindness of my old college mate and my father's former pupil, in preparing the able chapter with which we close the volume.

E. T.

M. E. College of Nebraska,
  York, Neb., March, 1885. }

CONTENTS.

CHAPTER I.

BOYHOOD.

CHAPTER II.

EARLY MANHOOD.

CHAPTER III.

FIRST CIRCUIT.

CHAPTER IV.

FIRST YEARS IN THE MINISTRY.

CHAPTER V.

AT NORWALK SEMINARY.

CHAPTER VI.

EDITOR AND COLLEGE PRESIDENT.

CHAPTER VII.

CONFERENCE RECORD.

CHAPTER VIII.

ANTI-SLAVERY SENTIMENTS.

CHAPTER IX.

A EUROPEAN TRAVELER.

CHAPTER X.

SECOND EUROPEAN TRIP.

CHAPTER XI.

IN DELAWARE AND NEW YORK.

CHAPTER XII.

LETTERS FROM NEW YORK.

CHAPTER XIII.

DEATH OF MRS. THOMSON.

CHAPTER XIV.

AS A BISHOP.

CHAPTER XV.

HIS ORIENTAL TOUR.

CHAPTER XVI.

WORK IN THE SOUTH.

CHAPTER XVII.

WORK ON THE PACIFIC COAST.

CHAPTER XVIII.

AMONG THE CONFERENCES.

CHAPTER XIX.

THE BISHOP'S LAST CONFERENCE.

CHAPTER XX.

CLOSING SCENES OF HIS LIFE.

CHAPTER XXI.

CHARACTER AND TRAITS.

CHAPTER XXII.

" Here was a unique blending of the strong and the gentle, the mystical and the practical, the dreamer and the thinker, the speaker and the writer."   JAMES M. BUCKLEY.

The ranks thin below, but thicken above.   The Master does not require long service for everlasting rewards.   Among the multitudes that gather at His feet, none will gaze with more devout delight upon that divine countenance, none sink in more adoring awe, none rise in more rapt and unutterable peace.   GILBERT HAVEN.

Like the morning star's, his spirit's course was steadily upward, still glowing with its own peculiar effulgence, till lost in the glories of the opening day.   In the fullness of his activities, with body, mind, and heart all occupied in the Lord's work, without protracted sickness, feebleness or suffering, he laid him down to die.   The Master said, "It is enough," and he passed at once from labor to recompense.   DANIEL CURRY.

THE LIFE

OF

BISHOP THOMSON.

CHAPTER I.

BOYHOOD.

EDWARD THOMSON, the subject of this biography, was born on Friday, October 12, 1810. His parents were Benjamin and Eliza (Moore) Thomson. He was the fourth of thirteen children, of whom seven were boys. Four children died in childhood or infancy. Three sons and two daughters are still living,—James Thomson, of Princeton, Illinois; Benjamin Thomson, a farmer, near Malcolm, Iowa; Henry A. Thomson, a farmer, near Topeka, Kansas; Mrs. Matilda McGugin, of Ironton, Ohio; and Mrs. Selina Richmond, of Dover, Illinois.

His father was reared in the Baptist faith. His mother was a devout adherent to the Church of England; but after her marriage, that there might be no schism in the family, and desiring that the children might be brought up in one faith, she dissolved her connection with the Church of her childhood, and became a Dissenter with her husband. Benjamin Thomson was a kind-hearted husband and a generous friend. He was always good-natured, and ready to aid any who might seek his assistance. His wife had received as elaborate a culture as was afforded to women at that time in England. Her mother died when she was a babe; but her father had her trained under the best instructors that could be found in the realm.

When Edward was born the family lived in a large brick house, on the corner of Queen Street and Southampton Row, in what was then called Portsea, a suburban town of Portsmouth, England, a bridge connecting it with that city. From the windows of the upper story of this house Edward saw the ships of every nation sailing in and out of that important English port; and over the waters he could view Gosport, Newport, Cowes, Spithead, and the Isle of Wight, "that beautiful gem, that looks like the last of earth or the first of heaven." Green fields were seen in all these localities, and the landscape was most enchanting, looking like a picture in the sky.

Portsmouth is, perhaps, the most historic city on the southern coast of England. Here are old fortresses, erected mainly by the Romans. The castle was built partly in the reign of Claudius, and partly in that of Vespasian. The dock-yard was used by Carusius in 286 A. D. After the defeat of Waterloo, Napoleon I, being forced to abdicate the throne of France, and unable to escape to America, surrendered to Captain Maitland, the commander of the English man-of-war *Bellerophon.* This vessel lay several days in the harbor of Portsmouth, while the English Parliament was determining what to do with the great enemy of Europe, whom all the crowned heads feared more than the tempest or the pestilence. Edward, then five years old, saw the great warrior, with his gray coat and cocked hat, pacing the deck from day to day, and one afternoon, going on board with his father and a few others, who were acquainted with Captain Maitland, was introduced to that greatest of all Frenchmen.

In 1817 his father, Benjamin Thomson, who had been carrying on a large retail trade in dry goods for a number of years, concluded to remove with his family to another country. His ample fortune had been largely depleted by going security for his friends. He was one of those men who could never say "No" to a relative or intimate acquaintance. Thus, in the course of years, he was obliged to pay large sums of money on account of the reckless business speculations of others, to whom he sustained the relation of surety; and he wisely decided to go some place where his friends would not be continually seeking his financial assistance. Accordingly, he moved to the south of France.

He was delighted with the climate and confident concerning the political prospects of the land. He could see before him a most enviable opening for business, but could not persuade himself, strong Protestant as he was, to raise his children in a Catholic country. Hence, on April 28, 1818, he sailed with his family, consisting of his wife, his daughters Jane and Elizabeth, and his sons James, Edward, and Benjamin, from Havre de Grace for New York.

After tarrying a few weeks in New York, Philadelphia, and Pittsburg, and thoroughly considering the matter of location, he crossed the Alleghany

Mountains in the Fall of the same year, and made a permanent home for his family in Wooster, Ohio. This town is the county seat of Wayne County, and at that time it contained but a few hundred people. Situated among hills of moderate altitude, which were covered to their summits with noble forests, and watered by a placid stream whose banks were shaded with lofty trees and pendant vines, it was a charming and romantic home for the early settlers.

But, in the midst of all this, they were forced to endure many trials and disadvantages, which are not incident to early settlements of new States and Territories at the present day. The intercommunication now is greatly facilitated by steam, on railroads, rivers, and canals, and the benefits of civilization, education, science, and arts are more rapidly disseminated than in former years. The serious want of roads was a matter which subjected the growing population to many discomforts. Communication was had with available markets only by teams, over mud roads. Up to 1823 only a few harbors had been opened along the southern shore of Lake Erie, and to those points the farmers and merchants within a radius of seventy to one hundred miles in the interior transported their produce by wagons, and brought return loads of goods and merchandise. This long wagon transportation greatly decreased the value of home products, and increased the price of articles of merchandise and consumption. Wheat, which would sell at port on Lake Erie at 60 or 70 cents a bushel, would generally cost from 25 to 30 cents a bushel to transport by wagons, so as to leave only from 30 to 45 cents for the home value. Merchandise was regularly wagoned from Baltimore and Philadelphia over the Alleghany Mountains, in Pennsylvania, by six and eight horse teams, at a cost of ten dollars a hundred pounds.

The completion of the Erie Canal through the State of New York, and of the Ohio Canal from Cleveland to Portsmouth, connecting the lake with the Ohio River, relieved the people from some of these disadvantages. Facilities which were then thought very fine were opened, and access by canal to Northern, Eastern, and Southern markets was offered. Journeys and pleasure excursions were then made in canal palaces, at the rate of four miles an hour, and canal freights were transported at the slow speed of twenty-five or thirty miles in twenty-four hours. Stage-coaches on most of the public highways seemed to be the successful rivals of canal travel; yet the merchants were fortunate if by these public carriers they accomplished their annual visits to Eastern cities after merchandise in less than three or four weeks.

When Benjamin Thomson arrived at Wooster he purchased lots and erected a building, a part of which he occupied as a residence, using the other part for the drug business, in which he was quite successful. After his death, which occurred in 1834, at the age of sixty-two, his wife and younger children continued the business for a number of years, at the old stand.

Among the inhabitants of this village were several families of intelligence and refinement, and there was a demand among them for the best of schools. Teachers who had been educated in European schools and in the best colleges of the Eastern States occasionally came West, and taught private schools. The oldest boys, James and Edward, were soon sent to the best masters that could be found. They were taught the common branches by a Mr. Whitehead, and the languages and higher mathematics by the Rev. Mr. Irvin.

Edward immediately manifested a fondness for study, and Mr. Whitehead is reported to have said that he was the best scholar in the school. Mr. Irvin said: " Edward Thomson has a fine texture of brain, and I predict for him a brilliant future, no matter what profession he may enter." He was very energetic, persevering, and industrious, always employing his time in some useful manner. He never had any fondness for games or plays of any kind. Books were his delight. Indeed, he did not take enough bodily exercise to develop a very strong physique. Yet he was always happy in disposition, and sometimes would join in a merry ramble with his playmates ; and when he did, he was as bright and cheerful as any of the company, as is evident from his recorded recollections of those days.

" My mind rushes back," he wrote, " to my earlier and better days—to the scenes of my youthful gambols; the school-house on the village green; the church where we held our moot-court and rude debate; the old haw-tree, through whose branches, on the Summer eve, the noisy prattle and loud laugh of joyous innocence rose up to heaven; the winding banks of the Kilbuck, on which, with our sisters, we gathered walnuts and crab-apples and plums; the spring, three miles in the woods, from which the friend of my better days brought clear, cold draughts, in the depths of Winter, to cool my parched tongue, when he thought I was dying; the sugar-camp, where

we stole sweet kisses from rosy lips, which we shall
see no more till we look for them in the choirs of the
upper sanctuary; and the old grave-yard, without a
vault or a monument, where we read on plain head-
stones the names of the loved ones that we buried
and the simple 'annals of the poor.' "

CHAPTER II.

EARLY MANHOOD.

BENJAMIN THOMSON determined to educate one of his boys for the medical profession, and, entertaining English ideas about primogeniture, offered the opportunity first to his eldest son. But James preferred business to professional life, and cheerfully gave up his chance to his brother Edward, who, thirsting for knowledge, readily accepted a proposition that would enable him to secure a thorough education. He accordingly went to Philadelphia in the Fall of 1828, and entered the Jefferson Medical College. This institution was then regarded as the finest school of the kind in the land.

The future bishop was at this time a sedate and mature-looking youth, who usually was thought to be twenty-two or twenty-three years old; and there was, indeed, a mental growth far beyond one of his years, that spoke from the pensive brow and thoughtful eyes. The elaborate notes which he took of the lectures he heard in the Winter of 1828–9 he copied carefully into a large blank book, which he preserved as long as he lived. He had made such progress in his medical studies and acquitted himself so well in his Spring examinations that he was granted a diploma to engage in medical practice.

He soon after returned to Ohio, and opened an

office in Jeromeville, a small town near Wooster. In a brief time he met with success in the treatment of his patients; but he was not well adapted to the practice. He possessed too sensitive a nature to enjoy surgical operations, did not even like the looks of sick people, and his sympathies were so great that he would sooner get down and pray for them than administer nauseous drugs. He was so generous that he did not charge what his services were worth, and would not collect even what he charged, unless his patients insisted on paying their debts. Nevertheless, in the course of a year he built up a paying practice. He was often called to the county seat for consultation, and to assist in surgical operations; for it was said he could use the knife most skillfully.

But he loved not these things; and God was preparing his mind for higher, nobler offices. It has often been stated that Dr. Thomson was at this time an infidel. Mr. James Thomson strongly denies this charge. He says:

"I was sorry to read in the obituary published in a New York newspaper that my brother Edward was at one time an infidel. This is too sweeping a charge, and unjust. The truth of the matter is simply this: When he commenced the study of medicine he was very young. He went to Pennsylvania, and studied with a celebrated physician, who, we learned afterward, was an avowed infidel. When my brother returned home he seemed to be blinded or befogged on the subject of religion. But my father and mother, who understood him well, had no fears of their son's ever embracing such pernicious doctrine. Knowing his investigating turn of mind, they believed that he would never entertain wrong views on any subject, especially on that of religion, but would make a thorough and prayerful investigation of the matter. The result was as they had anticipated, his firm and abiding belief in Christianity."

Dr. Thomson himself ascribes the occasion of his awakening to a sermon delivered by the Rev. Russel Bigelow, the unrivaled orator of Ohio Methodism. The young physician had been called to make a professional visit to a camp-meeting in progress three miles south of Wooster, late in the Summer of 1829. The horn blew for preaching just as he was about to leave the ground; but the urgent and polite invitation of friends in whose families he was physician constrained him to remain for one service. Three preachers sat in the stand—Adam Poe, Henry Colelazer, and Russel Bigelow. The doctor was in hope that either one of the first named would preach; for he had long dreaded the power of Bigelow's logic and the melting pathos of his appeals. But Bigelow arose. The doctor thus describes the occasion:

" All was stillness and attention when the presiding elder stepped forward. His text was, ' Come unto me, all ye that labor and are heavy laden, and I will give you rest.' As he commenced I determined to watch for his faults; but before he had closed his introduction I concluded that his words were pure and well chosen, his accents never displaced, his sentences grammatical, artistically constructed, and well arranged, both for harmony and effect; and when he entered fully upon his subject I was disposed to resign myself to the argument, and leave the speaker in the hands of more skillful critics.

"Having stated and illustrated his position clearly, he laid broad the foundation of his argument, and piled stone upon stone, hewed and polished, till he stood upon a majestic pyramid, with heaven's own light around him, pointing the astonished multitude to a brighter home beyond the sun, and bidding defiance to the enemy to move one fragment of the rock on which his feet were planted. His argument being completed, his peroration commenced. This was grand beyond description. The whole universe seemed animated by its Creator to aid him in persuading the sinner to return to God, and the angels commissioned to open heaven and come down to strengthen him.

"Now he opens the mouth of the pit, and takes us through its gloomy avenues, while the bolts retreat, aud the doors of damnation burst open, and the wail of the lost enters our ears; and now he opens heaven, transports us to the flowery plains, stands us amid the armies of the blest, to sweep, with celestial fingers, angelic harps, and join the eternal chorus, 'Worthy, worthy is the Lamb!' As he closed his discourse, every energy of body and mind was stretched to the utmost power of tension. His soul appeared too great for its tenement, and every moment ready to burst through and soar away as an eagle toward heaven. His lungs labored, his arms rose, the perspiration flowed in a steady stream upon the floor, and every thing about him seemed to say, 'Oh that my head were waters!'

"But the audience thought not of the struggling body, nor even of the giant mind within; for they were paralyzed beneath the avalanche of thought that descended upon them."

Dr. Leonard B. Gurley, who also was present, says :

"I listened with profound interest to the sermon. It was one of that great man's great discourses. In its range it swept the whole zodiac of theology. The introduction was exegetical, the body of the sermon was 'logic on fire,' and the peroration tempest, sunshine, and shower mingled together."

The effect on the mind of Dr. Thomson was such that he left the place convinced of the truth of the Bible, while his heart cried out, "O that I were a Christian." The doctor rode immediately to his office, and determined there that he would seek religion. But he had a vast amount of reading on some professional subjects which had been laid out for some months, and this would take up all the time he had at command. Yet he said to himself, "On the first day of the next year I will seek the Lord." And fearing he might forget the day thus fixed he concluded to write it in his note-book. Not finding any ink he took out his lancet, opened a vein in his own arm, and dipping his quill in the blood, wrote his determination in red letters on the page of his pocket memorandum. The time came, but he had lost the feelings of deep concern which he had when he made the bloody entry in his book. Thus he put off the period of seeking his salvation from month to month for more than two years.

Finally, on the morning of Sunday, December 11, 1831, he was reading in the Epistle of James, when he came to the words, "If any of you lack wisdom, let him ask of God, that giveth to all men liberally and upbraideth not; and it shall be given him," he fell upon his knees and asked in faith. Nor did he arise till his soul was renewed in the divine likeness. The evening of the next day he attended a class-meeting in Wooster, at the house of C. Eyster, and made a public acknowledgment of his trust in Christ. On Friday evening, the 16th, he attended a prayer-meeting in the Methodist Episcopal Church at Wooster, and when the opportunity was offered, he united with the Methodist society at that place, then served by the Rev. Henry O. Sheldon.

His union with the Methodists was very distasteful to his parents, and particularly to his father, who threatened to disinherit him for the act. Methodism in Ohio, at that time, had no fine churches or wealthy adherents, being mostly the faith of the poor and the less intelligent classes; and Benjamin Thomson felt that it was a great step downward socially and intellectually, and almost a disgrace to the family name, for one of his children, particularly the most promising of all, to ally himself with the despised people. But Edward felt, as he says in his essay "On Methodism," that "it was in these societies that the unwatchful were warned, the erring reproved, the ignorant instructed, the vicious reclaimed, the mourner comforted, the fainting encouraged, and all blessed and built up in the most holy faith; while affection cemented each to the other, and revived those scenes of primitive Christianity which made the enemies of Jesus say, 'See how these Christians love.'"

Often afterwards he said that he "joined the Methodists because they made a business of religion." Before his six months of probation expired the young doctor received a call from God to preach the Gospel.

But he told it to no one. Others, however, felt that his prayers were so spiritual, his talks in class-meeting so thoughtful, his manner of speech so impressive, that surely he must be a chosen vessel of the Lord. On one occasion Mr. Sheldon, his pastor, questioned him quite closely on the subject. And immediately thereafter this clergyman gave him a license to exhort, which bears the date April 30, 1832.

The day prior to this date he had been baptized by his pastor, by immersion, in Kilbuck Creek. For several months he retained something of the Baptist prejudice toward this mode of administering this ordinance, and also against infant baptism. But thorough investigation convinced him of his error. From this time Mr. Sheldon gave much attention to the young exhorter, and took him with him frequently in the rounds of the Wooster Circuit.

Many deprecated the association of the polished convert with this peculiar pioneer preacher. Henry O. Sheldon had many eccentricities, yet he was well posted in the history, doctrine, and usages of the Church, and was a zealous and useful minister. He was a fine penman, and for several years served the Ohio Conference as secretary. He was a wise counselor in the things of God, and could appreciate the genius and promise of the young doctor; and in after years Edward Thomson was his fast friend, and often assisted him in various ways, never forgetting the service Mr. Sheldon had rendered him as a spiritual adviser at the time when he was inquiring the way of the Lord.

CHAPTER III.

FIRST CIRCUIT.

ON July 1, 1832, Edward Thomson was licensed to preach, and recommended by the quarterly conference of Wooster Circuit, for admission on trial into the Ohio Annual Conference. Two days after receiving his license he preached his first sermon in a grove near Wooster. The effect of it was such that, at its close, sixty-five penitents presented themselves at the altar for prayers, and forty-five of them joined the Church.

Dr. Thomson now concluded that he must give up the practice of medicine and devote his whole time to the work of the ministry. As soon as this decision was announced at home his father was deeply grieved, and said, " You are very foolish to abandon the profession of medicine, for which you have been educated, and in the practice of which you have been successful, and to enter another for which you are not qualified. Heretofore I have cherished strong hopes for you, but such vacillation does not augur well for the future; but if you persist in refusing to follow the advice of your father in this matter, and are determined to be a clergyman, do not think of joining a Methodist Conference. They will put you on a large circuit. You will have hard work and poor pay, and, above all, the poorest social and literary advantages. If you feel that you can not enter the ministry of the Church in which you have been reared, go to the Presbyterians or the Episcopalians, and let your association be with a cultured denomination. Then I shall have no cause to be ashamed of you."

The doctor's mother remonstrated with her husband, and said, "Let us not say too much for fear we may be found fighting against the Lord." But Edward could go nowhere and be happy except among the Methodists, and, in after years, both his parents became reconciled to their son's action.

On the first Monday of September the young local preacher, who was now nearly twenty-two years old, started on horseback for Dayton, where the Ohio Conference was to convene on the 19th of that month.

The doctor had been, prior to his conversion, a fashionable young man, and dressed according to his rank in society. Now finger-rings, breastpins, and ruffled shirts were laid aside, and he put on the peculiar garb of a Methodist preacher—a broad-brimmed hat, round-breasted coat, and close-cut pantaloons, all of somber drab shade, with no vest, cravat, or other adornments. It was a wonderful change for him. Look at him as he dismounts at the door of the Dayton church. He is five feet six inches high, and weighs one hundred and twenty pounds. His features, however, are attractive; forehead full, dark gray eyes, nose large and straight, mouth large and lips well made, chin slightly projecting, complexion a fine brunette, with dark brown hair, neatly parted on the left side, and combed behind his ears.

At this time the Ohio Conference embraced nearly the whole of the State of Ohio, the peninsula of Michigan, and a part of Virginia. Various candidates for admission from different parts of this large field presented themselves at Dayton. Of them the following were admitted on trial: Obadiah Johnson, F. A. Timmons, L. L. Hamline, D. G. Deeter, John Kinnear, L. D. Whitney, Daniel Poe, Robert Cheney, S. G. Patterson, Joseph M. McDowell, Edward Thomson, M. Swift, E. Zimmerman, P. Sharp, David Reed, E. D. Roe, H. M. Shaffer, John Hasty, A. Dixon, W. Westlake, Hugh Dodds, George Smith, A. B. Elliot, Zachariah Games, W. P. Strickland, B. Ellis, and W. S. Thornburg.

Nearly all of this large class reached the rank of elder in four years, and some afterwards attained eminence in the Church. Most prominent of these was L. L. Hamline, who, in 1841, became editor of the *Ladies' Repository*, and, in 1844, a bishop. Dr. Thomson remained on trial in the Ohio Conference three years, and was ordained deacon in 1835. In 1837 he was ordained elder, being then a member of the Michigan Conference.

At the close of this session (1832), Bishop Emory, who presided, read out the name of Dr. Thomson in connection with Norwalk Circuit, H. O. Sheldon being senior preacher, and W. B. Christie, one of the great pulpit orators of that time, presiding elder.

The bishop's own description of his start in the itinerant life is as follows:

"Riding up to the door of my spiritual father, I awaited instructions. 'Now,' said the senior minister, 'call on ——, a merchant at N. Stay with P. all night, etc.' 'Nay, I can not take such liberties.' 'But,' responded the senior, 'the Church pays not unnecessary expenses. Moreover, if you avoid the brethren, you will be considered proud, and that will bar access to the people's hearts.' 'Well, I'll try.'" The bishop then describes himself in the third person.

" With fear and trembling, and many distracting doubts of his call to the ministry, and many depressing thoughts of his deficiencies, he rode out twenty miles through the woods, whose howling winds and falling and fading leaves were in harmony with his melancholy feelings, when he emerged into the beautiful village of N. In a hesitating manner he rode up to the door of Brother ——. Unpleasant were his feelings as he saw the merchant carelessly eying him through his store window while he hitched his horse to the post. Entering the store with all the confidence he could command, he introduced himself as the colleague of Brother S., and stated that he had called by request to present his friend's regards. Having asked and answered a few questions concerning his circuit and colleague, he seated himself in a chair by the stove, where, after he had 'mused till the fire burned,' he rose to depart. As he passed out, the merchant dryly asked him if he would stay to dinner, but the young man thanked him and said he would go a little farther. As he mounted his horse he found it difficult to dam up his tears or press down the feelings which choked him. Seated in his saddle, he said within himself, 'This is the first and last Methodist tavern I call at.' So, spurring his pony, he moved in a direct line toward a sign-post.

" On his way to it, as he passed with averted face the store of another Methodist merchant, whom he knew no better than the first, he heard a voice calling him. Turning around, he saw this merchant moving toward him, and by the time he could stop his horse, he found one hand of his new friend on the bridle-rein, and the five fingers of the other feeling for his own right hand, which was destined to a painful squeeze. 'Dismount, dismount,' said the merchant, 'no excuses.'

"Soon the young captive was ushered through the store to the parlor, and before he could be fairly seated, he saw through the back window his little bay nag trotting towards the stable. He was asked nothing about dinner except to say grace when it was ready."

This was his first day of itinerant experience, and in it he saw something of the lights and shadows of itinerant life.

His first field of labor was a large four weeks' circuit, bordering on Lake Erie, and had for its chief town Norwalk, the seat of the seminary, of which, a few years later, he became principal. The country embraced was comparatively new, and most of the religious meetings were held in school-houses and private dwellings.

The late Rev. Leonard B. Gurley writes of him at this time: "In personal appearance he was so delicate and diffident that at first sight the sympathy and fears of the people were awakened lest he should fail in his attempts to preach. But when he opened his lips, apparently without effort, beautiful thoughts clothed in golden words fell on the charmed ears of the audience. Among the preachers' homes on this circuit was the residence of my father, the Rev. William Gurley, a local elder. As he was a veteran,

who received his first license to preach from Mr.
Wesley himself in Ireland, the doctor was delighted
with his company and conversation. After hearing
Thomson preach, my father said: 'He is a small man,
but, mark my word, he will yet become a great one.'
The words were truly prophetic."

Concerning the result of his first year's ministry,
Dr. Thomson writes:

"Sometimes sweltering under a July sun, and sometimes almost frozen, I rode over the prairies. . . .
I received seventy-five dollars for my labor, and shortly
after gave a subscription of fifty dollars for the first
Methodist seminary of learning in Ohio; but I have
nothing but thanks for the kindness of my first circuit."

As to pulpit preparations, Dr. Thomson was careful from the beginning. Frequently he wrote his
sermons in full, but rarely used manuscript in the
pulpit. He always loved to write, and to him thinking
was not a task, but a pleasure. In youth he formed
habits of reflection. By this first year of intellectual
work he illustrated his own words:

"Reflection is more important than reading; as in
the physical, so in the moral world, industry must be
incorporated with our treasures to give them value.
Reflection is the mint which selects, refines, classifies,
appropriates, and stamps our knowledge, and fills the
mouth with golden words; without it knowledge is
rubbish, and study a weariness of the flesh."

He sought to cultivate the memory, the imagination, and especially the reasoning powers. He endeavored to abstract himself from surrounding objects,
that he might study more thoroughly the mysteries
of the inner world. For well he knew that "habitual

inattention to the outer world greatly promotes attention to the inner. The more we live the life of sensation, the less we do the life of reflection."

Dr. Thomson's so-called absent-mindedness, which was sometimes a cause of worry to his friends, must be attributed to this desire of his soul to study grand and glorious spiritual things rather than be attracted by the trivial incidents that were going on around him.

He was economical of time. Thus he became a scholar whose researches were extended over a wide range. He did just what he advised others to do:

"Take no more time for any object than is necessary for its accomplishment. Let the time for a given labor be fully consumed therein, while the full energies of your souls are brought to bear upon it with all the requisite advantages; such as silence, books, physical comfort. Do every thing by system. Divide the day, and assign to each duty its metes and bounds. In a life thus regulated the whole community of sciences may dwell in harmony, and derive mutual advantages from their very neighborhood. As, however, the customs of society will not allow you to make such a division with exactness, it is necessary that you acquire the habit of using fragments of time. Fortunes have been made from the shavings of horn. Time is money, and who shall duly estimate the value of its clippings?"

He was at this time, as ever after, a great reader. But he read not all books. He was as careful of his mental food as a dyspeptic of his diet. He read nothing out of curiosity, but always with a desire that he might grow better and wiser. And from his own experience he gives this advice:

"Books are indispensable for instruction, amusement, the formation of style, and the supply of mental stimulus; they must, however, be selected with caution. The press, by the power of steam, is wheeling off cart-loads every moment; yet the world, like the grave in a pestilence, stands with its mouth wide open, and cries not, It is enough. That this mass is all to be rejected, 't were madness to affirm. Much of the periodical literature of the day and many of its books are rich and instructive; but the precious must be separated from the vile, and the greater the preponderance of the latter over the former, the more difficult the task. A few hints only will be given. Old works are better than new. Old writers, like the bottles of old doctors, generally contain *multum in parvo;* but many of the mental quacks of our day compose according to the following receipt: Take of words, one hogshead; of understanding, one drop; of human depravity and coloring matter, a sufficient quantity. Mix, and filter through green or yellow paper. And although they get certificates of the clergy, on whom they practice gratuitously, it is perfectly safe to let their ' eye-waters ' alone.

"The contempt I have for the novels of the time is not indiscriminate. The pages of Sir Walter Scott, I doubt not, are enchanting, although I have never felt their power; but I have yet to learn who has been made better or wiser by their perusal, while I suppose that their tendency is the reverse of mental discipline—to relax the energies, intoxicate the reason, and fill the fancy with dreams of rapture and of anguish. It may be asked how I know their effects, never having felt them. Just as I know the properties of arsenic without ever having tasted it. What need we of the literature of a superficial and hurried age, when we have at command the works of Greece, Rome, and England, elaborated respectively in the Homeric, the Augustan, and Elizabethan periods?— above all, the oldest of all writings, which, blending philosophy and poetry in union, and affording mingled instruction and delight in forms ever varying, with ever-increasing charms, gleams at every re-perusal with new glimpses of the mind of God?"

The Bible, Milton, Shakspeare, and the classic authors were the books which he mainly read and studied at this time. And thus, as he rode over his large circuit, he coined the golden ore dug out of them into the current coin of his own mintage.

CHAPTER IV.

FIRST YEARS IN THE MINISTRY.

AT the session of the Ohio Conference held in Cincinnati in 1833, Edward Thomson was stationed at Sandusky City, then, as now, an important place on the shores of Lake Erie. Here he was thrown again into the constant society of his old friend Sheldon, who was now the presiding elder of Portland District, of which Sandusky was the leading station. In this field of labor he sustained himself so ably and his usefulness and eloquence became so well known that at the next conference, held at Circleville in 1834, he was sent to Cincinnati, where the best talent was demanded.

Joseph M. Trimble was his senior colleague. Mr. Trimble was of tall, wiry frame, classic features, and noble bearing. He was one of the finest pulpit orators of that time, a few years the senior of Thomson, both in years and in conference rank, and a valuable and inspiring associate. The intimacy which now began between these two ministers was most sweet and brotherly, and grew in depth and tenderness till death severed the tie.

Mr. Trimble rose to prominence, filling high positions in the pastorate and presiding over districts. He was for several years secretary of the Ohio Conference, and afterwards served in the same capacity in the General Conference. From 1860 to 1864 he was one of the missionary secretaries. Many years ago he became a Doctor of Divinity. He has been highly honored by the Ohio Conference, and has conferred honor upon it, having been elected by that body a delegate eleven times to the General Conference. Mr. Trimble being the preacher in charge in Cincinnati, Dr. Thomson was relieved of many cares that he had borne at Sandusky, and this gave him time to pursue again his medical studies, for which he still retained a fondness. He took a full course of lectures at the Cincinnati College of Medicine, and received the degree of M. D. from that institution. At this time the faculty was small but able. Daniel Drake was dean and professor of theory and practice; S. D. Gross, who afterwards became the most skillful surgeon of the country, was professor of anatomy; Joseph N. McDowell, of chemistry; Horatio G. Jameson, of surgery; Landon C. Rives, of obstetrics; James B. Rogers, of pharmacy; and John P. Harrison, of Materia Medica.

He never regretted the time spent in association with these men, and within the walls of that college. Though he reviewed the various systems of medicine, he was a confirmed believer in the old-school practice. In after years he permitted the practice of homeopathy in his family; yet he often laughed about it, saying, " Little pills are good for children, or for old women, when there is nothing the matter." But for himself, his favorite remedy was the " blue mass."

It was from this early and thorough study of medicine that he was led to think so much on scientific subjects, and use so many beautiful illustrations drawn from chemistry, physiology, and anatomy in his lectures and sermons.

While Dr. Thomson was in Cincinnati the presiding elder of the district was Leroy Swormstedt, one of the "sons of thunder," and one of the best business men of the Church. His superior talents as a manager of Church interests were properly esteemed when he became chief agent of the Western Methodist Book Concern.

In this metropolis of Ohio Dr. Thomson was very popular, drawing large crowds to his services; and he was appreciated by men of the world as well as by members of the Church. It was hoped that he would be returned the next year; but, his father having died a few weeks before conference, it was desired by his mother that he come to Wooster, and assist her in the administration of the estate. Hence, at his request, he was sent, at the conference in 1835, to his old home, with William Runnels, a kind-hearted, strong-minded man, as senior preacher, and Adam Poe, afterward, for many years, one of the book agents at Cincinnati, as presiding elder.

The next year (1836) the Michigan Conference was set off from the Ohio, and Edward Thomson fell into the northern division. He was stationed at Detroit, with William Herr as presiding elder. Detroit was then the capital as well as metropolis of Michigan, and the most important station in the conference. It was also a seat of fashion; and when the young minister appeared in the peculiar garb of a Methodist preacher, many of the good sisters were ashamed of him. When they heard his first sermon, their shame was turned to pride. But they determined that he should no longer be disfigured by the odd-looking coat and homely hat, and before a second Sunday they made him a present of a fine broadcloth suit, of fashionable cut, and gently suggested that they did not like the appearance of the old one. The doctor could, of course, do nothing but accept and use their present.

Here his power of oratory was displayed in its best style. He had a highly cultured auditory to please, and he rose equal to the demand. The distinguished Lewis Cass, Governor Brown, and others of intelligence and culture, were among his auditors. Here he wrote some of his best discourses, and delivered them in his best style; so that his popularity was unbounded. He had a silvery tongue, a magnetic eye, and an impassioned delivery. Sometimes he would so charm an audience as to take it apparently beyond the range of time and sense, while he drew the most brilliant pictures of the imagination, carrying his hearers to the pearly gates, through the golden streets, and seating them on the banks of the river, under the shade of the tree of life; or, with equal artistic power, he would lead them to the abodes of the lost, and ask them to listen to the groans of agony, the yells of madness, and the cries of despair. The impressions made were not merely temporary; for blessed revival influences attended his ministry.

At the conference of 1837, held at Detroit, he was reappointed to that station, and thus remained two years, at that time the limit of the pastoral term. Great was the regret of his congregation when obliged to part with him. The people of Detroit have ever since held him in the highest estimation; and the recollection of his work among them was always to him a source of pleasure.

While he was pastor here he was married, and, in the Summer of the first year, led to the parsonage his young and interesting bride. He had made the acquaintance of Maria Louisa Bartley while he was on Wooster Circuit, having been introduced to her by his presiding elder, at a camp-meeting held near Mansfield in the Summer of 1836. Miss Bartley was then a flaxen-haired, blue-eyed, laughing girl of sixteen years. Yet she was religious, and was an ardent Methodist. Her father, Hon. Mordecai Bartley, was a man of wealth and political influence. He was a Virginian by birth, and possessed an excellent English education. For eight years he had been a member of Congress, representing the Thirteenth Ohio District, which then included the large and important counties of Cuyahoga, Lorain, Medina, Huron, Seneca, Sandusky, and Richland. He was a good public speaker, and an excellent writer. His political documents were among the ablest prepared at that time in the Buckeye State. In 1842 he was elected governor of Ohio on the Whig ticket. The triumph of Mr. Bartley over his Democratic opponent was regarded as a compliment to his popularity and ability as a political manager. His son, Thomas W. Bartley, was at this time the acting governor of the State, and, although only thirty years of age, was one of the leading men of the Democratic party. Wilson Shannon, who was chosen governor at the previous election, had resigned his office to become United States minister to Brazil, and this left the gubernatorial chair to the younger

Bartley, who was speaker of the State Senate, and as such empowered to act as governor. When the inauguration of Mordecai Bartley as governor took place the son gracefully vacated the chair of State for his father.

Maria Bartley, being the youngest of the family, was the pet of all. Her childhood life was spent on a farm. When she was thirteen her father moved to Mansfield to give the younger members of the family the benefit of the school at that place. In a year's time she went through the studies as far as the classes were taken, and she was then sent to Norwalk Seminary, where she became a good scholar in higher English, French, music, painting, and drawing. Here and elsewhere she was ever after much in society and was remarkable for her sprightliness and vivacity.

At Mansfield and at Norwalk she listened to the Gospel truth as presented by such able men as Bigelow, Christie, and Adam Poe, and before she was fifteen years old she was led to Christ, and united with the Methodist Church. Within a year thereafter she was instrumental in bringing her father, mother, and other members of the family into the Church.

On July 4, 1837, she was married to Dr. Thomson. She knew what she was likely to undergo in consenting to become the wife of a Methodist preacher; yet, after fully counting the cost, she freely gave herself up to the itinerancy, with all its toils and privations. Nor did she ever regret making this choice, but with a true Christian spirit cheerfully endured all for Christ's sake. Her pleasant face, attractive manners, intelligence, culture, and social standing were of great help to her husband in his early ministry.

CHAPTER V.

AT NORWALK SEMINARY.

AT the Conference of 1838, held in Tiffin, Ohio, Edward Thomson was appointed principal of Norwalk Seminary. Here he began his literary career and his work as an educator, for which he seems to have been especially fitted by nature and by grace, and in which he was destined to achieve such brilliant success. Some of his friends felt that he ought not to leave the pastorate, and that he was not qualified for the place, since he had never been a teacher of youth. He, however, entered upon the duties of the position with a modest, yet cheerful, confidence in his ability to achieve success.

He knew, perhaps, better than any one else what he lacked of the requisite qualifications, and applied himself diligently to the study of those branches of learning with which he was not sufficiently familiar; and with his close thought, quick perception, retentive memory, and untiring application he became well rounded in all the departments of scholastic knowledge. And thus he pursued his studies, ever adding to his stock of literary and scientific acquisitions, and never forgetting what he learned. He made himself proficient in belles-lettres and psychology, two departments in which he was specially interested; but whatever he studied he mastered.

He was an attentive reader of history, and wherever he traveled in after years he called up with pleasure and with ease the various associations of places and of men and the incidents connected with them. When he was at the great city of the Turks his mind reviewed its entire history. Thus he writes:

"What a crowd of historical associations arise as we survey Constantinople, the Byzantine, Roman, and Latin empires, of which it has successively been the seat; the councils of the Church held within its walls; the earthquake which, in the fifth century, shook its foundations; the plague which, in the ninth, swept away three hundred thousand of its inhabitants; the storming of its gates in the fifteenth, which transferred it to the Turks; and the eagerness with which it has been watched and the zeal with which it has been fought over in later years by the great nations of the earth! Its very name brings before us one of the greatest characters of history, who reared the Cross over the Roman legions, and constructed a government and court that have been the model for all modern European monarchies."

It was late in the Autumn of 1838 that Dr. Thomson went to Norwalk. Alexander Nelson, afterwards a traveling preacher, and now an honored member of the North Ohio Conference, worthily bearing the title of Doctor of Divinity, accompanied him as assistant teacher. To Dr. Nelson the author is indebted for many facts, hereafter stated, relative to the seminary.

The opening of the school had been delayed because the new building was not ready for occupancy. From 1833 to 1836 a school, called the Norwalk Seminary, had been kept here under the principalship of Rev. Jonathan E. Chaplin, a gentleman of fine parts, who for several years had been a member of the bar, but was then a minister and an educator. He was aided by a select number of competent teachers, and good, efficient work was done during those years. But on the night of the 26th of February, 1836, the building in which the classes met for instruction took fire and was reduced to ashes, including school books, library, and apparatus. The loss was three thousand dollars, and there was no insurance. This was a severe blow to the institution, as it had no endowment, and it was considered doubtful whether an edifice of sufficient dimensions and such as the times demanded, could now be erected. But the friends of education thought it too great an enterprise to be allowed to fail without proper effort to rebuild. Hence with commendable zeal the work was undertaken and in due time accomplished.

The new building was forty by eighty feet, three stories high. The two sections on the lower floor contained each a school-room and two recitation-rooms. In the second story were two large rooms, one for chapel purposes, the other for the ladies' classes. The third story was divided into dormitories.

When the new teachers arrived the seminary building was only inclosed; hence the school term had to be opened in a private dwelling. The pupils at first were twenty or twenty-five boys from the village of Norwalk. In the course of two months the school-room in the west wing and two recitation-rooms were finished and furnished, and the school was transferred to the new building. By the end of the year the entire edifice was completed and occupied. In the Autumn of 1839 the ladies' department was opened with Mrs. A. Nelson as preceptress, and Miss A. E. Morrison, her sister, as assistant—ladies of superior qualifications, who had had experience in teaching in the Eastern States.

The seminary, which had been increasing in numbers and popularity, now took advanced ground, and became more generally known and patronized. The Catalogue of 1842 sums up the number of 265 male and 126 female students, making the total number for the year 391. The departments of teaching at first took a wide range, all the branches of study being attended to by the two first instructors. But afterwards, as teachers were added, the number of classes to each was reduced. Hence, at first, Dr. Thomson's department was belles-lettres, physics, and Latin; Mr. Nelson's was mathematics, natural science, and Greek. Thomas J. Pope, an advanced scholar, subsequently a member of the North Ohio Conference, was engaged to teach some classes, and afterwards James Mitchell, an adept in mathematics, was employed, and E. W. Done was made assistant in the lower English branches. H. S. Bradley was soon secured to occupy the east room on the lower floor. He subsequently entered the ministry, and rose to great usefulness in the Central Ohio Conference. A Mr. Sayre, a graduate of Kenyon College, was employed, but after a few months he took a fever and died. Then a Mr. Olney, a graduate of the Ohio University, at Athens, Ohio, was engaged. After a short time he resigned, to prepare himself for the ministry at Lane Seminary, Cincinnati; but he died before he was able to enter upon his ministerial duties. Shortly after this, Rev. Holden Dwight and lady, Eastern teachers, came to Norwalk, and were added to the teaching force at the seminary.

In the Fall of 1842 Mr. Nelson and wife received an urgent call from the trustees of Worthington Female Seminary to come and take charge of that institution, which was under the supervision of the Ohio Conference. After due deliberation, they accepted the invitation, tendered their resignation to the trustees of Norwalk Seminary, and their connection with the latter was dissolved. In after years Mr. Nelson entered the ministry, and became a popular pastor on the most important stations. He was twice a delegate to the General Conference, and wherever he was placed was a useful instrument in the hands of God. Holden Dwight and wife took the places of Mr. and Mrs. Nelson when they departed for Worthington. For a few months Mrs. Thomson, the wife of the principal, acted as preceptress and teacher of French.

The trustees at this time were Timothy Baker, Platt Benedict, A. E. Sutton, D. Squire, Thos. Dunn, and Walter Osburn. Tuition in the primary department was $2.00 a quarter; higher English, $4.00; mathematics, $5.00; Latin and Greek, $5.00; French, Spanish, and Italian, $5.00; ornamental branches, $5.00; music on piano, $10.00.

A historical and geological society was established in April, 1842, with A. Nelson, president, and H. Dwight, secretary. A literary association, known as the "Athenian Society," was formed among the students, and for a series of years was continued with great profit to those who took part in its exercises. Among those who composed it we find the names of L. A. Hine, L. B. Otis, W. H. Hopkins, and others who subsequently made their mark upon the world as men of mind and worth.

In 1840 the North Ohio Conference was organized, and Edward Thomson was elected its first secretary. He was well qualified for such a position. Accurate, careful, and an excellent penman, all his minutes were well kept. He held the place four years, and then declined a re-election.

In 1842 the Ohio Wesleyan University was chartered by the Legislature, and was located in Delaware, near the center of the State. At the first meeting for business of the Board of Trustees Dr. Thomson was elected president of the institution. But as nothing was contemplated for the present except a preparatory school, the services of the doctor were not immediately required; hence he continued as principal at Norwalk for a time longer.

The finances of the seminary were at this time in a bad condition. The debts of the old building, together with those of the new, became so oppressive that the minds of the trustees were filled with apprehension. For the purpose of aiding the trustees to meet their pressing demands, a society was organized in the Autumn of 1842, known as the Norwalk Education Society, the object of which was to raise funds for the liquidation of the debt of the seminary. Rev. Adam Poe was elected president, and other officers and agents were appointed. But the funds came in tardily and in small amounts, and the debts still remained, growing more and more burdensome.

In the Fall of 1843 the North Ohio Conference elected its first delegates to the General Conference, and Edward Thomson, the youngest member of the delegation, was the first chosen. The other delegates were elected in this order: John H. Power, Adam Poe, Elmore Yocum, and William Runnells; reserve delegates, H. M. Shaffer and L. B. Gurley.

The attachment of Dr. Thomson to Ohio and to his conference was very decided. It is, perhaps, not generally known that two very tempting offers were made him while at Norwalk, either of which, if accepted, would have deprived the Ohio Conference of his inestimable services. Transylvania University and the State University of Michigan both invited him to fill the highest chairs they had to offer; namely, the presidency of the former and the chancellor's position in the latter. His salary at Norwalk at that time was but six hundred dollars, while either of the places offered would have given two or three times that sum at least. Dr. L. B. Gurley says:

"I was his near neighbor at Norwalk and his presiding elder. He showed me the first invitation, and asked my advice. I referred to the condition of the South. The slave question was then being agitated. I dreaded the influence of a residence in a slave State, and urged him to give a prompt refusal, which he did. The proposal from Michigan came not long after. He was very much inclined to accept; but the General Conference was to meet in the following May, and I advised him to wait until it was over, and to say that, unless the General Conference disposed of his services otherwise, he would accept."

At the General Conference of 1844, L. L. Hamline, editor of the *Ladies' Repository*, was elected one of the bishops of the Church, and the friends of Dr.

Thomson in the delegation from the North Ohio Conference immediately put him in nomination for the chair which was thus vacated. The doctor was already known as a good writer. He had contributed articles to the Church periodicals, and one or two of his addresses had been printed and circulated in pamphlet form. In the East he was then but little known; but as he was named for the editorship by Ohio delegates, and Ohio was then as now strong in strong men, Dr. Thomson was elected.

At the close of the academic year he tendered his resignation of the principalship, with great regret on the part of all. A gentleman of Norwalk, well versed in all matters pertaining to educational interests, and especially to Norwalk Seminary, speaking of Dr. Thomson, says: "He was a man of fine literary attainments, of ripe scholarship, of pleasing address, of refined and gentlemanly manners, and of purity of life and character." Referring to this opinion, Dr. A. Nelson says: "He also might have added, for management of scholars and power over youth, exercised with prudence and skill, he was rarely ever equaled, and never excelled."

The Rev. John Burgess, M. D., of Keokuk, Iowa, furnishes a description of the doctor at Norwalk:

"In 1839 I entered the Norwalk Seminary in Huron County, Ohio, under the presidency of Dr. Edward Thomson. Never can I forget the noble reception and kindly welcome I received, when I handed him a letter from my father, committing me to his special care. No parent could have shown more interest for my physical, intellectual, and spiritual advancement than did he during all the time of my attendance at school. He and his amiable wife cordially received me at their house and to their table. The doctor, in addition to all my regular class advantages, took me under his private instruction, and at extra hours heard me recite to him; so that, at a much earlier date, he advanced me to higher classes than I otherwise would have reached. Never did I know any person more attentive to the welfare and progress of all his students.

"During these years, as he influenced hundreds of youthful minds, his own intellect was visibly expanding, and all seemed to see him rise in his mental powers toward the heights he afterward attained. He was a fluent and mighty writer, and an unsurpassed, if ever equaled, governor and instructor of the young. At times the doctor, in his ardent search after knowledge—for he was always a diligent student—appeared so engrossed that it was intimated by some he would eventually lose his mind. At times when pursuing a thought, or, as he once remarked, 'adding thought to thought,' he would apparently forget almost every thing else. We give two or three instances. Once our class in Latin was reciting. Each of us five had read and interpreted his part. When the last had finished we were all in silence, perhaps for five minutes. The long pause seemed heavy to us; then, all at once, the doctor lifted his eyes, and said : 'Gentlemen, why do you not proceed? Whose turn is next?' We all replied that we had gone through with our parts. He smilingly said : 'O, excuse me, gentlemen ; I was following the writer's thoughts. Please read it over.' We all, with him, had a merry laugh over the matter. At another time, after we had recited to him in his private room, as our hour was from 11 A. M. to 12 M., the bell began ringing for noon; and then, without his saying to us, as was his custom, 'You may retire, gentlemen,' he rose up, took his hat, walked to the door, passed out, turned the key, and left us in the study—so intensely was he engaged in pursuing the subject of his thoughts. His excellent wife was often amused at his mental abstractions, from his incessant application and deep searchings after knowledge. He was exceedingly prompt and exact to pay all his little debts; so, as he passed from the seminary to his home, on one occasion, he saw a farmer passing, whom he owed for a load of hay, and he hastened to get his money and go back and settle the debt. He went into his house, and opened the bureau where he kept his purse; then, taking it out, he carefully placed his hat in the drawer, and with the purse in his hand went to the door, and out on the step, where, missing his hat, he instantly recovered his thoughts, and attended to the matter he had in hand.

"For three years or more I sat at his feet, and gathered knowledge and learned wisdom from his lips in the blessed path of humility. His lessons have been to me a glorious barricade, and a perfect delight all my life. I roomed with Rev. Thomas Cooper, of whom the doctor, in his 'Biographical Sketches,' wrote a beautiful and life-like history. He was a young man of estimable character, and the doctor loved and appreciated him. He visited our room often, and on one occasion he dined with us, as we boarded ourselves, and said to us: 'Gentlemen, I will depend upon you more than any others to see that all things are well regulated in this institution, and that good order is kept. Your religious attitude will be to me of great value in conducting the school. I will look to you for assistance.'

"One Sunday, in addressing our class in the sanctuary on 'Close Thought,' a lecture which was afterward published in the *Ladies' Repository*, he unfolded those rich thoughts which we recall with delight. He said: 'Christianity is supreme love to God in the soul, and it will out. It will make itself manifest in all places, at all times, under all circumstances in prosperity or adversity, or even at the stake. We can not retain the love of God in our souls for selfish purposes; it will *out*. If we try to hold it within ourselves, our light will be smothered and go out, our profession will be vain. Love dwelling within our souls magnifies God to the world. The world will realize the results of what we feel in our hearts. The holy reflections of divine favor will be seen in all our lives. Can you place powder in that stove, upon the live coals, without an explosion? Neither can you have the love of God in your hearts without its coming out of your eyes, out of your mouths. It will be seen in the countenance of every one who possesses it. As the human soul filled with God's love emits the heavenly sparks, and as we seek the happiness of our fellow-beings, the rainbow of divine promise spans over us as an inspiration to love God and live for heaven.'

"A more gentle-spirited, kind-hearted, transparent, and God-fearing man I never knew, and, outside of our own household, I loved him next to God. If Moses was the meekest man, I think the doctor was second to him in that grace. He always manifested the simplicity and sweetness of a child in the presence of all, and the wisdom and nobleness of a royal saint. All who had pure intentions were at perfect ease in his presence.

"In our weekly prayer-meetings, which he always attended, his invocations and remarks were in the sweetness of Christian humility, showing deep experience in the things of God. I have often seen him cross the street to take the hand of a student, and say a pleasant, passing word of encouragement, and never one passed him without the notice of his eye. In him was a mighty power of attraction and of inspiration for all with whom he mingled. He always called me 'his boy,' by way of kindly appreciation, and urged me to make my mark high in life. Could I help loving him? At my house, years after I entered the ministry, he spent a night. His talk to, and his prayers for, my little family encouraged us as if an angel had entered our humble home. Years elapsed, and I met him next in Iowa, as a member of his conference cabinet. I acted as his private secretary, filling in the names and dates in all his ordination parchments. Then, in social counsel alone with him, I enjoyed his precious company, talked over much of the past, and received from him words of inspiration and advice, words of comfort, never to be forgotten.

"In the institution of learning he was assisted by three of the choice men of earth, as faithful, competent teachers,—Alexander Nelson, Holden Dwight, and Horatio S. Bradley. The doctor there left imperishable impressions for good upon hundreds of youthful minds and hearts, which are now, and will be for all time, developing for human happiness. He touched chords in our hearts which are still vibrating, and will continue through endless ages. Eternity only will circumscribe the gracious influences then set in motion by that holy man of God. O, what gems will sparkle in his crown of rejoicing!"

Rev. Holden Dwight, a man of education and scholarly ability, succeeded Dr. Thomson as principal of the Norwalk Seminary; but the claims of the creditors became so pressing and their demands so urgent that nothing would satisfy them but money or the institution itself. Hence, the building was sold for the benefit of the creditors, and Norwalk Seminary ceased to exist. Very few, if any, institutions of this grade and length of duration ever turned out more eminent young men or more discreet and well-educated young ladies than did this institution.

Every department of society in Ohio, as well as in other States, has been benefited by those who received their training in Norwalk Seminary. Some became statesmen, and entered Congress and the State legislative halls. Hon. Charles Foster, late governor of Ohio, obtained all his school education at Norwalk Seminary. Indeed, it was one of the most useful institutions of its day, and accomplished a grand mission.

CHAPTER VI.

EDITOR AND COLLEGE PRESIDENT.

WHEN Dr. Thomson assumed the editorial chair he exhibited the same characteristics of diligence and perseverance which he had manifested in other positions. His fondness for writing, his own cultured style of composition, and his excellent literary taste made his career as editor successful. Under his direction the magazine became more popular than before, and at the same time he made himself more widely known as a literary man. But he had served the Church scarcely two years as editor when the trustees of the Ohio Wesleyan University called for his removal to Delaware, to take full charge of that prosperous young institution, of which he had been nominal president for four years. Hence, with the consent of his conference and that of the bishops, he resigned the editorial chair, and B. F. Tefft, D. D., was chosen his successor.

Soon after Dr. Thomson's appointment to the editorship of the *Repository*, he received the title of Doctor of Divinity from Augusta College, Kentucky, and from the Indiana Asbury University. In 1855 the degree of LL. D. was conferred upon him by the Wesleyan University, at Middletown, Conn.

All acknowledged that Dr. Thomson possessed superior qualifications for the position of university president. He had been successful as an instructor and school manager at Norwalk. He was a fine scholar, and had not merely a book acquaintance with the various departments of literature, ethics, and philosophy, but he was also a thinker. Above all, he was persevering. He illustrated in himself at Delaware what he thus expresses:

"There is scarce any difficulty that can not be overcome by perseverance. Trace any great mind to its culmination, and you will find that its ascent was slow and by natural laws, and that its difficulties were such only as ordinary minds can surmount. Great results, whether physical or moral, are not often the offspring of giant powers. Genius is more frequently a curse than a blessing. Its possessor, relying on his extraordinary gifts, generally falls into habits of indolence and fails to collect the materials which are requisite to useful and magnificent effort. But there is something which is sure of success; it is the determination which, having entered upon a career with full conviction that it is right, pursues it in calm defiance of all opposition. With such a feeling a man can not but be mighty. Toil does not weary, pain does not arrest him. Carrying a compass in his heart which always points to one bright star, he allows no footstep to be taken which does not tend in that direction. Neither the heaving earthquake, nor the yawning gulf, nor the burning mountain can terrify him from his course, and if the heavens should fall the shattered ruins would strike him on his way to his object. Show me the man who has this principle, and I care not to measure his blood nor his brains; I ask not his name nor his nation: I pronounce that his hand will be felt upon his generation, and his mind enstamped upon succeeding ages.

"This attribute is godlike. It may be traced throughout the universe. It has descended from the skies—it is the great charm of angelic natures. It is hardly to be contemplated even in the demon without admiration. It is this which gives to the warrior his crown, and encircles his brow with a halo that, in the estimation of a misjudging world, neither darkness, nor lust, nor blasphemy, nor blood can obscure."

As so many years of Dr. Thomson's life were spent in Delaware, it may be well to give here a brief account of the institution with which he was connected. In the year 1841 Rev. Adam Poe—then stationed at Delaware—addressed letters to several of his brethren in the North Ohio Conference, stating that the "White Sulphur Spring property," adjoining that village, and consisting of a mansion and beautiful grounds, tastefully laid out with graveled walks and appropriate shade trees and shrubbery was in market; and that, if encouraged, the people of Delaware would purchase it and present it to the Methodist Episcopal Church for a seminary or academy. Dr. Thomson responded to Mr. Poe's letter, saying that the location—so central, so accessible, and so healthful—was suitable for a *college* or *university*, and that, if the Ohio Conference would unite with the North Ohio, such an institution could be organized, endowed, and well sustained. The hint was taken, and the citizens contracted for the purchase of the property, upon condition that the North Ohio Conference would establish the school, and appointed a committee to present the matter to the conference. The North

Ohio Conference received the committee with favor, and proposed to the Ohio Conference to become a joint partner with her in the enterprise. Commissioners were also appointed to co-operate with similar commissioners from the Ohio Conference, in case she did.

The latter wisely took the precaution of sending a committee to view the property before coming to any conclusion. This committee consisted of Drs. Charles Elliott, W. P. Strickland, and others; their report was favorable, and, having been ably sustained by the chairman, was, with considerable unanimity, adopted. A commission was then appointed with power to negotiate, in conjunction with the commissioners of the North Ohio Conference, a transfer of the property. The joint commission, consisting of Jacob Young, Charles Elliott, Joseph M. Trimble, and Edmund W. Sehon, of the Ohio Conference, and John H. Power, Adam Poe, Edward Thomson, William S. Morrow, and James Brewster, of the North Ohio Conference, met October 13, 1841, and exchanged the necessary papers. They also purchased some adjoining ground at a cost of five thousand five hundred dollars.

In March, 1842, a charter was obtained from the General Assembly of the State incorporating the "Trustees of the Ohio Wesleyan University," and securing the institution to the Methodist Episcopal Church by giving perpetuating and visitorial powers to the patronizing conferences. The board met at Hamilton, Ohio, on the 1st of October, 1842; and having organized by electing ex-Governor Trimble, president, and George B. Arnold secretary, authorized and established a preparatory school, and elected Dr. E. Thomson president of the University, and Rev. Solomon Howard principal of the preparatory department, which was at once organized by Mr. Howard. At the third meeting of the board, held in September, 1844, Rev. H. M. Johnson was appointed professor of ancient languages; Rev. Solomon Howard, professor of mathematics; William G. Williams, principal of the preparatory department; and Enoch G. Dial, assistant.

The salaries paid, or rather promised, to these men were gauged by the resources which the board hoped to have at their command at the end of the year. The president's salary was fixed at $800, the professors were to be paid $600 each, and the teachers in the preparatory department $400 and $350, respectively; but it was many years before even these meager salaries were paid as they became due.

Herman M. Johnson, was a graduate of Wesleyan University, Connecticut, and before coming to Delaware had held the chair of ancient languages in St. Charles College, Missouri, and in Augusta College, Kentucky. Professor Johnson had abilities as an instructor of the first order. His mind was analytic, and he had remarkable talent to explain and illustrate the subject that he taught; his scholarship was broad and thorough. After six years' service here he accepted the professorship of philosophy in Dickinson College, and was afterward raised to the presidency. In this office he died in 1868.

Solomon Howard held the office for only one year. He was subsequently, for some years, principal of the Springfield Female College, and in 1852 became president of the Ohio University, at Athens. He died in California in 1873.

William G. Williams was graduated at Woodward College, in Cincinnati, in 1844, and elected principal of the preparatory department in the university the same year. In 1847 he was promoted to the adjunct professorship of ancient languages, and in 1850 to the full chair of Greek and Latin languages. This appointment he held until 1864, when his chair was divided, and he became professor of Greek language and literature. In 1856 he became a member of the Central Ohio Conference, of which body he has for twenty-five years acted as secretary, and which he has represented in the General Conference.

Enoch G. Dial remained in connection with the institution only a single year.

Lorenzo D. McCabe came into the faculty as the successor of Professor Howard. He was born in Marietta in 1818, and graduated at the Ohio University in 1843. He then became a member of the Ohio Conference, and preached one year; but in the year 1844 he was appointed to the chair of mathematics and mechanical philosophy in his Alma Mater. This place he held one year. In 1845 he was called to the same chair in the Ohio Wesleyan University, and in 1860 was transferred to the chair of Biblical literature and moral science. In 1864, by a rearrangement of the college work, his chair was named that of "Philosophy." To this department he has since given his entire services, except in the years 1873 to 1875, during which he was also acting president. Dr. McCabe is a fine orator and an able writer, his best works being the "Foreknowledge of God" and "Di-

vine Nescience." He is a member of the Cincinnati
Conference, and represented that body in the General
Conference of 1864.

Frederick Merrick was born in the year 1810,
in the State of Connecticut, and was educated at
the Wesleyan University, at Middletown. In 1836
he became principal of Amenia Seminary, in New
York, and in 1838 professor of natural science in Ohio
University, Athens, and a member of the Ohio Conference. For one year (1842–3) he was pastor of the
Methodist Episcopal Church at Marietta. The next
year his conference appointed him financial agent of
the institution. In 1845 he was made professor of
natural science, and was acting president till Dr.
Thomson was inaugurated in 1846. Subsequently
(1851) he was transferred to the chair of moral philosophy, which he held till 1864, when he succeeded
Dr. Thomson as president. He retained this office
until 1873, when he resigned the presidency, and was
appointed lecturer on natural and revealed theology.
This relation he still sustains to the institution. Professor Merrick was offered the honorary degrees of
D. D. and LL. D., but declined them both. He has
represented his conference in the General Conference,
is a fine speaker on the platform and in the pulpit,
and is a terse and vigorous writer. During the last
few years he has written much and forcibly on moral
questions, and, being a thorough prohibitionist, has
ably advocated that cause both by pen and speech.

William L. Harris was educated at Norwalk Seminary, and joined the North Ohio Conference in 1840.
He was stationed at Delaware in 1845–6, and here he
first became connected with the university as one of

the teachers of the preparatory department. He taught, however, but one year. After preaching two years at Toledo, he accepted the principalship of Baldwin Institute, at Berea. In 1851 he was recalled to Delaware, as principal of the academical department, and was the next year appointed professor of natural sciences. In this chair he remained eight years, till 1860, when, by the appointment of the General Conference, he became one of the secretaries of the Methodist Missionary Society. He was a member of the General Conference from 1856 to 1872, and was the secretary of that body five terms. In 1872 he was made a bishop, and has become one of the ablest administrators of ecclesiastical affairs. In 1873–4 he made a tour around the world, visiting all the foreign missions of the Church.

These professors were assisted by several superior tutors. Edward Clinton Merrick served in this capacity from 1846 to 1849, and again in 1857–8. William D. Godman, the first classical graduate of the institution, taught in the college in 1849 and 1850. Mr. Godman afterward became president of Worthington Female College, professor in the North-western University, professor at Ohio Wesleyan University, president of Baldwin University, and of the New Orleans University. Thomas D. Crow, afterwards a prominent Ohio lawyer, was tutor from 1850 to 1852; and Owen T. Reeves in 1850–51. Mr. Reeves also became a practitioner of law after having served two years as principal of Baldwin Institute. In 1877 he became judge of the Eleventh Judicial District of Illinois and professor of law in Illinois Wesleyan University. In 1878 Monmouth College

conferred upon him the degree of LL. D. Samuel
W. Williams, a graduate of the university, became
tutor in 1851, and remained six years. He afterwards became, under Bishop (then Dr.) Clark, assistant editor of the *Ladies' Repository*, and continued in
that position as long as the magazine was published.
He acquired an enviable reputation as a facile writer
and painstaking editor. George F. W. Willey, afterwards professor in the Iowa Wesleyan University,
was tutor one year, 1851–52; Tullius C. O'Kane, the
most brilliant Sunday-school music composer of our
Church, from 1852 to 1857; and John Ogden, the
great normal specialist, from 1853 to 1855.

William F. King, Hiram M. Perkins, and William
O. Semans were appointed tutors of mathematics, natural science, and languages respectively, immediately
after their graduation in 1857. Mr. King left in
1862, to take a professorship in Cornell College,
Iowa. Soon thereafter he became vice-president, and
afterwards (1863) the president of the institution.
He was made a D. D. by Illinois Wesleyan University in 1870. He is a fine speaker and writer. By
his able administration he has made Cornell the first
college of the State. Tutor Perkins served in this
relation for five years, having entire charge of a department one year, during the absence of the professor. In 1865 he was appointed adjunct professor
in mathematics, and in 1867 was promoted to the full
chair of mathematics and astronomy, which he has
since occupied. Professor Perkins is a member of the
Central Ohio Conference. Tutor Semans served for
two years, and then entered into business in the West.
In 1862 he was appointed professor of natural sci-

ences in the Ohio Wesleyan Female College. In 1865 he was invited to a place in the university as adjunct professor of chemistry, and in 1867 promoted to a full professorship in the same department. In this position he yet remains. In 1875 he was elected mayor of the city of Delaware on the citizens' ticket, and served two years in this office.

William F. Whitlock was graduated in 1859, and was immediately appointed tutor of languages. In 1864 he was promoted to an adjunct professorship of Latin; and in 1866 was made a full professor. When the Ohio Wesleyan Female College was united with the university, he became dean of the ladies' department in the college. He was made a D. D. by Baldwin University in 1878. He is a member of the North Ohio Conference, and served as a delegate from that body to the General Conference of 1884. He married a sister of Bishop Thomson's second wife. He is one of the ablest speakers and best scholars connected with the institution.

These are the men who labored with Dr. Thomson during his presidency to make the Ohio Wesleyan University what it was when he left it, and what it is now. When he closed his work as president, the institution had been built up to a condition of permanence and prosperity, and it had acquired such a reputation and obtained such a position among the colleges that it was regarded among the foremost in the land. It must forever be an educational center of great power and usefulness.

Let us look at the material condition of the university when Dr. Thomson resigned the presidency. The campus is a beautiful grove of twenty acres, in which is a sulphur spring. The chapel building, of Grecian-Doric architecture is of brick and stone—eighty-eight feet by fifty-five, with two stories and a basement. The stories are high and rooms well arranged. The basement story is nine feet high, and is furnished with conveniences for the chemical and physical laboratories. The second story is occupied by recitation-rooms. The third story is the chapel proper, a beautiful room, seventy-one feet by fifty—exclusive of the vestibule—and twenty-three feet high, with an orchestra of ten feet at one extremity and a platform at the other. The entire building bears the name "Thomson Chapel."

On the north side of this building is one of substantial frame, and on the south one of brick, each sixty-two feet by fifty-two, and of the same style and nearly the same height as the central structure. In the rear, east of these, is another brick building not so large, called Morris Hall, and used as a dormitory for those students who wish to board themselves.

The library at this time was worth not less than twelve thousand dollars; the museum, including the Prescott and Mann cabinets, about the same amount; and the philosophical and chemical apparatus about half that figure. The total property, aside from endowment, was then valued at eighty-two thousand dollars, and the endowment fund was one hundred and sixteen thousand dollars. There were five professors, three tutors, and five hundred students.

But what were the elements of Dr. Thomson's success?

First, he entertained just views of his position: "The post of college instructor," he says, "is by no means an enviable one. The compensation, small; the honors, after death; the labors, arduous and incessant. I know no employment more heart-trying, spirit-wasting, health-destroying. Were all students amiable, talented, and pious, they would reconcile professors to their lot; but alas! in this land children are rarely trained by parents in the way that they should go; still we welcome them with hope; we spurn not, without trial, the surly, proud, self-willed youth." He went into the position fully knowing what he was undertaking, and he entered it with a determination to succeed.

Secondly, he devoted all his abilities as a lecturer and as a writer to the institution. His discourses delivered all over the State, for he traveled in all directions and almost incessantly during vacations, as well as his able articles, appearing in nearly all the newspapers and magazines of the Church, naturally attracted great attention to the institution over which he presided. Many students were thus drawn and friends made for the university.

Thirdly, he devoutly believed in a religious education, and had no confidence in that which was purely secular. He said: "You may educate your soul without religion, but you will only refine your misery. You may polish your speech without grace, but will only sweeten the food of the undying worm. You may render brilliant the flames that burn within your bosom, but it will be only to add brilliancy to the conflagrations of earth and hell. Am I challenged to a comparison of educated and uneducated states? I accept the challenge. Admitting, for argument's sake, that some cities of antiquity, where refinement was found, were free from grosser vices, it may be asked, Was not their superiority in moral character owing to their religion? For though paganism is false it has a substratum of truth, and its influences in restraining the multitude are potent. But we challenge Athens or Corinth or Rome, in her attenuated refinement to escape from the charge of criminality as brutal as disgraced the darkest barbarism that ever found a place on earth. . . .

"God has given you a son with all the elements of a man. Day by day you watch and pray over his unfolding powers, and rejoice especially to mark the ideas of right and duty and gratitude, the feeling after God, the aspiration after a better state. How painful would it be to see the light of his fine eye go out, or the power to guide his feet or stretch his arms fail, and then to see the light of reason and imagination and memory slowly extinguished, leaving him an idiot in your arms! But still you could carry him with tenderness if only there were left the idea of right, the power to love the good, to be grateful for your kindness and to breathe after a higher life. But O, to see the light of conscience go out, and though the form of man be left, though the intellect blaze forth with celestial brilliancy, yet the power of self-government and the power of being loved, and the connection with good men and angels, and the sympathy with God is gone! Let us have 'blue laws,' puritanical strictness, any thing rather than uneducated, neglected, put-out consciences."

Thus entertaining the highest views of the value of the soul he inculcated the proper kind of truth, and insisted on the culture of the whole man. One term he felt such a deep responsibility for the souls of his students that he had arrangements made for his classes, and he gave his whole time to the work of pastor, visiting his pupils and praying with them in their rooms. From this grew a wonderful revival, in which most of the students who were not already professors of religion, were converted.

Fourthly, he was an advocate of the most liberal culture. Young men who went to Delaware expecting to stay one year, under his influence were persuaded to remain until they graduated in the classical course; and they, in turn, became enthusiasts for a thorough education.

Dr. T. J. Scott, one of our missionaries in India, and a graduate of the university, says:

"His reputation as an educator and most admirable man drew me to the Ohio Wesleyan University in 1856. My first interview with him was with the object of settling a doubt I had as to the propriety of completing the classical course of the university rather than taking the shorter Biblical course in view of gaining time, and thus sooner entering the ministry. He advised the longer course, and ended by saying, 'If you were about to set in for a day's sawing you would gain time and make better work if you would sharpen your saw well before beginning.'"

Dr. Scott now finds practical use for all the culture and discipline he acquired as he labors in the theological seminary, preparing the minds who are to herald the Gospel through the valleys and over the mountains of that fertile and densely populated peninsula.

President Thomson believed that all men should

be well educated, but especially the man of God.
He says:

" Providence seems to have trained his chief instruments for religious purposes by an elegant education.
Moses was learned in all the wisdom of the Egyp-
tians. Paul was versed not only in Jewish history
and law, but in heathen poets, one of whom he quotes
with fine effect on Mars' hill. Did not his education give him influence at Jerusalem, at Athens, and
at Rome, and qualify him to plead his Master's cause
in the imperial city, and did it not also help him
before Agrippa and the Areopagus?

" When darkness and vice had overspread Christendom, on whom did God fix to bring in the light?
Luther was a professor in the University of Witten-.
burg, Knox a graduate of St. Andrews, Melancthon
a professor of Greek, Calvin, Beza, Zuinglius, and their
coadjutors were among the eminent classical scholars
of their age. When, at a subsequent period, the
English Church sunk into lethargy, who roused her
from her slumbers? Wesley and Fletcher were profound scholars and distinguished linguists."

Dr. Thomson gave not the least credence to the
hypothesis that a liberal education, especially the
study of natural science, would have a tendency to
weaken faith in revelation: " According to my observation," he says, " true knowledge has a favorable
effect on faith. Revivals of religion are as frequent,
as powerful, and as permanent in colleges and semi-
naries as in any of our Churches. Thousands of the
brightest ornaments of Zion were converted to God in
institutions of learning. I have seen much of Christian character in all its forms. . . . I have wit-

nessed it in the negro's hut, the sailor's hammock, the Indian's wigwam, the convict's cell, and the rich man's mansion. I have seen it in the ocean's storm, the chamber of sickness, the pillow of the dying, and house of the dead; but never have I witnessed a more triumphant faith, nor a more lovely exemplification of all the graces that adorn the Christian character than I have witnessed within the halls of learning. I have never yet known a man to enter a seminary a Christian and depart an infidel, but many have I known to enter the hall of learning infidels, who are now stars in the firmament of the Church."

Fifthly, his government was through love. He felt a real affection for all his students, and they seemed to know it. They feared to do wrong lest his great and paternal heart would be grieved. He was a great student of the face. When mischief had been done, he would refer to it in chapel, and watch the countenances of the students, and rarely failed to detect the offender. When reproof was necessary he gave it. He would set forth the nature of the offense and its inexcusableness, the sorrow of his heart, the grief that must come to the friends of the offender when they heard of his disgrace and the inevitable tendency of a course of folly in such a light that the student was nearly always melted to tears and awakened to a new life.

He expresses his own method of reformation when he says: "We throw around him arms of love, pour into his ears the voice of entreaty, and bedew his cheeks with the tears of fraternal sympathy; we read to him the commandments of God, preach to him Jesus and the resurrection, bear his name to the throne of grace, and often, in watches of the night, when deep sleep falleth upon man, we see the terrible vision of his danger, and our pillows can not bear up our aching head."

His love, though deep and apparent, was manifested with dignity. He was sociable, and endeavored to treat all with courtesy, yet he was not familiar. Professor S. W. Williams describes accurately this element of his nature:

"In addition to his usual Commencement levees it was his custom to give special entertainments at his own table to the members of the senior class and, upon occasion, to others. Of the trouble and expense neither he nor Mrs. Thomson made any account. Here he laid aside not his dignity but his mastership. Not as president but as friend he received his pupils. He was not now instructor sitting in the lecture-room, but elder brother and companion rather; and, like Plato, sitting among his disciples in familiar discourse, as the easy question and the humorous response, the witty statement or the sportive answer went back and forth, all felt at ease. If the students had heretofore only admired their president, they were henceforth to love him. He had learned well the lesson of old Polonius, and no one knew better than he where lay the border-line between friendliness and familiarity. He never strained a point toward either extreme of austerity or intimacy. He knew how to make a student feel at perfect ease in his company without inviting familiarity, and herein lay one secret of his power."

Sixthly, there was an inspiration about his presence which it is almost impossible to explain. It was, doubtless, owing largely to his constant walk with God. Dr. T. J. Scott says:

"Perhaps Bishop Thomson's power in the university, as an educator, was far greater in the stimulating and molding character of his presence and general influence than in his work as a teacher of text-books or mere science. Quiet and gentle as the most refined lady, yet he had a powerful and most impressive personality. The literary style of his lectures and Sunday afternoon sermons shaped many a student's pen and molded his thoughts. I have often heard students remark, 'Dr. Thomson's presence makes one feel like being a better man.' Years afterward, when he visited the India Mission, I heard a lady remark, 'After being in Bishop Thomson's presence one feels like being a better person.'

"I remember that while I was at the university he was suddenly stricken down, and was nigh unto death from a sharp attack of inflammation of the bowels. He was so low that he had to be lifted as a child. L. J. Powell, since professor in the Willamette University, was one of the students detailed to nurse him. Powell remarked that at the very gates of death the bishop was as serene as in his calmest daily mood, and that he was sweet and holy as an angel. All deeply regretted his removal from the university to the editorial chair. I recall that often afterwards, in reading his editorials, tears would start in my eyes. This was more from the image and tender memory of the man I carried in my heart than from the matter I was reading. The purity and guileless spirit of the writer re-enforced with great power what he wrote, for any one who knew him."

Another element of Dr. Thomson's power at the university is referred to by Dr. George L. Taylor, one of his pupils:

"The throne of his glory was in that peculiar and difficult thing to make popular, the college lecture-sermon. In this it is questionable if any American college ever boasted his peer. Never, for years, on any tolerable Sabbath, would the spacious chapel accommodate his audiences. Perhaps there was no other so cultivated auditory in the State. It comprised the faculties and students of two, and much of the time three colleges, the county bar, the medical corps, the clergy of ten Churches, and many other educated minds. No other interest could attract a hearing at three o'clock P. M. The students by scores were often crowded out of their seats by strangers staying in town over Sabbath to hear Dr. Thomson, whose pulpit was the Mecca of the State. No other in the country has ever had a more mesmeric power. His lectures were generally delivered from manuscript, and Chalmers never made his manuscripts glow and burn more than did Thomson. Often his audiences were completely electrified, and the toughest veterans among his hearers were bathed in tears and fairly lifted from their seats. His Commencement Baccalaureates were things of anticipation for weeks, and of admiration for months. But every lecture, year after year, seemed better than the last."

The Rev. O. Burgess, referring to the same things, says:

"Though small in person he often impressed others with the greatness of his soul. On one occasion, after he had delivered one of his wonderful baccalaureate discourses at Delaware, I was walking with several ministers, one of whom was a very large man, weighing about three hundred pounds, who said, in a doleful tone, ' Well, I am dissatisfied with the ways of Providence.' ' Why Brother B.,' one asked, ' what is the matter now?' The brother answered, 'The Lord has made some men all body and no soul, and others all soul and no body. I am discouraged, and feel, after hearing that sermon, that I ought never to enter the pulpit again'—so impressed was he with Thomson's greatness and his own littleness. But that man was then, and is yet, prominent in the Church."

CHAPTER VII.

CONFERENCE RECORD.

DURING the time that Dr. Thomson was at the university he was constantly growing in reputation in his conference. He was not talkative, nor did he seek in any way to make himself prominent on the floor of the conference; but he was an earnest worker on the committees to which he was assigned; and when the time came for a great debate on some vital question he was ready with an elaborate argument. He was a member of the committee on education from the organization of the conference till the time of his election as bishop, and was chairman almost every year. He was present at every conference session from the time he joined on probation, except in 1854, when he was in Europe purchasing books for the Sturges library of the university.

He represented the North Ohio Conference in the General Conference from the organization of the conference till he was elected bishop. In 1848 the associate delegates were John H. Power, Leonard B. Gurley, Adam Poe, John Quigley, and James McMahon. The reserve delegates were Henry Whiteman and Hiram M. Shaffer. At this quadrennial convention Dr. Thomson was strongly talked of as an editor of one of the Church papers. But he had so recently taken the presidential chair at Delaware, that the Ohio delegations felt that he must remain there for some time to come. And the doctor's wife was very loath to leave her native State again, in which all her relatives were located, and the associations so agreeable. Following is a letter which was written to her from the seat of the General Conference:

"PITTSBURG, PENN., May 22, 1848.

"MY DEAR WIFE,—I have been looking for a letter from you for some days past, but in vain. However, I write to you regularly on Monday. I hear no news of interest except what you find in the *Daily Advocate* I send you. Business in conference progresses slowly. To-day the committee on the state of the Church made a report, which will be the order of the day for Wednesday next. It recommends a disregard of the line established by the 'plan of separation,' and the submission of a proposition to the annual conference to arbitrate the property question. The prospect is that the report will be adopted with great unanimity.

"I have just returned from Beaver, where I spent the Sabbath very pleasantly. I was entertained by a lawyer, whose name is Agnew, and whose lady is a connection of the Christmas family. My health has not been very good for the past week. I am just recovering from a very severe cold. Brother Tefft is my room-mate, and a very pleasant one he is.

"The weather has been remarkably unfavorable for me. I walk nearly a mile, if not quite, to the conference, and very frequently all the way in the rain. We have had more or less rain almost every day since I entered Pittsburg.

"You must endeavor to be cheerful and contented a little while longer. I hope we shall adjourn in the course of ten days. Please tell me in your next what you want me to buy for you here.

"Dr. Dixon, the delegate from England has left, so also the delegates from Canada, except Brother Green. The commissioners from the South are still here, together with Drs. Early, Lee, and Parsons, and, I believe, Bishop Soule. They announced last Friday that they had given up the idea of obtaining their claim; had employed Daniel Webster as chief counselor, and several assistants; and had determined, at the rising of this conference, to commence suit simultaneously at New York, Cincinnati, and Philadelphia; but I believe we generally disregard their threats. Brother Power is well, as much so, I believe, as ever—so also the other delegates from the State of Ohio except Brother Young, who appears to be feeble.

"I am becoming more and more impatient to return home. You need not be informed how I love you and your dear babe, and how solicitous I am to render you happy. Give my regards to all, and believe me

"Your affectionate husband,

"E. Thomson."

"P. S.—At a caucus last night the following nominations were made: Editors of *Christian Advocate and Journal*, G. Peck and M. Simpson; editor of the *Western Christian Advocate*, C. Elliott. The caucus adjourned to meet next Wednesday. I have been urged by brethren here to be editor of the *Pittsburg Christian Advocate*. The Erie and Pittsburg delegations operated against my nomination elsewhere with a view to this. I could come here, I feel satisfied, if I would consent, but I would prefer to remain where I am. What say you to Pittsburg?"

John H. Power, who had charge of Delaware District, was made a book agent at this conference, and Dr. Thomson was appointed the presiding elder of Delaware District by Bishop Janes, and served in this capacity the remainder of the conference year—from June to September. As most of this time was during the Summer vacation given by the university the doctor was enabled to perform the work without interfering with his duties as president; and thus he had the honor of serving in this important, trying, and responsible position of itinerant life.

In 1852 the delegation from the North Ohio Conference to the General Conference was as follows: E. Thomson, John H. Power, H. Whiteman, Thomas Barkdull, John Quigley, Adam Poe, and H. M. Shaffer—with L. B. Gurley and W. L. Harris as reserves. The General Conference was held that year in Boston, and it was, in some respects, the most important session yet convened in the history of the Church. It was decided that four new men be added to the board of bishops, and Dr. Thomson was urged by some of his friends as an appropriate man for episcopal honors. Indeed, no other man from Ohio was put forward. But he declined, very persistently at first, to have his name mentioned in connection with the office. Three days before the election the Ohio men addressed him a letter urging him not to decline, and assuring him that they were confident of his election if he would consent to be a candidate.

This is his reply:

"Boston, May 24, 1852.

"*To the Delegates of the Ohio and North Ohio Conferences:*

"Dear Brethren,—I have always been an obedient son in the Gospel, and I always will be. I *dare* not say that I will not serve in any post which the Church may assign me, more especially if that post be one of toil and danger; but I am at liberty to say that I feel a strong disinclination to the office for which you have named me. This arises partly from a desire to remain with my brethren in Delaware, to whom I am greatly attached, partly from a fondness for retirement and domestic happiness, but chiefly, I think, from a deep sense of my unfitness for the office of a superintendent. I do not wish it. I go farther; I respectfully, but earnestly, *request* that you will not nominate me for it.

"I can not close this note without expressing my profound sense of gratitude for the honor you have done me. Next to the love of God there is nothing that so overwhelms me as the confidence of my brethren, and I pray God that I may never be put into any situation in which I can not fulfill their just expectations—this were a burden too heavy to be borne by your brother in Christ,

"E. Thomson."

There were four other prominent candidates: Dr. Simpson, editor of the *Western Christian Advocate;* Dr. Scott, one of the Book Agents at New York; Professor Baker, of New England, and Edward R. Ames, a prominent presiding elder from Indiana. It was conceded that two men must come from the East and two from the West. When the result of the election was announced these four were chosen—Edward Thomson having failed of an election by seven votes.

He now writes to his wife:

"Boston, May 27, 1852.

"My Dear Wife,—So the election is over, and your husband is not elected. Bless God that he has escaped such heavy responsibilities and arduous duties. It is a wonder to me that I received so many votes as I did. The elements were deeply agitated on the day before the election. It was stated that I was sickly, somewhat hard of hearing, inexperienced in the itinerancy, necessary to the college, and that I had declined being a candidate—all true; though some of my Ohio brethren felt themselves at liberty to deny the last statement. In spite of all I received sixty-eight votes; which, I suppose, came from the following sources: Eric Conference, 7; Ohio, 12; North Ohio, 7; Michigan, 6; Baltimore, 12; Rock River, 3; New Jersey, 5; West Virginia, 2. East Genesee gave me several votes through Dr. Tefft, I suppose. The rest were scattering. Only two or three from New England, which was arrayed against me on account of a report that I would not be tolerant to *pewed* churches.

"We are now progressing rapidly with the business of the conference. This morning we ordain the new bishops. We shall probably adjourn by next Tuesday, and you may look for me on Friday or Saturday of next week.

"Yours, affectionately,

"E. THOMSON."

The same day he writes a letter to his little son, then nearly four years old.

"BOSTON, May 24, 1852.

"MY DEAR SON,—Pa sends you a kiss, fresh and warm from his heart. I thought of you the other day, when I saw a poor man in the streets with a hand-organ, playing for a few coppers which were thrown from the windows. Usually such strolling players take a monkey with them, who sits on the instrument or dances below while his master plays the music; but this poor man had a little boy instead of a monkey. He was a pretty little boy, not as old as you, I judge. He wore a straw hat with a broad brim. He appeared very feeble and sorry, but quite good natured. O, thought I, how happy I am that my dear little son is better off than that poor boy; so, to show my gratitude to God, I gave the little fellow some money on your account.

"To-day I dined with Dr. Elliott. In the company was Brother Lyon, who told some strange stories about a Methodist preacher in Virginia, called 'Billy Cravens.' One of them was this: He compared Christians to wheat; 'Sometimes,' he said, 'you see wheat that looks very well, but it does not weigh sixty-five pounds to the bushel. And what is the reason? You take a grain and press it between your fingers, and out jumps a weevil. So take many a Christian, he looks well, but press him between the law and the Gospel, and out jumps a negro.' Tell that story to Brother McCabe.

"Be a very good boy; do not get angry with anybody. The other day, when two senators here got angry with each other and said naughty words to each other, a third senator made them both ashamed of themselves by telling the following story: 'In Japan it is said to be very warm, so that when legislators sit long to deliberate, they are immersed in cold water up to the chin. Now, if senators on this floor can not keep their temper, I shall move to put them in similar legislative coolness.' Would not this be a good way to punish bad boys when they get angry?

"I hope you are a good boy. You know how to be—love and obey your mother.

"When pa comes home you must get him some flowers. I trust you have pretty garden, and that you do not pull any thing when mamma forbids you.

"The little boys here seem to be very good. They do not run in the streets, but ride their little stick horses at home. They go to Sabbath-school and meeting, and sing out of their hymn-books. Many of them pray to God to bless them, and he makes them very happy.

"The people here are not allowed to drink whisky, and this is a very good thing. The men that drink are very bad men. You ought to pray for them that God would make them quit drinking. I want you to be a good temperance boy, and when you get old enough you can talk to the people about 'living righteously and soberly,' so that they may finally get to heaven. Pray for your affectionate   PAPA."

In 1853 Dr. Thomson, with several others, was appointed to prepare a report on Romanism, which subject was then attracting much attention, and the report was presented at the next session. At the General Conference of 1856 Dr. Thomson was spoken of for an editorial position, but he positively declined the use of his name for any place, preferring to remain at Delaware, in the post that was so agreeable to himself and family and where he was almost worshiped by students and citizens.

At the session of the doctor's conference in 1857, he preached the Missionary Sermon, which was a superior effort, and which the conference requested to be published with the minutes of the session, but he modestly declined to comply with the request.

At the same session (1857) W. B. Disbro presented the following resolution, which was adopted, namely:

"*Resolved,* That a committee of five be appointed to take into consideration the propriety of introducing a form of lay delegation into our annual conferences, according to the provisions of the last General Conference."

The committee were, E. Thomson, W. B. Disbro, T. Barkdull, G. W. Breckenridge, and T. Thompson. The committee reported, and their report was adopted and ordered to be published.

Also, at the same session, Adam Poe announced the death of Rev. James B. Finley, of the Cincinnati Conference; whereupon E. Thomson, A. Poe, James McMahon, and Jacob Rothweiler, were appointed a committee to draft resolutions expressive of the feelings of this conference on the receipt of the sad intelligence. The report was prepared by Dr. Thomson, and in it he makes a beautiful tribute to one of the pioneer itinerants, whose life is familiar to many:

"In the death of James B. Finley the Methodist

Episcopal Church has lost an able, eloquent, and faithful minister, and an interesting, useful, and successful author; one whom we have long been accustomed to venerate for his age, his services, and his public and private virtues; one, whose molding hand has been felt on the institutions of our State, in which he was a pioneer; whose eloquent voice was cheerfully raised in all the great interests of philanthropy, and whose purse was ever open to the poor, the suffering, and the oppressed, of whatever name, nation, or color; one who will long be remembered with respect alike by the sons of the forest, who once roamed over our plains, and the cultivated inhabitants, who have succeeded them, to both of whom he preached Christ crucified with intense earnestness."

The delegates, in 1856, from the North Ohio to the General Conference, besides Dr. Thomson, were W. L. Harris, J. H. Power, James Wheeler, William B. Disbro, Adam Poe, Henry E. Pilcher, and George W. Breckenridge, with L. B. Gurley and H. M. Shaffer as reserve delegates. In 1860 the delegation stood: E. Thomson, Nicholas Nuhfer, A. Poe, John T. Kellam, and H. Whiteman. The reserve delegates were W. B. Disbro and W. C. Peirce. In 1864 E. Thomson, Jacob Rothweiler, A. Poe, G. W. Breckenridge, and H. Whiteman, with W. C. Peirce and E. R. Jewett as reserve delegates. These were his prominent and able associates in those years.

CHAPTER VIII.

ANTI-SLAVERY SENTIMENTS.

THOUGH conservative on many subjects, where no vital principle was at stake, Dr. Thomson was always radical in defense of truth. A man of his tender sympathies could not be otherwise than on the side of the oppressed. On the floor of his own conference, and in the highest legislative body of the Church, he was an anti-slavery man. Dr. Aydelott, one of the early abolitionists of Ohio, says: "I never knew Dr. Thomson to do but one, as I feared, imprudent thing. Many years since, at a Commencement of the university in Delaware, I found myself standing up before a large and crowded audience, addressing it in behalf of a students' missionary society. Though in the days of strong pro-slavery hate, I did not hesitate—as I felt called—to declare my intense abhorrence of oppression in all its forms, its vile, unchristian character, its ultimate destruction of the freedom of the Church and our republican government. The instant I stopped, Dr. Thomson started from the back part of the platform and hastily coming to the front grasped me by the hand and exclaimed, 'I do, my dear brother, cordially approve every word you have uttered!' You have, thought I, my good friend, *voluntarily* brought down upon your own head an enormous load of odium!" But he cared not for odium; he was not a policy man; he would not wink at iniquity, but he dared to meet it boldly in the name of God.

To show how he felt, and what he thought on the subject of human freedom, we give the following extract from one of his arguments on the relation of government to slavery:

"But suppose, owing to the weakness of human reason and the strength of human depravity, that government is perverted? The question may arise, When is government perverted? The answer is, I think, simple. 1. When it fails to protect its subjects in the enjoyment of their rights; or, 2. When it requires its subjects to do wrong. But who are the subjects of government? Human beings, of course; and who are human beings? They who possess the essential attributes of humanity. What are these? They are not to be found in color or feature, or flesh or blood—they are reason, affection, conscience. These confer the capacities of comprehending, loving, serving God, and lift the being possessing them aloft above the mere animal creation. He who is capable of obeying God is accountable to God, and he who is accountable to God has the rights of man. What are the rights of man? We hold these truths to be revealed, that all men are sprung from the same father, plunged in the same ruin, and redeemed by the same Savior. A natural inference is that all have equal rights. Our revolutionary fathers held this to be self-evident, that among these rights—natural and inalienable—are 'life, liberty, and the pursuit of happiness.' Inferiority does not extinguish rights. If you claim control over another because of your superiority, another may claim you by the same title. Such a claim is, indeed, rarely set up. It is not the inferiority of the slave, but his status, on which the master rests; the more the slave improves, the whiter his skin becomes, the greater the infusion of Anglo-Saxon blood that floats in his veins, the tighter does the master hold him. Oppression does not cancel rights. If a man buys property of a thief, he gets a thief's title; if he sells it, he conveys a thief's title; if he bequeaths it, he bequeaths a thief's title. Ill gotten property may, in time, be rightfully acquired by possession, provided the original owner can not be found; but in man there is always a soul—an original owner; so that, however many ancestors of the slave may have been sold, the present master has no better title than the original man-stealer.

"Law can not destroy human rights; it is the province of law to confirm rights, not to annihilate them. The alleged incapacity of certain men for liberty, does not destroy their inalienable rights. How did such incapacity originate? Do you say it is natural? It were a paradox to say that God would perpetuate a race of human beings incapable of liberty. What rank would they hold in the scale of beings? What would be their position at the last day and beyond it? It were a libel both upon man and God. If the alleged incapacity is produced by our oppression, can this give us a title to the subjects of this oppression? Such a claim could be set up in favor of any tyrant. It goes to this point, that a man's rights over another are in proportion to the wrongs he commits upon him, and hence that the longer a man suffers wrong the less he is entitled to relief, until at length protracted oppression utterly extinguishes all his rights.

"Some rivet the chains upon the slave because he is content with his condition. If it be true that a man is satisfied with the condition of a slave, why is it true? Because slavery has embruted him. If a surgeon, by pressure upon your brain, were so to impair your reasoning powers as to make you satisfied to be his slave, would that insure him a valid title to what was left of you?"

In 1852 the North Ohio Conference appointed Edward Thomson, John H. Power, William B. Disbro, Henry Whiteman, and William L. Harris, a committee on slavery, and at the next session of that body Dr. Thomson, as chairman of the committee, presented the following report:

"WHEREAS, slavery exists in the United States of America; and, WHEREAS, it is destructive of human rights, contrary to natural conscience, and condemned by the written Word of God, and blighting in its effects both upon the slaveholder and the enslaved; and, WHEREAS, there has been a steady encroachment of the slave power upon the government, and an extension of slavery within our boundaries; and, WHEREAS, under the circumstances we can not be silent or inactive; therefore,

"1. *Resolved*, That the system of American slavery is a great evil, moral, social, and political, and the disgrace of the age.

"2. *Resolved*, That it is our duty to labor with untiring zeal, and in the use of all ecclesiastical, political, and commercial influences, but in the calm, considerate, and benevolent spirit of Christianity, for its abolition.

"3. *Resolved*, That the Church should bar from her communion all who hold slaves for the sake of gain.

"4. *Resolved*, That we rejoice in the establishment and prospects of the republic of Liberia, which, opening a home of freedom to thousands of emancipated slaves, demonstrating the capability of Africans for self-government, banishing the slave trade along the coast of Africa from the Gallinas to the San Pedro, and kindling up the light of civilization in a favorable position to illuminate both the border and the interior of Africa, has been of immense service to the cause of humanity.

"5. *Resolved*, That our government acts in a manner unworthy of herself in failing to recognize the independence of Liberia, and that we recommend our people to petition Congress on that subject."

Dr. Thomson was strongly in hope that some *peaceable* mode of emancipation might be devised, and that the Africans in America might be transported to Liberia; thence to work through the great continent in all directions, carrying the lamp of Christian civilization.

When the Nebraska bill was under discussion in the halls of Congress, Dr. Thomson gave utterance to his views in a public lecture. He said:

"In view of these things, many clergymen have spoken out against a certain pending public measure. For this they have been denounced in very high places and very low ones. For myself I have no apology. The question of slavery in the States is a difficult one—it is not simple, but complex—not abstract, but concrete; it relates not to a new evil, but an old one; one which has come down by the sin of both the British and American governments from the ages of darkness; it is inwoven with the institutions of the South, social, political, and religious. It has polluted her literature; it has shaped her manners, and fixed her prejudices, and bound itself up with her interests. We have been accustomed to pity and extenuate, and though we might still bear with the slaveholder, and wait for the truth to dissolve the chains of the slave as the south wind does the snow, yet we can think of no apology for the Nebraska bill. The question it presents is simple, abstract, novel. It proposes to render virgin soil liable to pollution; to render a surface of the map, already white, by law of peculiar force and solemnity, likely to be blackened; to open the way to indorse and imitate the iniquity of the past. It proposes, so far as a certain oppressed people are concerned, to submit the question of liberty—the fundamental purpose of government—the protection of society—to popular mercy, excluding from the polls, however, the oppressed people, and admitting to them those whose interests or prejudices may incline them to vote against their rights. And yet men tell us we don't understand it. Strange bill, that after being discussed for months, can not be understood! It has, however, a bright side, for however enigmatical to the North, it is clear to the South. It would be clear to all if Germans or Catholics were substituted for an oppressed race. I believe in popular sovereignty. Do you believe in liberty? Let us never, then, put it in jeopardy in regard to either black or white, Protestant or Catholic."

He attacked the Fugitive Slave law, which compelled, under heavy penalties, every citizen of a free State to act as a slave-catcher, if called upon by a United States marshal to track the runaway:

"A government may not only deprive its subjects of rights, but require them to do wrong. 'Who is to be judge when a government does so? For what may appear wrong to one man may appear right to another.' To a certain extent this is true. But there is a limit within which all is clear. To love God, to love man, for example, are duties which all must acknowledge. Cruelty, adultery, fraud, and theft, are condemned by every sane mind. If the legislature of Ohio should pass a law requiring us to chase down every man not more than five feet six inches high who should be trying to get his wheat to the Canada market, and enjoining us to distribute his wheat among his neighbors, and all this because he was not any taller, we should all agree that it was wrong. . . .

"That over which a government has power it may regulate. It can stamp its image on weights, and scales, and landmarks, and flags; it may, therefore, issue its decrees to mark boundaries, and regulate commerce, and measures, and fortifications, but when it comes to the human soul it finds another image there, and hears another voice: 'Render unto God the things that are God's.' Lift up your eye to the heavens; try to efface God's image from the sky and stamp your own there before you attempt to turn the human soul into gold and run it in your die. Stop the revolving earth with a stamp of your foot, or stay the sun in his course with your curse, before you prescribe the course of human thought, and feeling, and will. Bring on your chains! Kindle up your fires! 'He that sitteth in the heavens shall laugh.'"

And it was not with any inconsistency that he was a stockholder in the celebrated "underground railway." Many a poor fellow was assisted by him on his route to Canada and to freedom. He felt that the Fugitive Slave Law was unjust and inhuman, and he braved its penalties in his daring to help his unfortunate brother in black.

CHAPTER IX

FIRST TRIP TO EUROPE.

DR. THOMSON never took a tour for pleasure. His traveling was for the good of others, and his first long trip was in the interest of the university. In the Spring of 1854 Mr. William Sturges, of Putnam, Ohio, made a generous donation of ten thousand dollars for the purchase of a library for the university, and President Thomson was authorized by the trustees to go abroad and buy the books in London and Paris. Immediately after Commencement that year he set sail from New York. On his tour not only excellent bargains were made, but he was enabled to see some of the great objects of interest in the old world. He was present in the British Parliament when the queen opened it, and heard her address on the occasion. He visited Westminster Abbey, St. Paul's, the British Museum, the great parks, the Crystal Palace, the London Tower, etc. He also visited the south of England, viewing again his birthplace and the scenes of his childhood. Then he went to France and Switzerland, and looked upon the pleasant vales and the snow-clad Alps. He wondered at the opulence and grandeur of London, was charmed by the rich landscapes of Switzerland, and was delighted especially with the manners of the French.

"Take a letter of introduction," he says, "to an English gentleman and he will carefully read it, as if determined to settle the question of its genuineness, and, if satisfied, will formally bow to you once or twice across the room, and as formally after presenting you wine, authorize you to command his services if they are needed, and then bow you gracefully out. Go, under like circumstances, to a French gentleman, and rising to receive your introductory note, after giving it a mere glance, he will approach you with smiles, offer you his warm hand with all its fingers, and, perhaps, apply his other hand, that he may more closely grasp your own, and looking you in the face, with a countenance beaming with pleasure and benignity, will say, ' Welcome to France, welcome to Paris, welcome to my home, welcome for my friend's sake, welcome for your own.' Then inquiring concerning your health, your family, your country, your voyage, and your impressions of France, he will seat you in his own chair, and ask you to excuse him till he can direct his clerks in regard to the business of the day, and returning, gracefully announce that it will be his pleasure to devote himself to yours. It is vain for you to beg him not to encroach upon his time or impede his business for your sake. Ordering a carriage he will seat you by his side, and then request you to name the objects or scenes that you would first witness; and when the hour for dinner arrives he will land you at his own door. After meal, he may replace you in the carriage, and perhaps say, ' The only limit to our excursions and sight-seeing must be your inclinations, your engagements, or your approaching fatigue.'

"If an Englishman were to proffer like attentions you would find it easy to pay the expenses—and, surely, in this there were nothing wrong; but the Frenchman will pay all expenses and pay all fees, so speedily, so artfully, that you shall have no opportunity to share them, and as to negotiating concerning them his countenance banishes the thought. Not content with his own attentions, perhaps he sends to you next morning a polite clerk to say that he has been commissioned to be your pioneer in any direction that you may desire to go. He takes you to Versailles, to St. Cloud, to Fontainebleau; he guides you, he tickets you, he feasts you, and when you go to pay the bills, you find them all canceled. If you remonstrate with him he will say, "I do as I am charged, I must refer you to your friend, whose commission I fulfill.' If, oppressed by this generosity, you make bold to speak to that friend, or to place some napoleons in his hand, he will say, 'O, we must settle these things, not in France, but in America. Wait till I visit you at your own home.'

"But how shall I describe a French gentleman? He is more than civil, more than affable, more than courteous; he is polite, polished, refined. He respects your judgment, defers to your taste, recognizes your pretensions, appreciates your merits, anticipates your wants; he is solicitous for your comforts, studious of your wishes, condescending to your infirmities, forgetful of your foibles, tolerant of your errors, ready to make sacrifices for your enjoyment and to seek his own pleasure in your delight. His accomplishment is not the mere grace which may be acquired in the dancing-school, it implies the absence of every thing offensive in language, manners, and deportment, and the uniform possession of an easy, agreeable, and fascinating address, his charms are not merely exterior, not the automatic movements of one governed by artificial rules, they presuppose a skillful analysis of human character and human life, a keen observation of men and circumstances, a vivid perception of the influences which the most delicate attentions may exert upon their object, a facility of adaptation to the humors of men, a uniform flow of genial feeling, a perfect self-command, a kind and gentle heart, and an acquaintance with the forms of refined society.

"You may call this an art, but it is one of the liberal arts, and the complement of those arts which refine a cultivated people; it is a fine art, and the very finest of the fine. There is no painting or statue in the Louvre so pleasing to the stranger as the countenance of a friend beaming with unexpected benignity; there is no band in the Tuileries whose music is so delicious as that of the tongue of choice silver, no fountain in Parnassus so sweet as that mouth which is a well of kindness, nothing so softening and humanizing as the manners of a perfect gentleman."

All this greatly delighted Dr. Thomson, because it was congenial to his own tastes and habits—he was a perfect gentleman himself, and could appreciate gentility in others.

He admired very warmly French æsthetics, thus expressing his views:

"Beauty seems to charm all classes, and display itself in their dress, their habitations, their gardens, and their paths. In Summer seasons the ladies, as they enter the railroad cars, and the sweet children, as they follow their pretty mothers, are loaded with

nosegays and wreaths, so that you ride even over their
paths of iron in the midst of beauty and fragrance.
English mansions and castles may display more sump-
tuousness than French chateaus, but far less elegance;
and English country houses may have equal neatness,
but certainly not equal beauty with those of corresponding rank in France. The land is a land of flowers. England cultivates flowers as well as France,
but I think her soil and climate are not equally favorable to them, for I really believe the aster of France
is as large and lustrous as the dahlia of England.
Their public promenades, which are visited almost
daily by the wealthy, and weekly and semi-weekly by
the poorer classes, are well calculated to excite and
cultivate the love of beauty. Here ornamental balustrades, terminating in basements, from which rise
colossal statuary, inclose the areas; rostral columns,
bearing lamps, line the balustrades; and decorated
lamp-posts border the carriage ways; while groups of
statues on lofty pedestals adorned with historic emblems, meet the eye in every direction. Circular
basins, supported by cylindrical shafts, and embellished
with foliage, stand aloft on hexagonal bases; figures
seated around them with their feet on the prows of
vessels are separated by spouting dolphins; larger
dolphins, held by tritons and nereids, sport in the
ampler basins below; and upright figures of winged
children, standing on inverted shells, look down upon
swans spouting water at their feet. Here are parallel
avenues of lime and chestnut trees, there, beds of roses
and carnations; here are mounds commanding extensive views and crowned with cedars, there, labyrinths
with intricate and enticing paths, leading to pavilions,

which afford shelter and seats, where the weary traveler can look over the thronged city and the distant landscape; while ever and anon there arises before you some august monument of the past, such as the obelisk of Luxor, or the column of July, or some memorial of a distant land, as a palm from Sicily, a plant from the Cape of Good Hope, a buckeye from the banks of the Ohio, or a cedar from the summit of Lebanon.

" Evening and morning, as you walk the delicious shades, enrapturing music breaks upon your ear. Often in the Garden of the Tuileries, enjoying the fragrance of its gay parterres, or the shade of its majestic elms, or promenading in its alley of oranges, or gazing from its terraces upon the Seine, or reposing in its embowered seats, I have been overcome. The colossal statuary, the goodly palace—rich in animating associations, the enlivening strains of military bands, the delicious fragrance, the children swarming like bees around the flower beds, and the old men rejoicing on their crutches, were too much for me. But even the captivating gardens and walks of Paris are less beautiful than the places of resort in the vicinity, to which the whole population are wont to throng on Sunday or gala day, such as St. Cloud, Versailles, and Fontainebleau, where, in parks and palaces, in gardens and courts, in cascades and streams, in pavilions and terraces, art and nature seem to vie with each other in a doubtful contest; while within the buildings are grand vestibules adorned with statuary, marble staircases decorated with pilasters, and ceilings arched with gold and pierced with skylights; chambers, whose walls are sculptured with trophies, whose chimney pieces are portraits, whose ceilings—divided into compartments by mythological paintings—are hung with chandeliers ornamented with flowers; spacious saloons of statues and saloons of cabinets, saloons of Venus and saloons of Mars, saloons of Mercury and saloons of Aurora, saloons for feasting and saloons for sport; long galleries of paintings and galleries of antiquities, libraries with double tiers of loaded alcoves, chambers hung with tapestry containing copies of the richest paintings, and theaters and churches which my pen dare not attempt to describe. You must see for yourself the ample arches, the sculptured spandrels, the imposing painting of sacred story, the marble pavement wrought in mosaic, the balustrades of gilded bronze, the lofty columns, the architrave and cornice ripe from the richest chisels, the vaulted ceilings glowing from the noblest pencils, in the chapel of Versailles."

His volume of "Letters from Europe," published in 1856, and included among his works, contains an interesting account of this tour. To that volume we refer the reader for details.

CHAPTER X.

SECOND EUROPEAN TRIP.

DR. THOMSON made a second trip across the Atlantic in 1859. In the Fall of the previous year his mother died at Princeton, Illinois (whither she had moved to advance the financial interests of her younger children). She reached the advanced age of seventy-seven years; having been a widow twenty-three years. A part of her estate consisted of property in England, and the heirs requested their brother Edward to go thither in their interest, and attend to the sale and transmission of their title. Hence, in the Summer vacation of 1859 he set sail again for his native country. He landed at Cork, and made the tour of Ireland before entering England. The letters written home during that Summer abroad contain so much information, and are so characteristic of the author's style that we insert some of them here. They were contributed to one of our Church papers, but none of them has ever appeared in book form:

I.

CORK—IRISH GRAEFFENBURGH—BLARNEY.

Although in my early morning walks in Cork I met with no beggars, it was otherwise in the latter part of the day; it seems that beggars are not early risers. From the door of the hotel to the outermost wanderings, men, women, and children asking alms beset the stranger. Their eloquence is proverbial; they flatter you, pray for you, bless you, and coax you in all ways. They are often profane, using the name of God on every occasion. Usually the beggars are women and "widders" with twelve or thirteen "childer," and sometimes they show you one at the breast, tugging away as though it understood its business—perhaps it was borrowed for the occasion. These alms-takers are, however, easily put off—a penny or two is all they expect; and though they ask it "for the love of God," it is to be feared it often goes to gratify the love of whisky. Two things are not a little provoking—they cleave to the stranger, and especially the American, while they allow hundreds of the denizens to pass without the least molestation, and they are particularly clamorous when you mount the vehicle to depart.

Cork is a tolerably pretty city of about ninety thousand inhabitants. It is situated on both sides of the Lee. Some streets run up the adjacent summits, as they do about the hills surrounding the Queen City. Some of the public edifices are very fine, particularly Queen's College, the lunatic asylum, and the city and county jails. The commerce of Cork is considerable, it exports about fifteen millions of dollars annually. Many of the stores are very rich and attractive, and trade seems to be brisk. The Imperial Hotel is the best I have seen in the kingdom.

But we must take a jaunting car and go out to Blarney Castle and the Irish Graeffenburgh. The open jaunting car is a singular vehicle. Just at the horse's tail sits the driver; backward from his seat runs a long box, in which you may put your overcoat and umbrella—articles always wanted in this watery island—and upon which you may place a cushion and have a seat, or find a place for luggage; on each side of this box is a seat calculated for two or three persons; the passengers sit back to back, facing opposite sides of the street. When there is but one the driver sits opposite to him to balance the vehicle, which, resting upon only two wheels, might otherwise easily be overset; below each seat is a platform for the feet, which are protected at the sides by a board; below is an iron step by which you mount. Crack goes the whip and on we rush, pursued by the beggars, till the speed of the car becomes too great for them. Soon we are in St. Patrick's Street—the principal one—irregular, but business like, and, at certain points picturesque. And now we reach the Grand Parade; next through Great George's Street to the Western Road. Onward we rush passing the Convent of Mercy, the Cathedral of St. Finbar, etc., turning to the right we come to a double row of magnificent elm trees, whose tops intermingle to form a green canopy over a broad graveled walk more than a mile in length.

"What is that, driver?"

"It is the Mardyke; there the queen, when in Ireland, walked as straight as an arrow."

On the left we find the imposing structures of Queen's College and the county jail; on the right, beyond the Mardyke, Blair's Castle and numerous beautiful villas.

From the end of the Mardyke we see to the right, on an elevated summit, an immense pile of new buildings whose pinnacles rise above the trees, in which a choir of birds make melody. Alas! it is the lunatic asylum. Onward we career over magnificent roads, between stone walls, varying in height from five to twenty feet, crowned with ornamental hedges, now of privet, then of blackthorn, then of furze, then of a mixture of all, interwoven with the rose and the honeysuckle, and bordered below with the foxglove's purple bells. Generally the hedges are neatly trimmed, and sometimes portions are allowed to rise above the general level, to be cut into pyramids and other geometrical figures. Here, on one side, from the lofty walls rise precipitous heights, covered densely with an intermixture of pine, larch, fir, holly, and laurel up to their summits; on the other side, a vast expanse of cultivated fields separated by hedgerows and laden with barley, wheat, and oats, stretches out before you as far as the eye can reach. Here and there the wall is curved and pierced to allow an entrance, which is closed by a massive and lofty ornamented gate, through whose gratings you can see the graveled carriage-ways, with their bordering of aloes, rhododendrons, and arbutus, winding in graceful curves to the splendid mansion embosomed in fragrant shrubbery.

And now, on a hill-top, we pause to take an extended view of the charming valley of the Lee. The entrance to Cork was like the entrance to paradise— this is like paradise itself.

"What is that castellated building yonder, rising from that rock?"

"It is Carrigrohan Castle, recently restored and occupied by Mr. McSweeny."

Onward we go, still guarded on each side by massive masonry, charmed on every hand by some new and pleasing object and the song or twitter of the birds. Nothing to mar the pleasure, but now and then a mud-walled hut by the roadside or a beggar stretching out to you his imploring hat.

And now we reach the Irish Graeffenburgh. This hydropathic establishment is at St. Ann's Hill, about seven miles from Cork. To the right of the road to Tower Bridge, on the summit of an eminence commanding a magnificent prospect, stands the house and its surrounding cottages. A spring of fine water supplies both the house and the baths. A wood, with numerous walks, stretches northward and westward for two miles. In other directions are beautiful views of cultivated fields, amid which is Blarney Castle and its famous grove. It is curious to observe the use made of sticks in building covered ways, summerhouses and their furniture. We saw a row of cottages built of turf and plastered inside and out—the cost was fifty dollars a room.

Here there are water baths, vapor baths, vapor chambers, etc. In addition to all these the Turkish baths. These are to give a temperature to the body higher than can be given to it by other means. You can not use water at a higher temperature than 103°, Fahrenheit, nor vapor higher than 105°, but in this Turkish bath you can raise the air to 200° or 300° without inconvenience. A man can not remain in a vapor bath over ten minutes; he may remain in the Turkish bath for hours. This bath is, indeed, a succession of baths; water is poured over the patient from time to time at a temperature most agreeable to his feelings. We were taken into the Turkish bath, and found the rooms most admirably and elegantly furnished. There is, first, the tepidarium, or warm room; then the sudatorium, or hot room; then the divan, or cooling room, where the patient, reposing on luxurious couches, undergoes the process of shampooing. The whole arrangement is sumptuous. Splendid carpets cover the floor; colored glass in the windows soften and enrich the light; while artificial fountains play in the center. Of course, we had not the privilege of seeing a gentleman enjoying his luxury, but we were permitted to enter one of the heated chambers; we did not advance beyond 130°, which perfectly satisfied us. We were permitted to look upon a horse that had advanced beyond this, for it is used for the cure of inferior animals. I thought, however, that he enjoyed the opening of the window through which we looked upon him, more than the temperature of the chamber.

The terms in this establishment vary from £2 7s. to £3 5s. per week, £1 1s. consultation fee entrance, and fires extra; blanket for packing, sheets and towels for bedroom use and for bathing purposes furnished by the patient; private sitting-room, £1 7s. 6d. per week extra; Turkish baths, 3s. extra; and oxygen inhalation, 4s. extra. The expenses are, I suppose, about twenty-five dollars a week, without servants. Hydroppathy as a system of sanitation will have its run, and run out.

Up, now, for Blarney. Well known is the spot. In the park around the castle is an old woman, well dressed and civil, who furnishes you with a key to the castle. You ascend to the top and walk upon the walls, looking for your footing. A sense of security is given by the matting of ivy on each side. The view must be seen to be appreciated. The hills, groves, and lake are all immortal; but

> "There is a stone there
>   That whoever kisses
>   O, he never misses
>   To grow eloquent.
>   'T is he may clamber
>   To a lady's chamber,
>   Or become a member
>   Of Parliament.
>   A clever spouter
>   He 'll soon turn, or
>   An out-and-outer
>   To be let alone.
>   Do n't hope to hinder him
>   Or to bewilder him,
>   Sure he 's a pilgrim
>   From the Blarney Stone."

On the top of the wall you must lie down, and, taking hold of an iron clasp that supports the stone— for it is broken and would else fall—while a friendly party holds your feet, you must crawl forward and put your head down to the talismanic slab. The ladies merely kiss *at it*, that is, kiss the hand. It is amusing to see the intense desire to kiss this stone. How the kisses smack alike from American Democrats and Irish Tories. "Did you kiss it?" Yes, indeed. So look out for me.

II.

KILLARNEY.

From Cork we proceed to Mallow by rail. Here we make a short stay to glance at one of the best country towns in this part of Ireland. It is well situated on the Blackwater, and was once a resort for fashionables, on account of its mineral waters. It is said to have a large retail trade. To us it wears a gloomy aspect. It is approached through a long walled lane; its streets are narrow; its houses nearly all alike in shape and color, stuccoed or slated, and without ornament; beggars sit at the public places; a policeman is seen at every turn; artillerists throng the street or gather around the drinking-houses; and ill-clad children encumber you as you pass. Looking through the cross streets up to the old portions of the town, you see low, thatched-roofed dwellings, indicative of any thing but thrift and comfort.

From Mallow we proceed, by Lombardston, Millstreet, Kanturk, Shinnagh, and Headford, to Killarney. The country is much less charming than that we have seen; beautiful prospects of hill and valley, with hedgerows and woodland, open before us, but the land is rich and less cultivated, in some places overgrown with furze, in others, presenting extensive peat bogs. These last look like overgrown brickyards; the turf extends in some cases to the depth of eight or ten feet; it is cut into the shape of bricks, and piled up in regular rows. It is burned in grates like coal, and makes a beautiful fire, with a bright blaze, without smoke, and radiating great heat. I asked the price of the turf on a new-made kitchen fire that I saw brightly burning, and was answered, a penny. About £100 are expended annually in turf to furnish the Royal Hotel at Killarney. Turf is a great mercy to Ireland. The town of Killarney is about a mile from the shore of the lower lake, and contains many excellent inns; but, owing to its depressed situation and the intervention of the woods of Lord Kenmare's estate, it commands no view of the enchanting waters. We, therefore, take carriage and drive out one mile and a half to the Royal Victoria Hotel, within whose spacious gates we pass before we get a glimpse of the lake. At first view I was disappointed; the lake is so small compared with our great lakes that I felt a little contempt for it, and was disposed to ask, " Why have you made so much ado in the world?" and to say within myself, we need not go beyond America to see the works of nature. Looking up to the mountains and wandering along the beach, the feeling of disappointment was followed by admiration, and as the quiet moonbeams lighted up the woodlands and played upon the waters, I lingered, delighted and filled with gratitude and praise, till a late hour at night.

Arrangements must now be made for the morrow. We hire a jaunting car, a four-oared boat, and a guide. At the waterside we inquired of a boatman who was the best guide. The elder Spillane was mentioned, and the boatman added, " O, he is a *swate-speaking* man." And so we found him. The day dawns brightly, and a good breakfast awaits us in the coffee-room ; on going out we are beset at the door by a man selling arbutus canes, and by several women at the garden selling various articles, chiefly manufactured from the same wood or from the bog oak. Mounting the vehicle we were surrounded by beggars, chiefly girls, with various articles for sale. The driver cracks his whip, but they follow till, at length, in mercy, we promise to buy or give on our return. The boat having proceeded with a good supply of sandwiches, rolls, etc., for luncheon, we drive round to meet it at the upper lake, passing on the right by the ruins of

Aghadoe, the estates of Lady Headly, and Mr. James O'Connell—brother to Daniel O'Connell—and on the left by the seat of Mr. Mahoney. Not the least interesting object in the drive is Dunloe Castle. At length we arrive at the famous "Gap of Dunloe." At the approach to it is a roadside *posada* kept by a descendant of Kate Kearney, who, as we drive up, comes out to sell us goat's milk and mountain dew. A slight pause, and we drive till the path is inaccessible to the carriage, when dismounting, instead of taking a pony, we resolved to walk. Advancing, we come midway of the gap to the house of "fighting Paul," and entering it find only a few goats and a donkey. At different points in the gap are fine echoes, which are awakened by the bugle of the guide and by the firing of cannon, which had been provided in anticipation of our coming. The guide, "guessing correctly," played with exquisite taste, at the first echo, "Hail Columbia." You can not imagine my feelings as I sat upon a fragment of rock, and, yielding to the spirit of romance, looked up to the cloud-capped mountain and listened to it playing our national air, and to the three cannon fired in succession afterward, each calling from the mountain four distinct reverberations from as many different peaks. At the center of the gap we ascend an elevated point and look each way; the distance from mountain-top to mountain-top is probably sixty English miles. O, what a charming sight! It seems as though an angel had torn the mountains asunder here to give us the goodly vision. Just now our feelings are disturbed by a Scotch gentleman of American ideas, who cried out, "What a fine sheep pasture! I would take this at once." "No," said the guide, "sheep have been tried here; but the green plant at the foot of the mountain destroys them. They like it, and it brings on the dropsy—*anasarca*—of which they are sure to die in a year or two; but look up to the summits of the mountains—the Reeks—they are not birds that you see. Yonder are sheep, those are cows. Alas! one often gets entangled in the clefts of the mountains and perishes of hunger."

Reaching the termination of the gap, the Corn a Dhuv, or Black Valley, breaks suddenly upon the view. The contrast between the gloomy scenery of the gap and the cheerful prospects of the glen heightens greatly the effect of the latter's matchless beauty.

Pursuing the winding road we come to Lord Brandon's cottage, now occupied, and passing round it we soon come to the point on the upper lake where we meet our boat. Seated at the base of a beautiful holly, boatman, guide, and travelers all engaged heartily in devouring the "substances and fluids" which had been prepared to nourish the wearied system and revive the exhausted spirits, or rather keep up the exhilarated spirits. Nothing sweeter, thought I, than those sandwiches since I left my mother's breast.

Luncheon over, we embark to view the lakes. The upper, though the smallest, is the gem. Surrounded by mountains and full of islands, it is a diamond set in emeralds. We stopped to visit Ronancy's island, the most interesting of this water. After coasting numerous bays we proceed to the Long Range, which is a narrow channel that leads to the middle lake. It presents a variety of charming scenery, but its most interesting object is the perpendicular cliff, in which is contained the eagle's nest. You come upon it suddenly by reason of a turn in the channel. Here the boat stops, and the guide landing proceeds some distance below the cliff, and concealing himself, plays his bugle. All listen breathless for the echo. At first we seem to hear only the original notes; at length we discover that it is only the reverberated ones that greet our ear, and "load the trembling air" with rich and various melody. A mile further and we come to the old wire bridge, consisting of two arches, which so confine the channel as to render its passage dangerous at times. A short distance below is the "meeting of the waters." Here the channel divides, one branch leading to Glena Bay, the other to the middle lake. We take the latter. We stop to view Dinis Cottage, the cottage of Mr. Herbert, M. P., a lineal descendant of a hero who was knighted by Henry V, and the owner of large estates in this quarter. Proceeding to Glena Bay, we land to view the sweet little cottage of Lord Castleross, son of the earl of Kenmare, which it will be a pleasure to me some day to describe to you, as it affords many hints on cottage building in America. It is just finished.

From this point we proceed to the Island of Innisfallen, pronounced by Arthur Young the most beautiful spot in Europe. It is famous not only for its natural beauty but for its historical interest. It was chosen by some monks, twelve centuries ago, as the site of a monastery, whose ruins are not the least attraction of the traveler. Fancy an island indented with most graceful bays, creeks, and hollows; encompassed with dense woods—oak, beech, elm, holly, sycamore, in their most magnificent proportions and interiorly molded into the most pleasing forms of hill, valley, dell, glen, adorned with myrrh, myrtle, furze, purple heather, daisy, buttercup, dandelion, rose, and honeysuckle, woven in a surface of shamrock; while the ruins of one of the noblest convents of the olden time stand before you, reminding you that light shone upon that sacred spot when there was darkness upon the continent; that here prayers were offered and treasures preserved, praises chanted, philosophy studied, and history written through many ages, and you have an idea of Innisfallen. There is somewhat peculiar in the soil or the atmosphere which makes vegetation flourish here. We measured an ivy that was holding up an arch in the abbey, and found it twenty-eight inches in circumference; a holly, and found it twelve feet; and yew, thirteen to fourteen feet. Considering the slowness with which these trees grow, we may say with a distinguished botanist, the age of these trees is to be estimated by centuries, or even by thousands of years. The island is unoccupied save as a pasture. The proprietor hired a daring Scotchman to plow the graveyard; his assistant soon ran off, terrified by the frightful sounds—he himself soon followed in great alarm, declaring that no price could hire him to complete the work. He still lives, and declares he is not feigning. He lost his place by not fulfilling his task. No wonder imagination should have power in this charmed spot, and shall we complain that she guards its sacred precincts? I cut some shamrock for the editor (a native of Ireland), but found I could not carry it.

Next day we proceeded through the grounds of Mr. Herbert to Muckross Abbey. This consists chiefly of the ruins of a church and convent of the Franciscan friars, who are supposed to have erected it in 1440, though the beautiful site has been occupied for religious uses from a much earlier period. The original abbey is said to have been consumed by fire in A. D. 1190. Luxuriant vegetation encompasses these interesting relics of antiquity, still beautiful in their decay, so that the stranger is quite near them before they strike his eye. This was the favorite place of burial for many of Ireland's ancient chiefs, whose tombstones may still be seen in various stages of decay. The architecture of the building is much admired—a visitor observing the elegant paneled and ivy-encompassed doorway which forms the entrance, remarks: "We have not improved in architecture for ages." In the center of the cloisters a yew-tree, thirteen feet in circumference, lifts its venerable head, on which the sun has probably looked down as long as on the abbey itself. Wandering among the tombs I copied some of the inscriptions, such as "*Dum spiro spero,*" "*Mea gloria fides,*" and, ascending to the top of the wall, surveyed the surrounding scenes.

III.

SABBATH AT KILLARNEY—ARBUTUS—ROSS ISLAND.

Having on Saturday introduced myself to Mr. Higgins, pastor of the Wesleyan Chapel in this place, I received from him a kind invitation to preach the next day, which I accepted. In the morning I set out from the hotel on foot. Killarney is a town of about ten thousand inhabitants, containing some neat buildings, but generally structures of the old, gloomy style, stuccoed or slated, and arranged on narrow and irregular streets. It has no manufactures, except those of articles made of arbutus wood, and but a small trade, mostly retail.

The place has grown up chiefly within the last century; for it is said that in 1747 it had only thirty or forty thatched cottages and a few slated houses, in the midst of which stood the residence of the earl. It has a few good hotels, but no public buildings worthy of notice, except the new Roman Catholic cathedral. Before leaving the place I passed through this edifice, and was delighted with its beauty. A priest, of gentlemanly manners and an appearance indicative of good habits, was polite enough to inform me that $100,000 had been expended upon it, and that $85,000 more was needed to complete it, the tower not having been yet carried much above the roof.

"Where," said I, " do you get so much money?"

"The late bishop subscribed $20,000 out of his revenue; the earl of Kenmare, $10,000 ; the Americans have sent us $10,000 ; the rest has been obtained from the people of the diocese."

As I passed through the town on my way to church, a crowd of boys surrounded me, each crying, "Give us a penny, sir!" "What do you want a penny for?" Some cried, "To buy bread;" others, "To buy a book." "What do you want a book for?" "To get our lesson, sir." "Go home and say your prayers ; I can not give a penny to boys that beg on Sabbath." Some cried, "We have said our prayers." A sort of leader among them said, "Let the gentleman alone; we will see him Monday morning;" whereupon they all left me.

At the end of the street, and fronting on the first cross street, is the market space. Here are the market women, selling vegetables, as briskly as on any week-day, and the streets are crowded with merry idlers as on a gala-day. Behind the market space is a remarkable building, doubtless intended for public uses—perhaps for meat-market, town hall, etc. The front part of the upper story has fallen, or been taken down. On the wall of the back part is a good place to stick bills, and it has been used for this purpose. Covering all others is an immense yellow bill, with the words, "The American Circus is Coming," in flaming capitals. The lower story, which still stands, with house-leek growing above it, is divided by an archway into two apartments, in both of which the windows, having had their glass knocked out, are protected by loose boards. Over the one are the words, "National Evening School;" over the other, "Temperance Hall." Turning to the left, and advancing a square or two, we find close to the police barracks the Wesleyan chapel. It stands in the back yard of the parsonage. The premises, both chapel and parsonage, are owned by one of the members of the Church, and rented to the society for ninety dollars a year. The parsonage is a comfortable but humble dwelling; the chapel is about twenty feet by forty, painted white outside, and slate color inside; the seats and pulpit are oaked. The light comes through semicircular windows on one side. The pulpit is a semi-octagonal box, supported by a single column. It is quite deep, concealing most of the preacher's person, and is not large enough to admit any one else. There are no pews, but families sit together in their appointed seats. The order of worship is singing, prayer, reading the Scripture, singing, preaching, singing, prayer, closed by benediction, without any interval between it and the prayer. I supposed that the Common Prayer of the Church of England was used; but the pastor tells me that among the Irish Wesleyans it is used only in the cities. In prayer the minister stands, the people sit. In singing, the hymn is repeated in couplets, or, as we say, *lined*. There is no instrument of music or choir.

The congregation consisted in the morning of thirteen persons; in the evening of nine. Four persons followed me in the morning from the hotel, out of politeness, I suppose; but they did not attend the evening service. Mr. Higgins invited me to preach in the evening, remarking the Sabbath was his last, and his people were expecting a farewell sermon from him, but adding that he would preach that after my evening discourse. Of course I declined, wondering at the extreme clerical courtesy which induced him to make such a proposition. I, however, attended the service, and heard a good sermon, founded on the words of Paul's farewell discourse to the Church of Ephesus.

At the close of the services the congregation, at the suggestion of the pastor, stepped into the parsonage, with myself, when I was introduced to them severally. We had a very pleasant conversation of an hour, in the course of which I learned a few things that it may not be uninteresting for you to know or for me to reportt. The Wesleyan mission was commenced here about six years ago. The first missionary preached in the streets, but was driven away by violent persecution. Another was sent, who, by prudent management, laid a foundation. He was succeeded by the present pastor, who has just closed his third year, and, therefore, must depart. His people seemed very sorry to lose him. He has preached twice every Sunday and once every Thursday, held a prayer-meeting every Tuesday, and visited during the other days of the week eight other appointments, as occasion offered ; some weekly, some fortnightly, etc. The membership in Killarney is 12 ; the congregation rarely exceeds 20. This little band is closely united. They seem to be very intelligent and pious. On entering the church they all reverently kneel, and during the service seem profoundly attentive. They suffer no little persecution. One of Mr. Higgins's children was severely beaten in the street the other day for no other reason than that he was a Protestant. His father brought the case before the magistrate, who, I believe, inflicted no punishment on the offender, but bound him to keep the peace in future. Men are afraid to join lest they should lose their business or suffer otherwise. The whole number of Protestants in the place is about a hundred. Such of them as are not Wesleyans attend the parish church. This did nothing till the Wesleyan mission was commenced. For many years the congregation consisted of the curate, the sexton, and a Methodist local preacher. Of late they have made more exertion, and have gathered in a congregation of thirty or forty. Lord Kenmare nominates the rector, and, as he is a devoted Catholic, it can not be expected that he will select one very active in the cause of Protestantism; nor can it be supposed that a rector so appointed will feel any very great obligation to oppose the papacy. The present rector, it is said, spends most of his time in England, leaving the parish in the hands of the curate, who, instead of co-operating with the Wesleyans, opposes them. Mr. Higgins has changed his hours of worship at different times; but the curate has made corresponding changes, so as to prevent him from deriving any advantage from it. This is a pity, and it is to be hoped that, in this forlorn hope of Protestantism, Protestants will learn that union is strength.

The Wesleyans could not worship without the protection of the police. A policeman is regularly detailed to guard them whenever they hold service. The people here all profess to be religious. No wonder; for the Roman Church is powerful at this point, having the aristocracy, the magistracy, the business, every thing in their hands. But it is pretty evident, as might be expected, that there is a deep undercurrent of skepticism. The salary of Mr. Higgins is £54, exclusive of house-rent and fuel. His wife does not seem satisfied, and sometimes hints to her husband the propriety of seeking in America or elsewhere higher attainments pecuniarily; but the good man admonishes her to guard against worldly motives. At a late hour I returned to the hotel accompanied by the pastor, and charmed with the beauty of mountain and lake, of art and nature, which presented itself on all sides, under the beams of a bright moon. Can we be surprised that men should cleave, even in poverty and persecution, to a land so charming, or forget to pray that its moral charms may correspond to its material?

Before I parted with Brother Higgins he informed me that he was distressed about a debt of fifteen or twenty dollars that had been incurred by the Church for painting. Have you no subscriber interested in our work on this island that would take pleasure in sending this amount to the little struggling Church?

Before I leave Killarney I must mention more particularly the arbutus, as it is one of the beauties of the scenery, and one of the sources of the revenues of this region. It is a tree-shrub, *Arbutus unedo*, whose leaves, of a peculiarly bright green, give a rich variety to the foliage of the forest, and whose scarlet berries and clusters of flowers adorn these mountains and islands in the autumnal season. It is uncertain whether it is indigenous, though it grows all over Ireland, but nowhere with the luxuriance it exhibits around this enchanted spot.

Its wood is of great beauty and durability, and the root, the trunk, and the branches, having different colors, it is molded into the most beautiful forms of useful and ornamental articles, such as paper-folders, card-cases, needle-cases, checker and chess-boards, writing-desks, tables, etc. I visited the principal factory in company with a traveler, who bought articles to a large amount. The proprietor showed us a table similar to the one purchased by the Prince of Wales during his visit last year, and the price of which, if my recollection serves me, was $500. While in the establishment, I took occasion to ask the proprietor what wages he gave the workmen who made such exquisitely beautiful furniture. He said, I believe, from six to eight dollars a week.

Ross Island, which afforded me much pleasure, I think I forgot to mention. We sailed to it the first day, but did not land. Near the landing and beneath the castle is the celebrated echo of Paddy Blake, to whom one of our boatmen paid his respects, and from whom we received the usual attention. On a subsequent day, we visited the island by land. Here are graveled walks, and flower gardens, and seats placed in positions to command the finest views. But the castle is the chief attraction. It is surrounded by a lofty iron railing, painted green, which incloses a spot around the castle that is in most perfect order, both as to its green slopes, and its graveled walks and terraces.

The noble old ruin is a massive square building that rises from a limestone rock, and is supported landward by strong buttresses; it is covered with ivy, and is a very picturesque object of the lower lake. Its historical associations add to its charms. It was the stronghold of the O'Donoghue family, and held out resolutely against the forces of Cromwell, but at length yielded under the siege of Ludlow and Waller in 1652. Many legends, with which some of your readers must be familiar, add to its interest.

Ascending by a spiral stone stairway the round tower of Ross Castle, and walking upon the crumbling walls, you have the most beautiful prospect I ever beheld. The varied colors of the mountains, the silver surface of the lakes, and the long vistas of cultivated fields interspersed with woodland, the modern palaces, and the crumbling ruins, form such a mixture of sublimity and sweetness, of rising beauty and decaying grandeur, as the earth rarely presents. I lingered, not without danger, on the walls, and looked through all the windows of the tower as I descended.

IV.

DUBLIN.

We must take a ride through the city. Off we go in a jaunting car. All at once we are stopped; the street is full of wagons, carts, and cars, and as it is now narrowed in consequence of repairs which are in progress, we can not pass; our driver permits several to go by him while he stands, but seeing the advancing procession interminable, he occupies the way and they are brought to a dead halt. And now he begins to remonstrate, but in vain; the driver of the vanguard of this opposing host makes no reply, but seems to say, " I can stand still as long as you can," and the long train behind appeared to draw up to endure with patience a long siege. This is all the more provoking to our excited driver, and what might have happened we can not tell, but luckily a police officer arrived and prevented violence. Commanding the first driver opposed to us to pass us, he forbade the others to advance, and so left an avenue for us. We wanted our driver to take another route when he found his way blocked up, even though it were longer, but he was obstinate.

"Here," said our Irish friend who played the cicerone, "are the four courts—Court of Exchequer, Court of Common Pleas, Court of Queen's Bench, and Court of Chancery. As to the Courts of Exchequer and Common Pleas, they might as well be called the devil's courts." Onward to the Phœnix Park, said to contain 1,000 acres, and to surpass any park of London. Here is the Wellington memorial, on which are inscribed the victories from Assaye to Waterloo, and which George IV called an overgrown millstone. "Here is the Royal and Military Hospital of Kilmainham, established in 1675, on the site of a priory founded by Strongbow; there the commander of the forces and some other old fogies live. Here is the vice-regal lodge, where the Lord Lieutenant lives in Summer, and where the queen was entertained on her late visit. His salary is $100,000 a year, and what he can steal." "But you don't have stealing among your officials, I hope." "O, yes, indeed; it is easy enough to get five hundred by giving a thousand." "But you will not accuse your newly appointed lord lieutenant of such a wickedness." "Well, I believe he is among our purest officials." Here is the Phœnix Column, with the rising phœnix on its summit. Opposite the lodge is the "fifteen acres," where Daniel O'Connell shot Mr. D'Esterre, a member of the corporation. Happily, dueling is now frowned down, alike by English and Irish nobility. We are just in time to witness on this spot, which is the usual place of parade, a grand review under Lord Seaton. The troops are of all arms, and about six thousand in number, and the evolutions are admirable. It is difficult to say which is best, artillery, cavalry, or infantry. The music, the marching, the rattle of musketry, the booming of cannon, as you may well judge, were inspiring. I called in question the perfection of the horses, but was assured that they were all carefully selected and the best in the world;

their long bodies and heavy tails did not, however, strike me as beautiful. After the troops were dismissed, Lord Seaton and staff passed within a few feet of us, giving us a fine opportunity to mark him. He is a well-made, good-looking old gentleman, with hair and whiskers white as snow. His face is not unlike Wellington's, and his attitude and manners indicate a calm and self-possessed spirit. He rides a very large gray steed—white seems to be a favorite color with generals. The troops leave the field in order—a thing which seems to be very natural and easy, yet Wellington once said there were but few men in England that could take ten thousand men into Hyde Park and lead them out again without disorder. Riding along one of the regiments as it was going to quarters, I remarked a great want of precision in marching, but was told that the soldiers were not then considered as marching—that it was deemed too fatiguing after field exercise to exact precision of step in going to barracks.

There has been quite a war panic in the United Kingdom, which everywhere shows its indications to the stranger's eye. The militia are called out twice a year for three weeks' drill, when they are uniformed, and lodged, and furnished with arms by the government, and receive about twenty-five cents a day. As the drill, though daily, is not exhaustive, and as the pay—$13\frac{1}{2}$ pence per diem—is equivalent to ordinary wages on farms—mechanics only get ten shillings a week in Winter, and twelve in Summer; farm laborers only nine, usually—they do not grumble when under orders; but this year, as they were called out generally in the middle of hay harvest, when wages are high, they would have had cause to complain but for the excited feeling of the country. People now begin to .think that there was no occasion for the alarm, and as they are to be called on to pay four pence in the pound extra income tax before Christmas for their extra military expenses, they feel rather sore. The news that France is about to reduce her army and navy to a peace footing with all convenient dispatch, is most welcome and refreshing. Men breathe more freely in every English home; yet still there are lingering doubts of Napoleon's honesty. Now and then you hear an Englishman say, "I hope Napoleon will make war upon us, we shall soon be ready for him; we might suffer at first, but he would soon kill off our old fogies, which would be a great blessing to us, and would call forth competent men to fill their places." Nevertheless, there may be some mistake in this. Positions in army and navy are still bought and sold. We traveled with a captain who had been wounded at the Crimea, and who had just sold his commission for $10,000. Even in the militia this system prevails. The colonel of a militia regiment is a well-qualified officer, and he is generally taken from the regular army, and there are a few other officers of skill and energy associated with him; but the rest are usually young men, sons of the wealthy, who have money to buy commissions. When will wars cease? Mr. Bright suggests that by interweaving commercial ties more closely between England and France, government is to perpetuate the peace between them, and he is right. If the destruction of London would be as ruinous to French pockets as to English, it would not be done by French cannon. I mean no offense to the English by this allusion; they generally think the idea of invasion ridiculous, and the encampment of a French army in a London park utterly impossible.

The peace between Austria and Italy has taken Great Britain by surprise. Both the mode and the matter of the treaty are the subjects of severe animadversion. It is deemed most unnatural and unfortunate that the peace of Europe should depend upon the will of two emperors, who draw the sword and sheathe it without consultation with others, and even without the intervention of responsible ministers.

The results of the war are not likely to be satisfactory to any party, and to be most distasteful to some. After the loss of one hundred thousand men, and perhaps one hundred million of treasure, Italy, to say the least, is *in statu quo.* Never was an enterprise more " bloated in the promise," more " lank in the performance," than Louis Napoleon's Italian campaign. Instead of planting the flag of Italian independence on the shores of the Adriatic, he has planted the flag of Italian subjugation on the fortresses of the *quadrangle.* Austria, by entering the Italian confederation, virtually extends her power over the whole peninsula. There is no more hope of a free state entering this confederacy than fear of a monarchy entering ours. The exaltation of the pope to a nominal presidency must give a temporary check to his declining influence.

Who, then, can be pleased with the issue? Not Austria, disgracefully beaten and forbidden to restore by force the expelled Italian dukes, although she knows they can not be restored without it. Not France, reduced in men and means, and compensated only by a little military glory, which is a poor offset to the moral disgrace of disappointing the excited hopes of Hungary and Italy. Not Sardinia, though enlarged somewhat in her territories, yet crippled in her influence. Not Protestants; for the Pope has been exalted. Not Papists; for the most devoted and powerful support to the pope has been beaten and humbled. Perhaps Napoleon alone is satisfied. His life is said to be devoted to three things,—the restoration of his dynasty, the revision of the treaty of 1815, and the revenge of Waterloo. This war accomplishes the second step of this programme.

There is much discussion as to whether the British will take any part in the settlement of the details of the treaty whose bases were laid at Villafranca. The John Bull feeling is, " You have got into a bad fix without consulting me; get out of it as well as you can." But perhaps better counsels may prevail, and something be done for the Italians.

What a mystery is Napoleon ! Who can fathom him ? A year or two hence he may land an army in Kent. The British are slow and persistent; the French are quick and enthusiastic. The former could not be beaten in a protracted war, but would develop increasing energies with the advancing conflict. But the sudden landing of Napoleon might possibly occur. This, by breaking the charm of British prestige, would answer Napoleon's end, and thereupon he might offer a *generous* peace. But I did not intend to write of current news, as you get that by telegraph.

The business of Dublin, though small compared with that of London, is, nevertheless, large. A commercial friend introduced us to one of the principal houses, that of Pym Brothers, Quakers, who politely showed us through the different departments, in which they employ daily two hundred and forty clerks and $750,000 capital, realizing, probably, a profit of $150,000 per annum.

We must not forget the castle. It stands on an elevated point in the southern part of the city, and, you know, is rich in historical associations. But little of the ancient structure is left, and, with the exception of the Birmingham tower, it is said, the original shape of the castle has been altered. It contains at present two parts—one for the public offices, and the other for the apartments of state of the lord lieutenant. Numerous soldiers appear to be quartered in it, whom you may see early in the morning marching and countermarching in the court and adjoining avenues and streets. The chapel of the castle is new and exquisitely beautiful. The interior is oak carving; around the gallery is carved the coat-of-arms of every nobleman who has served in the capacity of lord lieutenant. The pews of the lord lieutenant are in the center of one of the side galleries, and those of the bishop directly opposite. The other gallery seats are for the officers of state and their families. Below are a few open seats for visitors. The pulpit rests upon a single ornamental shaft—the column of faith, surmounted by the heads of the four Evangelists, each bearing his own Gospel. Opposite the pulpit shines the grand organ, with its enameled pipes, while the effect of the whole is heightened by the light from the stained windows. The sight is worth the shilling you give to the pleasant Irish girl who shows you through.

The evening before leaving I called at the castle,

to pay my respects to the lord lieutenant, to whom I bore a letter of introduction from a common and much-esteemed friend. Unfortunately for me, he had not yet reached the city, though he had been hourly expected for some time. I left my letter, and a few days afterward received a complimentary note from his lordship, inclosing a ticket of admission to the gallery of the House of Lords.

Early in the morning we bid farewell to Dublin, intending to take breakfast at Kingston, and spend a little time in observing the beautiful port before setting sail. Kingston, formerly known by another name, was thus called in honor of George IV, when he visited the island. Its large rows of splendid houses and the heavy shipping in the port indicate activity, comfort, and thrift. Great improvements are in progress to make the harbor more secure. Here we take leave of Irish railroads. The Irish boast of their railway king, Mr. Dargen, a man of great talents, energy, and generosity. He was the chief instrument in getting up the late exhibition at Dublin. When the subscription was found inadequate, he subscribed the deficit. He was visited by the queen quite unexpectedly, and offered knighthood, which he declined, preferring to be called Mr. Dargen. "Why, sir," cries a friend, "Mr. Dargen can tell you at a glance the height of a mountain, and how long it will take and what it will cost to carry a railroad round or through it." He has, perhaps, been poorly paid for his services; for, although reputed wealthy, his means consist chiefly in railroad stocks, which, in this country as in ours, are fluctuating and precarious, and he is often close pressed for a thousand dollars. It is said he is now getting fond of the bottle—tarries long at the wine. We hope not.

We have seen Ireland to great advantage. The weather has been most charming. With the exception of the shower that fell upon us in the cove of Cork, we have had nothing but sunshine. Every thing has contributed to our comfort, health, and delight,—sunbeams within and sunbeams without.

"Bless the Lord, O my soul!"

V.

LONDON.

In many respects English usages and customs differ from ours. These differences are generally interesting to us. I am not unwilling to give you details, because they are just what books do not give, and what, after all, throw the best light upon the life and character of the people.

Having been charged with a little secular business by some American friends I learned somewhat of English law practice.

All deeds and other evidences of property in England are registered at Somerset House, London, where they are examined very critically, and rejected if defective or informal. Married ladies signing deeds must be examined apart from their husbands by two commissioners appointed by court for that special purpose. Among the papers committed to me was the acknowledgment of a lady; in the papers containing this acknowledgment her name, by unpardonable carelessness, is spelled three different ways; once correctly, namely, in the commission. In consequence of this discrepancy it is rejected at the registrar's office. What is to be done? If sent back it will require two months nearly to replace it. The commissioners may be absent, the lady may be absent, the papers may be miscarried. Learning that in case of an error not deemed vital, the court might order the document to be filed, I came up to London to make application to a judge to order the acknowledgment referred to to be put on file.

To Lincoln's Inn Field, where the lawyers congregate. The process is very simple and inexpensive, though by no means sure to be successful. I state the case. The attorney drafts an affidavit, and directs me to call at such a day that it may be examined, then to call another day when he will attend me to one of the commissioners, before whom I may swear. The affidavit being sworn and papers referred to produced and certified by the commissioners, the judge is applied to for an order, and it is granted.

The charges of lawyers in this country are more specific than those made on the other side. This case, for example:

	s.	d.
To examine you with a view to ascertain what affidavit you could make,	6	8
To take instructions for affidavit,	6	8
Drawing affidavit,	18	0
Attending your reading over draft,	6	8
Engrossing,	6	0
Attending you to get sworn,	6	8
Preparing five exhibits,	5	0
Oaths and exhibits,	7	0
Attending judge praying order to register certificate,	6	0
Attendance to draw up order and attending registrar as to form in which it should be drawn,	6	8
At judge's chambers thereon order and filing affidavit,	6	0
Copy to keep,	2	0
Attending to filing certificate,	6	8
Paid,	5	0
Paid on filing order,	2	0
Attendance to obtain office copy,	6	8

Walking to the court, I said, "How many lawyers have you in the city?" "About fourteen hundred solicitors do the business; then we have barristers very numerous. As to those admitted to practice they are innumerable. Thousands of them are supported by their friends or by private fortunes."

The judges are all on circuit except Baron Martin, who, the solicitor remarks, is considered one of the best and purest, and who is now sitting at chambers. He is a fine-looking old gentleman—patient, thoughtful, and grayheaded, without the John Bull ruddiness and rotundity.

Lawyers here have the same character for shrewdness that they have with us. They tell a good story of a miserly merchant who invited a lawyer to dinner, and when he had well drunk, indirectly popped a legal question and received a satisfactory answer. The lawyer a few days after sent him his bill for advice. The merchant sent to him a bill for his dinner, specifying the different courses and the different wines of which he had partaken. The lawyer sent him notice that unless he withdrew it he would prosecute him for selling wine without a license.

This is a city of magnificent distances. The omnibuses are counted by thousands, and are usually built to carry twelve inside and as many outside. Many, however, are much larger, and are called barges. Seats run along the center above, and three passengers may be accommodated by the side of the driver. Omnibuses are generally drawn by two horses, though often by three or four; they are driven with speed, and in the principal thoroughfares are so numerous as to arrest each other and intercept the passage. It is dangerous for a stranger to cross Cheapside, Threadneedle Street, Fleet, the Strand, Oxford Street, etc. If you wait for a clear passage, as strangers sometimes do, you may wait a great while. You must thread your way through. Irish jaunting-cars would not answer here; a man mounted on one would soon find his heels tripped up. Cabs, flies, and hansoms are the private conveyances of strangers. The last is the favorite. In this you are comfortably shut up; the driver is behind you and the horse before; and in the midst of the jam and confusion and whirl you may go to sleep, as many do, after a night's debauch, when on their way to lodgings in the morning.

The conveyances are all numbered and licensed and under the strictest regulations; the drivers claim that they are the best in the world. All those whose numbers are above ten thousand are Sabbath-keeping conveyances. The omnibuses are owned by companies, of which there are many. An idea of this business may be found from the fact that one company realizes from sixty thousand to one hundred thousand dollars a week.

A gentleman's cab is somewhat larger and neater than the ordinary one, and is called a brougham. It is four-wheeled, and drawn by a single horse. They are common vehicles for the families in moderate circumstances. The rich have their splendid carriages, a great collection of which may be seen in Hyde Park every evening, and they are a sight worth seeing, especially to one who can admire fine horses. -

The common people, when they take their Monday excursion, ride in vehicles called vans, very large and high, such as on ordinary occasions are used to transport furniture. In these multitudes of women and children may be stowed. Sometimes you may see a string of forty or fifty of these vans, filled with poor, but happy people, on their way to Epping Forest or Hampstead Heath, decked with gay ribbons and holding little flags, their countenances indicating the utmost delight.

It is Sunday morning, and I must go to hear Mr. Spurgeon. "How far is it to Surrey Gardens, where Mr. Spurgeon preaches." "Seven miles." Perhaps I did wrong, but I hired a carriage and started. By Kensington Gardens and Hyde Park, through several toll-gates, along streets built up with most spacious, tasteful, and even extravagant houses, we drove mile after mile, reaching the Gardens just in time. A policeman meets the carriage and tells the driver where to post himself, and where he is to be found after service. At the door another policeman asks you if you have a ticket, and if you have not, he directs you to the lower part of the house.

VI.

MR. SPURGEON.

The great music hall at Surrey Gardens was filled when I entered. All seats, both in the galleries and below, were filled, and there was scarce standing for another person in the side aisles. I was lame and weary, but determined to hear; so, pressing my way to one of the columns that support the lower gallery, I leaned against it till the close of the service.

Mr. Spurgeon was reading the 44th Psalm, and making expository remarks upon it so extensive that

I was at a loss to know whether he intended them for his sermon or not. Some of these remarks were strongly Calvinistic. At this I took no offense. When I hear a Calvinistic preacher, I expect to hear a Calvinistic doctrine, and to hear it proclaimed as if the speaker believed it—distinctly, boldly, emphatically, and without apology—and thus does Mr. Spurgeon preach it. Having gone through the psalm, he gave out the hymn, "Come, Holy Spirit," etc., stanza by stanza, and thus it was sung by the whole audience, a gentleman beneath the pulpit leading. Now and then there was some confusion, different parts of the house sending in their contributions of music at different times; but before the singing of the hymn was concluded, Mr. Spurgeon, by dint of exhortation, succeeded in getting pretty good time.

Then came prayer. Mr. Spurgeon's sermons are usually reported and published; his prayers are not. I may be allowed, therefore, to say that he prays like a humble, earnest, believing Christian; his petitions being carefully composed, and distinctly, clearly, and powerfully uttered. Some of them I recollect, as they struck me as peculiar: "O, God, hear us! Thou knowest that we feel; if we never were in earnest before, we are in earnest this morning. We can not let thee go unless thou bless us. O, God of St. Paul, God of Chrysostom, hear us! God of Luther, hear us! God of Whitefield and Wesley, hear us!"

After prayer another hymn was sung, in the same manner as the first. The text was Psalm xliv, 1–3. The skeleton, as I sketched it, is as follows:

Introduction: How contemptible our nursery tales! How different were those of ancient times!

I. The marvelous stories which our fathers have told us of the olden times, such as the flood, the crossing of the Red Sea, the smiting of the Amorites, the expulsion of the Canaanites, the overthrow of Jabin, the triumphs of David, the destruction of Sennacherib, the planting of the Gospel, the day of Pentecost, and the fall of idols. Have you never heard of more recent wonders—the success of Chrysostom, the uprising of Luther, the labors of Zwingle, and of Calvin, and of Wiclif, and of Wesley, and of Whitefield? The passage in relation to these last, as it shows Mr. Spurgeon's liberality, I give in full:

"The Churches were all asleep; irreligion was the rule of the day; the very streets seemed to run with iniquity. Up rose Whitefield and Wesley, men whose hearts the Lord had touched, and they dared to preach the Gospel of the grace of God. Suddenly, as in a moment, there was heard the rush of wings, and the Church said, 'Who are these that fly as a cloud, and as doves to their windows? They come! they come! numberless as the birds of heaven, with a rushing like mighty winds that are not to be withstood.' Within a few years, from the preaching of these two men, England was permeated with evangelical truth. The Word of God was known in every town, and there was scarce a hamlet into which the Methodists had not penetrated. In those days of the slow coach, when Christianity seemed to have bought up the old wagons in which our fathers once traveled—where business runs with steam, there oftentimes religion creeps along with its belly on the earth; we are astonished at these tales, and we think them wondrous."

Observe, God works, 1. Suddenly; 2. By feeble

instrumentalities; 3. By men of faith; 4. By men of prayer.

II. The disadvantages under which these stories labor. Men set aside their force by saying, 1. They occurred long ago; 2. Under peculiar circumstances; 3. Their like does not occur now.

III. The inferences to be drawn—1. We should be led to gratitude and praise; 2. We should be led out of our self-dependence; 3. Incited to earnest prayer.

Application—1. To saints, pray; 2. To backsliders, return; 3. To sinners, repent. In the last exhortation he stated his Calvinism, and yet seemed to burst through it. "It will come to this yet—God the Holy Spirit will have you. Give way now, but remember that if you succeed in quenching the Spirit you are lost."

Mr. Spurgeon is a well-proportioned man, of medium height, youthful appearance, and a pleasant countenance. He has a voice of tenor key, great compass, and flute-like melody, which he sends out distinctly, with all his mutes and semi-vowels, to every one of the twenty thousand ears that are uplifted to catch them. His tones and attitudes and utterance, all indicate humility and sincerity. I could but thank God, as I heard him, that his amazing popularity had not turned his head. He speaks boldly, confidently, and as one who speaks what he believes, and feels that he is right. He rarely argues, but speaks as one having authority, regarding religion as a matter of faith, and not of reason.

He is untrammeled. Little cares he what the *Times* may say, or the mob or the ministry. What comes uppermost with him comes out, as if it were from God. Hence he utters a great many silly things and a great many strange and uncouth things, but a great many bold, strong, effective things also, which but for this ultraism he would restrain.

Put together these elements—a pleasing person and address, a melodious voice, a distinct utterance, a novel doctrine (for such is Calvinism in the pulpit now), an earnest manner, an unbounded confidence, and an untrammeled mind—and you have an explanation of his success.

That he is an orator I would as soon doubt as I would doubt that Napoleon was a warrior. A man that can gather ten thousand hearers in the center of London, and hold them year after year, must be an orator; for the center of London is a region of darkness, though it is encompassed by a region of light. That city is like pandemonium surrounded by paradise.

"How do you like Mr. Spurgeon?" said some of my London friends to me.

"Well, very well. Nor did I see any extravagance or eccentricity in him. Throughout he spoke like a sensible and holy man."

"O, but you should hear him in his own chapel at Park Street, where he indulges himself freely."

"Are not the reports we hear about his bitterness and bigotry and eccentricity apocryphal?"

"Some of them may be; but I know some that are authentic. For example, he said, speaking of Arminians, 'I would not worship such a bread-and-butter God as yours.' Again: 'Your Lamb is not like ours. Ours is like a good leg of mutton; you can cut and come again all the year round.'"

Well, we must not deal harshly with one of those honest, outspoken men. If they say improper things they repent of them. I wish we had a thousand Spurgeons. I have no doubt they would grow wiser and better, though less popular, with every year's experience.

Mr. Spurgeon's great chapel is a great mistake, though it may do for him; but what will become of his successor in a wilderness of empty pews?

12

CHAPTER XI.

IN DELAWARE AND NEW YORK.

THE house of Dr. Thomson at Delaware, which the family occupied for a dozen years, was a pleasant and attractive one. It was a two-story brick building, of modern style, with a double porch in front, and two long verandas on the east. It occupied a commanding position on the north side of the street, leading directly west from the university grounds, and its upper windows overlooked the town. Grapevines, honeysuckles, the English ivy, and climbing roses were trained up the walls on all sides, and shaded the verandas. In the front yard were flower-beds of various shapes, in which bloomed flowers of almost every shade and variety. There were also ornamental shrubs and trees,—the flowering almond, mountain ash, horse-chestnut, arbor-vitæ, larch, hemlock, fir, pine, and spruce. Immediately back of the house was the garden, in which Dr. Thomson took his regular morning and evening exercise. And in the rear of this was a northern slope, containing nearly an acre of orchard-ground and lawn. Both the doctor and Mrs. Thomson took great delight in the adornment of their home, and they loved to gather the flowers, the berries, and the larger fruits which grew in their grounds.

While in Delaware, four children were born to them,—Elizabeth Maria, in 1846; Edward, in 1848;

Eliza Selina (now the wife of Hon. Thos. E. Powell, of Delaware, Ohio), in 1852; and Louisa Matilda, in 1854. The oldest and youngest died in infancy, Maria in 1850, and Louisa in 1856. When the first-born died, Dr. Thomson wrote in the family Bible: "Every hour of her life she was a blessing to us, and we trust her death has been sanctified. How sweetly did she sing God's praise, and pray to her heavenly Father! How gently did she suffer her last sickness, and how calmly she fell asleep in Jesus!" When he recorded the death of Louisa he added: "She passed gently away to heaven, after having endeared herself to us on earth. Deeply we grieve, but say, 'Thy will, O God, be done!'"

To Maria he dedicated the following acrostic lines:

> "**E**very hour I seem to hear
> **L**ost Maria, fresh and fair,
> **I**n her little elbow chair,
> **S**inging in a voice so clear:
> **A**ngel sounds, from regions blest,
> **B**reak upon my midnight rest,
> **E**ver saying, 'Papa, list!
> **T**here is Jesus, here is love;
> **H**appy I in realms above.'
>
> **M**any eyes their waters shed
> **A**t thy gentle cradle bed;
> **R**ested not this weary head
> **I**n the day the weepers said,
> **'A**ngels come—Maria's dead!'
>
> **T**hroned in light—by faith I see thee,
> **H**appy in redeeming love;
> **O**n the temple's threshold mark thee,
> **M**ingling with the throng above.
> **S**oar, my child, with seraph's wing,
> **O**nward in those realms of light,
> **N**ever more to cease thy flight."

The children were a source of great joy and comfort to their parents. In their tender years they always expected papa to kiss them in the morning, before he started to college ; and at noon and evening they often watched a full hour for him to return, and when they caught the first glimpse of his smiling face, ran with glee to meet him and receive his fond embrace. After supper the whole family adjourned to the sitting-room, and for an hour or more all were children. They played "blind-man's buff," "pussy wants a corner," or wrestled and romped, with noise and laughter. Then followed an hour of historical tales. There were various courses,—the English kings, the French dynasties, the Christian fathers, the holy martyrs ; and the pictures thus painted by Dr. Thomson can now be recalled with vividness by his children. Next came the solemn hour of prayer, and the children, kissing each other and their parents, retired for the night. On Sunday, instead of the playing and history, the catechism was taken up, recited, and explained. Thus the children were made familiar with their parents, and trained to love and fear the Lord.

When, in 1860, Dr. Thomson became editor of the *Christian Advocate and Journal*, at New York, it was very hard for the family to leave their pleasant home and take up their residence in a crowded city. The students and citizens of Delaware felt that the president of the university must not move. As soon as the news of his nomination to the editorial chair of the *Advocate* was telegraphed from Buffalo, the seat of the conference, the mayor and others called a public meeting. At a very short notice the largest hall in the town was filled with interested citizens, and resolutions deprecating the removal of the doctor from the presidency of the university, and urging him to remain, were unanimously passed, and telegraphed to him. But the Church had for him new duties to perform, and to him its voice was the voice of God.

On the day of his return from Buffalo, a commitee of thirteen ladies waited upon him at his residence, and presented a petition signed by themselves and four hundred and fifty others, beseeching him to continue to make his home in Delaware. However gratifying it would have been to his own feelings to remain, and he was deeply affected by all these expressions of regard, he hesitated not to undertake the labor or perform the duty imposed upon him.

In matters of reform the Church is always ahead of the State. From 1844 the antislavery sentiment of the Church in the North grew stronger year by year. There were, however, two parties, one radical and the other conservative in views. The latter, for a long time, held the most prominent positions. But before the country was ready to elect an anti-slavery President, the Church said that these positions must be filled by radicals. At the General Conference held in May, 1860, it was determined that strong and outspoken anti-slavery men must be put in all the editorial chairs; and Edward Thomson was selected to conduct the leading organ of Methodism. He desired not the position; but when it was thrust upon him, at this critical time in political and ecclesiastical history, he felt that he could not decline. His salutatory expresses the feelings of his mind in accepting this new field of labor, and we here reproduce it.

"The new editor offers Christian salutations to his readers. He comes from a quiet village to a crowded metropolis, and from a life of comparative ease and tranquillity to one of turmoil and anxiety. He comes at the sacrifice at once of feeling and of interest, and with reluctance, regret, even grief. A sedentary life has impaired his health, and he had fondly anticipated, erelong, a season of relaxation and retirement, or at least a return to the healthful, inspiring labors of the regular itinerancy.

"But the Church calls, and as 'a son in the Gospel' he obeys. This implicit obedience, against both one's judgment and feeling, may be deemed the mark of a mean or superstitious mind; but he can not help thinking that the voice of the Church is to him the voice of God, and he yields his judgment in this instance, as well as others, to that of his brethren, without accusing them of cruelty, or even of unkindness.

"The post assigned him calls for a mind in the freshness of its faculties and the fullness of its strength. It is associated with some of the most illustrious names in the Church. Dr. Bangs, Dr. Samuel Luckey, and Dr. George Peck still linger among us, and their labors and praises are in all the Churches. Dr. Bond, a man of noble intellect and generous heart, rich in the means that convince, nor wanting in those that charm, gentle as the Summer breeze to the friends of Zion, terrible as the wintry storm to her foes, though now 'with God and his angels,' is still fresh in the memory of our Church. Dr. Stevens, the astute tactician, the ready writer, the glowing historian, has left the impression of his mind full upon us. If the new editor be found wanting, let the readers remember that he is tried by no mean standard.

"The crisis is a painful one. Our Church is agitated, discordant, distracted. Brother meets brother, and force meets force, in hostile array. Happily, our conflicts are of policy rather than of principle, and are indicative of vitality and ominous of good. Your editor comes with no new principles or new controversies; he needs make no declaration of opinions. A ministerial life of nearly thirty years has given him a record. His views, whether right or wrong, have been clearly conceived and boldly declared, and they are in harmony with those of the great body of the Church. On the 'vexed question' his position has been deliberately taken, and will be *firmly* and *fearlessly* held. He has no wish to enter the arena of controversy; and if he must, he hopes to do so with that charity which 'thinketh no evil.'

"We all know with what difficulty error is avoided and truth secured; with what slowness sin is forsaken and righteousness attained. It is his fixed purpose to avoid all personalities; to treat all opponents with respect; to assign no bad motive where a good one can be found; to dip his pen not in a brother's blood, but in the milk of human kindness; and when reviled, to revile not again. This may entail weakness, for men are stronger in depravity than in righteousness; it may involve difficulty, for it is easier to descend with nature than to rise with grace; but let us sit at the feet of Him that was 'meek and lowly,' and learn how, while we are weak in ourselves, we may become 'strong in the Lord.'

"There is no harm in controversy if it be not

attended with bitterness, and there is great good in it; it is God's ordained path of progress. We must exchange thought for thought, argument for argument, opinion for opinion, if we would enlighten others or be ourselves enlightened. When this process is properly conducted it brings both parties under obligation, and should increase their respect for each other. Still, the editor hopes that it will not be necessary to appropriate much space to controverted points, and he is determined that his paper shall not be devoted to one idea, however grand that idea may be. He will make his sheet, as heretofore it has been, a well-balanced one, symmetrical in doctrine and precept. Still may it go forth the herald of news, the messenger of the Churches, the medium of communication between distant parts of our common Methodism! Still may it be the friend of the family, the admonisher of the sinner, the monitor of the saint, breathing in all its pages, 'Peace on earth, good-will to men, and glory to God in the highest!' May it never bear the sad tidings of disunion, or the more disastrous news that righteousness has been sacrificed to peace.

"Our illustrious predecessor closed his labors with an allusion to an evil prediction of his own, and a prayer that it might not be fulfilled. We begin ours with a contradictory prophecy, and shall *hope* and *work* up to it. The head and heart of the Church are sound, and will radiate a genial influence and pump a healthful blood into its extremities Earnestly asking your prayers, the editor will firmly pursue his path with an eye upon the tomb to which he hastens, and the retributions which must follow, reposing his head, in every trial, on the bosom of 'Our Father,' whose providence has strangely called him to unexpected and unwelcome duties."

• He was called to this position in the most critical period of our national history, and conducted the mother of *Advocates* through her most trying quadrennium. When he took his seat a storm of opposition was raised by a respectable minority throughout a large part of the patronizing territory of the paper, and after the election of Lincoln, matters became still more complicated.

As indicative of the spirit of the pro-slavery members in certain localities, and particularly in New York City and vicinity, we might state that a document was presented to the New York East Conference at its session in 1860, just before that body proceeded to the election of delegates to the General Conference, soon to convene in Buffalo, in which the preachers of that conference were implored "by your love for us to vote for no one, whatever may be your personal regard for him, who you are not morally certain will, if elected, stand in the General Conference as a rock against any change of the General Rule on Slavery." And this was signed by many prominent and wealthy laymen of New York City and suburban towns.

The "Laymen's Union" made great exertions to secure the election of delegates who would be opposed to the much feared alteration in the Discipline. It sent up to the seat of the General Conference a strong force, which held meetings, and attracted so much attention as to have its debates reported in the *New York Herald*. It threatened that if Dr. Stevens were not re-elected to the *Advocate* an opposition paper would be started in New York. The same party carried out its threat, and the *Methodist* came into life as an organ of the border, pleading for the repeal of the new rule on slavery.

The most abusive letters were written to Dr. Thomson by laymen and ministers in Northern and border States, censuring him for espousing the cause of the oppressed, and denouncing him for having assisted in the election of Abraham Lincoln, and thus bringing war and probably ruin to the nation. Subscribers withdrew by hundreds and gave their support to the opposition paper, and it managed to have the backing of nearly all the wealthy laymen of the great city, and drew to its columns much of the most able talent of the Church. George R. Crooks, John McClintock, Abel Stevens, and others of equal ability, gave their powers to the building up of the *Methodist.* Many supposed that the *Advocate* was doomed, and that its editor was so timid and sensitive that he must surely resign his place in a few months. But they found that he possessed all the elements of power, and that a great ordeal only developed them. One of his associates in the university, who knew him well, said of him: "All that was most gentle, and lovely, and pure in our holy religion, his heart clung to with affection; any thing the opposite of this, he shrank from as a timid child, except when the voice of duty commanded; then the lamb was a lion. Neither favor nor fear could affect his life-long fidelity and his great ability. Straight forward he moved in the conduct of the paper, which had never before been so full of thoughtful, charming editorials. In this new position his great qualities were equally exhibited—unwearying industry, large resources, and unfailing zeal. A single instance of his capacity for work, of his fertility, is given in a passing remark made in a private note to one of his friends, that he had that week, besides other editorial labor, written eleven columns for the *Advocate*."

The Methodist, however, scarcely got an opportunity to open out on the slavery question. The war came on. The country was all excitement. The great mass of the people in the North demanded the preservation of the Union, and the new paper became, very wisely, a supporter of the administration. Thus when, by the shock of war, its occupation was gone, it dropped the slavery question and became the great advocate of lay delegation.

Dr. Thomson was, at heart, favorable to lay delegation, and felt that just as soon as the laymen in the Church should, by a fair majority, express a desire for representation it would be wise to grant it. As far back as 1856 he was moving in a prominent way in his own conference towards measures favorable to that end. But since the opposition paper had taken up the cause and was claiming that the vote expressed by the membership was not the real sentiment of the Church, he felt called upon to answer on behalf of the party that had placed him in his position. Many of his editorials on this question might be given, and they would still be read with interest. We merely extract a brief answer to a committee of the laymen's convention held at St. Paul's Methodist Episcopal Church, in New York City, in 1863. Those of our readers who remember something of the agitation will appreciate the points thus strongly made:

"The committee has both failed to show that lay delegation is expedient, and to devise a satisfactory plan. At either of these points we might have stopped, but let us see how they meet objections. The agitation of the Church by elections they do not touch, because their plan obviates it. The objection that the laity is not represented in their plan they remove by saying, Let a more popular plan be adopted. If this is not reasoning in a circle, what is?

"Surely one with but half an eye can see that if the plan is restricted the second objection stands; if it is popularized, the first objection. But one or the other must be done in case of lay delegation; therefore either one or the other objection stands in all its force. And here we must say that the committee departs from Christian charity by imputing to the editor of the *Quarterly Review* a want of candor. He can speak for himself. For ourselves we say, *on our conscience*, that if we are to have lay representation we hope every male member may be permitted to vote for the representative. We honestly believe that the Church will be safer in the hands of the whole membership than in the hands of a part. There is certainly as much spirituality, zeal, and attachment to the Church in the hearts of the masses as in that of the stewardship.

"The answer to the objection arising from the vote is a curiosity. Let us suppose that in the State of New York the clergy were not eligible to a seat in the Legislature; that the question of a representation of the clergy, as a class, had been agitated since the organization of the government; that a failure to get it had occasioned frequent migrations; that twelve years ago a new party arose, and after agitating the cities by the various methods adopted for such purposes, had petitioned the Legislature, power being possessed by it, to grant the request for such representation; that in 1860 that body had kindly resolved that they were willing to admit the clergy if the people favored it, and submitted to the citizens, lay and clerical, two years from that time, the question of so altering the constitution as to provide for it; that of the people one hundred and fifty thousand should vote against it and fifty thousand in its favor, and of the clergy in their conventions about two to one should vote against it; and suppose that a party should maintain that this adverse vote did not estop the Legislature. If by this they meant that it would not diminish their constitutional power, we might assent; but if they meant that it did not present any moral reason, any political propriety against the change, we should certainly think they were wild. Any legislature that would run athwart the public will, legally solicited and expressed in regard to a fundamental principle of the constitution, would be doomed.

"The committee go further, and say that the vote does not express the wishes of the Church; and why? Because it had not been reasonably discussed, owing to the shortness of time between the General Conference and the taking of the vote, and owing to the condition of the public mind. But our people have been called on to make up their mind on political questions in a much shorter period, in the same condition of the public mind.

"If the subject was not *reasonably* discussed it was

not the fault of lay delegationists, for they had the discussions all to themselves. Suppose the vote had been two to one of the laity and three to one of the clergy in favor of the change, and a party issue circulars, get up conventions, appoint committees, and draft addresses to convince the General Conference that the 'enlightened and reliable judgment of the Church' was against lay representation; in other words, that the majority were ignorant people that did not understand their business, and the minority the 'enlightened and reliable' people, and express their opinion that, 'on this appearing,' the General Conference 'will accept their judgment' and act 'judiciously,' that is, not admit lay delegates, would their committee find access to *The Methodist?* Would the gentlemen of the committee compliment them on their wisdom and propriety? Would the political world imitate their bright example and oust candidates elected by majorities, because the votes of the minority express the '*enlightened and reliable judgment*' of the country?"

Dr. Thomson had as his assistant editor, for the first year, the Rev. W. P. Strickland, D. D., a Methodist author, and one well qualified for the place. Soon after the great war broke out, he was in such deep sympathy with the cause of the Union, that he resigned his position, and became a chaplain in the army. The Rev. George Lansing Taylor, A. B., the brilliant poet, then a young graduate of Columbia College, was employed as the successor of Dr. Strickland. Mr. Taylor left the place in about two years to enter upon active service in the itinerant ministry. He has since become a distinguished preacher, and has received the degree of doctor of divinity. Then Mr. Stephen B. Wickens, who had been connected with the office for many years as a proof-reader, and had acted as assistant to Dr. Thomas E. Bond during a part of his long and able editorship, took Mr. Taylor's place, and labored with Dr. Thomson till the close of his term of service.

The correspondents which Dr. Thomson employed were not, at that time, so distinguished as the dozen brilliant names emblazoned on the first page of *The Methodist* as its "Special Contributors." Scarcely any of them had attained prominent position; nearly all were in the pastorate, and had not then reached the first places in this line of work. Some of the best talent of the East was arrayed against *The Advocate*. Still, many of the men who assisted the editor in making his paper one of excellence were strong and polished writers. He allowed no inferior communication to enter his columns, and encouraged the able men, some of whom were young and almost unknown, to write frequently; and thus *The Advocate* was, all the time, at least the equal of *The Methodist*.

Among Dr. Thomson's contributors may be mentioned Gilbert Haven, Daniel Curry, Daniel Dorchester, George W. Woodruff, Robert Allyn, Henry W. Warren, and James M. Buckley, now historical names.

Dr. George L. Taylor, well acquainted with all the facts, sums up Thomson's services during this quadrennium:

"Conscious of the trials of the position, he accepted the editorial chair as a duty he owed to the progress of the Church in the great reform of human

liberty. A rival sheet was sure to be started by the
party defeated at the General Conference, and with
capital and talent to support it. Confident expectations were entertained that the organ of the Church
would be a deserted craft, a foundering concern in a
twelvemonth. The conservative society of New York
received the unpretentious and, externally perhaps,
unprepossessing radical with a coldness that sorely
wounded his sensitive nature. Many who in the later
years of his life were ambitious to bask in the honor
of his acquaintance then treated him with unchristian
bitterness. But it was only of a piece with the lot of
reformers and warriors for the truth before him, and
he bore it in meekness and silence. The paper became at once a classic in the grace and elegance of
its editorials, which were widely quoted. The strongest radical minds of the Church rallied to its columns.
Although forced into distasteful and harassing controversies, no braver or knightlier pen than his was
ever lifted against an antagonist. His ability and
suavity made friends by hundreds from the ranks of
those who began as his enemies; and he brought the
paper through his term of office, in spite of the cru-
sade against him and the ravages of war, with a larger
subscription list than he found. The paper was among
the most patriotic of the day, and an editorial in the
New York Tribune justly remarks that ‘few religious
journals in the land did the country better service
during the war for the Union than *The Christian Advocate.*’ In all respects Dr. Thomson’s editorship was
a fine success, that could only have improved with
continuation.”

CHAPTER XII.

LETTERS FROM NEW YORK.

WHEN Dr. Thomson was appointed to the editor-ship of the *Advocate*, the condition of his wife's health was such that she could not safely take up her residence continuously in the city. The dampness of the sea-breeze seemed to intensify her affliction, which was a complication of inflammatory rheumatism and heart disease. Hence, most of the time she remained with the children at the family home at Delaware, spending only a few months each year with her husband in New York. He was willing even to deny himself home comforts, if thereby he might render his family happier and at the same time serve the Church to which he had devoted his life.

Many letters passed between him and the family during the months of separation. His letters to his son, who was then just entering the most important period of youth, embody much of the wisdom which he had gathered in the training of the young; and as they were written during a most interesting time of our national history, some of them are here given. The address and subscription of each letter are omit-ted, as not necessary; only the date is given.

"New York, July 15, 1861.

. . . . "The city is still alive with military display. On Saturday the Ninth Massachusetts Regiment passed through. There are now about three or four thousand at

Camp Scott. The tents make a beautiful sight. I should like you to see them. In looking into one the other day, I was pleased to see Bibles on the shelves. I hope every soldier will carry his Bible, and do his duty in the fear of God. I hope and pray that when you are a man, there may be no more war, so that you may never feel it your duty to bear arms against your fellow-man. I want you to be a good soldier of Jesus Christ.

"It is said that when Origen, one of the great lights of the early Church, was a boy, he used to read the Scripture to his father, asking him to explain not merely its literal but its spiritual meaning. The father felt proud of his son, though he never told him so. Often, when the boy was sleeping, the father would go to his bed, and, raising the covering, kiss the breast of his son reverently, as a temple in which the Holy Spirit was about to fix his dwelling; then, raising his weeping eyes to heaven, he would thank God for so great a treasure.

"With much solicitude and prayer does your father look upon you. May you become a holy man, that, after a happy life here, you may find an eternal crown!"

"New York, April 23, 1862.

"On arriving from Troy last Monday, I found your letter, and was much pleased to read it, although it was not written with sufficient care. You must bear in mind what my father used often to say to me, 'Whatever is worth doing, is worth doing well.'

"Accept my thanks for the beautiful flowers you send.

"Do not engage in any quarrel with your neighbors. Speak kindly to young S. His dog, I trust, will not do much damage to your yard. When I return home I will talk to his father, who is a kind man, and will do any thing reasonable. All through life we may expect more or less trouble; but kind words and a gentle spirit will carry us through.

"In regard to your studies, I have only to say that you

should be advised by your teachers. I wish you to understand thoroughly every thing you study, and therefore I am not anxious that you should take advanced classes. If there is a commencing class in Latin, you should enter it; for it is time you began your classical studies. I want you to have enough to engage your attention, but not enough to imperil your health.

"Be very kind and unassuming, both to your fellow-pupils and your professors. The president and his associates are your friends. They labor for the good of their students. You must always be found on their side, sustaining the government, reverencing their persons and respecting their instruction.

"Pray to God daily. I hope you will soon be a Christian. It would rejoice me to hear you had joined the Church.

"P. S. I send you a part of the white flag sent from Fort Pulaski when it surrendered. Dr. Strickland sent it to me."

"New York, April 30, 1862.

"I am satisfied with your arrangement for study; but I beg you will not forget your private spelling, nor omit to practice penmanship. It is very important to learn how to spell correctly and write plainly. It seems to me that mamma should arrange some regular hours for a short spelling lesson and writing exercise every day or every other day.

"You must be very kind and obedient to your mother. Boys of your age often think too much of themselves. I hope you will not be so silly. Never set up your judgment in opposition to ma's. I trust you will never leave the house, or enter into any company, or engage in any enterprise, without your mother's consent.

"Be punctual at prayers and at Church, and behave not merely like a gentleman, but like a Christian. Set the example of kneeling in the house of God, and seek his blessing on all your studies and enjoyments."

"New York, May 7, 1862.

"You have done well to commence the Latin. You will find it easy, as you advance, and I hope you will continue till you become a fine scholar in that language. The languages should be acquired early in life, as the faculty which they chiefly tax is the memory, and that is more retentive in youth than in later periods. It is not so with the mathematics; they strain the reasoning powers, which are imperfectly developed in youth, and ripen with advancing years."

"New York, September 17, 1862.

"You seem to be entirely too much excited about the war. You are too young to take any part in it yet, though if the contest be long protracted, you may. I trust, however, that God, in his kind providence, will soon bring the conflict to a close, and give us a righteous and lasting peace. War is a dreadful calamity, and a source of demoralization to a people.

"You do well, however, to cherish the most lively patriotic attachments. Respect the flag, which is the emblem of our national life; respect the ruler whom Providence appoints over us; and be ready whenever the government may call upon you to defend the nation. At present you can best serve your country by a close and diligent attention to your studies.

"I presume you will get along with languages well; but you must not neglect the lower branches. Study arithmetic until you *master* it; seek to be thorough in geography; spell every evening, and read to your mother once or twice a week. Show yourself a gentleman in all your intercourse with others, and shun rude or vulgar company.

"I inclose you a picture on paper made out of rice, which Brother Nathan Sites sends to you from China. All well at Mrs. Belden's. Among the boarders is the poet, N. P. Willis."

"New York, September 24, 1862.

"Yours of 20th was received to-day. I am glad that you are at your books. The time with you is precious; you ought to improve every hour. Try to make yourself agreeable at your boarding-place; do not expect to have every thing to suit you. Learn to be contented in every situation in which Providence places you. Be very kind and attentive to your mother and affectionate to your sister.

"I send you an autograph of General Hunter, which Dr. Strickland sent me from Port Royal. It is attached to a form of certificate which is issued to the colored persons who are made free by coming within the military lines. I hope you will preserve it as a curiosity.

"Endeavor to master whatever you study. Be careful to show proper respect to your teachers, and treat all your fellow-students kindly. Do not neglect your Bible or your prayers; but give your heart to God, and seek a place early among his people."

"New York, October 30, 1862.

"Yours of the 26th, which was duly received, was very carefully and prettily written. If you continue to improve as you have done the last month, you will soon have an excellent penmanship. You are right in reading your commentaries; but I hope you will not go too rapidly. A few verses each day, well studied, will be far better than whole chapters hastily perused.

"Your attendance at the German Sunday-school pleases me. I trust Eliza will go also. It will be a great pleasure to you both to be able to read the German Bible and much of the German literature.

"Your mother's last letter makes me melancholy. She tells me that she has asthma and that you are troubled with chronic catarrh. Now, my dear son, I fear you do not take exercise enough. You are too anxious to succeed in your studies. This is all well; but you must not neglect your health. What will your knowledge do if you get sick?

I wish you had a gymnasium in the college. If you are going to be afflicted in Delaware, I must bring you to New York. We have gymnasiums here, in which you could take exercise daily.

"Give my love to all. Do all you can to render every body about you happy, and pray for your affectionate papa."

"NEW YORK, November 4, 1862.

"Yours of the 1st is before me. I can not give you six dollars to be spent in such a vain and foolish way as the buying of a secret society badge. Money is the gift of God, and in spending it I regard myself as his steward. I would much rather send you six dollars to give to the poor. I am willing to give you any thing that you need, but nothing to encourage you in pride and vanity. You have money of your own that you can spend as you like, and if you must have the badge, you can take some of that.

"Now, my dear boy, do not think I am unkind. You are just as I was when I was a boy, and I do not blame you; and you must not blame me for withholding when I see an improper use is to be made of money.

"Remember me to all. I yearn for home, its slopes of green, its streams of milk and honey, and its kisses of love. You do not know how much I pray for you. Mamma says you have been troubled again with catarrh. Take fresh air and plenty of exercise. These will do you more good than medicine."

"NEW YORK, January 24, 1863.

"You can not imagine how grateful to God I feel for the news contained in your mother's letter that you have united with the Church. And yet I can not say that I am surprised. I have so long prayed for it that I came to expect it.

"With your mother I agree that your case is all the more hopeful because you have taken this step not under the influence of any excitement, but calmly and deliberately. We should enter upon the service of God from principle.

"You have long been in the habit of praying, and I have no doubt God has heard your prayers and regenerated your heart. The proofs of regeneration which are most satisfactory are to be found in the life and spirit. We know when Spring comes by the springing of the grass, the bursting of the buds, and the return of the birds; and so we know when the grace of God is in the heart by the graces or virtues of the Spirit; and these are love, joy, peace, long-suffering, gentleness, etc. There is one special fruit of regeneration mentioned; that is, 'love for the brethren'—love for good men because they are *good* and delight in the sanctuary and worship of God. I trust you will attend your class-meeting regularly, and make yourself a useful member of it even while young. The surest way to grow in grace is to help others to do so.

"I hope you will be careful to spend some time every day in healthful sport or labor. You must not sit up late, and therefore I would not have you attend night meetings if they continue late. Do what you can to influence your associates by private conversation and a Christian spirit; but I think you should not attend the night meetings, on account of your health.

"Tell mamma I am about as I was when I last wrote, but am still doing all my duties. Feeble as I am, I seem tough as leather."

"NEW YORK CITY, February 11, 1863.

"Yours of the 6th, with Eliza's and mamma's of the 7th, came to hand to-day. It was very gratifying to hear that you were all well.

"You are right in attending the singing-school. Singing is a noble art, and you have a fine voice. It will promote your health to exercise your lungs moderately every day. You are generous in appropriating a dollar of your pocket-money to purchase a book; but I think this fortunate, since you will be more likely to value the instruction. Children often disregard knowledge because they do not have to pay for it.

"The city has been excited over Thomas Thumb's wedding to Miss Warren. The little couple received many valuable presents from those to whom they issued tickets, and received a great many calls at the Metropolitan. The marriage was solemnized at Grace Church. I was walking home to lunch as they returned from the church. There was a double row of carriages from Ball & Black's to the church, and the crowd was so great near the Metropolitan that I could not get through, but turned aside, as did the omnibuses, into an adjoining street. A large police force was on hand.

"We are all upside down at the Book Room, having a general renovation preparatory to the meeting of the book committee—women scrubbing, men plastering, white-washing, painting, etc.

"Last Sabbath I preached at Yorkville; next I go to Brooklyn—Summerfield Church.

"You may all expect to come in the Spring, if you desire to do so. I have written mamma to say when I shall come for you. Give my love to all."

"New York City, February 18, 1863.

"Since I last wrote you I have had an interview with Archbishop Hughes. It occurred in this way. A friend from Troy was in my office yesterday, lamenting that the Catholics had purchased our college at that place. I advised that a proposition be made to repurchase. So we went first to the chancery of the archbishop, where his secretary kindly received us, and gave us a letter of introduction to the archbishop. Getting into a stage we proceeded to his residence, 198 Madison Avenue. The house is a noble one, and elegantly furnished.

"A female servant introduced us into the reception room and took the letter. Here we noticed a card from the city council inclosing a resolution of honor for the archbishop's patriotic services, and inclosed in an elegant gilt frame. We also saw a fine historical painting. A male messenger soon appeared and said that the archbishop was indisposed and suffering much, but would be pleased to see us in his chamber. So we walked up, noticing some choice statuary in the hall and paintings beside the stairway. His reverence was in bed, with his morning gown and night-cap on. He said he suffered from constipation. He is old and feeble. His bearing was very polite, and even courteous; he beckoned us to his bedside to shake hands with us. After a few friendly remarks had passed between us, we asked if he would sell the college. 'No, gentlemen; I reflect before I move, and when I advance it is never to go back. There are eight bishoprics in my province. I desire the college for youth from all these, who aspire to the priesthood, for theologians and philosophers. There the young men may be educated and the aged devote themselves to study. But if the people of Troy prefer to purchase I will sell it for a hospital for disabled soldiers. We need a *Greenwich* or an *Invalides*. I will not sell it for a Methodist or Presbyterian college. They can not support such an institution. Have you any proposition to make? If so, I will consider it. I have none to make myself.'

"We then asked what he would take for it for a hospital.

"'O, that I should have to consider,' he said; 'I care nothing about profit. By the way, you have a mortgage for fifteen thousand dollars. I told my secretary to send you up the amount for an investment, for I consider real estate better than greenbacks now.'

"'The secretary offered me fourteen thousand five hundred dollars,' said my friend.

"'Ah,' said he, 'I care nothing about discount.'

"'How do you like the building?' said I.

"'Well, pardon me, doctor, for what I am about to say. Whenever I have visited Troy I have looked up at

your college and laughed—now you will not be offended—
I said within myself, these Methodists have no architectural taste. Those little towers would become a mosque
rather than a Christian building. But do you think, after
I got it into my own hands I was better *reconciled.*'

"I was about to quote from Solomon, 'It is naught, it
is naught, saith the buyer, but when he goeth his way then
he boasteth;' but the conversation turned upon Catholic
architecture, and we had a long and pleasant chat about
the cathedrals of the Old World. For the purpose of
drawing him out I spoke of Westminster Abbey and York
Minster. 'Ah,' said he, 'these are all Catholic. The
Minster was once a monastery. All the fine structures
are ours.'

"After uttering this sentence his strength seemed to
fail, so that he could say no more to us. A priest, who
was in the room, continued the conversation, but was not
nearly so courteous in his conduct as the archbishop.

"I called on Mr. Drew recently, and was received
very kindly. Give my love to all. Pray for your papa."

"NEW YORK CITY, February 28, 1863.

"Your last letter was received a day or two ago. It
is an improvement upon preceding ones. Let *excelsior* be
your motto when you sit down to write.

"It pleased me much to know that you can go through
the storm to church and class; but why should you not
when your father can go through it much farther to
preach?

"Mr. Carey called on me yesterday noon, and we
spent the afternoon together. We went to the Cooper Institute, Mercantile Library, Astor Library, Zoölogical Institute, and Ball & Black's. The latter institute is a new
thing, and is likely to be permanent. We did not witness
all the performances, but staid long enough to see one
elephant dance, while another played a hand-organ.

"At Ball & Black's they were very polite, and we

were greatly delighted. I had no idea that they had so many curiosities; they allowed us to use one of their ten thousand-dollar diamond rings. They have now an excellent assortment of pictures, clocks, and music-boxes. Among other curiosities they have a rocking-chair which plays tunes as you rock yourself in it. They say it is the first one of the kind ever made.

"We had one or two collisions yesterday, of which I send you a published statement. I will also send you an account of the approaching marriage of the Prince of Wales.

"To-morrow I am to preach in the course of the South Church Lectures, and I expect to dine at Dr. Durbin's on the way. This afternoon I expect to spend with Mr. Carey visiting the parks, etc.

"Give my love to all my friends; kiss mamma and Eliza; and be a good boy. Determine to be faithful in all relations, and above all, faithful to God and faithful even to death.

"York, Pa., March 7, 1863.

"On my way hither I took a very severe cold, from which I have been suffering, though I am now better. The conference received me very kindly, and by resolution requested a copy of my sermon preached on Wednesday evening for publication. I am to preach again at the ordination of elders on to-morrow.

"The weather has been remarkably cold, and it is now snowing and has been all day. It is my intention to start for Washington on Monday next at 11½ A. M., and arrive there on the same day at 6 P. M. I should have gone to-day had I been well. I dread March traveling very much, and think I shall not return West before April.

"It relieves me much to think that Eliza is getting so well. It is painful for me to be separated from my family, especially when any are sick. I hope when I hear from you next I shall receive the intelligence that you are all well. Take care of your health; endeavor to develop your muscular system by manly exercise. You can not have a sound mind without a sound body.

"I have good hopes that by correct habits you will acquire a physical frame much larger and more healthful than your father's. Now especially is the time for you to form those habits that will enlarge and invigorate your bodily members. At the same time I hope you will be able to keep up your studies, and give to your sister such assistance as she may need. My love to mother, and sister, and all friends."

"NEW YORK, March 16, 1863.

"On returning from Washington I found your letters, and was much pleased with them. You have, no doubt, received my last, written at York, but mailed at Georgetown, D. C. My health, which was bad from cold, is now pretty good, though I still have a little sore throat.

"On Saturday I took tea with a number of preachers at the house of Mr. Ridgaway, pastor of St. Paul's. The conversation turning on dogs, one of the company said that he called the other day at a house where he was surrounded by a pack of dogs. Supposing himself in danger, he was about retiring, when the owner of the house cried out, "Do n't be alarmed, we keep a dog boarding house." I find that there are a number of establishments of this kind in the city, where persons having sick dogs leave them for treatment, and persons going into the country leave their dogs to be taken care of. Perhaps there is also a cat boarding house; if so, Eliza might bring her pussy.

"It is said that when General Butler was here last, he went to Grace Church with a rough overcoat on and took a seat forward. The sexton, however, took him back by the door. A spruce-looking lieutenant entered soon after, and was taken forward to the place which the general had been called to leave. In the course of the service General Butler threw off his cloak, and when the sexton saw the stars of a major-general on his shoulders, he invited him forward, but he refused to go. You see how foolish it is to judge by appearance, and how wrong to make distinctions in the house of God.

"The war seems to wear a more favorable aspect now, but we are accumulating a fearful debt. We owe now $1,000,000,000. If this were reduced to cents, and if Adam had commenced counting them as soon as he was made, and counted six hours a day from that time to this, do you think he would have finished?

"Give my love to all, and write often.

"P. S.—Be faithful to God and the Church."

"New York, May 6, 1863.

"We have had a long, cold storm since Monday morning, and it still prevails; the wind blowing terrifically from the north-east. I never saw such a storm in the month of May before. I am in the double room occupied by us at Mrs. B.'s, and I find it very cold. My health is good, though I am kept very busy.

"Your mother's letter came to hand to-day, and gave me great comfort and encouragement. I trust you are all doing well. The visit of Bishop Morris was very pleasant for you. Rev. Dr. Foster was at the office to-day to invite me to Sing Sing, where I am engaged to spend Sabbath, the 30th inst. Dr. Strickland called also; his wife is no better; the rest of the family are well. Rev. Gilbert Haven, of Boston, spent an hour with me this morning, and insists that I shall agree to be a candidate again for the editorship. Bishop Ames is here on his way to Germany; he also called on me. Rev. Mr. Abraham, of Trenton, spent nearly the whole afternoon at the office. So you see I had not much time for writing, and was obliged to postpone my letter to you till evening.

"The continued storm has prevented me from going anywhere this week. I hope it will clear before Sunday; for I have an engagement at Claverack then, one hundred and twenty miles from the city.

"I trust you will be a good boy in all things. I feel

much less reluctant to leave you at home now than formerly, seeing that you and Eliza are able to render your mamma so much assistance.

"You may take lessons in elocution if you wish. I think it will do you no harm, and perhaps some good.

"Give my love to all; kiss mamma and baby for me, and believe me, as ever and forever, your affectionate father."

"NEW YORK, May 21, 1863.

"Yours of last Saturday came to hand duly. You are too sensitive about allusions to your father. It was, I suppose, Dr. Wayland, instead of Dr. Whately, who was quoted against me in your discussion. Perhaps, however, there was no conflict after all. Dr. W. speaks of *ordinary* conflicts; I speak of *decisive* battles, those which have decided the fate of empires, and marked the great epochs of the world.

"The warm weather is coming on now. The first fly I have seen in New York this season presented himself to-day.

"The set of doctrinal discourses which was preached last Winter in South Street Church is to be published. I was called on to-day for my manuscript.

"My Sabbaths are all engaged until my departure for Ohio, besides many Commencement discourses.

"I hope you are getting along with your studies; and I infer you are, because you make no complaints. Bear in mind my command to be kind to your mother and sister and courteous to all."

"NEW YORK, May 30, 1863.

"Be assured I often think of you. A son may be unmindful of his father, but a father can not forget his child. Lamech said of Noah when he was born, 'This same shall comfort us concerning our work and toil of our hands;' and thus have I thought concerning you. As I grow old, it is a consolation to me that my son is growing up to take my place. You know not how often I pray that you may rise up to holy and honorable manhood. This is the prayer of every father who fears the Lord for his son. The first prayer on record is the prayer of a father for his son: 'And Abraham said unto God, O that Ishmael might live before thee!' I am the more solicitous for you, because I can not be with you to exercise authority over you, and give counsel and encouragement to you. The Almighty said of the patriarch just referred to, 'For I know him, that he will command his children and his household after him, and they shall keep the way of the Lord to do justice and judgment; that the Lord may bring upon Abraham that which he hath spoken of him.' Mark first, strict family government; secondly, a righteous and godly posterity; thirdly, a great and mighty nation.

"Your rejoicing over the taking of Vicksburg was rather premature. I hope, however, that we shall soon have official information of that event. Grant has certainly shown himself an able general. His five successive battles in the rear of Vicksburg constitute the most remarkable campaign of the war thus far, and display the highest military genius. I hope the government will sustain him by ample reinforcements.

"You are, I trust, making a good use of your time. It is very precious, and your character and success in life will depend very much on the forming period. Take good care of your health. You will, I trust, grow stronger from day to day in physical strength and in virtue.

"Let me be assured of your kindness and politeness to your mother and sister and all your associates. Attend Church, Sabbath-school, and class-meeting, and let your influence upon the Church be felt for good.

"Remember me to friends and neighbors. Kiss mamma and Eliza for me."

"NEW YORK, June 6, 1863.

"You have now entered your fifteenth year. I hope you feel the importance of preparing for manhood. Be more thoughtful, more sedate, more considerate; in fine, more manly. I am very much pleased that your mother, in her last letter, speaks of both yourself and your sister as very good.

"Walking out with Mr. Stoddard the other evening, we called at a police station, and were politely treated. The captain told us that the police force is about 2,000; the stations, 31. Each station is under a captain. His force is divided into two platoons; each platoon into four sections. One-fourth is on duty at a time. The day is divided into four watches. Each station has sleeping wards, in which each policeman has his bed. All the stations are connected by bells and telegraphs.

"While we were at the station the captain asked the station of a distant ward for a lost child, by the bell signals. The answer came immediately. In the rear of the station is the prison, which is divided into cells, in each of which there is nothing but a bench fixed to the wall. On this hard surface the prisoner sleeps all night, with no covering but his clothes. Just before we entered, a man was brought in for stealing a pair of shoes on the Bowery. We walked through the wards, the library, the office, and around the cells. Only three prisoners had been brought in then; but we were told that the cells would all probably be filled by midnight. In one room we saw the clubs worn by the policemen. They are called 'billies,' and are generally made of rosewood or lignum-vitæ. Truly the way of the transgressor is hard. It seems strange that any one should sin, since Providence is so sure to punish, sooner or later.

"The regiments whose time has expired are returning from the war. When a regiment comes in, some of the city regiments turn out to escort it. This makes the city lively with military music and display.

"The *Wood* faction is growing bold and threatening trouble. Ex-Mayor Wood was defiant as well as disloyal at the late meeting, and his worst utterances were applauded to the echo. This is a dark day. Let us trust in God, and pray to him for the salvation of the country."

"New York, June 13, 1863.

"Your note, as well as Eliza's, and two letters from mamma, awaited me on my return to-day from Boston. My trip, as I wrote your mother, was pleasant, though marred somewhat by the cold weather, for which I was not prepared. My route was by the steamer *Bay City* to Fall River; thence by railway to Boston; thence by rail, through Lawrence, Manchester, Andover, etc., to Concord, the capital of New Hampshire. Manchester is quite a city, the largest in the State. Andover is the seat of the oldest theological institution in the country, the one in which the distinguished Dr. Stuart was long a professor.

"Concord is a pretty place of twelve thousand inhabitants. I took tea with Ex-Governor Berry, who went out of office last week, and also with Dr. Prescott and Dr. Patten. Mrs. Patten is an aunt of General McClellan's wife. Governor Berry was once a Democrat; but he broke with the party when they refused to nominate Richard M. Johnson for Vice-president.

"Concord is the most celebrated place in the world for wagons. I was at the manufactory. They tell me they have large orders from New Mexico, Australia, Oregon, California, etc. They make none but the best work, and charge accordingly.

"Mr. Fox, of New York, was my companion at Bishop Baker's. He told me a good story, which, as you like a little humor, I will here relate. A good deacon of Dr. Haven's Church, Hartford, has a very long nose. One Sabbath morning, while shaving, he touched the end of it with a razor. Looking around for some sticking-plaster, he saw a round glued surface, which he thought just about large enough; so he put it on. It happened to be from the end of a spool of thread, and on it were printed the words, 'Warranted two hundred yards long.' The deacon, all unconscious of the figure he made, went to Church, and as he passed from pew to pew to take up the collection, he was surprised that the people all smiled, and some of

them laughed outright.   It was not till he went home that
he discovered the cause.

"I long to hear that your dear mother is well."

"NEW YORK, June 20, 1863.

"It is gratifying to know that you are pleased with
your elocutionist, from whom you will no doubt derive
great benefit.   You must know, however, that your academical studies should be first in your estimation.   Store
your mind with knowledge, discipline it by study, exercise
it in continued thought, and you will be able to speak.
A mind charged with thought, like a cloud with electricity,
will discharge itself effectively whenever occasion offers;
and when the lightning makes its way, the thunder will
naturally follow.   The advantages you derive from your
eloquent instructor will be more due to his example and
his spirit than his rules.   He will inspire you with a correct taste and a love of oratory, and thus influence your
expression and animate your studies.

"A clergyman of Indiana wrote me that he had a son
in the army in disgrace, and wished me to see General
Wool in his behalf.   The general granted me an interview,
and told me that the youth had been condemned to be shot
as a deserter, but that he would remit his sentence on the
ground that he was liable to aberration of mind, as his
father assured me.   General Wool is a plain but polite
man.   He was dressed in a black suit, while his staff
around him were in regimentals.   He told me that if you
would call with your autograph book, he would at any
time write his name in it.

"The course of the Democratic party in Ohio alarms
and afflicts me.   They will, if they continue their policy,
necessitate division of the country, anarchy, or military
despotism.   I trust you will be found at all times firmly but
mildly for your country.   Get into no quarrel, for this would
disgrace you and injure your influence; but stand true to
the Stars and Stripes under all circumstances."

"New York, June 27, 1863.

"I have just returned from Lima. You will see an account of the Commencement there in our next issue. Whilst there I dined with Major Lyon, the chief of General Sigel's staff. He tells me that the general is a man of unblamable character, cultivated mind, and amiable manners; not fond of fighting, but ready to do his duty from principle. He is a genuine republican, and thinks that the principles involved in this contest are the same as those for which he has all his lifetime contended. He is a man of the highest military skill and genius; his reports have been described as models, both in the United States and abroad. He has, since this rebellion occurred, been offered the highest commands in the Prussian service, and also in the Austrian, but he prefers to remain in a free country. General Hooker told Major Lyon that he considered General Sigel the best military officer in the United States, whether in the Northern or Southern army.

"In answer to the question, Why General Sigel is not in service? Major Lyon said, in substance, as follows: He was senior general in the Army of the Potomac, and he has repeatedly been superseded; the government has repeatedly adopted his plans, but never called upon him to execute them. His corps is the smallest in the army, and too small for effective action by itself, although it is often isolated. He felt it due to his officers, as well as to himself, to offer his resignation; for a brigadier-general under him has scarcely so large a command as a colonel under another, and a major-general under him is not equal to a brigadier under another. The President declining to accept his resignation, he asked leave of absence for a week, in which to recruit his health. When that expired he asked an extension, and finally an indefinite extension, and this is his situation now. He would gladly be recalled at any time if he could be treated as others are. He is at the Springs at Bethlehem, Pennsylvania. He is a small man, about my size, and very nervous.

"I could but ask how he came to be so badly used. And Major Lyon says he was opposed from the first by the Missouri delegation in Congress because of his anti-slavery principles and policy; he is regarded by the West Point officers with jealousy, and he has been eyed askance by politicians because he is a foreigner. I hope he will erelong be appreciated. No one seems willing to bear the blame of his persecution. When Major Lyon remonstrated with the President he was referred to General Hooker, and when he went to General Hooker he was referred back to the President.

"Returning to New York I stopped at Albany and visited the home of Mr. Secretary Seward. I came from Albany by steamboat. My health is now quite good. To-morrow I am to preach in Brooklyn.

"Your mother can direct you in regard to books and every thing else. Treat her with the utmost affection. Do every thing you can to render her happy. Be good to your sister, and keep up your studies faithfully. Above all, take care of your spiritual interests. Kiss mamma and Eliza for me.

"East Greenwich, July 4, 1863.

"Your last letter was written more carefully than your previous ones, and contained but one error in orthography. I was, however, a little grieved with the spirit of it. Heretofore you have shown a proper respect for your father's opinions, you now seem to have fallen into the error, so common to young people of your age, of supposing your judgment better than that of your seniors. This is a double error in your case. Youth should always defer to age, and a son should honor his father. I would by no means discourage independent thought, nor the expression of adverse opinion, but I would have a young man modest and deferential when he utters an opinion different from that which his superiors have expressed. Perhaps, however, you were merely trying your skill in argument, and would have your father encounter you in an intellectual battle, as he used to sport with you in mock physical combats, and thus strengthen and train your mental powers, as he was wont to invigorate your natural or muscular ones.

"What, then, is your proposition? Is it that elocution is the only, or the principal, or the best element of power or means of distinction? Alas! it is but an outlet; as a channel without a stream. What avails the most perfect vocal organs, the most graceful attitudes, the most perfect methods of controlling the voice, if you have no truth to convey? On the other hand, if the mind be full of knowledge and inflamed with elevated feeling it will utter itself in unexceptionable manner, as a spring issuing from a mountain side will make a channel—nature will show how without study. Though I would not discourage the study of manner, yet I regard it as only negatively serviceable—that is, in teaching us how to avoid improper habits and mannerisms.

"You refer to Cicero. Very well. Cicero would not have been the orator of Rome had he not long and carefully studied those ancient arts and languages which you affect to despise. Who would have ever heard of Demosthenes in this age, had he not possessed a mind wonderfully cultured? It was not the sound of his voice or the majesty of his attitude that gave him his posthumous fame. These things were, indeed, an advantage to him, and increased wonderfully his power over the people; but had his fame depended upon them he would have been forgotten a few years after he was entombed. That which has given him his immortality is his pen. His style has never been surpassed or even equaled. It is marked by an elegance, energy, condensation, and majesty that no man can acquire without long years of patient study. He must have been a master of grammar, of language, of the elegant arts and sciences of his day, as Cicero was of his.

"When you can write Greek as the former or Latin as the latter, or construct English sentences that may be compared with either the orations of Demosthenes or Cicero, I shall be content to let you devote your chief attention to utterance; but mark, my boy, you must spend many years in running the collegiate curriculum before you accomplish the feat. Still you may some day do it, for I mean to afford you every advantage. When Demosthenes attributed the chief power of the oration to *delivery* he meant merely *temporary* effect. Be a good boy then, *study* well, but take care of your health and of your soul, and your mother and your sister also."

"New York, July 11, 1863.

"I am happy to learn that you spent the 'Fourth' in an interesting and patriotic manner. Your early rising and military drilling will promote your health.

"Your lessons in elocution have, no doubt, been useful, nor would I discourage you in relation to your elocutionary practice; but I would not have you rely on mere mechanical or muscular means to move an auditory. An orator without sense would be, as Æschines once said (though improperly) of Demosthenes, 'a mere bugle from which, if the mouthpiece be withdrawn, there is nothing left.' In order to have a good basis of thought we must study. Hence Cicero recommends the orator to compass, as far as may be, the whole range of knowledge; and he says of himself, 'I have been made an orator, if, indeed, I am one at all, or such as I am, not by the workshops of the rhetoricians [elocutionists], but by the walls of the academy.'

"Learning and thought are not, indeed, all that is necessary. Thought, without feeling, would be like gunpowder without the spark. Hence Quinctilian gives us to understand that the heart must be cultivated as well as the head, and intimates that no bad man can be a great orator—that virtue is essential to genuine eloquence.

"I am in great anxiety in regard to the battle on the Potomac. Love to all. Kiss mamma and Eliza for me."

CHAPTER XIII.

DEATH OF MRS. THOMSON.

AT the close of the year 1863 the Thomson family was clothed in mourning, for the wife and mother had been taken by the hand of Death. A few weeks previously, while attending divine service in Washington Square Methodist Episcopal Church, Mrs. Thomson had a stroke of paralysis, from which she partially recovered; so that on the day before Christmas she walked out with her husband, and selected presents for the children. While on this walk she said: "This will be my last Christmas with you all; I want the children to have nice presents by which to remember me; and I hope we shall have a happy day." But alas! on the morrow another stroke came, depriving her of speech and ultimately terminating her life. She died on the last day of the year. During her illness, Mrs. Thomson received the kindly ministrations of Mrs. Governor Wright, Mrs. W. B. Skidmore, and Mrs. Dr. J. P. Newman, who were angels of mercy to the weeping children as they sat in the darkness of their great sorrow.

On the evening of the same day an informal funeral service was held at the family residence, in which Bishop Janes, and Drs. Porter, Newman, Crawford, and Fox took part. At the close of the services

Dr. J. P. Newman, the pastor of the family, received her son Edward, then fifteen years of age, into full connection with the Church. He had served out his probation, and would have been received on the succeeding Sabbath; but, as the family would then be in a distant State, to gratify his young and sorrowing heart, he was admitted into the full communion of the Church beside the coffin of his departed mother.

In the midst of a severe snow-storm on New-year's morning, 1864, at half past five o'clock, the remains were taken to the railroad depot, attended by the family, and accompanied by Bishop Janes, and Drs. Newman, Porter, and Crawford. They were thence conveyed by the cars to Delaware, and laid by the side of the two children who had preceded her to the heavenly land. There they sleep, waiting for the blissful morning when the dead in Christ shall awake to life immortal.

We have already referred to the assistance rendered by Mrs. Thomson to her husband in the early days of his ministry. While at Norwalk, she was an essential helper in the office of preceptress for several months. When not engaged in that position she gave much attention to the pupils, seeking in every possible way to advance their interests and happiness. When her husband moved to Delaware she took a deep interest in the happiness and well-being of the university students, enticing the wandering from the paths of error, and interceding for their pardon, where she could see any ground of hope; while she encouraged the diligent and upright to continue in the way of duty.

When the war broke out in 1861, she was greatly

concerned for the success of the Union armies; and though in feeble health, she did all she could in sending comforts and delicacies to the hospitals, and encouragement to the men in the field. As a single instance we ought to mention that she, in connection with a number of other ladies, prepared and sent to the 121st Ohio Regiment a most beautiful silk banner. And with it Mrs. Thomson transmitted the following letter of presentation:

"*To Colonel William P. Reid, Officers, and Privates:*

"In behalf of the ladies who have contributed, in the counties where you so nobly responded to the call for 'three hundred thousand more,' I address you. With this flag—emblem of our National Union, the temple of our liberties—we send hearty greeting. The women of America to the soldiers—the hearthstones to their defenders—send greeting. And with greeting we send prayers that you may trust in the God of battles, be strong and courageous, and bear aloft this beautiful banner with never ceasing fidelity. We send prayers, too, that you may win victory in the field, and return speedily with honor, to enjoy the fruits of a righteous peace which you have contributed to secure.

"Your cause is that of truth, of liberty, of union; and your conflict one which is looked upon with interest by the whole civilized world. Go, husbands, brothers, friends, and may God shield you and bless you until you send the welcome news that our flag floats in all its original luster down to the Gulf. First victory, union, liberty; then peace, honor, home.   M. L. THOMSON."

From the funeral discourse, delivered at Delaware by Dr. J. M. Trimble, we extract the following:

"Sister Thomson possessed an excellent mind, trained under moral influences for usefulness and happiness. As a wife, she was most devoted to the happiness of her husband. She sought to relieve him from care and labor in household affairs, anticipating every want, and by her own genial spirit causing sunshine around the hearthstone of home. In sickness she was an angel of mercy, ministering cheerfully to the wants of the suffering. To the poor she was attentive, kind, and generous. To the stranger she was cordial without freedom, and hospitable without ostentation. To the Church of her choice she was strongly and conscientiously attached. While entertaining liberal views and catholic sentiments, she rarely entered any other Church than her own, deeming that her highest usefulness would be secured by limiting her labors to her own communion. Her associates in the Church will not soon forget the services she rendered in various ways to the advancement of the good cause in their midst.

"For the last six months she had evidently been ripening for the heavenly world. She had a presentiment of her death, and contemplated the event with Christian composure. Though she could not speak upon her dying bed her mind was clear, and she gave every evidence possible that Jesus was precious to her in the last trying hour. Feeling that her exit was near, she beckoned her family to her bedside. Imprinting a kiss upon the cheek of her dear son and daughter, and most affectionately embracing her husband, she kissed herself away from their companionship to join the sainted multitudes above. A faithful friend, a devoted mother, a true and loyal wife, a loving sister, and a child of the living God, has gone to rest."

The Rev. Oliver Burgess, of Cleveland, Ohio, says:
" My acquaintance with Maria Bartley (afterwards
Mrs. Thomson) began in 1834, in Norwalk Seminary,
when Rev. J. E. Chaplin was the principal. There
we formed a strong friendship, which continued until
her death. I often visited her father's house in her
youth, in Mansfield Ohio, and frequently met her,
after her marriage, at Norwalk and Delaware, and
found in her a faithful friend, a lovely companion, an
accomplished woman, devoted to her honored husband, and fond and proud of her children. May they
meet her in heaven!"

The faculty of the Ohio Wesleyan University, who
knew her so long and well, tendered the following
testimonial to their bereaved ex-president:

" WHEREAS, We have learned with deep affliction
the decease of Mrs. Thomson, the wife of our beloved
Dr. Thomson; therefore,

" *Resolved*, 1. That we do deeply sympathize with
our former president and our warmly cherished friend
in this bereavement. We have been witnesses of his
happiness, and are able in some degree to measure the
greatness of his sorrow. We have had the honor to
be partakers in the fellowship of his prosperity, and
we esteem it among the noblest privileges to drink
with him the bitter cup of this grief. If there be in
human sympathy a sweetness fitted to beguile, if but
for a moment, the agonies of a rent spirit, we humbly
tender it as our offering. We could wish the power
of a charm were in our words that we might create
the dewy freshness of a June morning about the sad-
dened heart of our friend. We are sure, however,
that he knows of a fountain of health and a garden

of ever fresh delight and a spiritual presence of an
infinite wealth of sympathy and love; that so we need
but ask the privilege of communing with him there,
having much to receive and little to give.

" *Resolved,* 2. That we remember with pleasure
the many virtues of our deceased friend.   Her cheerful and benevolent spirit, her active usefulness, her
domestic happiness, her religious sociality, her devotion to the Church and to the university, her kindness to students, and considerate attentions to citizens
and strangers, have all made a lasting and ineffaceable
impression on our hearts."

Dr. Thomson dedicated to her the following lines,
which he wrote in her album, and which never have
heretofore been published:

"TO MY WIFE.

" Around us in the solemn night,
Around us in the morning light,
Around us in the twilight gray,
Around us in the blaze of day,
    There is a God.

When up we run our ravished eye
Along the arch of stellar sky,
Or, turning from remotest star,
Survey the mountains from afar,
    All round is God.

When we read the historic page,
When we muse with the mystic sage;
When on the tide of heavenly song
Our raptured souls are borne along,
    We trace our God.

When Science, with her cheerful light,
Threads the labyrinth with delight,
And, scattering mists of error's age,
Shows us the cavern all ablaze,
    We 'll worship God.

When we behold the infant breathe,
Or see the new-born soul believe;
When we observe the breath depart,
And feel the cold and pulseless heart,
    We 'll trust in God.

When tempests o'er the ocean sweep,
And terrors rise o'er all the deep;
When break the billows o'er our head,
And briny make our daily bread,
    We 'll look to God.

When we unclose the closet door,
With reverent spirit to adore;
When in the holy courts we stand,
And worship with uplifted hand,
    We 'll feel our God.

When bowed beneath the load of sin,
And pressed by passion's force within,
Our Savior on the cross we see,
As a Lamb slain for you and me,
    We 'll own our God.

And when our work on earth is done,
And the last hour of life is come,
May angels bear, on pinions bright,
Our spirits to the world of light,
    To praise our God."

CHAPTER XIV.

AS A BISHOP.

AT the General Conference of 1864, held at Philadelphia, it was decided that the episcopacy must be re-enforced by three new men. Among many competent men, it was not surprising that Edward Thomson, who, had come within a few votes of being chosen at the last election of bishops, and had conducted the leading organ of the Church so ably during the past four years, should now be thought of as a prominent candidate.

On the 20th day of May, when the election occurred, Davis W. Clark, then editor of the *Ladies' Repository*, received 124 votes, and Edward Thomson 123, both being chosen on the first ballot. Calvin Kingsley, editor of the *Western Christian Advocate*, was elected on the second ballot. On the 24th of the same month they were consecrated to the highest and most laborious office in the gift of the Church.

Bishop Thomson's episcopal labors lasted scarcely six years, yet they were continuous, efficient, and extensive. His first tour as a bishop was greater than any made by the apostle Paul. Wherever he went he manifested the spirit of the "beloved disciple." He wrote with the strength of Paul and the beauty of John, and from his lips flowed the eloquence of Apollos.

Following is a table kindly prepared by Bishop Simpson, which represents, in brief, the labor performed by Edward Thomson in the episcopal office:

1864.—He visits the missions in the East.

1865.—*West Wisconsin*, August 31—September 5, at Brodhead, Wisconsin. J. B. Bachman, Secretary.

North-west Wisconsin, September 14, at Menomonee. T. M. Fullerton, Secretary.

Minnesota, September 21—24, at Faribault, Minn. Jabez Brooks, Secretary.

Rock River, October 4—9, at Aurora, Ill. E. Q. Fuller, Secretary.

Mississippi Mission, December 25—27, in New Orleans. J. P. Newman, Secretary.

1866.—*East Baltimore*, March 7—13, in Williamsport, Penn. J. H. C. Dosh, Secretary.

Providence, March 21—26, in Bristol. M. J. Talbot, Secretary.

Wyoming, April 18—24, in Oswego, N. Y. R. Nelson, Secretary.

Cincinnati, August 29—September 4, Ripley, O. W. H. Sutherland, Secretary.

Indiana, September 12—17, in Vincennes. C. Nutt, Secretary.

Southern Illinois, September 19—24, Centralia, Ill. R. Allyn, Secretary.

1867.—*Kentucky*, February 24—March 4, in Lexington, Ky. G. W. Johnson, Secretary.

West Virginia, March 14—18, Catlettsburg, Ky. Alex. Martin, Secretary.

Pittsburg, March 6—11, Massillon, O. I. C. Pershing, Secretary.

Oregon, August 7, Portland, Oregon. C. C. Stratton, Secretary.

Nevada, September 5—9, Carson City, Nevada. Warren Nims, Secretary.

California, September 18—24, Santa Clara, Cal. J. B. Hill, Secretary.

1868.—*Missouri and Arkansas*, March 11—17, St. Louis, Mo. L. M. Vernon, Secretary.

Kansas, March 25, Lawrence. G. S. Dearborne, Secretary.

1868.—*Nebraska*, April 2—4, Peru, Neb. H. T. Davis, Secretary.
  North Indiana, April 15, Warsaw, Ind. M. Mahin, Secretary.
  East Maine, June 11—15, Machias, Maine, B. S. Arey, Secretary.
  East Genesee, August 26—September 2, Bath, N. Y. K. P. Jervis, Secretary.
  North Ohio, September 9—15, Wooster. W. D. Godman, Secretary.
  Central Ohio.—September 17—20, Lima, O. W. G. Williams, Secretary.
  North-west Indiana, September 30—October 5, Valparaiso. C. Skinner, Secretary.
1869.—*Philadelphia*, March 17—22, Philadelphia. R. H. Patterson, Secretary.
  New England, March 24—30, Lowell, Mass. E. A. Manning, Secretary.
  New York East, April 7—13, Middletown, Conn. G. W. Woodruff, Secretary.
  Vermont, April 15—20, Waterbury, Vt. R. Morgan, Secretary.
  Iowa, September 1—6, Muscatine, Iowa. E. H. Waring, Secretary.
  Southern Illinois, September 15—20, Vandalia, Ill. R. Allyn, Secretary.
  Illinois, September 22—28, Lincoln, Ill. W. S. Hooper, Secretary.
  Central Illinois, September 29—October 4, Canton, Ill. O. S. Munsell, Secretary.
  South-west German, October 8—12, Burlington, Iowa. W. Koeneke, Secretary.
1870.—*Lexington*, February 24—27, Louisville, Ky. E. C. Moore, Secretary.
  Kentucky, March 2—7, Maysville, Ky. D. Stevenson, Secretary.
  West Virginia, March 10—14, Charleston, W. Va. J. L. Clarke, Secretary.

Before his election to the episcopal office many who were not well acquainted with him thought he would not be well adapted to the exacting labor of this position. They should have considered that a man who had managed affairs so skillfully at Norwalk and built a university at Delaware must have administrative abilities of a rare order. Dr. George Lansing Taylor describes him quite accurately:

"His matchless politeness and unvarying kindness made him one of the most faultless models of the Christian bishop. While inflexible in his decision upon occasion, he was at the farthest remove from that brusque bluntness which excuses its incivility under the plea of duty. Although one of the most relentless workers, he never made work a drudgery, and from his invariable ease and courtesy of manners he seemed to be always at leisure. He was never too busy to be a gentleman, nor too emphatic to be a Christian."

Dr. C. C. Stratton, president of the University of the Pacific, says: "He was easy in the chair and accessible." The Rev. E. A. Manning, who was secretary of the New England Conference, when he presided over that body, says: "I can now recall the rare faculty he had of facilitating the business of a conference session by his genial manner of presiding. My regard for him was so greatly heightened by that brief week of sitting by his side, that when the news of his death came it was with keen regret that I read the mournful announcement."

When he presided over the North Ohio Conference that body, in passing the usual vote of thanks to the presiding officer, did the unusual thing of saying that it had a "high opinion of his *administrative* ability." At the session of the Rock River Conference above referred to, Bishop Ames was present for a day. After adjournment that noon he said to Bishop

Thomson: "I have been regarded for years as the best man in our board of bishops to push business through, but I must take off my hat to you."

The Rev. I. C. Pershing, president of the Pittsburg Female College, who was secretary of the Pittsburg Conference when Bishop Thomson presided over that body, thus writes of his presidency:

"Great satisfaction was felt by the members of the Pittsburg Conference when the announcement was published that Bishop Thomson, so long known as president of the Ohio Wesleyan University, and subsequently as editor of the *Christian Advocate*, was to preside at its coming session in Massillon, Ohio, March 6, 1867.

"The bishop had become widely known through the great force and purity of style evidenced in his published 'Essays' and 'Letters from Europe,' as well as through his successful management of the university, and expectation was on tiptoe and curiosity keen to see the man who had stirred the Church by his brilliant writings, and done so much to give tone and character to its educational enterprises. Not the least element was the desire always felt by both ministers and laymen to see the men clothed by the General Conference with episcopal honors and responsibilities. To a Methodist there is much in the name bishop, but in this case, as in many others there was more in the man.

"The hour for opening the session came—an hour spent by many whose fields of labor are widely separated, and who have not looked into each other's faces for a year, in kindly greeting—but a desire to see the new bishop had gathered an unusually large number

to the conference room. Promptly at the appointed
moment he appeared and took his place on the platform. Not the least effort at display was made in the
opening services. The lesson and hymn were well
and impressively read; and the conference was led in
a prayer of remarkable simplicity, but beautiful and
comprehensive. Every want of the members, their
families, and the Church at large, seemed to be included in its petitions. The business of the conference was at once taken up; and all doubts, if any
previously existed, as to the capabilities of the new
bishop as a presiding officer soon vanished. All felt
that beneath that quiet exterior there was a reserve
power equal to any emergency. This was fully evidenced in the promptness with which the business of
the then large conference, numbering two hundred
and forty-four members, was dispatched. And yet in
no instance was there any appearance of undue haste.
Patience, courtesy, and kindness were constantly manifested; and each member cherished the conviction
that so far as a 'godly judgment' could guide the
appointing power, the best thing possible would be
done in assigning fields of labor, for the coming year,
to his fellow-toilers in the Master's vineyard. Nor
were they disappointed. When the appointments
were announced, each felt that he had in the bishop
a personal friend, one full of tender sympathy; and
that if his allotment was not all that he desired, it
was the very best of which the circumstances would
admit. The writer does not recall a single case in
which there was the least dissatisfaction.

"By Saturday evening all the work of the conference, even to the minutest details, had been attended

to; and nothing remained for the Monday morning session but the reading of the appointments and the minor matters incident to the closing hour.

"Sabbath morning brought together an immense audience that literally packed the church from end to end. After the opening services, the first and second verses of the twelfth chapter of Romans were announced as the text. The exposition of the reasonableness of the duty enjoined by the apostle was clear and logical, classical in diction, and full of unction. The premises granted, the conclusion was irresistible, and was enforced in such a way as to leave a profound impression on the audience. It was eminently adapted to men who had laid, body and soul, time and talents, upon the altars of the Church. If any one entered the house that morning tempted by the toils and sacrifices of the itinerancy to retire from the field, he left it with a purpose to leave the sacrifice where he had placed it, and toil on until he could

> "'His body with his charge lay down,
> And cease at once to work and live.'

"We are aware of the fact that to some it may appear a mere form to adopt a resolution of approval, but far more than a mere form was intended by the members of the conference when, by a rising vote, they adopted unanimously the following:

"'WHEREAS, This session of our conference has been favored, for the first time, with the services of our beloved Bishop Thomson; therefore,

"'*Resolved*, That we hereby express the great pleasure we have enjoyed in having him to preside over our deliberations, and our appreciation of the Christian courtesy and signal ability with which he has discharged the duties of a presiding officer; and assure him of a warm greeting whenever the episcopal plan of visitation shall permit him to visit us again.'

"This action was subsequently emphasized by the vote of thanks, the last item of which was as follows: 'And finally, to our most excellent Bishop Thomson, who in this his first visit to us has greatly endeared himself to us, and justifies our largest expectations of him as an executive and episcopal officer.'

"Little did we then dream that that first visit was to be his last as well; and that he, who had so honored the Church of his choice, was so soon to leave us, and join the general assembly and Church of the first-born on high."

The Rev. Robert Allyn, president of the Southern Illinois Normal University, thus writes of "Bishop Thomson in Conferences:"

"In September, 1866, Bishop Thomson presided at the session of the Southern Illinois Conference, held that year in Centralia. I had known him in Ohio, and was delighted with the idea of having him for our presiding bishop. I was chosen secretary, and was set down to be entertained at the same place where he was located with his wife—whom he had not long before married. He came among us with the reputation of a scholar who frequently read his sermons. And, as he was small in stature and of a gentle and innocent appearance, there was much curiosity both to see him and, I rather think, to test his administrative force. The abstraction of his manner, making him seem to hear indistinctly, added not a little to the general desire to know exactly 'what he was made of.' He was, however, most cordially greeted by several of our men, who had voted for him two years before, and who had learned to know him somewhat.

"When he opened the conference he made a few remarks on the proprieties of the conference session and on the intercourse of the preachers among the people; and the members and visitors at first looked at each other as if wondering whether he really knew the import of his own words. He spoke of the character of a minister being such that all innocent people always welcomed his coming. 'But,' said he, 'if it were a gang of copperheads that had this morning advanced along these streets, would young children and women come out to meet and greet them?' It was too soon after the war for men not to think of certain partisans whose names were prominent at the time. And not a few gave him credit for intending to convey a political lesson. When I told him one day, in presence of his wife, what many thought of his meaning, how archly he looked when he replied: 'Could any body be so suspicious as to believe I meant men when I named snakes?' But he had used his illustration of the copperheads crawling along the street so felicitously that every body got a rich lesson, whatever they may have suspected. The five minutes' talk gave the conference an insight to his soul—transparent as crystal, and clear as a diamond.

"He dispatched the business with precision and rapidity, often enlivening the dryness of conference details and statistics with a pious remark or a witty suggestion, which very soon won all hearts. I remember well the impression made by his address to the candidates and his sermon on Sunday morning, though I can not recall the topics. The address came in as a sweet strain of holy music, and melted every heart. The trials of a young minister were alluded to; and his own early circuits among the plain people of the Western settlements, and the glories of communion with God and saints were infinitely touching and overwhelming. The sermon was on the Christian life, with the love of Jesus pervading it all, and exhaling a divine odor which refreshes all who come near the soul. 'There is,' said he, 'a mosque in Smyrna, into which if you go, or even if you approach it, a stimulating perfume wraps your sense in an ecstasy of delight. When Omar built it he mixed all the mortar with particles of musk, and a thousand years have not dissipated the power of the odor. So build into every fiber of your life the divine perfume of Christ's love, and it will exhale all around and delight to all eternity.' His manner was more than the words, and the most captious was glad that the good bishop read his sermon.

"He attended our conference in Vandalia in 1869, and was received with, if possible, more than delight. Here his address was still more highly appreciated. He argued for simplicity of thought and language in preaching, and for the simple every-day topics of love and duty. I think that address—a carefully written one—not exceeding fifteen minutes in the reading, was the best I have heard in more than forty addresses from different bishops. I can not so clearly recall his sermon. But his dispatch of business and his intercourse with the preachers was Christlike.

"I saw him at another conference in Missouri, at

which time there had been a trial of a preacher for
indiscretions if not immoralities with women.   He
made allusion, discreet and courteous, to the trial in
his address; and then proceeded to set forth what a
man should be who is trusted in a thousand families
and welcomed as a noble minister is and ought to be;
and he did it with such tact and power and yet in
such plain words that, while his thought almost made
the flesh to creep, the words could not offend the delicate ear of a woman.   Many of the older men were
amazed at his matchless fidelity and skill, and said
such art could only be gained by the most intimate
communion with the Infinite Wisdom and Tenderness.   I have never heard or read any thing approaching it for truth and gentleness.

"I saw him one day as he presided in the General Conference in Chicago, in 1868, when the body
was, to say the least, a trifle tending toward anarchy.
He evidently was perplexed and a little mortified.
An hour afterwards, when he was to make report on
his journey to India, he found his chance and said,
'Dear brethren, when I was in India, they put me up
to ride an elephant, and what with the long strides
of the beast and its loose slipping skin, and its sway-
ing gait I had a hard time to keep my seat.   But I
think I have known a more difficult position'—they
never heard the end of the sentence.   But there was
'great sensation,' and before long business moved as
though every wheel had been oiled.

"He seemed to me to have the happiest art to say
the most innocent things exactly when they were
needed, and to convey by them instruction, reproof,
correction even, in such a way as to strengthen with-

out offending, and to encourage while it admonished. In this he certainly had as much of the wisdom of the serpent as was ever joined with the harmlessness of the dove. Other bishops came to our conference and were honored and revered, but he was loved and trusted quite as much as any of them all. Bishops Janes and Simpson have been particularly favorites with us. But neither of them won hearts sooner than Bishop Thomson, or held them with a firmer grasp. They are remembered as men of power and eloquence, he as a man of love and without guile."

In a personal letter to the author the Rev. William H. Sutherland, of the Cincinnati Conference, says: "He impressed us all as a man of strong thought-power, broad culture, and exquisite literary taste; and yet of Christ-like simplicity, humility, and sweetness of disposition. I was secretary of our conference for fifteen consecutive years, and during that period was associated with all, or nearly all, the bishops of our Church; and yet none of them ever drew me so closely to him in affection as did your noble father. I still sincerely mourn his premature departure."

He might well be regarded as a model bishop—kind and courteous towards the members of his cabinet, thoughtful of the needs of the preachers and their families, prompt and firm, but not blunt and harsh in his decisions, swift but thorough in his dispatch of business, dignified yet unassuming, popular with both the poor and the rich, at ease in the mansion of the merchant, at home in the cabin of the negro preacher, a gentleman in travel, a prince in literature, and an orator in the pulpit. In this last particular he always attracted attention.

At conference sessions a bishop is expected to preach the leading sermon, and so when he appears in the pulpits of the larger cities, he has usually the finest audiences who expect the best sermons. The writer has not heard of an instance where Bishop Thomson ever disappointed the people by preaching a mediocre sermon. He was not always equal, it is true, but he did not fall below himself.

The New York correspondent of *Zion's Herald*, in noting various Methodist affairs, says: "Bishop Thomson, on Sunday morning, in the Seventh Street Methodist Church, delivered a sermon on 'Dealing justly, loving mercy, and walking humbly with God,' that very few ministers in our denomination or any other could duplicate. The whole sweep of the discourse was wonderful in its keen analysis, its beautiful imagery, its ethical power, and its evangelical spirit. I hope the sermon will be repeated all through our work. It is needed everywhere."

The following appeared in the *Christian Advocate* the next week after Bishop Thomson held the New York East Conference at Middletown: "The sermon before the New York East Conference, on the occasion of the ordination of deacons, was delivered by Bishop Thomson. It gave universal satisfaction, many clergymen present pronouncing it the ablest effort they ever listened to. The bishop selected his text from Acts iv, 12, 'There is none other name under heaven, given among men, whereby we must be saved.' His theme was the necessity of a divine Christ as a Redeemer, argued from a negative standpoint. He discussed the attempts of man to gain piety and holiness or religion under three heads: 1. Government;

2. Education; 3. False Religions. Under the first division he treated of monarchy, aristocracy, democracy, anarchy, and communism. Under the second he dwelt upon the various systems of education, ethical, metaphysical, and æsthetical. Under the third he reduced the various false religions to three, idolatry, Mohammedanism, and deism, or natural religion. All these systems of moral reform had miserably failed, and there remained but one resource, the acceptance of the atonement. The sermon was an eloquent and masterly vindication of the claims of Christ to be the only hope of the world's salvation."

His sermons were always thoroughly orthodox. Though broad in his culture and range of reading he was not in sympathy with what is falsely called "liberal theology." He was not unsound on a single point in any one of our doctrines. With unction he declared the *terrors* as well as the beauties and consolations of divine truth. We give below a passage from one of his discourses in illustration: "Some hope to escape through the love and sacrifice of Jesus. We must recollect, however, that Jesus was holy. A man of obscure perceptions, feeble mind, and uncultured conscience will have but little indignation against wrong; but it is otherwise with an enlightened and holy man. If, in proportion as our minds are enlarged, our hearts purified, and our consciences cultivated, our abhorrence of wrong and aversion to it increases what must be the moral indignation of the infinite and holy God against wrong doers? Men sometimes hold up the mild God of Christianity in contrast with the stern deity of the Hebrews; but little do they know about either. The lamb is, in-

deed, the emblem of love; but what so terrible as the
wrath of the Lamb? The depth of the mercy despised is the measure of the punishment of him that
despiseth. No more fearful words than those of the
Savior! The threatenings of the law were temporal,
those of the Gospel are eternal. It is Christ who
reveals the never-dying worm, the unquenchable fire,
and he who contrasts with the eternal joys of the
redeemed the everlasting woes of the lost. His loving arm would enfold the whole guilty race, but not
while impenitent and unbelieving; the benefits of his
redemption are conditional."

We also give an outline of the discourse delivered before the East Genesee Conference at Bath,
on the "Divine Call to the Ministry:"

" Every man employs his own laborers. It is his
right. So God appoints all that he has made, even
the worm, to its position; he chooses his own ministers, and gives them their work. Will he take and
send unconverted men? How can sinners preach
that which they do not believe, and which they have
not experienced? The Church recognizes those whom
God calls. How is this call distinguished? By the
Holy Spirit's influence attending the ministrations,
and by the results following? How is this call as-
certained by the person himself? By his motives—
not for the applause of men; not ambition; but to
save souls; by the inward, burning desire to preach
the unsearchable riches of Christ; by his success; by
the indorsement of the Church; by the way being
opened up before him, while, perhaps, in every
worldly occupation there is a want of success or a
closing up of every avenue.

"There are many duties implied. When the Church invites, the called should enter the vineyard. We have no right to refuse. We should, as far as possible, obtain the necessary qualifications. Some seem to expect that God will endow the minister with the gift of tongues. There is no hope of this. If we are to preach to the Chinese, we must study their language. Dr. Morrison felt called of God to go to this people, yet he had to study dictionaries and grammars. Why not do the same thing if we preach to an English-speaking population? Wesley required of his ministers close study. Our Church is not satisfied with preliminaries, but prescribes a course of study also. If a man has a hard day's work to do in chopping timber, he will gain by taking sufficient time in the morning to grind his ax. How can a preacher do more in the regular work than preach two or three sermons a week, and pursue his conference studies, unless he is an intellectual Colossus?

"He who has a divine call should devote himself exclusively to his work. Let no minister engage in secular business. It is impossible to handle the world without soiling the fingers. Paul worked at tent-making, but he preached to heathen; besides, he had no missionary society to fall back upon. We can not follow successfully two kinds of business. The interests will clash. Suppose one of the Siamese twins should engage in the practice of medicine and the other attempt to perform the duties of a minister, would they not pull heavily on the umbilical ligaament?

"How can we secularize without violating our ordination vows? We have promised to devote ourselves to the work of the ministry. Does God call *half* of a man or the whole? What said the apostle? 'This one thing I do.' We must focalize the rays of mind to accomplish any thing for ourselves or others. If we take half of our time for business, can we wonder if our people complain, or if they withhold half our wages?

"May this call be canceled? Yes; but only through our sinning against God; for 'the gifts and calling of God are without repentance.' Would that we could send forth our preachers now as formerly—as Wesley did, as Christ sent his apostles—by two and two.

"It is no fault that our youth prefer ministers who are imaginative and emotional, but it is a fault that age and gray hairs are ignored and unappreciated. But is it not, brethren, too often the fault of the minister himself? Let him be diligent in study. Let him keep his heart warm with Jesus' love. And what reason is there why he may not compete successfully with his younger brethren, and be sought after as much as they?

"A minister ought to defer to the judgment of his brethren in regard to retiring from actual service. They are frequently better judges than we. If we are needy, God will raise us up friends; and if we are not, we ought not to hold on against the convictions of others.

"Again, we should do all the work of the ministry. If we fail at any point, it will mar our entire efforts. A chain is no stronger than its weakest link. Among our duties, pastoral visiting holds an important relation. By this we know the wants of our people, and what is the needed remedy. A hospital physician, who should cast into each ward a promiscuous supply of opium, quinine, and pills, and trust to Providence for the administration of them, would hardly be successful. Neither can a minister who, neglecting to visit his flock, remains ignorant of their spiritual condition. If he would hit, he must take aim; and to do this he must know where the game is, and this knowledge must be obtained by beating the bush. A minister must execute and enforce discipline, and cut off those who are incorrigible.

"All the duties of the ministry must be performed with a single eye to the Divine glory in order to lead men to Christ, and that they may finally reach heaven. Do somewhat as Lyman Beecher directed, 'fill your heart chock full of the subject, and then *let natur' caper.'*

"Some seem to have a roving call. They run around from conference to conference, and if they are not suited, they are offended and talk of locating. Beware of leaving the ministry before your work is done. When it is, God will tell you; till then, though you may have infirmities, you must work. Nelson lost an eye, but he was Nelson still. If you lose one leg, preach on the other; one eye, see with the other. Neither leave for fear of death. Die, if need be, the first good chance you get, and go to glory. All things here below are given to change, but the Word of God endureth forever. Atheism, pantheism, deism, have sought to destroy it, but it still remains for your support and comfort.

" Who will read Milton and Homer a million years hence? But a thousand millions of centuries in the future we shall still read that 'God so loved the world that he gave his only begotten Son' for our redemption. O, why will not every Hannah say to-day before the Lord in his temple, 'I have lent my son unto the Lord? As long as he liveth he shall be lent unto the Lord.' Let every father say to his son, 'Go, thou, and preach the Gospel!'

"You, brethren, are about to be ordained to this work. Angels might envy you the privilege. They are not permitted to preach the Gospel. Christ spoke to an angel and sent him to Peter. He, not the angel, was to preach salvation to Cornelius. Garibaldi said to his legions: 'I offer you hunger and thirst, sufferings and privations, wounds and death, in the cause which we espouse. Whoever accepts the cause let him follow me.' They did not hesitate, and accepted the choice. We may in our work meet with trials and disappointments, hardships and even death, but, brethren, your, our, reward is in heaven. Let us be faithful and cry,

> "'Happy, if with my latest breath
> I may but gasp his name;
> Preach him to all, and cry in death,
> Behold! behold the Lamb!'"

At the New York East Conference which sat in Middletown, Conn., April 7–13, 1869, Bishop Thomson delivered the following address to the young ministers who had served out their probationary period, and were now to be admitted as deacons into full membership. After the usual disciplinary questions were put and answered, he said in substance:

"Our first question is, 'Have you faith in Christ?' The scope of this question is sometimes not sufficiently appreciated. Faith in God is not enough to answer this question. You are proposed as ministers for the Church of *Christ*. What have you to do in the Christian pulpit without faith in Christ? Christ is the combination of all theology. He is our ' wisdom, and righteousness, and sanctification, and redemption;' our 'alpha and omega' in redemption, in salvation our all in all. As all the firmament above us, all the solar system is filled with light, and all that light is from the rays of the sun, so all doctrine, all morals, all saving truth is filled with rays of celestial light from Christ. If you have not an intimate and saving faith in Christ, how can you do the work of a Christian minister?

"Your personal religious experience is here a subject of solemn inquiry. It is presupposed that you are already converted men. But the question is, 'Are you going on to perfection?' If you are going *on* at all, you are going on to perfection. Going backward is not going on. Where else are you going if not to perfection? You *must* go on. A Christian is like a velocipede. He must go ahead or he will fall over. He can not go backward. We demand perfection in all our temporal matters; perfection in our walks, our bread, our daily conveniences. We have perfection in nature all about us, perfect atmosphere, perfect water, perfect sunlight; every work of nature is perfect. We demand perfection in art. See the progressive development of the steam-engine. What toil of thought to perfect the telegraph! I passed the other day through the factories at Lowell. Visitors are admitted only by tickets. Why is this? Why, but because improvements are constantly being made in machinery, appliances, and processes, giving greater and greater perfection to manufacturing, and manufacturers are careful to whom they exhibit their improvements? Why should not Christian experience be governed by the same laws, and in like manner move forward?

"'Do you expect to be made perfect in love in this life?' Do n't be afraid of this word, nor of the doctrine, nor ashamed of the experience. Of course you are not to expect to be made perfect in wisdom, or in knowledge, but in love—love to God and love to men. Why should we doubt the power of God's grace to make us perfect in all the breadth and depth of Christian charity? This is that grand action of Christianity without which the highest attainments in faith and knowledge are empty. I have been alarmed at an apparent tendency to discount the promises of God; to narrow and shadow and almost to negative them in this respect. Let us rather enlarge our comprehension of all their length and breadth and depth and height. If we 'count not ourselves to have apprehended,' still let us say, 'This *one* thing I do, forgetting the things which are behind, and reaching forth unto those things which are before, I press' forward, forward, ever forward; never to be satisfied with any thing less than that moral perfection of which our Lord Jesus Christ is the standard, and to which he is our mighty aid. Let us experience that the greatness of the grace and power that raised up Jesus Christ from the dead can also lift us into life in him.

"You are to be 'devoted to your work.' All Christians are stewards for God of whatever they possess. The Christian minister must be particularly such, an example of devotion to all. All his time, talents, acquirements, abilities of every kind, of mind and heart, must be devoted to his work. But we are not only inquiring into your fitness for the ministry in general; we want to know if you are fit for Methodist ministers. You have read our rules, you promise to conform to our rules, both for the membership and the ministry. Do not be afraid of reading them too frequently. You may spend years of study upon our Articles of Religion, and years more upon our practical economy, and yet find room for progress. Here are our *first, tenth,* and *twelfth* rules, which are especially emphasized: 'Be diligent. Never be unemployed; never be triflingly employed; never trifle away time, neither spend any more time at any place than is strictly necessary.' 'Be punctual. Do every thing exactly at the time.' 'Act in all things, not according to your own will, but as a son in the Gospel. As such, it is your duty to employ your time in the manner in which we direct: in preaching and visiting from house to house; in reading, meditation, and prayer. Above all, if you labor with us in the Lord's vineyard, it is needful you should do that part of the work which we advise, at those times and places which we judge most for His glory.' What wonderful rules are these! Let a man keep them, and who can measure their effects? 'Never spend more time at any place than necessary.' Let a man keep that alone, and what wonders it will work for him! It is not the genius, but the plodder who wins the race in life. The genius has the advantage in the outset, but it is the man who goes straight forward, up hill and down, over mountain and plain, who first gains the goal. You all have brains enough and heart enough to accomplish grand things for God if you will work, work, work. 'Be punctual.' If you lose half an hour with a congregation of a thousand people waiting, you lose a thousand half hours, and set your people a demoralizing example. They will sooner learn your failings than your virtues. Do not 'mend our rules, but keep them.' This is a progressive age, and you are, we hope, progressive men. But something is due to the wisdom of the past. There are some things in which progress is impossible. We can not improve upon revelation, nor upon the moral law, nor upon the precepts of Jesus. Something is due to institutions which have the sanction of the aggregated wisdom of ages. It is easier to destroy than to build up. A boy with a handful of shavings may lay in ashes a city which a million of men have toiled through centuries to rear. You may recall the classical fable of the daughters who were ambitious to have their ancient father rejuvenated. They consulted a magician in the matter, and he directed them to cut up the old man and boil him down and remould him. The cutting up and boiling down were easy enough, but how to get the old man out of the caldron again! Ah, there was the rub! So when you have torn a Church or a system in pieces, who shall gather up the fragments of your ruin? With all your progressiveness, therefore, hold with a true conservatism to the old foundations.

"Again, will you do the work assigned you? Our itinerant system has its disadvantages. It has its advantages also. The system of a settled pastorate has the same. We have chosen this system; you have chosen it. Now rest in it and do your work. Is it honorable, after accepting this system, to say 'I will go here, but I will not go there?' If you had said so here you would not have been accepted. We compel no one to come, or to stay; but while you stay we expect you to be loyal. But we believe this system to be good, and we advise you to stay. One of our brethren, the Rev. D. Dorchester, well known as a statistician among us, has shown that among the other denominations of New England the average ministerial life, that is, life spent in the active ministry, is about six years. You all know that ours is much longer than that. But he has also shown that removals are actually more frequent among them than among us. Now, in moving, I prefer to roll smoothly along on wheels rather than to jar along on parallelograms and rectangles. I prefer to move by machinery, and when I expect it, rather than by an arbitrary chance.

"You have, moreover, no necessity for watching and negotiation to secure a place to work. A few days ago I dined with a friend in another denomination, whose Church had been three or four years without a pastor. I asked him, 'How do you supply your pulpit?' He replied, 'By candidates.' Then I saw in imagination that long line of candidates ascending that pulpit and standing there trembling as on a Fairbanks hay-scales, while every man before them, every woman, every child even, claimed the ability and privilege of weighing them to a hair's weight, as one after another their heads rolled into the basket where those of their predecessors had gone, while the people lavished on them their hospitality, and said every pleasant word but 'Come.'

"But in your case the Church assumes the responsibility of keeping you in work, and you may dismiss all anxiety on that point. You may also be assured that you will receive fair treatment in the designations of your fields of labor. Sometimes ministers seem to forget this. At a recent conference, after I had announced the appointments, a young man came to me with an air of 'sweet simplicity' and said, 'Bishop, you made a mistake in my appointment. I was down for such a place.' Do n't fear about the mistakes. Here are five men, your presiding elders, men of experience and wisdom, men whose honesty and piety have been tested, who look over the whole field, and know every man and every charge. They know the charges better than the ministers do, and the ministers better than the charges do. If they have prejudices or partialities, those of one cancel those of another, and a just result is almost certain. Their own success as overseers of the work demands wise adaptation between men and work, and if they fail in judgment, here is an impartial umpire to decide the question. But if you labor as you should, and qualify yourselves for your work as you ought, you are independent of all aid or hinderance. You can defy presiding elders and bishops and conferences to keep you down. O that we had more of that sanctified heroism that inspired our fathers in this respect! My venerable and departed friend, Adam Poe, known to you all by reputation, when once asked by his bishop if he would go to such a place, replied: 'Bishop, if you appoint me to the moon

I will go, if I can get there by land or water!'
Another minister of my acquaintance resented as an
imputation upon his honor a report that he was unwilling to go to a certain place, and said to his bishop:
'I want it understood that if you appoint me to
preach the Gospel in the mouth of hell, I'll go, if
you can tell me how to get there!'

"And don't overlook the children. An old
physician of my acquaintance said to me, 'When I
want to estimate the amount of a man's practice, I
ask him how many children he attends. If he gets
the children he gets the parents.' Go from house
to house. You have a great calling, the greatest on
earth. Angels in heaven envy you your places to
work on this planet! You are called to dispense
God's greatest benefaction to mortals! You are his
ambassadors to this earth! If I were a young man
to-day, and felt no call to this work, I would kneel
down this moment and ask God to give me some little
spot on this globe where I might preach his Gospel."

CHAPTER XV.

HIS ORIENTAL TOUR.

THE day after the bishops' annual meeting in 1864, when it was determined that Bishop Thomson should visit the missions of the Church in the Orient, Dr. Durbin, the missionary secretary, said to him: "I am glad you are the man to go, for you will give us the most elaborate information and present to the Church, in a luminous form, the condition of our Oriental missions." This the bishop did in the two volumes which he prepared in the last Winter of his life, and which were issued shortly after his death. The letters written to his children Edward and Eliza, jointly, during this long and perilous journey are here given, as they contain incidents in his life not heretofore published:

"ROYAL MAIL STEAMSHIP *Persia,*
"ST. GEORGE'S CHANNEL, September 2, 1864.

" We have just passed Queenstown, where some of our fellow passengers disembarked, and we are now speeding towards Liverpool, two hundred and forty miles distant, where we hope to arrive some twelve or sixteen hours hence, our progress being dependent somewhat upon the tide. Our passage was, at first, much impeded by fogs and head winds, which the sailors ascribed to me, saying that it was because they had a *bishop* on board; but after we reached the longitude of about 40° the wind became favorable, and the passage pleasant. Indeed, yesterday we made three hundred and forty-one miles. I told the officers that if the sailors ascribed to Jonah the fogs and foul winds they should credit him with the fair wind, and in that case there would be a balance in my favor.

"The captain (Lott) is a remarkably pleasant man, who takes good care of his ship, and yet is attentive to his passengers. He invited me to officiate in divine service on Sabbath, which I did, and he not only thanked me for my sermon, but sent me some wine with his compliments, the next day, of which, as you know, I would not partake.

"'The discipline of the ship is admirable—in this respect the British excel. The company of passengers is measurably small, not exceeding seventy. They are of several different nations, German, French, English, and Spaniards, as well as Americans. The Spaniards are chiefly from the West Indies, particularly Havana—some from Venezuela and New Grenada. Of the Americans, I think all are of the Democratic faith except myself; and all, or nearly so, I am sorry to say, sympathize with the South. One has fought in the Southern army and, for a year or so past, has been carrying on unmolested a contraband trade with the South at Memphis. Another says he hopes the South will maintain her ground and establish her independence. He leaves the country without a passport, because he will not take the oath of allegiance, although he is a delegate-elect to the Chicago convention. All except one, who is a war Democrat, not only denounce the administration, sneer at greenbacks, praise the Confederate money, but talk loudly of federal repudiation. Can we wonder that foreigners should feel as they do when this is the character of the Americans who go abroad? There are a few friends of the North in the company. Among these is an Englishman and some Germans. The latter are strong and earnest for us.

"Nothing unusual has occurred on the voyage. The most noteworthy incident is that in the fog we narrowly escaped a collision. I was sitting on deck when I heard the cry of ' *Helm-a-port,*' and knowing there was danger I ran forward just in time to see a ship across our bow. As she fell safely astern her crowded deck sent up a shout of gratitude (I suppose) for their narrow escape. The vessel was an emigrant ship, the *Prince Albert.* As we were nearing the Irish coast a wearied bird, probably driven from the shore in a storm, alighted on the bosom of a passenger sitting on deck. The sailors tried to catch it, but it flew from point to point and escaped. After it had regained strength it set out again for the land. After we had passed Cape Clear the telegraph boat came out for our news, which was thrown into the sea in a sealed tin case for the boat to fish up.

"We have the usual amusements of shuffle-board, quoits, etc., among the men, but the women are generally sick ; some have been during the whole passage. Many are making their appearance in the cabin to-day for the first time. The weather, when I started from New York, was hot, and I had thrown off my flannel and sent my trunk into the hold. I had reason to regret this, as the sea air is so damp and cold. Indeed, after the first day out, I felt the temperature too cold for comfort. The only place to remain is by the steam pipes on deck, and when the weather is wet it is not practicable to avail ourselves of this expedient. My health, however, is good. Strange to say I never take cold at sea, am never sea-sick, and never lose a meal or a night's rest. When the weather is pleasant I enjoy sailing. I like to stand at the helm and see the prow dip down and up. It is a magnificent see-saw. When we have a beam wind and the ship rocks from side to side I eat as in a rocking-chair and sleep as in a cradle. If voyages are short I can enjoy them. but these long voyages soon grow wearisome and monotonous, with all their luxuries and amusements. Our meals are not well arranged. We have breakfast at 8 o'clock, luncheon at 12 M., dinner at 4 P. M., tea at 7.30 to 9 P. M.

"In two weeks or less I expect to sail from Southampton for Alexandria. I am told I shall have a good
vessel, but as my time of sailing is the equinox I suppose we shall have storms on the way. Praise God that
I have got along so well. And now, my dear children, be
good, trust, love, and fear God; make yourselves agreeable and useful in the families where you abide. Let
Edward be kind to Mrs. H., and give her as little trouble
and as much politeness as possible. Let Eliza be good to
John and the baby, respectful to the doctor, and perfectly
obedient and submissive to Mrs. M.; she, for the time being,
stands to her in the relation of a mother, having all her
responsibilities and much of her affection towards her.
I pray daily for you in my state-room when only a little
plate of iron is between my knees and the great deep."

"Marseilles, France, September 19, 1864.

"My health is good, though I am somewhat altered in
appearance. My face is bronzed from exposure to wind and
sun, and I wear a white cravat and carry a card. My English friends insisted that I should do these things, and Dr.
Jobson devised the card for me. I send you one inclosed.
I presume it is necessary in going abroad to go in character.

"This is a fine city. The palace of justice, the bourse,
the city hall, and the museum are elegant structures, and
look as if fresh from the chisel of the artist, and all are
adorned with elegant statuary. The parks are numerous
and beautiful, shaded by the plantain, a tree like our sycamore, and the French elm, a tree which very much resem-
bles our elm. There is one park which is elegantly laid
out and ornamented. It is on a hill overlooking the city,
the castle, and the bay, and is named in honor of Napoleon
I. This is the largest seaport of France, and one of its
most rapidly improving cities. It has a very mixed population, and there are strangers from all parts of the Mediterranean. Many of the travelers at our hotel are Egyp-
tians, and among them is the brother of the viceroy.

"I have met no American here except the consul; but have found some English friends and relatives. I am beginning to speak French again, and can order my meals and make my wants known very well.

"To-day I sail for Egypt in the French steamer *Peluse*. Every friend I meet discourages me, and expresses his wonder that I travel alone. In England, especially, all assured me that my voyage and journeys were arduous and perilous, implying, probably, that I would never return. My apology for having no companion was that, owing to the depreciation of our currency, it was necessary for the Missionary Society to save every cent, and therefore the missionaries going out were sent by sail vessel instead of with me. 'What will you do if you are sick?' said every one. I replied, 'God will take care of me.' 'Yes,' said they, 'but it is cruel to send you alone.' However, I do not allow my mind to be depressed, and I have all confidence in the good providence of God.

"I am more than ever convinced of the importance of temperance principles. In warm countries, pure wine may be safely and perhaps usefully employed; but a man will rarely, if ever, lose any thing by total abstinence, and he may suffer fearfully from indulgence. I have seen new proof of the danger of tippling, and if I ever return to America, I shall be as much as ever an advocate of temperance principles. You know that I have abstained from spirits even when they have been prescribed by physicians, and I do not regret it. Bear in mind my example and instructions during my absence, and give all your influence in college to temperance principles and abstemious habits.

"I hope you will be faithful to the Church. If I were dying, my last charge to you would be: 'Love God, accept Christ, and remember affectionately the Church of your father.' I trust you will worship together and attend the same Sunday-school, rendering yourselves useful as far as possible. I want you to do your part financially, and not only put five or ten cents in every collection, but pay

at least $5 each quarter as quarterage. You should learn
to give to the Lord while you are children and from your
own allowance.

" You must remember me to all my friends, and tell
them I would write to them, but my personal and private
expenses are very great, and every letter I send costs me
nearly a dollar of my salary.

" The Chicago platform seems well enough, but I
see not how the Democratic party standing upon it can
give peace to the country any more speedily or certainly
than the party in power; for they dare not offer any terms
which the existing administration would not accept. And
if they should be willing, in case of success, to abandon their
platform, I fear the United States will be the most unhappy
of nations, and Gen. McClellan the most unfortunate of
men. But my trust is in God. He will do right. Blessed
be his name.

" I have not had much opportunity to gather opinion
in France; but so far as I can learn, it is as much against
us as in England. If we succeed in putting down the rebellion, we shall excite at once the surprise, the admiration,
and the jealousy of the nations. In France the lower
classes are against us and the upper in our favor; while it
is the reverse in England. Some powerful arguments for
the North have lately appeared in the French papers. I
wish I had the time to translate a few extracts.

" God bless you, my children."

"ON BOARD THE Tigre,
On her passage to India, Oct. 3, 1864.

" It is now more than six weeks since I left home, and
I have had but one brief line from Delaware, and that
reached me before I left New York. You may imagine
how I feel. You know not how I love you. God alone
does; and my relief from anxiety is in commending you to
him. I fear you will not find friendly counsel in Delaware.
The people there will not reprove you if you go wrong,

lest they should offend me. Remember that they are your best friends who tell you of your faults. May you maintain a character void of offense. But, if you do wrong, I hope you will find some kind reprover, and so far from being offended with him, give him your warmest thanks.

"I am beginning to feel the perils of my voyage. My sufferings from the heat in this sea are great. One more day of safe sailing will bring us through the straits, and we shall soon be in the Indian Ocean. If we meet with no misfortune, we shall reach Calcutta the 20th of this month. Praise God he has thus far preserved me!

"Since I last wrote you I have washed my feet in the Mediterranean, drunk the waters of the Nile, and bathed in the Red Sea. I have looked at the spot where Moses led the children of Israel from the house of bondage, and where Miriam raised her song over the pursuing hosts. I have caught a glimpse of the spot where it is thought Moses was exposed in his ark of bulrushes, and have had a glance at the summit of Mt. Sinai. I shall have much to tell you when I return. I am now conforming to Eastern habits in my style of living. We take a bath in the morning, are fanned at dinner, and sleep on deck at night.

"Attend faithfully to your studies, master every thing as you advance, and regard your teachers as your best friends; and all the more so when they administer righteous discipline. One of the great dangers of our literary institutions, and one of the great drawbacks to their efficiency, arises from the tendency of youth to deem itself wiser than age. Indeed, the great danger to our country lies in this direction. And what a country we have! None know how to appreciate it except such as go abroad. In the fertility of its soil, the intelligence of its people, the freedom of its institutions, there is nothing like it on the earth. It is the hope of mankind. May God preserve it.

"Pray for your affectionate papa."

" Point de Galle, Ceylon, October 15, 1864.

" We arrived here on the 13th, expecting to meet the steamer *Alpha*, belonging to our line, to take us to Calcutta; but we found that a severe cyclone or tempest had swept down the bay of Bengal by which more than a hundred vessels were wrecked, and the *Alpha* was disabled and compelled to put back, badly damaged, for repairs. The company has chartered another vessel, less safe and commodious, however, which left Calcutta on the 9th, and is expected to reach here on the 18th. But as the northeastern monsoon has already set in, there is no calculating about the results.

" Providence has thus far very much favored me. Except the exhausting heat of the Red Sea, I have not suffered at all. The southern monsoon gave me a ' touch of its quality' on the Indian Ocean, but nothing that disturbed me, as you know I am a good sailor. The heat on the Arabian Sea and on the Indian ocean was very great, but by taking a cold bath of sea water every morning I endured it well. The greatest annoyance I suffered was from the insects that swarm the vessels in these latitudes.

" We are now within fifty miles of the equator. Ceylon presents the Oriental vegetation and scenery in its perfection. The palm on all sides, monkeys on the trees, paroquets in the jungle, perfumes on all sides. The tavern is all open; part of it on one side of the street, part on the other; no glass in the window, no coverings on the bed, no fastenings on the doors. The floors are brick and the walls stuccoed. The servants are black as negroes and nearly naked. So with all the coolies of the island.

" The rainy season has commenced, and we have it very wet; it literally pours, so that I have not been about as much as I wanted to be. I have visited the mission and two of the most prominent priests of Buddha, by whom I was very kindly received. I have also seen the temples and images.

"I trust you are doing well. Do not forget to pray for papa. I am going through great danger. The cholera has attacked our mission at Fuhchau (according to the China mail), and Rev. M. Martin and child have died. I feel that God has been wonderfully kind to me. Blessed be his name! Give my best regards to all inquiring friends, and say to them how much I love them and prize our country and sigh for its peace and prosperity.

" Let Eliza show herself a lady both at home and at school. I shall hope to learn soon that she has given her heart to God. Tell Professor McCabe and all other friends that it would rejoice me to hear from them. I am hungry for letters from home."

"CALCUTTA, INDIA, October 27, 1864.

"To prevent any uneasiness on your part, I write to inform you of my safe arrival here in good health on Tuesday morning of this week. Our passage from Ceylon was not pleasant on account of the crowded state of the vessel, and of the storm which affected us during part of the voyage. We all felt very grateful, however, for such accommodations as we had. The vessel, ' *The River*,' was not the regular one, but was specially chartered to convey us, our vessel being compelled to put back to shore for repairs in consequence of the cyclone. The first cyclone of the month was probably the most severe ever experienced upon these waters. Almost every vessel we passed in the bay was more or less damaged and the ' *City of Poonah*' was totally dismasted.

"From the entrance of the Hoogly to Calcutta, over a hundred miles, the river seemed strewed with wrecks. In one of them three hundred and twenty souls went down to a watery grave. Some large steamboats were carried clear over the bank, and were hopelessly high and dry. This city itself bears marks of the calamity, in trees uprooted, fences and iron railings crushed, and houses partly or wholly demolished. This fearful cyclone your papa, by the great mercy of God, just escaped. The second, which occurred a few days after, we felt, though less than we otherwise would, had we not fortunately been detained a few hours at Madras. As it was, we just skirted its outer circle, though we felt the groundswell for some days. I feel exceedingly grateful to God, and it seems to me that his mercy is the fruit of prayer.

"The very day I arrived here, Dr. Butler, superintendent of our missions, met me, to conduct me to our mission field. To-night, at 9 o'clock, we shall be off for Benares, where I am to preach next Sabbath.

"Be good and happy, and remember me in prayer. The Lord bless you evermore."

"Shahjehanpore, India, November 29, 1864.

"God bless you. This is my constant prayer. I trust you pray for me. The little children of the missions tell me they have been praying for me since the day they heard I was coming.

"My health is good, and through all my dangers I have been safely brought. Since I wrote you I have been traveling and working night and day. We travel by night because the men who bear us wish to avoid the heat. We required twenty men to carry us (Dr. Butler and myself) every ten miles. Four for each palanquin, four to change, and four to carry baggage. We often go fifty miles at a time. Where the roads will permit, we go by horse or garey, and once I traveled by elephant. Sometimes in ascending the mountains we go by dandy—a very light conveyance for one passenger—which is carried by two men, with a change every ten minutes.

"The grandest sight in the world is that of the snowy range of the Himalaya from the top of Cheena. The ascent itself of Cheena is wonderful. I was carried up in a dandy on a narrow path. I could not look down the sides of the path without growing giddy and fearing lest the men should make a false step and send me down the moun-

tain side. The mountains are infested with a great number and variety of wild beasts—tigers, elephants, leopards,
bears, etc. The last named are black in the valleys,
brown on the lower heights, and white near the snow.

"I have seen in India the oldest city, the most beautiful building, and the loftiest mountains in the world. I
stopped, up the Ganges, at all the great cities. I am now
half-way round the mission circuit; and shall soon, with
God's blessing, reach Lucknow, the seat of the conference;
though I am so pressed for time that our arrangements
will not bring me to Lucknow before the 8th prox., when
conference begins, and that will require me to travel all
the night previous. It is wonderful that my health and
heart keep up so under such incessant toil: for even while
I am halting I am kept busy delivering addresses, administering ordinances, preaching, examining property and
deeds, and inspecting schools.

"In case you are sick, call the very best physician;
and to heal your souls apply to Jesus. Remember me to
the students; tell them they ought to feel grateful to God
that he has cast their lines in pleasant places. God bless
and preserve you."

"CALCUTTA, INDIA, December 19, 1864.

"You know not how I grieve over the fact that I do
not hear from you. May God have you in his holy keeping. Pray for me. My daily earnest prayer is for your
salvation.

"The vessel in which I am to sail for China does not
leave till the 21st. It is an opium steamer—'*The Thunder;*'
and the '*Lightning,*' of the same company, leaves a few
days later. The captain promises me a rough passage.
But I have had so much land traveling lately that I am
ready for a change. I still expect to adhere to my pro-
gram; and hope to reach Alexandria, Egypt, early in
March.

"I hope you are getting along well in your schools.

Take care of your health, attend Church, give as little
trouble as possible where you board. You have, doubtless,
money enough. I hope you will use it prudently. Do
not be too saving—allow yourself every thing needful;
but do not spend any thing uselessly. I write in great
haste. God be gracious to you, and preserve you unto
eternal life."

"Hong Kong, China, January 14, 1865.

"This morning, at 9 o'clock, we arrived at this port.
My voyage from Calcutta hither was the most fearful that
I have ever endured. To me it was like a protracted
funeral procession of three weeks and three days. The
boat was one of those which, on my arrival at Calcutta, I
had seen high on the main land, borne thither by the cyclone. She had been dug out and floated, her old engines
being replaced. Painters, carpenters, etc., were still at
work upon her. My cabin was freshly painted. I knew
not the state of things until it was too late.

"The seamen were Lascars, or native sailors, who can
be had very cheap, and do very well except in a typhoon,
cyclone, or other severe storm, when they lose presence of
mind. The cargo was chiefly opium, and every other
place being filled up, large quantities were stored away in
the cabins. We had a few deck passengers, but they were
Bagdad Jews, and could not speak English. We had
three cabin passengers, who were Calcutta Armenians, two
of whom could speak a little English.

"The passage down the bay was not especially bad,
though our discomforts were great, and, I confess, my ap-
prehensions also, for we stopped a number of times to fix
our machinery—a circumstance which had never occurred
in a vessel in which I sailed before. At Penang we
stopped, and I took a drive and dined with the consul.
At Singapore, where we arrived December 31st, it rained,
rained and poured all day. I, however, went ashore and
called on one of the old missionaries. The captain forbade
me to stay ashore, for he said he must be off by six o'clock

in the morning. Sabbath came, and the rain continued to descend; but the boat was taking in cargo, and as all the passengers left here except myself, the cabins were generally filled up with fish, butter, etc.; some of the latter being rancid, the smell was intolerable.

"Monday the ship sailed. I went up to see the surrounding islands, although the wet weather continued. The sea was rough even in the harbor, and as soon as we passed the light-house it blew a tempest. When I went down to my state-room I found that the steward had not closed my port; and my books, papers, etc., which had been placed in the upper birth, were saturated, as well as bedding and baggage. And now commenced two weeks of horrors. Scarcely a day were the decks dry. So did the vessel roll and pitch that it was well-nigh impossible to stand or even be in bed without holding on. It was the north-eastern Monsoon that was upon us in more than its usual fury.

"When the passage was about half over, the small-pox appeared among the crew; and the patient was brought into the cabin and put into a vacant state-room, two doors from mine. Other cases were reported to have occurred towards the latter part of the voyage. One man with the disease was slyly shipped ashore at Singapore. There was no doctor on board.

"In the course of the voyage the jib-boom was literally torn from the foremast, and the figure-head broken, so that the ship presented the appearance of having had a collision. My health bore up astonishingly until the last week, when I had a severe bilious attack, and thought I should have died. I began to realize what my English friends said of the perilousness of the voyage and the cruelty of sending me alone. But my heart has not murmured. I have called in a physician, and he speaks encouragingly. His first prescription has come in, and costs five dollars. What his fees may be I know not. I am here without a single friend or acquaintance; and the American consul is at Macoa, whither he has moved for his health and comfort. God bless you.

While on board the *Feelong* on her passage from Fuhchau, China, to Hong Kong, he wrote thus to his son:

February 9, 1865.

"The only letter from you which has reached me since I left New York, came to hand whilst I was at Fuhchau, and about a week ago. It was dated October 4, '64. Of course I read it with unspeakable joy. It called forth gratitude to the Father of mercies which I can not express. It informed me that you and Eliza were well, and that you were prosecuting your studies according to my wishes. I am pleased that you are in the second preparatory year, and regular. You will have studies enough. Preserve your health. As a general rule, take exercise every day, and not less than three hours. The election news is very gratifying.

"I rejoice that you are so patriotic, but you ought never to disturb a meeting of any kind. If you do not like the proceedings, you can stay away. Always behave yourself like a gentleman, and do unto others as you would they should do unto you.

"The death of my dear friend, Mr. Cary, struck me with great force. Seldom have I heard of a death which so grieved and surprised me. I trust he was prepared and that the event will be sanctified to the good of his family and friends. I am now fairly on the way home, and it awakens unspeakable joy in my breast. At Hong Kong, as I wrote you, I was taken sick. As soon as I was able to start, I set sail for Fuhchau.

"Every thing here is very costly. For one visit at Hong Kong the physician charged me $5. For two calls at Fuhchau the physician charged me $18. I soon dismissed the first doctor at Hong Kong, and called on an eminent one who told me that I needed only nourishment and mild stimulants. At Fuhchau, when I arrived, I had sunk down again, and it was necessary to give me quinine, but I rapidly recovered, and I now feel in my usual health.

"God has been very gracious to me. On the *Thunder*, as I wrote you, a small-pox patient was placed close by me. On my arrival at Fuhchau I was vaccinated, and the kine pox was communicated clearly and unmistakably, thus showing that I was susceptible to the small-pox, although I was preserved from it. I feel more and more your mother's death. O, how appalling was the anniversary of it at Singapore! It seemed as dreadful as the sad scene itself. My loneliness I could not endure but for the grace of God. No one to sympathize with me! No one to receive the gushing love of my warm heart! No one to alleviate my sorrows, nor minister to my wants! And must this be the case for the rest of my life? Must I see my children grow up and leave me, and old age come upon me in dreary solitude and neglect? I fear I must. May God, in whom I trust, enable me to bear it! But what will become of you at the most critical period of life without a home and the counsels of a mother? But I must leave this unpleasant theme. Pray for your father and yourself. Give my love to Eliza; tell her I hope to find her in the Church when I return."

He next writes to his two children jointly:

CEYLON, March 18, 1865.

"I wrote you at Fuhchau, or rather on my way from Fuhchau to Hong Kong, but did not post my letter at the latter place, because I am traveling as fast as the mail. I shall probably take this letter also with me and mail it with several others at Alexandria, should Providence kindly permit me to reach that place.

"My voyage from Hong Kong to this place—over three thousand miles—was most pleasant. The days were bright, the nights starlight, the ocean calm and smooth as a mirror save when it was ruffled by a passing breeze. The captain treated me with the greatest attention; and yet the voyage was a sad one, for we had two burials at sea, and we lost one of our stewards by drowning. I officiated on both of the funeral occasions. A bench was placed before the open gangway, a plank was inclined from this towards the sea; the flag was spread over this gloomy but simple apparatus. The corpse, followed by sailors, was then brought from the bow of the vessel at the tolling of the bell. The minister and passengers met it coming from the cabin. The service was read with extracts from the Scripture, and when the words 'we commit his body to the deep' were uttered, the sailors raised the coffin by a rope and it plunged into the waves. One of the deceased was the child of a German missionary, whose mother was conveying it to Germany. The other was a young merchant who went to China to make his fortune, and was returning with his effects. He was the son of a canon of Bristol Cathedral.

"These warm seas, however pleasant, are excessively exhaustive. The thermometer stands steadily at 85°, very little variation in the twenty-four hours.

"On arriving here, we are told that the *Nemesis*, which is to convey us to Suez, is very crowded. She entered the port of Madras as we entered this, and was telegraphed hither. I trust I shall find a berth somewhere in her, for my health requires that I should get out of the tropics as soon as possible. You know I am bilious, and the excessive heat has a bad effect upon me. Still I have endured the voyage from China better than I expected, and am now, thank God, nearly four thousand miles nearer home than when I was at Fuhchau, and am hoping that after I pass through the Red Sea, I shall recruit fast, although I dread the visit to Constantinople, for all Europe south of the forty-fifth parallel is hot and exhaustive to a citizen of Ohio.

"I think none of my colleagues will ever go through what I have. Too much has been undertaken in so short a time.

"On taking a ride this afternoon to Richmond Hill, the seat of the Wesleyan Mission, I found to my great surprise and delight a letter from you, conveying most gratifying intelligence. You are doing well in your studies, and, what is better, in your religious life. I know not whether to rejoice or regret that you should be licensed so young. Do not let this interfere with your studies. It is *seed time* with you, not harvest. Do not let your friends press you into service against your judgment. When you do speak to the people, be humble in your manner, simple in your matter, and earnest in your spirit. The story of the cross is soon and easily told, and this is the sum and substance of preaching. Do not, therefore, aim at great things. Elaborate reasoning may do for you by and by, but not now. Any attempt at display would be a failure, while a simple statement from an earnest and prayerful soul must be a success. In saying this, I would not discourage you from preparation. Never speak without it."

The next letter was written by John J. Jones, supposed to be a missionary of one of the English societies, and addressed to Rev. John P. Durbin, missionary secretary at New York. It was penned at the dictation of Bishop Thomson, who was unable to sit up and write himself:

"Steamship *Nemesis*, off Suez, March 18, 1865.

"Dear Brother,—I bore the voyage from Fuhchau to Hongkong well, and also from Hongkong to Galle. In both cases I was fortunate enough to have every necessary accommodation; but on boarding the *Nemesis*, where I found the minimum of comforts and the maximum of discomforts, my biliousness returned, and reduced me so low that I thought I should find my last resting-place in the Red Sea.

"God has graciously heard prayer and revived me, so that I hope to reach Alexandria with the ship's company or soon after. There I hope to recruit, and shall be governed by the indications of Providence—either to go to Constantinople or to Southampton. Think of five passengers pressed within a space of eight by twelve feet, in a temperature between 85° and 95°, and you may judge somewhat of the sufferings through which I have passed. God be praised for all his mercies. I shall pursue the line of duty while life lasts. Please advise my children of my condition."

His next letter to his children is dated:

"ALEXANDRIA, LOWER EGYPT, March 27, 1865.

"One week ago I arrived here a sick, but convalescent man, having been brought hither in a car fitted up for the sick, and in charge of my nurse.

"My voyage from Point de Galle, Ceylon, to Suez—a distance of three thousand four hundred and forty-two miles—was the most distressing I ever experienced. The ship was crowded beyond her capacity. All the stewards and officers, even the captain, were turned out of the berths to accommodate the travelers. I had the misfortune to be assigned to a berth in a cabin with four others. The steady heat and stillness of the air were exceedingly exhaustive to me. When a little breeze sprung up the ports were closed, for the *Nemesis*, though a fine vessel, was not built for tropical seas, and lies so low in the water that a small agitation of the sea sends the water through her ports. I endured for a time, but at length my peculiar physical trouble came upon me, complicated inflamation of the stomach and bowels, and I thought I must be buried in the sea. But God heard my prayer, and by his strange mercy raised me up, when every thing seemed to be against me. How often has he heard my prayers!

"Since my arrival here I have been steadily, but slowly, improving. To-day I took a donkey ride. To-morrow I expect to sail for Constantinople by the Austrian steamer *Adria*. It may be venturesome, but I trust in the Lord that he will enable me to complete my mission.

"I hope you are good children. I rejoice that Edward is doing so well, and I believe that Eliza will not be behind him. I trust I shall see her a subject of grace and a member of the Church, if God permit me to return. Whenever I have kneeled before God, whether in the cities of India or China or Arabia, or on the Red Sea, the Indian Ocean, the bay of Bengal, or the China Sea, I have remembered my Edward and Eliza, prayed God to bind them to himself. Continue to pray for papa, that his life may be spared, his mission completed, his soul sanctified, and his life rendered more holy and more useful to the Church. Last mail I could not write you; bless God that I can now. The Lord be with you, my precious ones."

"CONSTANTINOPLE, April 6, 1865.

"The *Adria* brought me here at eight o'clock on the 3rd inst. The cold weather of this latitude was too great a change from that of the tropical seas, and I suffered on the voyage very much. There were no fires except in the furnaces of the engine.

"My bilious trouble came back on me, and I have suffered with it ever since. I am under the care of Dr. Millingar, one of the imperial physicians. The sultan has seven, one of whom, in turn, spends a day and night each week at the palace. Dr. M. came from England to the East in 1823, and has resided in this empire ever since. He was Lord Byron's physician, and was with him in his dying hours.

"My bed is so situated that I can look out over the Golden Horn and feast my eyes on the mosque and minarets of St. Sophia. When I remember that Chrysostom there preached the Gospel of Christ from his golden mouth, my indignation is awakened to think that the Turks are ruling here. It is an anomaly that a few Mohammedans should rule sixteen million Christians in Europe. Although willing to leave the world whenever God calls me, I feel that there are many blows which I should like to deal against the battlements of error, and my zeal for the Gospel is greatly stirred. Notwithstanding I have had an arduous journey and a hard time, I do not regret that I was sent upon my mission; and, although my case is precarious, I have great cheerfulness and good hope that I shall get home to clasp you once more in my warm embrace. Indeed, I feel now near home. When I saw the Mediterranean I felt like the troops of Xenophon when on their retreat they shouted, 'The sea! the sea!'

"I am within three weeks of New York. It is my purpose, as soon as I am able, to resume my journey, to go to Fulcha, a town on the Danube, where we have a mission; thence proceed up that river to Vienna, thence to Liverpool, and from there to New York. You may, therefore, if all is well, expect me home in the month of May.

"I see by the papers that there has been a revival of religion in Delaware, and that students in both colleges have been subjects of renewing grace. I must say that my heart leaps within me at the prospect of finding my dear daughter as well as my son a member of the 'household of faith.'"

"Rose Cottage, Sunbury, England, May 5, 1865.

"I wrote you last when on the sea. We arrived safely in Liverpool next day.

"I preached at the oldest Wesleyan church in the city on Sunday. Next day I went to Chester, and next to London. Calling at the mission house I was told that I was to be entertained at Mr. Lycett's, Highbury Grove. I went there next day, and was pleasantly received. The place is beautiful indeed, having park, summer-house, garden, and meadow, all inclosed by a high wall. The living is sumptuous. We usually have about ten courses at dinner, including fish, game, poultry, puddings, pies, sweetmeats, jellies, nuts, fruits, and wines.   .   .   .

"Often, as I visit England, I am reminded at every turn that I am in a strange land, and my wanderings only make me more than ever in love with my own country, its people, and its institutions. The English are very kind, and bestow upon me much more than I have any right to expect; but America is my home, and my daily prayer is that our Union may be righteously and permanently restored. Then the United States will be the best country on earth.

"The pronunciation of the English is quite different from ours, and the modes of expression also. For instance, at Liverpool, I lost my carpet-sack, and inquired of a baggage-man concerning it. Another official standing near asked, 'What is the matter?' The reply was, 'The man is short a bag.' On approaching a house I inquired the occupation of the owner, and the reply was, 'He is a small merchant in the chimney-pot way.'

"On Sunday last I preached at Lambeth in an old chapel built over fifty years ago. It is near the palace of the Archbishop of Canterbury, and on the south side of the Thames, and within the limits of London. I have taken passage in a French mail steamship, which leaves Marseilles on the 19th. To-day I ran down to see my cousin, Mrs. King, and expect to go to-morrow to London and leave next day for Paris.

"You must be good children. I have been dreading the vacation, for idleness is greatly to be feared. By the time this reaches you the term will have commenced again. I trust you will employ all your time diligently. Remember the old Latin maxim, '*Festina lente*,' and that old English proverb, 'Whatever is worth doing at all is worth doing well.' Do not hurry through your course, but master what you undertake. Leave no enemy in the rear. Let your foundations be well laid, your preparatory studies well understood. You have plenty of time, and as long as your father lives, you shall have enough to pay your way.

"I feel very gloomy at times. I sometimes picture to myself my house carried down the valley by the floods and fast approaching the ocean, the expanse of water on both sides preventing all hope of gaining the shore, and myself alone, walking from room to room through the floating ruins, with not even a dog to break my solitude. While my children were with me, my desolation did not seem complete, but now the loss I have sustained comes upon me with all its power, and I walk even over the green lawns of this beautiful island with a deep shadow on my path. Yet do not understand that I murmur. No, God is just and he is good, and blessed be his name! I cry from the deep of my bleeding heart, 'The Lord is my shepherd.' To you I must look for my only earthly consolation. If you are good and holy, my heart will heal; but if not, I shall soon go down in sorrow to my grave. Now pray for yourselves and for your father, and remember that, though your earthly papa is absent, your Heavenly Father sees you and sees through and through you. May he bless and sanctify you through and though."

The bishop's visit to the Oriental missions was of great value to the Church, and a special inspiration to the missionaries. The Rev. Dr. T. J. Scott thus speaks of the effect of this episcopal visit in India:

"His power of quiet, accurate observation was very great, and was manifested after he became bishop as well as at the university.

"When he visited the Indian mission in 1865, many of the brethren thought he was dreamily passing around and hardly seeing any thing. The superintendent of our press remarked that he had quietly passed through the press establishment, but he doubted if five days afterward he knew that we had a press in the mission. But in an opening address delivered before the missionaries who were about to be organized into an annual conference, he electrified us all by flash after flash of brilliant statement and minute observation. Poetry, philosophy, history, and practical fact were poured upon us in a luminous shower. We were surprised during the session of conference to find how familiar Bishop Thomson had become with the facts of our work, and how readily he could call the names of towns, and villages, and persons.

"At this session, the first of the conference, the bishop proved himself to be the right man in the right place. He had been sent out to organize the conference with an episcopal veto in the transaction of business. The home authorities had mistrusted the ability of the mission to assume the complete functions so far from home. A very considerable feeling existed among the missionaries over the subject. A meeting had been held, and a protest was drawn up against being organized under the veto power. A stormy and rebellious session was anticipated by some, but the bishop's sweet and persuasive manner disarmed all opposition, and we had a quiet and delightful session.

" The bishop was endeared to all, and the memory of his visit is cherished to this hour. Our leading native preacher 'Joel' remarked of him, 'An angel came among us.' Though dead, Bishop Thomson yet speaks in India."

To show the impression made by the bishop in China, we quote the lanquage of Tang Yeu Keong:

"When I beheld the bishop's face, my heart greatly rejoiced. When I saw his feebleness, and considered that it was for Christ's sake he suffered, that he crossed the wide oceans to come for God's people, and that he did not fear the discomforts and dangers of the voyage, only desiring to aid the few sheep in these ends of the earth, truly my heart is lost in wonder and love. I thus knew him to be a genuine bishop. (See John x, 2.) His visit and his example has been a great blessing to us all."

The bishop was in the deepest sympathy with the missionary work of the Church, and regarded it as an honor and a privilege to go forth, at the peril of his life, on this errand of love to distant lands. Thus he speaks of the work of the missionary :

"It is no small matter to bid farewell to home and native lands, to settle in a climate which is pretty sure to disturb our health, if it do not abridge our life; to rear our children under influences and institutions which we disapprove, and forfeit for them literary, social, and political privileges, to which in our own land they would have fallen heirs, to move amid foes and to be regarded as intruders. It is a still greater trial, far from a land of Sabbath bells, separated from the watch-care of the Church, and deprived of the communion of the saints, to be subjected through every sense to pagan influences. He who moves amid the temples of idolatry, moves in a great moral pest-house. Nothing but open, perpetual, prayerful resistance to the forces that play upon him can keep him safe.

" Penetrated with your high calling, you are ready to deny yourselves, endure afflictions, make full proof of your ministry, and through perils either by sea or land, by robbers or false brethren, remain unmoved; willing if need be to die for the Lord Jesus, and when you do, to commend to your children the battle you fought, committing them confidently to the care of your Father and of their Father, to whom you ascend through the grace of his Son."

In the address which he delivered at the opening of the India Mission Conference held at Lucknow he uttered words of hope, and gave his theories of mission work:

"The human mind having reached its limit of false theology, must recoil. Hindooism is like a building whose walls are honey-combed and whose rafters are tunneled by ants. That a system so monstrous has stood so long, we can easily comprehend. The power of the priesthood has been cemented for ages; the religion is inwoven with the national life and social habits of the people. . . . Moreover, all religion has a foundation in truth; namely, that the universe is under the guidance of supernatural powers. . . .

"Harmless as doves, let us be wise as serpents. In pouring contempt upon the Puranas, and exposing the institutes of Menu, we may point Hindoos to their more venerable and pure theology. The Vedas afford us a stand-point. The nation that was among the first to syllogize and geometrize, and to reason up to the sublimest heights of metaphysics, can be shamed out of that idolatry which so degrades and stupefies man, and misrepresents and abuses and slanders God; substituting blocks and beasts for Him who makes the clouds his chariot, the thunder his voice, the earth his footstool, and the heaven his throne. The incarnation is admitted by Hindoos; we have only to identify Christ with it. . . .

"We must teach the *natural sciences*, and show how the universe is governed by fixed laws, devised by an infinite and eternal mind, who, nevertheless, answers prayer according to his promise, not perhaps by altering physical laws, but by adjustments of humanity to them through the higher laws of the spiritual world. . . .

"We must *teach the young*, both because of the ease with which impressions are made upon their minds, and because of the durability of such impressions, which are interwoven with the very texture of the soul. If you would write your words in a book; if you would cut them on the lead with stylet of iron; if you would drive them with chisel and mallet into the rock; if you would send them down the ages, and centuries, and millenniums, aye, into eternity, write upon the *young* soul. . . .

"In estimating your work, men may count your one hundred and sixty-four converts. Look rather to your thirteen hundred and twenty-two scholars. . . . Especially may we regard with hope the *education of females*. Inferior, ignorant, as the Hindoo mother may be, her influence is well-nigh irresistible. She needs but breathe her faith upon the little one; and though her lord may instruct, and argue, and confound, she knows, alas! too well, how to intermix grateful digressions,

> "'And solve high dispute
> With conjugal caresses.'

"From her lips flow sweeter things than words. Even British officers have painted themselves and danced to idols, to please woman less than wife. Satan needed not to trouble himself about Adam after he had captured Eve. Nor will India be retaken from him until we imitate his tactics, and attack it at that side, which, though strongest for our defense, is weakest to our assault, for woman is oppressed and depressed by idolatry. If she lost Paradise by her desire of knowledge, may she not be induced to regain it by tasting the same inviting fruit?"

CHAPTER XVI.

WORK IN THE SOUTH.

BISHOP THOMSON'S work in organizing or presiding over the conferences in the South about the close of the year 1865, was a matter of great importance both to the Church and society. While there he writes thus to his son:

"GALVESTON, TEX., December 15, 1865.

"After an unpleasant voyage during which we had rain almost every day, I arrived at New Orleans on the 11th inst., and was warmly welcomed and elegantly entertained by my sister-in-law, Mrs. S. B. Day. After having obtained all necessary information, I set out for Texas in the steamer *Rapidan*, accompanied by my friend, Dr. J. P. Newman. Our voyage was exceedingly disagreeable; we had a chopped sea and a beam wind, and, as a consequence, a sea-sick company; children crying, mothers distressed, fathers grumbling. A few old sailors only were able to visit the table. To make matters worse the temperature was very low, the thermometer at 32° to 35° Fahrenheit, and we had no stove.

"We entered the harbor this morning at 11 o'clock. We had to go to five different houses before we obtained boarding. Business is revived, refugees are returning. Every house is full. Every article is extravagantly high. Our passage from New Orleans cost us $60.

"The people of Texas are very disloyal. The reasons of this are: They have never been whipped; they have not suffered by the war; they were brought into the Union reluctantly, and they like the institution of slavery. A report having been spread abroad that the British had declared war against the United States, led to the organization of bands to assist Johnny Bull. Governor Hamilton is truly loyal, and they say if the troops were withdrawn he would have to retire with them.

"I hope that you and Eliza are well. I have received not a line from Delaware since I left. It is exceedingly distressing to me to be compelled to travel so far and so fast that I can not keep up communication with loved ones. Be diligent. Take care of your health, and, above all, of your soul.

"I leave to-morrow for Houston, and shall probably soon return and set sail for New Orleans. Pray for your father. He was never on a more unpleasant, and perhaps never on a more perilous errand. A gentleman said to me and others, that there would be no prosperity for the South until the radicals were all killed. I am told that Northern men in the interior are shot down without mercy. This, however, moves me not. I go where duty calls, ready to die if need be by the assassin's hand."

A week after he writes again as follows:

"NEW ORLEANS, LA., December 22, 1865.

"Yours of the 4th and of the 11th reached me to-day on my return from Texas. . . I have no doubt that you will be wise and business-like in the management of matters, and that I shall be pleased with all you do. Your proposition to board yourself, however, does not strike me favorably, though I am pleased with the economical spirit which prompted it. We will talk about it.

"Now, my dear boy, there is no being in heaven or earth, except God, whom I love more than you. Do not in any way diminish the joy which I have in reflecting upon you, or mar the hope which I entertain respecting you. . . .

"The colored people, so far as I have gone among them, are gladly and promptly returning to the 'Old

Mother Church,' as they call ours. I expect to organize a conference next Monday.

"My trip to Texas was very unpleasant; the gulf was stormy, the passage long, the accommodations poor, and the expenses enormously high. Galveston and Houston are crowded with people, and we could scarcely get a bed for any consideration. We paid $4.50 a day at a private house, seventy-five cents at a restaurant for six oysters, and $5 for conveyance from the depot to the tavern. The people of the South are rather bitter towards the North, but this is to be expected, and I can bear with it. My impression is that it is best to deal magnanimously with them.

" I shall probably start home next week, spend a few days in Vicksburg with Uncle Henry, and then set out for Delaware *via* Cincinnati. Remember me lovingly to your dear sister—dear to me as yourself and as the apple of my eye."

On the day referred to in this letter, December 25th, he organized at New Orleans the Mississippi Mission Conference, to include the States of Louisiana, Mississippi, and Texas. Dr. J. C. Hartzell thus writes concerning this event fourteen years after it occurred:

"It was regarded in that city, if noticed at all, only with derision. Four or five white men and perhaps a score of colored brethren received their appointments and started out upon their mission in the midst of nearly 3,000,000 of people, in a territory larger than all New England, New York, Pennsylvania, Ohio, Indiana, Illinois and Iowa combined. ' How absurd!' sneered the editor of an *Advocate* in a sister Methodist Church. And that sneer was echoed from lip to lip and from paper to paper all over the South, and some in the North caught up the refrain and said also, ' How absurd!'"

But the sequel deserves to be noticed. Small and unpromising as were our beginnings in the South, they were prophetic of greater things to come. There was no going backward; and the Church of to-day is established on a broad and stable foundation. Wisdom is again justified of her children. Dr. Hartzell says:

"Now what have fourteen years brought of triumph for our Methodism in the territory covered by that conference? Here is the record: In New Orleans 18 churches with over 3,000 communicants, while we lead all other Churches save the Presbyterian in the number of Sunday-school scholars. In the State of Louisiana, 114 churches, worth $230,323, nearly 11,000 members, and Sunday-school scholars in proportion. In Mississippi, 300 churches, worth $120,165, and over 25,000 members. In Texas, 208 churches, worth $240,168, and over 21,000 members. To these results must be added the schools in New Orleans and La Teche, La.; at Holly Springs and Meridian, Miss.; and at Marshall, Houston, and Austin, Texas, in which are nearly 1,000 students, mostly of advanced grades. And still further, it must be remembered that this territory has almost wholly supported a weekly Christian *Advocate*. This, then, is the sum. That little company of apostles sent out by Bishop Thomson in 1866, report in fourteen years, 626 churches, all of them manned with ordained ministers. These churches, to say nothing of the parsonages, are worth $590,656, and count of communicants worshiping in them 57,000, by whom a weekly Christian *Advocate* is nearly supported, and who send from their midst nearly 1,000 students into our schools of high grade. Call up the record of any handful of God's faithful laborers among any people on any continent, and I doubt if a parallel of success can be found in the modern Church."

This, then, was the work which Bishop Thomson was appointed to inaugurate in the South. It was a work in which he was deeply interested. The freedmen of the nation had a warm place in his heart; and he pleaded their cause all over the North. To show the sentiments which he entertained concerning them and their needs we give the following extract from one of his addresses:

"Providence has two methods of evangelizing, one is by sending Christians into pagandom, and the other is by bringing pagans into Christendom. Behold, then, our great providential domestic African mission! The relation of these people to us is something intimate. Although freedmen, they have been born on our soil, reared in our institutions, trained in our domestic habits and customs, and educated in our language and religion. Could we say the same thing of the wild tribes throughout Africa a thrill of joy would seize upon Christendom. Their destitute condition appeals to our charity, for though they are civilized to a certain extent they are to a large extent without lands, without credit, without trades or professions, and, what is worse, without those habits of prudent husbandry and wise forecast which ages of freedom are necessary to mature.

"It is unreasonable to expect from a people whose powers have been paralyzed by slavery, that they should be energetic and successful equally with the people of free countries, England, France, or Ireland. Then the injuries which they have suffered at our hands commend them to our sense of justice, for we must not forget that we were all more or less implicated in slavery. Our fathers covenanted to protect the institution, gave half the soil of the country up to slavery, and gave respectability to the institution, both at home and abroad. It is not right, it is not fair that we should leave to the South this entire work of educating and supporting the freedmen. We should thank Providence if, by charity to the emancipated, we may be excused for our complicity with slavery. We should reflect that for many generations the unpaid labor of these black men has contributed largely to the wealth and prosperity of our common country. By the aid they rendered us during the rebellion they contributed, in no small degree, to the preservation of the Union. Without murdering masters or burning villages or desolating fields they, by giving information to our generals, by shielding the wounded loyalists, by entering our lines one hundred and seventy-eight thousand strong, they, in all probability, turned the scale in our favor. They prevented the recognition of the Southern Confederacy in foreign courts. They prevented the recognition of the rebellion in France and England. But did they not also prevent the recognition of the rebellion in a higher court? Who that believes in prayer dare say otherwise?

"By discharging our duty to this people we may derive inestimable benefits from them in the future. They are here and they must remain here. We can not transport them, and we can no longer think of enslaving them. If left uneducated and unchristianized, they must be vagabonds, thieves, liars, and curses to the soil and expense to the State, a corruption in the body politic. Educate them and they will become industrious, moral, and useful citizens, a revenue to the State, increasing the value of every such of ground, and increasing the prosperity and happiness of all its citizens.

"This people, if properly educated, may be of service beyond the nation in which they live. There are upon this continent nearly ten millions of Africans, nearly all of them in a very low intellectual and moral condition. They are destined to remain and to spread over our intertropical regions. White men can not cultivate these fertile regions. We want these colonies of cultivated, Christianized black men to carry with them the arts and sciences, and make it a civilized and Christian country.

"Look at Africa, that great continent, in the very center of the world. Christian Europe has not been able to settle it, or even to explore it. As America was civilized by colonies from England, so Africa must be civilized by colonies from some quarter, and, as they can not be colonies of white men, since the climate forbids, they must be black men; and where can such colonies be cultivated and sent forth as from the United States. We must send back to Africa the sons we have stolen from her, and send them back civilized and Christianized, thus furnishing the means by which the great continent shall be roused into life. Could we send colored missionaries into Africa, India, and China we would be able to keep good our mission forces without annual reinforcements, for they would root themselves in the soil. They would affiliate with the natives, and even intermarry with them without a sense of degradation, and be received at once to their intimacy. These educated, refined, Christianized colored men would not take the place of the white missionaries and drive them out altogether, but would act as their auxiliaries.

"It may be said that after all these are only colored men we are talking about; that they are inferior beings, inferior in intellect. Reverdy Johnson has told the English people that it is as absurd to say that a black horse does not belong. to the same race as a white horse, as to say that a black man does not belong to the same race as a white man. The same witness says that the black man is as capable of acquiring knowledge as the white man. To say that the negroes will not study, though under the strongest inducements to do so, or to say that surrounded by our civilization they must needs relapse into barbarism, or even to say that they must needs undergo a fiery forty years' preparation, is well-nigh to deny their humanity. Whatever may be their radical inferiority they certainly have shown superior sagacity. They contributed to the success of our cause during the war, and since then they have made many improvements. Two hundred and fifty thousand of them can already read and write, and they are anxious to acquire knowledge. If, with all their disadvantages, they have shown such sagacity and such love of knowledge, what may we expect of them when we furnish them with the requisite advantages?

"Supposing the negro is inferior in intellectual capacity, what sort of a heart has he? Is he inferior there? Is he not capable of loving God? If he be, he has the highest attribute of humanity. As mind is superior to matter, so is love superior to light.

"In conclusion, I believe this to be a country in which all men are entitled to equal rights and advantages. I would say to the Asiatic as to the negro, Welcome. 'The earth is the Lord's and the fullness thereof.' Let them come, whether they be Christians or pagans. Away with caste, which would degrade God's people because their skin is dark, or because of any other circumstances over which they have no control. It is a curse more causeless and cruel than slavery itself, and more anti-christian. Christianity, like heaven, is ecumenical."

On the 9th of May, 1866, after his return from his work in the South, Bishop Thomson was united in marriage with Miss Annie E. Howe, of Delaware, by his old friend, Dr. Lorenzo D. McCabe. The lady was then nearly thirty-three years of age, and had been known to the bishop for several years. She was tall, with dark eyes and hair, regular features, and a face beaming with intelligence and good nature. In literary taste and temperament she and the bishop were well mated, and most happy was their brief wedded life. She was fond of literary pursuits, was gifted as a writer of poetry, and contributed to several of the Church periodicals. She traveled with her husband in some of his episcopal tours, and wherever she went adorned and beautified the lofty position of a bishop's wife.

When the family was gathered together and moved to Evanston, Illinois, in 1867, she became a model step-mother to the children of his former wife. There in 1868 her only child, Paul Morris, was born. She survived her husband several years, and died July 29, 1877, in Delaware, O., whither she had removed after

her husband's death. As a fair specimen of her
poetry, we quote the following verses from her pen:

BABY PAUL.

Up in the early morning,
  Just at the peep of day,
Driving the sleep from my eyelids,
  Pulling the quilts away;
Pinching my cheeks and my forehead
  With his white fingers small,
This is my bright-eyed darling,
  This is my Baby Paul.

Down on the floor in the parlor
  Creeping with laugh and shout,
Or out in the kitchen and pantry,
  Tossing the things about;
Rattling the pans and kettles,
  Scratching the table and wall,
This is my roguish darling,
  This is my Baby Paul.

Riding on papa's shoulder,
  Trotting on grandpa's knee,
Pulling his hair and whiskers,
  Laughing in wildest glee;
Reaching for grandma's knitting,
  Snatching her thimble and ball,
This is our household darling,
  This is our Baby Paul.

Playing bo-peep with his brother,
  Kissing the little girls,
Romping with aunt and uncles,
  Clutching his sister's curls;
Teasing old puss from his slumbers,
  Pattering o'er porch and hall,
This is our bonnie wee darling,
  This is our Baby Paul.

Nestling up close to my bosom,
  Laying his cheek to mine,
Covering my mouth with his kisses,
  Sweeter than golden wine;

Flinging his white arms about me,
  Soft as the snowflakes fall,
This is my cherished darling,
  This is my Baby Paul.

Fair is his face as the lilies;
  Black are his eyes as the crow's;
Sweet is his voice as the robin's;
  Red are his lips as the rose.
Bright is his smile as the sunbeams,
  Beaming when 'er I call,
This is my beautiful darling,
  This is my Baby Paul.

Dearer, a thousand times dearer
  The wealth in my darling I hold
Than all this earth's glittering treasure,
  Its glory, and honors, and gold.
If these at my feet were now lying,
  I'd gladly renounce them all,
For the sake of my bright-eyed darling,
  My dear little **Baby Paul.**

CHAPTER XVII.

WORK ON THE PACIFIC COAST.

IN the year 1867, in the arrangement of the episcopal work, Bishop Thomson was appointed to hold the conferences on the Pacific Coast. His visit among them was of great service to the Church there. He remained several months, and in the interval of conferences traveled extensively, delivering lectures, dedicating churches, and in various ways giving an impetus to Methodism which was felt for years. At the time of his visit there were two routes to California; one overland by stage, the other by sea, *via* the Isthmus of Panama. He chose the latter, and took Mrs. Thomson with him. Just before leaving New York City he wrote to his children, who were still at school in Delaware:

"New York, June 21, 1867.

"We are about to depart for the ship. Grace, mercy and peace be with you. May you love God and grow daily in wisdom and grace. Some approach Christ through the mind, others through the heart, others the conscience. May you find all three currents bearing you to the cross. Pray for your absent parents."

Immediately after their arrival in California he wrote:

"San Francisco, Cal., July 13, 1867.

"We arrived safely at this city this morning. Mrs. Thomson suffered much from seasickness, but is evidently improved by the voyage. The passage was uu-usually pleasant, although we had four or five days of stormy weather. This, though unpleasant, was of advantage to us, as it prevented us from suffering from the heat of the tropics.

"The passage of the Isthmus was very exciting to Annie, as it presented to her for the first time tropical vegetation and population. We passed through a number of small negro villages which afforded us a good view of the inhabitants, many of whom crowded the cars to sell mangoes, ginger-bread, wine, etc. Panama is an old Spanish town. Those ancient turrets, tiled roofs and stone walls remind me of Castile. The bay is as charming as that of Naples. We found the Republic of Colombia in a state of revolution. The president, Mosquira, who had declared himself dictator and imprisoned Congress, was arrested. Though the states were not agreed as to their action, the richest of the eight—Antioqua—is strongly opposed to him. It is not unlikely that the republic will be dissolved. Panama is desirous of independence. The railroad over the Isthmus, which is a leading interest, is supposed to have much to do with the political affairs of the country. Mosquira is opposed to the present company and is in favor of selling the road to a British one.

"Acapulco is a small Mexican town where we stop to coal. Its harbor is perfectly land-locked, and looks as if it had once been the crater of a volcano. The natives in canoes come round the vessel to sell fruit—mangoes, pine-apples, bananas—shells, etc. Here we learned of the shooting of Maximilian. One of his officers who had escaped and is now here, came on board.

"We celebrated the Fourth of July on board with appropriate ceremonies. After refitting here, we shall set sail for Oregon on the 17th inst. I am to preach here to-morrow and lecture on Tuesday. I will write again from Oregon. I trust you will be good and happy in every situation. Try to be useful in all circumstances."

The *California Christian Advocate,* of July 18th, contains this notice: "The bishop reported for duty at once, and delivered a most impressive discourse on Sabbath morning in the Powell Street Church. On Tuesday evening he delivered a lecture in Howard Street Church in aid of the funds of the university at Santa Clara. Though the notice was brief a good audience was in attendance. The subject of the lecture, 'Constantinople,' was treated with rare intelligence, taste, and skill. Its historical groupings, its appreciation of principles, and sketches of characters and scenes, afforded a treat rarely offered to a San Francisco audience. The bishop sailed for Portland yesterday."

From Portland he writes to his children:

"PORTLAND, OREGON, July 23, 1867.

"We left California on the steamship *Continental* the 17th inst., and arrived here yesterday at twelve o'clock at night. The sea was tempestuous and the boat not staunch, so that we had some fears, one night, that the upper deck would be swept away; but by skillful management we rode out the storm safely. Once we hove to (or bore up against the wind) for several hours.

"The coast between Astoria and San Francisco is generally dreaded, as the sea is rough, and there are no harbors in which a laboring ship may find refuge. Indeed, between San Francisco and Puget Sound there is nothing but open roadsteads. At the mouth of the Columbia the bar is much dreaded, and upon it many vessels have been wrecked. We reached it Sunday night before dark, but did not venture to cross it until morning. We stopped at Astoria for a few hours and then left for this city. Mrs. T. was very seasick and often alarmed, so much so that I almost concluded that it was not best for her to go voyaging with me.

"We are pleasantly situated here—guests of Ex-Governor Gibbs, whose garden is like the field that the Lord has blessed, alike for its fragrance and its fruits. The scenery is the grandest I have ever seen in America. Puget Sound, and the Willamette River separate the coast range from the Cascades. The city is surrounded with beautiful slopes clothed with evergreens, and from various points it presents fine views of Mount Hood, Mount St. Helena, and Mount Adams, and many snow-clad summits. The first and second are volcanic, and their craters are distinctly visible from here. The citizens often perceive smoke rising from them, and occasionally flame. Our books state that the first is fourteen thousand feet high, but a recent measurement proves it to be 17,640 feet, which shows it to be but a few feet lower than Mount St. Elias, the highest mountain in North America.

"The climate here is mild and equable. There are no hot days in Summer, and no very cold ones in Winter. The land is good, and produces the finest fruit and cereals. Rain falls very frequently west of the Cascades, and very rarely east of them; for a reason at once perceivable—hence eastern Oregon is but sparsely settled. Even western Oregon is but slowly filling up with population, owing to the great expense of removing hither from the Eastern States."

Dr. C. C. Stratton, now president of the University of the Pacific, at Santa Clara, California, who was secretary of the Oregon Conference at this session, says: "I enjoyed his sermons and addresses. They had the finish and charm which characterized every thing that proceeded from his lips or pen. I remember yet the clear and cogent way in which he grouped the reasons for supporting the Church at the dedication in East Portland. His sermon before the conference was remarkable for the manner in which he mingled Gospel and scientific truth. It was manifest that to him the universe, no less than the Bible, **was** pervaded by the omnipotent Spirit."

Of his work in Oregon the *Oregon Advocate* thus speaks: "Bishop Thomson has shown himself a tireless worker since his arrival in Oregon. All his time is profitably employed. He is, indeed, an example to the preachers. His sermon, on the Sabbath of the conference, was regarded by all who heard it as surpassingly logical, able, and eloquent. It was a masterly vindication of revealed religion. The various popular forms of skepticism and infidelity were clearly refuted. Those who listened felt more than ever fortified in the truth."

From the seat of this conference he wrote to his son:

"Salem, August 8, 1867.

"We had a very pleasant and, I trust, profitable conference at Portland, and adjourned on Monday morning last. The preachers are, I think, rather more intelligent than our preachers generally, though but few rise above their fellows. They are also better off in worldly goods. I wish I could add that they are more spiritual. They have been injured as itinerants by their settlement upon large tracts of land, and perhaps, too, by their excessive devotion to politics. There is, however, a sensible improvement now. A greater number of the preachers give themselves wholly to their work, and since the war there has been a decline of political excitement.

"This conference has a special apology for interference in politics, for if they, during the war, had been indifferent to the condition of the country, the Pacific coast might have been carried over to the enemy. The State was settled largely by emigrants from the Southern and South-western States, and was strongly Democratic in early days. An indication of this you will see upon the map; for the counties of the lower portion of the country, which was first settled, are many of them named for Democratic leaders; viz., Jackson, Benton, Polk, Lane, Linn, and Douglas. The counties of the western part of the State, which have been named since the war, bear the proof of a change—such as Grant, Baker, Union. Still the State is at present pretty equally divided between the two political parties, and attempts have been made by the opposition party to attract disfranchished traitors from Arkansas, Missouri, etc., in sufficient numbers to carry the election. God rules in our affairs, national as well as ecclesiastical. I give myself no uneasiness about them. Let us always do our duty *faithfully*, and trust in God's good providence for the results.

"The climate here surprises me. Judging by the latitude, you might suppose that this region is a cold one, but it is otherwise. The thermometer has been as high as 106° Fahrenheit this Summer at Salem, and 104° at Portland. The skies are bright, and the heat is rendered tolerable by the pleasant breezes that make the nights quite cool. Usually the Summer days are at Summer heat, and the nights much below this. The Japan current warms the coast and moderates the cold in Winter. As the wind is from the sea usually in the Winter months, and as the vapor is condensed upon the Cascade range, this season of the year in Eastern Oregon is generally rainy, much like an English Winter, and so mild that cattle need neither food nor shelter except what the pastures afford.

"The valley of the Columbia all the way from its mouth is picturesque, and often it presents scenes of scarcely surpassed grandeur, especially where it passes the Cascade range. The banks are bold and sometimes present perpendicular rocks of great height, with here and there waterfalls and shapes that resemble immense castles, and lofty columns of basaltic rock. The low portions of the country are covered with willow, elder, cotton-wood, hazel, etc., and the hillsides with fir and pine. Of the former there are three varieties, *Abies grandis*, *Abies Doug-lassi*, and *Abies taxifolia.*   Of the pines, the most belong to the species *Pinus ponderosa*, a name significant of its weight.

"Since we passed the Cascades we have been in the middle country—which lies between the Cascades and the Blue Mountains. It is a desert-looking district at this season of the year, and is too dry to be an agricultural region, unless some new methods of irrigation are discovered. In the Spring of the year (as I am told), the surface is green, but now it is brown. Still the cattle thrive upon the dry grass, and thousand of sheep and oxen live on ranges where I should suppose at first sight, that one would starve to death on a hundred acres. The grass is more nutritious than the dry grass in the Eastern States, and they say more so than our hay, because there is no rain to wash out its nutritious qualities. A large portion of the State is not arable; indeed, of its sixty million acres, only ten million are tillable. This region—and I suppose the whole plateau of middle Oregon is like it—reminds me of Arabia, by its dry and rocky appearance and its abrupt mountain ranges. It has, however, some value for stock and mineral treasure.

"This place is rapidly declining, owing to the fact that supplies for the mining region east of it are now purchased at Umatilla, Walla Walla, and other places higher up the stream. This was once the seat of one of our missions, and here, under the labors of Perkins, it is said that one thousand Indians were converted."

After spending a month in Oregon he returned to California. The California *Christian Advocate* of Thursday, September 5th, thus mentions his arrival: "The bishop reached this city by the *Oriflamme* on Wednesday, the 28th ult. On Sunday, the 2d, he dedicated the church at Napa, and on Monday started to Carson City, the seat of the Nevada Conference."

And in the issue of the same paper for September 12th, the following note is made of the Nevada Conference: "The services of the Sabbath were especially interesting. The new Methodist Church was dedicated, Bishop Thomson preaching and conducting the services. The sermon was of rare excellence, as indicating the value of the Christian religion comparatively, materially, and positively. It was most appropriate to the occasion, and can not fail of permanent good effect. The bishop remained in Carson City to lecture on Tuesday. He will spend next Sunday at Stockton, and will open the California Conference at Santa Clara next Wednesday. He is doing the labor of an apostle, though not constitutionally strong nor in the best of health."

From the seat of the California Conference he wrote to his children:

"Santa Clara, Cal., September 18, 1867.

"Since I last wrote you, we returned to San Francisco and visited Nevada. After the conference at Carson City, we went to Lake Tahoe, visited some warm springs, and then started back for San Francisco by way of the Big Trees, in Calaveras County, and the city of Stockton. On my way from Stockton I was attacked with a severe nettle-rash, the result of either gastric disturbance or poison, I know not which. It has been very severe, especially at night, kindling a furnace over my whole person, but I am gradually overcoming it.

"The conference has commenced to-day, and has thus far progressed pleasantly and satisfactorily. There is a camp-meeting in the vicinity which will be continued through the session. We shall probably close the conference about the 24th inst., and start for New York by Panama on the 10th of October.

"May God bless and guide you and bring you every day nearer to himself. There is nothing worth living for except the grace of God. Pray for your father. Write often to your kindred; never be ashamed of them. I wish you would write to my brothers James and Henry and Benjamin and Alfred, and my sisters Selina and Matilda, and to Mr. Arnold and Uncle Thomas and grandpa. Go to work earnestly at your studies. Your time and privileges are valuable. You will never know their worth until you enter into life. Excuse my haste. I have scarce a moment to spare."

The California *Christian Advocate*, in reporting the proceedings of the conference at Santa Clara, says: "The bishop then read his opening address, occupying full fifty minutes in its delivery, but commanding the most rapt attention every moment of the time. It was an exhibit of the Pacific slope as respects its extent, population, resources, productions, and future prospects, closing with impressive deductions as to the duty of the Church. The address was replete with the soundest practical sense, yet embodying some of the rarest beauties of composition, and most pathetic touches of sentiment. It showed the scholar, the traveler, the patriot, the statesman, and the earnest Christian. The large number of ministers and people who heard it will remember it as a rare and interesting entertainment."

On the closing day of the session, the conference passed the following resolutions:

"*Resolved*, 1. That this conference records with gratitude to God, and warmest fraternal love to him, the pleasure of communion with our beloved Bishop Thomson, and its high appreciation of his presidency, his counsels, and his ministry.

"*Resolved*, 2. That the presence of his estimable companion has afforded us and our families real delight, this being the first occasion of the visit of a bishop's wife to our shore.

"*Resolved*, 3. That Bishop Thomson and his lady will be most welcome to our borders, our homes, and our hearts, whenever through the providence of God and the order of the Church they may come among us."

As a further token of their high appreciation and esteem, the conference presented an elegant gold watch to the bishop, and a beautiful ladies' gold watch to his wife.

In the California *Christian Advocate* for October 5th the bishop's sermon on Sunday is thus noticed by the editor: "Bishop Thomson's sermon was a most convincing argument in support of the truth of revealed religion. He did not pay court to the whims of modern skepticism, but boldly stated and maintained the old ideas of miracles and of the resurrection of the body. The discourse was masterly, and will long be remembered for good. The presidency of Bishop Thomson was marked by great courtesy and a rapid dispatch of business. He has won for himself, by his ministry, his affability, and kindness in social intercourse, and his manifest supreme devotion to his great work, the profound consideration and fraternal love of the whole conference, and of the people who have had the opportunity to hear him and make his acquaintance."

On October 5th the bishop and his wife sailed for New York, which they reached on the 30th. They encountered a severe storm on the way, but were mercifully preserved from harm, and arrived safe.

CHAPTER XVIII.

AMONG THE CONFERENCES.

THE following letters were written by the bishop to different members of his family while on his conference tours, and show something of his travels and of the episcopal labors performed by him. They also show the spirit of the man as father, counselor, husband, and friend. The first letter is addressed to his son.

"MENOMONEE, WIS., September 18, 1865.

"As to my health, it holds out better than I anticipated. I have been working more constantly and severely, I think, than ever before, and the heat has been, until within a few hours, intense most of the time since I left you. The thermometer has been 95° at noon, or very near it, every day. We have just closed a peaceful and pleasant session of the North-west Wisconsin Conference. I preached twice yesterday, besides ordaining elders and deacons, and am to lay the corner-stone of a new church to-day. . . .

"My time has been constantly employed; for, as soon as one conference closes I must start to another, and during sessions I have not one moment to spare. I have risen every morning at five o'clock and worked on till nine or ten at night.

"Excuse my haste, as I am to jump into a buggy as soon as the corner-stone is laid and be off at a gallop for Faribault, Minnesota."

He next writes to his children, jointly, the following letter:

"St. Paul, Minn., September 26, 1865.

"I have closed my third conference very pleasantly. It gave me an invitation to settle in this city by a unanimous rising vote. This is a pretty and improving place, but the latitude is too high, the Winters too cold. The Fall season this year has been very warm thus far, and I am assured it is always delightful. A peculiarity of the climate is frequent thunder showers, followed by charming weather. The surface is mostly a plain abundantly watered and beautifully diversified with lake and hill.

"I hope you are now fully employed in school and making progress in righteousness as well as knowledge.

"God has been gracious to me, preserving me in health and protecting me from danger. Blessed be his name. I never forget to pray for my dear children, doubly dear to me since the loss of my affectionate Maria. Never forget to pray for your father."

To his son he addresses the letters next given. We can not use all that he wrote, and are compelled to make a selection:

"New York, November 9, 1865.

"God bless you. I have you daily in my thoughts, and most fervently, do I beseech God to have you in his holy keeping. It is a great source of joy to me to find you improving your mind and maintaining your fidelity to God and his Church. You can not imagine how busy I am. Scarce a moment is left for conversation or correspondence. We meet at 9 A. M. and adjourn at 5 P. M., and by the time I am through my business it is time for sleep.

"The bishops met on Tuesday; the Centenary Committee on Wednesday; the Mission Committee to-day. Then we shall be engaged until Tuesday morning. I think I shall go to Philadelphia next week, and to Baltimore the week after."

"Baltimore, Md, February 28, 1866.

"I wrote you from New York a few days since. I expect to speak next Sabbath in Harrisburg, and leave that city for Williamsport on Monday. I shall hope to hear from you there.

"Do you recollect the giant at Barnum's Museum? He attended the Swedish Bethel ship a short time ago, and went forward for prayers and was converted. He is as humble as a child, and promises to be faithful and useful. He is a Norwegian by birth, but, at an early age, he entered the Swedish army, and was in the life guards of the king of Sweden, but was expelled for knocking a man down and almost killing him by a blow of his fist.

"Conference is in session here. I attend as an associate bishop—Scott presides."

"Williamsport, Pa., March 6, 1866.

"I spent last Sabbath in Baltimore and preached twice—once in Light Street Church and once in Charles Street. I shall probably spend Sabbath after next at Elmira or Harrisburg. If you write me immediately direct to this place, but otherwise to 200 Mulberry Street, New York. I shall pass through the city on my way to Bristol Rhode Island. My health is good. To-morrow I begin the labors of a large conference. I find revival influence everywhere. We have taken in about three hundred members during the last three weeks in our churches in this city.

"Give my love to Eliza. It grieves me that she does not write me. God bless, preserve, and keep you. Do not forget to pray. The sure way to heaven is on your knees."

"Roscoe, June 14, 1866.

"I fear that you are losing your spirituality. I know, however, how to make allowance for you. You have been flattered and caressed too much. No one of your age could receive praise that you have received without being injured. Now, my dear boy, whom I love as my own soul, do fall upon your knees and wrestle with God for a deeper baptism of his Spirit, that you may, while none the less diligent and acute, be more humble, more prudent, more amiable, more faithful, more believing, and more earnest for the salvation of your own soul and the souls of others. No talents, nor learning, nor activity, nor success can atone for the want of devotion. I am sorry you have a room-mate, for I fear this prevents you from spending much time in private prayer. O do not think of growing in grace without much and earnest prayer and faithful study of God's holy Word.

"I must express to you the great obligation I feel to both my children for their kindness to my wife. I want to have a peaceful and happy home."

"Ripley, O., September 3, 1866.

"I was disappointed at not seeing yourself and your aunt at this place, and still more disappointed to find no letter explanatory of your detention.

"The cholera is still prevalent. We have lost our greatest man by the disease, Rev. Michael Marlay, D. D., and we have also lost the representative from the Irish Conference, Rev. Robert Wallace, who left us on Saturday, and died in Cincinnati yesterday at noon. Some of our members are in some danger from the disease, having the premonitory symptoms, but I hope we shall adjourn without further loss of life.

"I shall probably leave with Mrs. Thomson on Wednesday, and stop a day or two in Cincinnati. We are on the line of danger, but we go trusting in God.

"Pray for us. Be a good boy. Keep humble, and strive to leave a good impression behind you. Do not act independently in your social intercourse. Remember your youth and your obligations. May God bless you abundantly."

"NEW YORK, November 9, 1866.

"The arrangements for episcopal visitation have been made, and I am to go South in December, hold conference in New Orleans, and organize a conference in Texas; returning, hold conference in Kentucky and Ohio, meet the bishops in Pittsburg in April, and start in June for the Pacific coast, where I am to hold the Oregon, Nevada, and California Conferences, and returning, probably reach New York the last of October. We shall spend a week or two in Delaware before I go South.

"Be a good boy. I am sure that my advice to you to keep at college was right. I would be exceedingly grieved and discouraged if you were to surcease classical study before you graduate. How many preachers are distressed when they are compelled to desist from preaching, but if they were educated men, professional chairs would be open to them as long as their health would permit them to labor.

"Finally, my dear boy, practice what you preach, and may God make you a burning and a shining light."

"ST. LOUIS, March 13, 1868.

"Your affectionate letter was duly received, and it afforded me great gratification. You are a reflection of myself, and I pray that you may be a bright one. My hopes are strong as my prayers are fervent in this respect. Dr. Kidder tells me that you are doing admirably in college.

"Be kind to all around you, and do all you can for the elevation and spiritual improvement of the family and college."

To his wife he wrote as follows:

"ST. LOUIS, March 14, 1868.

"DEAR WIFE.—Your kind letter by Dr. Kidder came duly to hand, and laid me under great obligations. The verses inclosed were very musical and very sweet. You know not how tenderly I feel towards you. My daily prayer is that you may be happy and holy. Keep close to God.

"I am in good health, though I am surprised that I am, for I get no time for exercise, and my nervous system is strained to its utmost from morning till night. The conference is large, the appointments difficult to be supplied, and the preachers difficult to be satisfied. This arises from the condition of the country, which has not yet recovered from the war. Full reports of the conference proceedings are published in the city dailies, one of which I send by mail, a copy every day.

"God bess you all. My heart is very thankful for my household, though I feel sad to think that you seemed unhappy and anxious to return to Delaware. I hope that feeling will subside. I am passing the conference with a calm and peaceful heart, and no other desire than to do God's will."

The next letters were written to his son:

"LAWRENCE, KANSAS, March 25, 1868.

"I have been very hoarse, but am now rapidly recovering. Conference commenced to-day and I got along very comfortably. Kansas is exceedingly beautiful, and the weather has not merely been clement, but warm. The thermometer has been as high as 90°, and for a good part of the time during the last week it has been as high as 80° every day.

"Do your duty, live near to God, improve your mind, and God will make you happy and useful. Remember me most affectionately to mamma, sister, and baby, and believe me yours as ever.

"PERU, NEB., April 4, 1868.

"Yours of March 30th is received, and although I ought to be preparing for a missionary speech to-night and a sermon to-morrow, I take a moment to express my gratification at the Christian tone of your letter. I hope your anticipations as to your health and progress may be realized. The more you love God, the more you will love his children, and especially those to whom he has placed you in intimate and endearing relations. We have adjourned the conference, and there is nothing to prevent my leaving here on Monday, so that Providence favoring, you may expect me Thursday next.

"The country is beautiful and fast filling up, but the immigrants are poor and their struggle is hard. In some cases they are living in adobe houses; in others, in tents; in others, in holes in the hillsides covered with turf. In one instance I have heard of a family living in a house made of turf alone. The preachers of course get but a limited support. Some have to work hard at intervals in some secular occupation to supplement their scanty stipends, but they do it cheerfully for God's cause. I heard of one case where a preacher's family, after gathering wild plums and crab-apples for the preserves at home, gathered enough to give $5 each to the missionary cause.

"It is not surprising that ministers sometimes leave their work. I believe, however, that they rarely do so without backsliding. One of the members of this conference who pursued this melancholy and sinful course, came back last conference a most deeply penitent and humble man. In alluding to years of wandering, he said: 'If by walking on my hands and feet from Omaha to the Rocky Mountains, I could hope with my bleeding stumps to wash out the paragraphs of the three past years of my history, I would bend my aged body to the task at once, and continue it without a murmur until I had either accomplished it or died on the way.' Such is sin! How terrible! The poor old man is, I have no doubt, restored to God; but alas! he can never be what he was, and he goes with a tearful eye and a sorrowing heart.

"Bear me up in your prayers, that my life may be more and more pure. Give my warmest love to my dear wife and daughter, and kiss for me the dear little Paul. I sigh to be restored to you all, but I am comforted by the prayers which ascend every day at every conference for my home.   O, if you could know how the Church feels for us, you would be incited to higher, nobler life.   I can scarce refrain from weeping sometimes when the brethren are praying for my house, my household, and my happiness. I fancy that blessings are falling on my home like snow-flakes, soft, white, silent, until all around is covered with heaven's own purity.

"Now may God bless you, my dear boy, and bless all my dear ones, and keep you for his heavenly kingdom."

"DELAWARE, OHIO, August 14, 1868.

"It strikes me that your impression about joining conference *this Fall* is a delusion.   You say your way is open, but to me it seemed closed.   You can not join without a recommendation from a quarterly conference.   Your way is open to the college, where you know I will gladly support you until you complete your course ; and your way is open to the Biblical Institute also, where you can complete another course.   If you enter conference before graduation—mark my words—*you will regret it as long as you live.*   You will, in that case, I fear, be doomed to inferior positions and inferior work.   Such a course is not worthy of my son, nor expected by your friends or the public.   Say what you will about genius, it is the educated man who does the eminent service in the ministry, as it was the graduates of West Point that won the battles in our late war.   Sooner or later civilians gave place to them, and they went to the head of the army.

"The best investment I can make for you is to give you an education, and the best thing you can do is to spend the next two or three years in earnest intellectual and moral preparation for the ministry under the best masters. There is no excuse for neglect in your case.

"Now you have my mind emphatically.   Let me add, if you choose to take a different course, I can not prevent it. You will soon be of age, and if you take a precipitate route to ministerial duty, I must submit; and if you plead as your excuse that you are under solemn conviction of religious duty, I must grieve in silence.

"God knows I would not divert you from the path of duty. I want you to work in the vineyard, but I would have you enter it with sharp tools."

"Boston, Mass., October 26, 1868.

"God only knows how I love you! I trust you are living in obedience to his laws and in communion with his Spirit. Be diligent in your studies. Beware of falling behind your class. Aim to get better day by day—Excelsior.—Shun that 'little end of the horn' at the end of the session. Let the term close upon you advancing with fresh spirits and onward footsteps. Look well to Eliza. Encourage her to a higher spiritual life.

"Last Sabbath I preached at Trinity, Charlestown, under the shadow of Bunker Hill Monument. It is a new church, one hundred and twenty feet in the clear with galleries all around, and a grand organ. It was well filled. To-day I began my course of lectures, and had a good audience, mostly preachers and students. If life and health are spared, I shall deliver a lecture every day this week and next, preaching on Sabbath at Bromfield Street Church, where my lectures are delivered."

The lectures alluded to in the foregoing letter were a course on the Evidences of Revelation, preached before the Theological School of the Boston University, and repeated before the Garrett Biblical Institute at Evanston, Illinois. The hearers in both cases expressed an earnest desire for their publication, but they were not issued from the press until after the bishop's death. They were published in a duodecimo volume by the Western Methodist Book Concern in 1872.

The following letters were written by the bishop to his wife:

"Boston, Mass., November 6, 1868.

"My Dear Annie.—Very sweet indeed is your letter of the 3d inst. How well suited we are to each other, and how God blesses our union! Let us live nearer to him and pour out our hearts in gratitude and obedience. My lectures closed to-day. I have had a delightful time. The Institution has asked me for the publication of the lectures in book-form, and the outsiders have invited me to remove to the city.

"My home at present is at Brother Rich's. I should have gone there at first, but his house was full of company at the time of my arrival. He lives in grand style; his house is worth I suppose $100,000, and is furnished throughout in elegant manner. He is a man of substantial wealth. Three blocks in the business part of the city, one the finest I have ever seen, belong to him. His wealth is not only more solid than Mr. Drew's, but it has been made in a more honorable way; that is, in the ordinary path of upright business. He began life with a wheel-barrow, and has gone up regularly, until now his ordinary transactions are over two millions a year. He is very liberal, and has recently built a library at the Wesleyan University at a cost of $40,000, and has given $50,000 to the Theological Institution here.

"This afternoon I dine with President Warren; to-morrow set out for New York. I shall probably spend the Sabbath at Wilbraham, the seat of our oldest literary institution. They have earnestly invited me to visit them. On Monday I go to New York, where I am to be entertained by Mr. Elliott, 302 East Fifteenth Street.

"Now farewell, my dear wife. God only knows how I love you and how precious you are to me. . . . All the time my heart is saying, 'God bless my dear ones at home.' Remember me to all."

"LOWELL, MASS., March 29, 1869.

"MY DEAR ANNIE.—It is sad that I can not hear from you. My consolation is that I fail not to pray for you all, and that I have no doubt you pray for me. We have passed along very pleasantly thus far. The Sabbath was bright and peaceful. I preached from Psalm ii, 5, 6. My congregation was very large and attentive; even the aisles and vestibule were filled. If you were here you would be most heartily welcomed and very happy.

"Lowell is the second city of the commonwealth, and first in manufacturing interests. Its water power is wonderful. New England Methodism is truly evangelical and heartily loyal. Many brethren have said, 'Why do n't you come to New England; why do n't you settle in Boston.'

"Bishop Baker was with us a few hours. He looks well, but does not venture to engage in any public duties. I asked him to take the chair, but he declined. My home is with the pastor, who is very kind. My companions are Dr. Hascall and Brother Sherman.

"I often think of you, and as often as I do, I thank God that he has given me so sweet a wife. My heart reposes in you without wavering. I have no doubt of your love or fidelity ever towards me. The dear Paul often comes before my mind, and I hear his tottering steps and mark his peaceful smile. I thank God also that Edward and Eliza seem to be maturing into Christian manhood and womanhood. I trust they will prove blessings to the Church and to the world. Our missionary meeting Sabbath night was a good one. Your husband presided. I lived my missionary life over again while brothers Parker and Walker were speaking.

"My sermon in the morning was, I trust, appropriate and useful. One brother said to me as we were leaving the church, 'I was hoping you would preach the sermon I heard you preach in Philadelphia, but before you concluded I was glad you did not.'

"May God bless and prosper you all. My love to you all. I wish Harry [Mrs. Thomson's brother] would become religious. You should feel more for him and say more to him on the great concern. A sister's influence is not easily resisted, especially when seconded by a mother's. We are fast passing away, and shall never be permitted to return to earth to make up for the neglect of time. Pray for yours affectionately."

CHAPTER XIX.

THE BISHOP'S LAST CONFERENCE.

A SHORT time before the bishop started on his last episcopal tour, he visited his brother James. The latter reports that he said he felt as strong mentally and physically as he ever did, and as well able to perform labor, and he could hardly realize that he was then fifty-nine years old. He continued pleasantly, " James, can't you make it a little less?" Then he told his brother that he thought it to be every one's duty to prepare for the great change, and remarked, "As for myself, when death comes to me, I have no fears but all will be well."

He presided over the Lexington Conference, which met at Louisville, Ky., February 24, 1870; then attended the Kentucky Conference at Maysville, March 2d to 7th; and passed up the Ohio River to the West Virginia Conference, which met at Charleston on the Kanawha, March 10th. In opening this conference, he made an address to the preachers present, from which we give the following extract:

" We meet to-day on historic ground. The echoes of the conflict have died away. The mailed hosts that swept this beautiful valley have disappeared. The sword that flashed along the line of a thousand miles has returned to its scabbard, never again to be drawn, we trust. The flag, planted on the crest of the Rocky Mountains, throws its shadows to both oceans over a united people." The Rev. W. M. Mullenix, now of the Ohio Conference, who was present, says the effect of the speech was electrical.

From Charleston he wrote the following letter to his son:

"CHARLESTON, W. VA., March 11, 1870.

"As I do not frequently hear from home I must comfort myself by frequently writing home. Yesterday I wrote to your mother, to-morrow, may be, I can write your sister, though the spare moments I have are whilst I am waiting for dinner. Charleston is on the banks of the Kanawha, on a level tract flanked by lofty hills; but at present it is inaccessible except on horseback or by carriage or boat. A railroad is finished to Covington, Virginia, and will soon be extended to this place, by the valley of the Greenbrier to the New River, thence down the Kanawha to this place, from which it is to be taken across the country to the mouth of the Guyandotte.

"Bishop Morris was born in this neighborhood, and the conference passed some kind and complimentary resolutions commemorative of him. When they were under consideration one of the brethren told this story: 'When the bishop was on his way to one of his early appointments, a Baptist preacher, with whom he was traveling, gave him this advice: 'Let your himes be suitable to the *composting* of your subjects.''

"This locality was once the great source of American salt. The manufacturers of the article brought slaves into the valley, but in the mountains around there was no use for them. Hence the motto of this new State, ' *Montani semper liberi*,' which was glad to be emancipated from the eastern part of old Virginia, whose interests it was supposed were favored by slaves. Here the use of slaves operated against the salt manufacturers; it prevented them from availing themselves of the advancing science and improved methods of the times. Their selfishness also operated to their injury. They diminished the production with a view to raise the price. The result was that they stimulated competition on the Ohio, and even abroad, for Liverpool salt has been sold in the streets of Charleston. Selfishness is always bad policy.

"Our work here is in a healthy condition; most of the preachers left a revival behind them; the work of church building goes forward; the preachers are better paid, and the benevolent institutions of the Church better sustained than heretofore. Some of the elders, however, and preachers too, have hard work. One has traveled five thousand miles the past year.

"My health is better. I had a bad cough when I left Louisville, but I am satisfied that it was sympathetic, the result of a diseased liver. My liver is now acting freely, and I am relieved. I mention this because I believe that, in many cases of bronchitis, the patients are injured by confinement and medicine. But if I were sure I had the consumption I should keep *out* and keep *on* as long as I could.

"My prayers go up without ceasing for you. Behave yourself like a good Christian man in my absence. Keep your thoughts pure, shun even the appearance of evil, cultivate your religious emotions, be faithful to your studies, and be much on your knees.

"God bless you all. Tell mamma to write me often, Eliza to grow daily in grace, and Paul to be obedient.

"My host lives in the style of an 'F. F. V.' He has many luxuries, his garden smells of crocus, and from his orchard we have shaken fresh filberts."

On Sabbath morning of this conference he seemed perfectly well, and his voice was clear and strong. He chose for the text of his sermon, 1 Cor. ii, 1–2: "And I brethren, when I came to you, came not with excellency of speech or wisdom, declaring unto you the testimony of God. For I determined not to know any thing among you, save Jesus Christ and him crucified." The Rev. W. M. Mullenix, in a personal letter to the author, thus describes the effect of this discourse:

"The sermon was delivered in the Methodist Episcopal Church on Virginia Street. The house was densely crowded. There were people present who had *walked* over the mountains of that picturesque land, some twenty and some forty miles, to be present that day. The bishop seemed to be in good health, and his utterance was as free as a mountain spring. His unassuming manner, the dignity and splendor of his thought, the wealth and pertinency of his illustrations, the classic beauty of his diction, his intense earnestness, delighted and impressed all who heard him. There was a solemnity in his bearing, and a sweet and touching, I think peculiar, tenderness in his tone and eye and manner. I know his strange tenderness that morning affected me profoundly. I looked around and saw that preachers and people were bathed in tears. He looked like a seraph, and preached like an angel.

"That night," continues Brother Mullenix, "your father heard an aged member of the conference in the same place. The sermon was sound in doctrine, yet full of grammatical errors, but delivered with great unction. At the close the bishop said to me, 'I enjoyed the sermon. Brother T. is a type of a race of preachers fast passing away.' Before we left the church he said to me, 'William, if I spend next Sabbath in Wheeling, will you let me preach for you?' Of course I was delighted that he contemplated such a thing, and told him so. I shall always think that he owed his death to exposure on the Kanawha River. I was with him on the 'hurricane deck.' The ground was covered with snow, and the wind was keen and cold. I left the boat at Parkersburg and went by rail to Wheeling to prepare for his reception the next day. The boat reached the city several hours earlier than usual. When I reached the landing I learned that he was ill, and had been removed to the Grant House. The only trouble on his mind, in his last sickness, was the absence of his family.

"Your father, in natural endowments, in culture, in purity of character, never had a superior in Methodism; but to me the great charm of the man was his wonderful and unaffected simplicity. He was absolutely without pretense. His place has not been filled."

To show further the impression made by Bishop Thomson on his last conference we quote the resolutions passed.at a meeting of the preachers at Wheeling the morning after his death:

"WHEREAS, by a wise, but inscrutable Providence, our beloved Bishop Thomson has been removed from us:

Resolved, 1. That it is with melancholy pleasure that we recall the able, yet genial manner in which he presided over the deliberations of our conference at its recent session in Charleston, West Virginia, and the very eloquent and profound discourse which he delivered before the conference on Sunday morning, in which he more than sustained his reputation as an able and evangelical minister; and also the address to the young men about to be ordained deacons, in which he seemed carried away with his subject, describing with a master's hand the duties, privileges, responsibilities, and reward of the faithful Christian minister.

" *Resolved*, 2. That in his social intercourse with us at the conference, and *en route* to and from the conference, by his sweet spirit and instructive and entertaining conversation he drew all our hearts to him as by cords of love.

" *Resolved*, 3. That as ministers of the Gospel, having just received our appointments at his hands, we will endeavor to follow him as he followed Christ, that our last end may be like his. 'Mark the perfect man, and behold the upright; for the end of that man is peace.'

" *Resolved*, 4. That the Methodist Episcopal Church has lost one of her greatest lights, the country a scholar of rare attainments and capacity, and society a courteous and kindly Christian gentleman."

CHAPTER XX.

CLOSING SCENES OF HIS LIFE.

WHEN the bishop wrote his last letter to his son he was feeling better of the cold which he had contracted some weeks before, and seemed to be rapidly recovering his usual health. On Saturday night, March 12, 1870, a heavy snow fell. On Sunday morning the sun came out bright and warm, and the walks were covered with slush at Church time. The bishop walked through this some distance from his stopping place to the church, without overshoes, and remained in the pulpit during the hour and a half of the services with damp feet.

On Monday noon he closed the conference session and, in company with a number of the preachers left Charleston early that afternoon on the steamboat *Kanawha Belle*, and passed down the Kanawha, sixty miles, to Gallipolis, Ohio. Here, at two o'clock on Tuesday morning, he was transferred to the *Mattie Roberts*, and started up the Ohio for Wheeling, on his way to meet the Newark and New York Conferences. On Tuesday afternoon and night a violent snow-storm prevailed, and the dampness was driven in by the winds through all the crannies of the old and inferior boat. Before the storm came on, while the wind was blowing strongly from the East, the bishop was on the hurricane deck, and part of the time with his hat off engaged in conversation with the preachers, and admiring the beautiful scenery as they passed along. He was so much interested that he forgot his personal comfort and welfare. On Tuesday night he could not sleep, and during Wednesday he was quite hoarse, and complained of chilliness. In the evening these symptoms increased, and, in addition, there was nausea and pain in the stomach. But he slept quite comfortably that night. The next morning, March 17th, he landed at Wheeling.

He had expected to stop with his friend, Brother E. J. Stone, but his residence being a long distance from the landing, and the day being stormy, Brother Stone did not deem it prudent to expose the bishop so long to the weather by taking him home, and so conducted him to the Grant House, where he was at once provided for comfortably by the proprietors, who were warm-hearted Methodist people, and every attention possible was shown him. One of the best physicians of the city was sent for, and he prescribed for the bishop, but said he thought his patient needed only rest from care and labor for a few days.

Though able to receive the calls of friends, he did not leave the house during the day. On Friday he felt much better. In the morning he attended to his correspondence, and wrote a number of letters and an article for *Zion's Herald*. In the afternoon he took a walk of over a mile, crossing to one of the beautiful islands in the river. Returning, he stopped for tea with his friend, Dr. T. H. Logan. But before the meal was over he complained of severe pain in the region of the stomach, and was conducted back to his rooms at the hotel. Dr. Bates, a leading physician of the city, was called. The bishop rested but little that night, and by noon the next day, decided symptoms of pneumonia were developed. From that time until his death, the disease, baffling all medical skill, progressed with fearful rapidity. A telegram was prepared to be sent to his loved ones at Evanston, but he prevented its transmission, fearing that they, in their anxiety to reach him, might start from home on the Sabbath day. By some unaccountable delay, the telegram did not reach them till Monday noon. His wife and son started on the first afternoon train, but had proceeded no further than Columbus, Ohio, when they received a dispatch announcing his death. They thought it unnecessary then to continue their journey, and immediately went to Delaware.

During his last sickness, all that Christian friends, with hearts full of tenderest sympathy, could do was done for him to relieve his pain and minister to his comfort. The proprietors of the Grant House were unremitting in their kindness, and Dr. T. H. Logan and Brother E. J. Stone were the best and most constant of nurses, one or the other of them being always in the room to administer lovingly to all his wants.

On Monday night a little past the midnight hour, the bishop was conscious of a great and sudden change. He called Dr. Bates, his principal physician, to his bedside, and requested him to speak plainly of his condition and danger, saying that he was prepared for any event in God's will. The physician explained the nature of the case, and the probability of an early and unfavorable termination. With great calmness, the bishop gave directions concerning his temporal affairs, and sent messages to his family which he signed with his own hand. Turning to Dr. Logan, he said, "If this be dying, it is very easy."

"A short time after," says Dr. Logan, "he opened his eyes with an expression of the greatest composure and tranquillity, and looking at me, I was encouraged to ask him, 'Bishop, have you full peace.' His reply was, 'O yes, O yes!' Toward morning he slept for short periods and seemed quite comfortable, although exceedingly feeble and his pulse rapid. At seven o'clock Tuesday morning, I gave his stimulants and nourishment, which he accepted with more than usual relish. He inquired if it was a pleasant morning. I told him it was, and at his request the shutters were opened to admit the sunshine. I then bathed his face and hands, brushed his hair, and rearranged his bed, after which he asked me to 'conduct morning devotions.' I inquired if he would select the Scripture to be read. He replied, "You select it.' I then read the twenty-third Psalm, knelt at his bedside with my hand in the bishop's, and prayed with him, and for him and his.

"At eight o'clock the pain in his stomach returned in increased intensity. I sent at once for the physician. Before his arrival the bishop began to comprehend that his life was fast ebbing away, and that no human power could stay its flow. He asked again and again the hour, being previously informed in answer to his inquiry that Mrs. Thomson could not reach the city before twelve o'clock noon. How painful to tell him that it was only eight o'clock, and afterward, in answer to another inquiry, only half past eight, and again only nine o'clock! His thoughts

were reaching out to his family, and he felt that the
hours which were to bring that family to his side,
were too slow to overtake the swift running sands of
his earthly life. This was the great trial of his dying
hours. He referred to it with great emotion and
tenderness, praying that God would give him grace to
bear it. At one time looking up, he said, 'The
Master said to Peter, "Satan hath desired to have
you that he may sift you as wheat; but I have prayed
for thee that thy faith fail not;"' and then he repeated
the last phrase, 'that thy faith fail not.' A short
time after he said to Dr. Homer J. Clark, who had
come in, 'Doctor, pray for me that my faith fail
not;' evidently referring to this great trial, under
which in the last hours, he was passing in obedience
to the will of the Master.

"The painful condition of his lungs and his extreme debility prevented him from speaking much;
and, under the direction of his physician, he was not
encouraged to speak except when his own will would
suggest."

About half an hour before his death Dr. Clark
expressed to him the hope that he felt underneath
him the everlasting arms, and that he found abundant
support in this hour of trial. The bishop replied:
"O, yes; that is the best, that is the best." This was
his last audible expression. He ceased to breathe at
10.30 A. M., Tuesday, the 22d of March. He was
not, for God took him.

With his characteristic dislike of observation, he
had directed that if he should die no curious gazers
should be admitted to the room; but the demand of
the citizens of Wheeling was too strong, for the whole

city was moved to sorrow by the sad event. Hundreds came and dropped their tears beside the cold remains of the stranger who had died away from his home and his dearest friends and kindred. The casket was crowned with the rarest and sweetest of blossoms, and some fair hands had made a large and beautiful cross of white azalea flowers, which was laid on the breast that had throbbed so long in purity and love.

As soon as the news of Bishop Thomson's death reached Delaware a meeting of the faculty of the Ohio Wesleyan University and of the resident clergy was held, at which President Merrick and Rev. D. D. Mather were appointed a committee to accompany Prof. W. F. Whitlock, the bishop's brother-in-law, to Wheeling for the remains. They arrived at Wheeling the next morning, and left on the first return train. Before their departure, at two o'clock P. M., an informal funeral service was held at the Grant House, affecting addresses being delivered by President Merrick, Dr. Homer J. Clark, and other prominent ministers present. A throng of ministers and citizens formed an escort when the burial casket containing the body was carried to the Baltimore and Ohio railway depot.

On Tuesday, at noon, the committee arrived at Delaware, and the remains were conveyed to the residence of the bishop's father-in-law, Mr. Abraham Howe, an immense concourse of students, alumni, and citizens following in procession. Flags were displayed at half-mast, bells were tolled, and court was adjourned for the day. On Friday the remains lay in state at William Street Church, in charge of the alumni, and were visited by hundreds of citizens anxious to look once more on the face of one so dear to all; for the bishop, by his long residence in Delaware, had endeared himself to the people irrespective of class or condition, and every one who knew him felt himself personally stricken.

It had been determined to have the funeral on Tuesday, the 29th, and Bishops Janes and Morris had signified their intention of being present. But many of the relatives from a distance having arrived in expectation of an early interment, who would not have been able to remain till Tuesday, it was thought best to have the funeral on Saturday, the 26th. This prevented the attendance of very many from a distance; however, there was a large attendance of ministers from abroad. The services were under the direction of Prof. William G. Williams and the Hon. Homer M. Carper, who very appropriately arranged to have three classes represented in the exercises— ministers, college faculty, and alumni. The pallbearers were Rev. John Wheeler, president of Baldwin University; Rev. Park S. Donelson, president of Ohio Wesleyan Female College; Rev. Joseph F. Kennedy, of the North Ohio Conference; Rev Isaac Crook of the Ohio Conference; Hon. Leander J. Critchfield, of Columbus; and Col. Joseph W. Lindsey, of Delaware.

William Street Church, where the services were held, was tastefully draped in mourning, as was also the exterior of the university buildings. Business in the city was generally suspended, and Sabbath stillness was over all. Notwithstanding the rain came down in torrents, the large church could not accommodate the multitude seeking admission. The pastor,

D. D. Mather, presided. Rev. William Goodfellow announced the hymn "Servant of God, well done," after the singing of which Rev. J. M. Trimble led in prayer. President Wheeler read the 23d Psalm, and a part of the 15th chapter of 1st Corinthians, beginning with "It is sown in corruption, it is raised in incorruption." The choir, under the leadership of Prof. T. C. O'Kane, then sang "Come unto me, all ye that labor," and the obituary addresses followed.

Rev. L. B. Gurley, representing the ministry, spoke first. He said:

"We have met to-day in sadness and sorrow. Yet the sadness is not all sadness, and the sorrow not all sorrow. The cloud has its silvery lining; we sorrow not as those who have no hope. Precious in the sight of the Lord is the death of his saints. We come as ministers to look for the last time upon the lifeless form of our beloved bishop. As citizens you come to look upon the remains of one who was more than bishop to you—the friend, the brother of your hearts. We come to say, 'Dust to dust, ashes to ashes'—precious dust that enshrined a spirit, adorned with all culture, enriched with the graces of the Holy Ghost.

"I came, expecting to sit somewhere among the mourners as near the coffin as might be, and then re-call his virtues and shed my tears of love and sorrow, expecting that some of his honored colleagues would be here to address you. Far from anticipating a duty like this, I had thought when my own lamp should go out, that perhaps the bishop would be present to say a word over my remains.

"I am not here to tell you what Bishop Thomson was. That were needless here; and where is there a city on this continent where it would be needful? for truly his light has gone out to all the world, and his words to the end of it. But we may recall some of his virtues. A recent writer has said that the fall of a great worker is a national misfortune. There was no greater worker than Bishop Thomson. For thirty-eight years he worked incessantly; and ceased at last at once to work and live. Many things invest his life with interest. Let me mention a few of them.

"*The peculiar period when he entered the ministry.* It was the morning of Methodism in North-western Ohio. He gave his youthful cheek to the wintery blasts that swept over your Erie; sought cabins in the wilderness where he might preach the Word of Life; traversed pathless forests and bleak prairies; and never shrank, never cowered. He was a golden link between our own and the heroic times of such men as Finley, Christie, Poe, and many others whose record is on high.

"*The peculiar work to which he was called.* When God has a peculiar work he raises up the workers. He will call him even as Moses was called, and Elisha, and Paul. The deceased believed in a Divine call to the ministry, and bade adieu to parents and home with such a sense of consecration to his work that he never cast a longing, lingering look behind; never turned aside for a day or an hour after any worldly object; presenting in this respect a model for us and for those looking toward the ministry.

"*The variety of work assigned to him, and his wonderful adaptation to it.* He was pastor, educator, editor, and bishop. If Norwalk and Cincinnati, Wooster and Detroit, could answer, they would say that as a pastor he was loving and beloved. Where was want, and sorrow, and distress, there was he to relieve, console, and direct. But in the great work of teaching he was best known. In Norwalk and Delaware he was surrounded by a noble band of young men, who felt that they surrounded a master spirit. He could not create genius, but like the angel that liberated the imprisoned Paul, he could discover genius, however hidden and obscured, shake open its prison house, strike off its fetters, and bid it come forth. He did not create genius, but he often struck the spark that kindled its fires, and sent it blazing through the world. Some of his pupils have gone before him; others are here who remember the debt they owe to his counsels, prayers, and example.

"His work is done, his labors are ended. No, not done; his works will follow him, they will never be done. Influences put in motion, deepen, and widen to eternity. A wandering peddler left a book at the door of Baxter's father, which led to his conversion. Baxter's writings in turn were instrumental in the conversion of Doddridge, whose "Rise and Progress" led Wilberforce to the Savior; Wilberforce wrote what led to the conversion of Legh Richmond, whose "Dairyman's Daughter" has been instrumental in the salvation of untold souls. Results thus link themselves together in an endless chain. Who can tell how many such mighty influences the departed, by his example and writings, set in motion; influences that shall widen until they reach the eternal shores? "The workmen die, but the work goes on."

"But, turning to his more personal characteristics, he was a man of *remarkable conscientiousness.* I remember being with him at Huron one Saturday night, on our way to conference at Ann Arbor. It was during the celebration of the British Centennial of Methodism, and he had an appointment to preach in Detroit the next day. At about midnight the tardy steamer made its appearance. Other ministers went aboard, and urged him to do likewise. "No," was his reply, "I have preached to that congregation that they should keep the Sabbath holy, and now I shall not set them the example of breaking it." And that was only an indication of what his life was in all its relations.

"His was *a warm heart.* Associating with you in business, in social life, in your Churches, he was full of love and sympathy for all. You never received a harsh word from him. Kindness was the law of his lips. You never will forget his friendly greetings; nor the wondrous play of his social nature in the circle of congenial spirits; nor his Sabbath services heard by eager and entranced listeners from all denominations. I was his neighbor as pastor and presiding elder for ten years; and after the death of his first wife, he boarded for several months in my family.

"Of his industry, his studious habits, his cheerful disposition, his tender heart, his humility, charity and benevolence, I might say much, but others can do this better. Such was his wisdom and sympathy in counsel, that I am inclined to say:

> "Of all the men of noble mind
> I've met along the path of life,
> Few have I found so true, so kind,
> So wise in counsel, calm in strife,
> In every virtue so refined.

O friend! O brother! oft to thee
  Through weary years my heart hath turned,
As mariner on doubtful sea
  To beacon light; for well I learned
Thou hadst a heart of sympathy.

I 've watched thy footsteps from the hour
  When first thy youthful cheek was given
To wintry winds and pelting showers,
  O'er prairie wild by tempest driven;
But never have I seen thee cower.

I 've marked with glad, unenvied eyes
  The upward path thy feet have trod,
Rejoicing as I saw thee rise
  In favor with both man and God;
The guide of thousands to the skies.

The brilliant stars, how fast they fall!
  But yesterday they shone so bright;
How sudden oft the Master's call,
  Their glory quenched in deepest night.
The inevitable fate of all.*

"We can but sorrow that he could not have fallen among his kindred. In affliction we instinctively turn to home and friends. Doubtless as our brother lay there, gazing over the river, he turned his eyes wistfully toward those who were coming from the far-distant home, yet only to say, 'Thy will be done.'

"Jacob's dying request was, 'Bury me with my fathers in the cave that is in the field of Machpelah, which is before Mamre, in the land of Canaan. There they buried Abraham and Sarah his wife; there they buried Isaac and Rebekah his wife; and there I buried Leah.' So, doubtless, he longed to die in this place, where he so long labored, near the classic shades he loved so well, amid scenes so endeared by the sacred

---

* These lines were composed by Dr. Gurley on this day.

associations of the past, and to be buried where his loved ones sleep, and where others not less loved and loving may drop the tear of affection on his grave.

"But he has gone. His sun has set. He has sunk to his rest, and soon his moldering remains will be consigned to the grave.

"'Leaves have their time to fall,
    And flowers to wither at the North wind's breath,
And stars to set; but all,
    Thou hast all seasons for thine own, O death!

We know when moons shall wane,
    When Summer birds from far shall cross the sea,
When Autumn's hue shall tinge the golden grain—
    But who shall teach us when to look for thee?'"

The speaker then closed with a few touching words to the afflicted and sorrowing family.

The Rev. William D. Godman, D. D., spoke for the alumni of the Ohio Wesleyan University. He said:

"I will endeavor, as well as I may, to speak for about three hundred young men, scattered over the earth, some of them in useful positions in our own land, some doing noble work beyond the shores of the Pacific, and some mingling in the classic life of the historic lands of Europe; and we would, if we could, concentrate the feelings of these three hundred in a single utterance of the unutterable experiences of the hour. We have lost a friend. Our *father* has gone from us. Of this Spartan band, every one counts it among the highest honors of his life that he has a diploma bearing the name and the sign manual of Edward Thomson. He attached us to himself. He knew how to kindle the hearts of the young. There was magic in his paternal glance. There was fascination in his manner. It always seemed a favor to take his cordial hand; and, to the students of the university, the offer of that hand was the reward of virtue and fidelity.

"It may not be amiss to note briefly some of the obligations we feel to the loved and honored departed. What are some of the chief treasures of that brilliant legacy he has left us?

"1. There is, first, his *character*. To this reference has already been made. None knew Dr. Thomson without feeling the impress of that which was inherent in him. None met him, even casually, but was attracted to his superiority. It seemed as if a heavenly intelligence had embodied itself in humanity. In any multitude he was marked, in any community he was a power. Perhaps the most prominent impression his character made on his friends was that of completeness, harmony, finish.

"It is not possible to delineate character—especially so rare a one as this—in more than general outline. But in him there was such harmony of intellect and passion, such balancing of the forces that make up the available power of life, as made on a contemplating friend the impression of a Corinthian column, the most happy combination of strength, beauty, and grace. It is not too much to say that every alumnus would adopt as his own this sentiment of a poet concerning his friend:

> "'Death! ere thou hast slain another
> Learned and wise and good as he,
> Time shall hurl a dart at thee!'

"There was, in our beloved father and friend, a vein of what some one, philosophizing, would call stoicism, but which might better be termed *Christian faith.* Those who have known him in sorrow have observed it. Perhaps his last utterance was, in this particular, characteristic. When in the throes of the death-passion he inquired when those whom he loved would probably arrive. Being informed they could not reach him before a certain time in the afternoon, he threw back his arms, said calmly, 'God's will be done,' and died.

"He was warm in affection, though not demonstrative in manner. He admitted few to his intimacy, but those few were his jewels. Among students he was tender of their faults, and made them feel that the possibility of his displeasure was the most painful anticipation. He could gain the heart by the most delicate addresses and condescensions. When in his first great domestic sorrow he sent for one of the youngest students to come to his house. 'Sit down,' said he, 'and write to my mother, and to such and such a friend. Tell them of my sorrow.' That request and confidence bound the young man's heart to him forever.

" 2. Secondly, we cherish his *instructions.* He was the most apt teacher. He always made truth attractive and winning. Every sharp blade of truth thrust into the conscience was freshly whetted and doubly polished by him at the thrusting. The Bible was his book. We remember how he went through it, as a fairy through her realm, flowers springing in every footstep, and delicious fragrance filling the air. We have not forgotten how he illuminated the Sermon on the Mount; how he made the wisdom of Solomon shine with new luster; how he made Elijah under the juniper-tree more eloquent than on Carmel. He had the power of so pointing and compacting truth as to give it a permanent lodgment in the memory. How, in that eloquent lecture on 'The Path to Success,' he exclaimed, 'Let others sing,

> "'Let me be little and unknown,
> Loved and prized by God alone;'"

and how the good old couplet went suddenly out of our hearts never to return! How often and how forcibly did he urge the thought that '*Learning dissociated from holiness—knowledge unsanctified—would be only an increased power for evil.*'

"3. We have, thirdly, his *eloquence*—an inspiration that can never die. Many of us, and some who were never his pupils, will call to mind the first appearance of Dr. Thomson's lecture on Education, first delivered before the Ohio Conference, and afterward published in the Ladies' Repository. That lecture was the foundation of systematic education among Methodists of Ohio. But its eloquence was rare. Some of us, who had been, in our school-boy associations, inspired by the eloquence of John Adams and Patrick Henry, were, by that lecture, introduced to a new and sacred style of oratory, that has been thrilling in us to this day; and that lecture, the discourse on 'Close Thought,' his Inaugural Address, and the lecture entitled 'The Path to Success' were, perhaps, his most perfect productions, and will never lose their charms.

"He wrote with such ease and rapidity that a casual acquaintance might prompt the judgment that his work was unfinished. Agatharchus boasted to Zeuxis of his rapid and easy painting.

Zeuxis replied, 'If I were to boast, it would be that I work slowly.' One not well acquainted with our beautiful exemplar might say he should have worked more slowly. But he, like Daniel Webster, was perpetually engaged in unwritten composition, thinking in finished sentences and rounded periods. Thus he ever had his quiver full of arrows, his head and heart stored with treasures fit for bestowal on an appreciative public.

"His writings, like himself, are finished. They ever suggest the use of the *stylus*. When he was composing, the inspiration of his seraphic intellect brought thought to ready command. They clustered around him like Spring flowers, or they came to him like mailed warriors. It has been said of the architectural monuments of Pericles, that 'as each of them so soon as finished had the venerable air of antiquity, so now they are old, they have all the freshness of a modern building. A certain bloom has diffused itself over them, preserving their aspect untarnished by time, and making them appear as if animated by a spirit of perpetual youth and unfading elegance.' So were our master's thoughts finished, and so will they live for time to come. He was our master, inasmuch as he inspired and molded us. His character, his works, his family are dear to us. Upon the shrine of our souls—in undying devotion—in the innermost sanctuary of our hearts, where life's deepest loves abide, will be enshrined forever the name and memory of Bishop Edward Thomson."

After this address President Frederick Merrick, of the university, read an interesting biographical sketch of the bishop, describing with great beauty the last hours of his life. He closed with these words:

"As his colleague during the entire time of his connection with the university, I may say, his administration of the affairs of the university was eminently successful. His wide popularity as a writer and speaker tended to draw attention to the institution, while his pleasant bearing toward the students, his wise counsels and effective teaching, and perhaps, above all, his instructive and eloquent lectures, tended to attach, both to himself and the university, all who came under his care. His bearing toward his colleagues was full of Christian courtesy; and his relations with them all were ever of the most amicable character. Highly appreciating, as I do, his valuable services in all the departments of labor to which he was called, I am inclined to think that in no field did he labor with more satisfaction to himself, or benefit to the Church, than as president of the university. But his work on earth is done. 'Mark the perfect man, and behold the upright; for the end of that man is peace.' Such was his. His life made sure a peaceful death. The religion of Bishop Thomson was never demonstrative, and in this respect, as in others, he was in death as in life. Calmly as an infant falls to sleep, he slept in Jesus. And yet he seemed not to sleep; the expression which lingered upon the countenance was too intelligent for sleep; it was rather as if the eyes had been closed to enjoy some thought or scene which was filling the mind with holy joy. Who will say it was not the expression of the first felt rapture of heavenly bliss?

"Farewell, brother and friend, farewell! Ours is

the loss; thine the gain. We hope to meet thee when life's work is done."

At the conclusion of the president's address the choir sang softly and sweetly,

"Cast thy burden on the Lord,"

after which the corpse was conveyed to the cemetery, where the burial service was conducted by the Rev. L. D. McCabe, of the university, and the Rev. P. S. Donelson, of the female college, the choir singing at the close,

"We shall sleep, but not forever."

After the benediction all withdrew and left the precious remains to the keeping of Him "whose eye never slumbers nor sleeps."

CHAPTER XXI.

CHARACTER AND TRAITS.

THOSE who knew Bishop Thomson held him in highest esteem. Gilbert Haven, editor of *Zion's Herald*, in Boston, at the time of Bishop Thomson's death, speaks of him as "the beloved disciple," and says: "Few men ever carried about in their bodies more strikingly the dying and the living of the Lord Jesus. 'A sweeter spirit ne'er wore flesh about him.' He was of modest and retiring manners, yet courtly and easy, with a well-bred air, that made him at home in any society. He was of fine culture, and of fine qualities out of which to make rare culture. The marble was worthy of the statue. His scholarship was very superior in some departments, especially in the literary and scientific. . . . His rhetorical finish was of a very high order; his imagination strong and trained. Had he been a resident of this vicinity, and in favor of the school that claims to represent its chief culture, he would have had no superior among them in rank and popularity. The most famous houses would have rejoiced to publish his essays and discourses. The last president of Harvard expressed the highest admiration of his gifts. His wit was keen and kind; his temper sunny and serene; his will strong, yet so handled as never to give his adversaries offense."

The Rev. W. D. Godman, D. D., president of New Orleans University, in referring to his own address at the funeral of Bishop Thomson, thus writes to the author: "In reading it over, I am impressed with the inadequacy of all that was said. I have known many men; but I have not yet known one so near perfection as your father."

Dr. George Lansing Taylor says: "His moral nature was almost faultless. Naturally of a shy and recluse taste, he never courted the world or its honors, in the Church or out of it. He was the most modest man of his powers we have ever known, while at the same time he had the most generous appreciation of others. No man could be further removed from selfishness. He was ever ready to honor others before himself, and the self-abandonment of the Gospel was never more complete than in him. He was one of the purest, sweetest spirits that ever walked the earth. A jest or hint of equivocal purity, even among his equals, would have been impossible in his presence. Yet the most timid child never feared him, and the most troublesome intruder never found him rude. In the Church he was the idolized Achilles of Methodism in the West, but an Achilles whose wrath never brought woes upon his friends. It is doubtful if he had a personal enemy in the world. His well-known absent-mindedness was the result of his mental type, and never alienated those who knew him."

The Rev. B. P. Aydelott, D. D., a distinguished Presbyterian clergyman of Cincinnati, and formerly president of Woodward College in that city, says: "I never heard any one of any Christian body speak otherwise than with respect and loving kindness of this early departed, faithful laborer in Christ's cause. I knew him well in all his offices and relations, and I know not in which I most admired him. Naturally he was very cheerful and of inexhaustible kindness. His mind was well cultivated in the sciences, but especially in literature. It would not be easy to say in which, public speaking or writing, his genius manifested itself most attractively. You could not be in his company one hour without being sensible of the beauty of Christian love shining out in his looks and in all his tones and actions. He was, however, firm in his principles and decided in conduct; and yet few men were more void of offense to those who differed from him. In a word, he seemed to be a striking embodiment of wisdom, love, and manliness. One other *crown of excellence:*—he could see and appreciate true piety, however he might conscientiously differ in many respects from its possessor. I was struck with an instance of this in one of his New York editorials. A correspondent had *coarsely* found fault with him because he did not give sharp blows to the different denominations around him. He replied that he could not but love true religion in whatever Church or individual it appeared; and he felt assured that he could do more real good to his own denomination by employing his strength and time in building it up than in quarreling with Christians outside of it. 'When,' said he on that occasion, 'I look back on my early childhood, I can not but recall the image of my dear mother taking me into her closet, placing her hand on my head as I was kneeling before her, and pouring out prayer for my conversion and usefulness in the Redeemer's cause. That dear sainted mother was a *Baptist.* How, then, can my heart love to quarrel with my *Baptist brethren?*' "

There are certain elements of his character which have been casually mentioned in the preceding pages, to which we desire to call more particular attention.

1. He was a man of *catholic spirit.* He counted as his friends all who were the friends of Jesus. It mattered not what was their denominational name or where they lived, or to what nation they belonged; what were the articles of their creed or the rites of their worship; so long as they called God their Father and Jesus their Savior and the Holy Spirit their sanctifier, he treated them as brethren in the Lord. "He is a true Christian," he says, "who loves Jesus; and the measure of this love is the measure of his spiritual life. He dwells in God, and God in him; he lives a life whose sources, principle, and sustaining power are hid with Christ in God. Without this love, even though we had the tongues of men and angels, all knowledge, all mysteries, all prophetic gifts; the faith to remove mountains; the generosity to give our goods to the poor, and the fidelity to die for our principles,—we are but sounding brass or a tinkling cymbal; and with this, whether we be baptized in a love-feast or at the altar of a cathedral; sing David's psalms or Wesley's hymns; wear the beard or shave the chin; be an Armenian in Persia, a Raskolnik in Russia, a Catholic in Italy, or a Protestant in America,—we are fit for heaven, and therefore for any Church on earth."

2. His *happy disposition* was an attractive element of his nature. The smile on his face was not dra-

matic; it was an involuntary expression of the soul. He was always pleasant in his family and to all his associates. He met every one with cheerful words and faced misfortune without a frown. The secret of all this was his determination to be happy and enjoy life under all circumstances. He had his regular hours for work and pleasure, and his periods of recreation were seasons of especial delight to his children, who generally accompanied him in his city walks or country rambles.

3. His *devotional spirit* was felt by all who came in contact with him; for they saw that he "walked with God." Regular and frequent were his hours of prayer. Daily he offered the morning and evening sacrifice in his family, and when away from home he observed the same hours of devotion. He spent much time in secret prayer, and thus held the sweetest communion with the divine Father, and drew from Omnipotence the strength required for every time of need. He permitted nothing to interfere with the regularity of his devotions. At the hour of prayer the door was locked, and no one allowed to enter till prayers were concluded; and if persons were present they were invited to join in the solemn services. His communings with the divine Spirit were deep, tender, loving, and showed the soul humbled with divine grace, full of profoundest adoration, bowing at the eternal throne.

4. His *affectionate nature* was a strong element of his power. His students were to him as his children, and he treated the preachers of his conferences as brothers and fathers. His love was not spasmodic, but deep, pure, and abiding.

As a son he ever showed the utmost deference to the wishes of his parents, and cherished their memory with an undying regard.   As a husband and father his heart constantly yearned towards his family, and his letters to them, some of which are given in this volume, attest the strength of his affection.   Nor was he wanting in love for those who were bitter against him.   From the first there were men who were jealous of his success, and anxious for his preferments. These were ready to misrepresent his sentiments and under-estimate his abilities.   But he never complained of their treatment.   Sometimes he said to his children that he "wrote insults on the sand and favors on the marble."

5. He endeavored always to *look on the bright side.* He saw something good in every body for whom Christ died.   If the bad elements of some one's character were referred to, he would instantly call attention to the good ones if he knew them, and suggest the possibility of the man's reformation.   No man in town was beneath his smile and a pleasant "Good day" whenever they met.   Once when attacked by "roughs" and robbed of his pocket-book, he spoke out, "Now stand back, brethren, and let us pass by."

6. *Modesty* was a leading trait in his character, and has often been remarked upon.   Though conscious of his own strength, he never vaunted himself, and in society he was as simple as a child.   Dr. Edward Eggleston called him "the most modest of the Methodist bishops," as well as "one of the greatest." Bishop Wiley, when editor of the *Ladies' Repository,* wrote of him as one who was "always and every-where retiring, unassuming, unambitious, rather un-

derestimating his own worth and capabilities, and ever esteeming others better than himself. He never sought preferment, never obtruded his own claims or opinions. For every position he held in the Church, the Church sought him. He even needed urging and the inspiration of encouragement from others to bring out some of his most valuable literary productions."

7. He was a man of unstinting *benevolence*. He scrupulously gave away one-tenth of his income every year, and sometimes much more. He was a leader in public Church benevolence, and used opportunities to give in private. He was constantly giving to the poor and afflicted, and frequently denied himself comforts to make some poor soul happy. When in Delaware, if he heard of a case of affliction, he sought at once to assist the sufferer and help to bear his burden. The poor found in him a never-failing friend. After he moved to New York he spent many an afternoon hunting up the destitute in their hovels of misery and ministering to their necessities. He would go to a policeman and ask to be conducted to families that were in pressing need. And while carrying loaves of bread and pieces of meat, he talked of the One who could supply the needs of the soul. Many tenement-houses and dark cellars and garrets of New York received his sweet words and pleasant smile.

A number of the students at Norwalk and Delaware were carried through their course of study by money given or loaned to them by their president. Indigent students who were working their way through college and boarding themselves, always found a friend in him. He really became their almoner, loaning money to them whenever they needed it; but doing his banking in a peculiar way—never charging interest.

When a new chapel building was required at the Ohio Wesleyan University, he sold his little home which he owned in Cincinnati, to give the first thousand dollars on the subscription. When he went South in 1865 and organized the colored work in Mississippi and Texas, he saw the necessity for the education of the negro preachers, and gave his draft to Dr. John P. Newman for five thousand dollars, to start the first Biblical Institute in the South.

8. His *patriotism* must not be forgotten. Though born in another country he was a thorough American, and evinced his attachments to the United States on all suitable occasions.

By pen and by speech he advocated the Union as the chief hope of the American people, and indeed of the world. "It diminishes," he says, "the hazards of foreign wars and the dangers of domestic violence. It secures to us uniformity in the administration of justice, respectability in the eyes of the nations, and the perpetuity of our free institutions. It harmonizes the conflicting interests and weakens the sectional prejudices of a people bound by the ties of a common origin, a common conflict, a common language, a common literature, a common religion, and inhabiting states broken by no natural boundary. It exhibits the only example of democratic government on an extensive scale that the world has ever seen; it holds out the hand of welcome to the oppressed of all lands but one, and animates the friends of liberty throughout the earth."

When the civil war broke out, he used all his influence in behalf of the administration, and conducted the *Advocate* so as to strengthen the hands of its friends. He never despaired of the republic, and looked forward hopefully to a reunited people and a more stable government. "The Church," he says, " regards the war, terrible as it is, as, on the part of the government, unavoidable and righteous, arising out of the existence in some of the States of an institution incompatible alike with the genius of our republic, the spirit of our age, and the principles of our religion ; an institution toward which in former days she was tolerant and hopeful, but which she has now placed under unequivocal ban. Seeing that law, liberty, and light are on one side of this conflict, and rebellion, slavery, and darkness on the other, we can but hope concerning the issue. Should the war end as we anticipate, it will leave us a stronger government, a more homogeneous people, and a higher civilization, while it removes the only motive for disunion. Then shall our land be the hope and refuge equally of every tribe, kindred, tongue, and color. At such a consummation men might utter praise, and angels halleluiahs."

No sketch of Bishop Thomson would be complete without some notice of him as a public speaker and a writer. In pulpit oratory he excelled, and William Morley Punshon called him "The Chrysostom of American Methodism." Dr. George Lansing Taylor thus describes his manner of speaking :

"He addressed both mind and heart. At one moment he sounded humanity to its springs, the next he thundered and lightened through the conscience; then he bore the imagination on wings sublime ; then taste and fancy caught a falling rain of flowers ; then reason, lifted and inspired, marched onward to spheral harmonics. The graces of rhetoric, the keenness of logic, the glitter of wit, the witchery of philosophy, the copiousness of learning and knowledge, all poured from his lips in a stream of gold. His style had the purity of sculpture, the splendor of painting, the majesty of architecture, the inspiration of poetry.

"His auditors came devoutly and went away entranced. To his students he was at once the magician, the seer, and the brother. Their minds in his hands became plastic as Parian paste, which, once molded, hardens into a marble. No man ever left a nobler or more imperishable impress upon minds of a texture to receive it. . . .

"Few great orators have ever more electrified a New York audience than did his report of his missionary tour at the Steinway Hall anniversary in 1866. Hundreds of his auditors in that hour awoke to the consciousness that they had entertained an angel unawares. The whole Church felt and proved the power of that single speech. Few scholars of the age could have absorbed so much of China in such a trip; none could have crystallized more of it into half an hour."

His discourses were never conversational. There was nothing common, trite or condescending in his words or manner. He spoke on great themes, treated them from lofty stand-points of thought, and in the purest and richest diction. He never used slang or any form of expression that was not scholarly, and never told an amusing anecdote in the pulpit. He felt that he had a sacred message, and that it must be delivered in a solemn and loving manner. He never ranted or bawled, no matter how moved his soul might be.

His manner never became boisterous, nor were his tones ever flat or harsh. His voice was like the Æolian harp, susceptible of the most various intonation, sweet, pathetic, and inspiring. He stood quietly behind the desk, rarely varying the position of his body, and making but few gestures. Yet his silver notes and impressive pronounciation charmed and often electrified his audience.

He was not always equally eloquent; indeed, there were times, especially in his early ministry, when he failed to meet the high expectations of the people, when it really seemed as if he did not care whether he preached well or not. These occasions, however, were not frequent, and were probably the result of some temporary depression or stagnation of mind. If there was any thing to arouse him, he always responded equal to the emergency. Dr. L. B. Gurley gives us an illustration:

"When he was principal of Norwalk Seminary, I frequently took him in my carriage to my quarterly-meetings on the district. On one occasion I noticed that he seemed depressed in spirit, and I feared a failure in his pulpit effort that forenoon. So apparently half in sport and half in earnest, I said, ' Doctor, I shall follow your sermon with another, in about fifteen minutes from the time you close. I give you fair warning that I shall eclipse you if I can.' He smiled and said modestly, ' No doubt you can.' I saw he was aroused as well as amused, and he delivered an able and beautiful sermon from the text, ' He endured as seeing him who is invisible.' "

The Rev. Oliver Burgess says, "I first heard Dr. Thomson at the old Ohio Conference, assembled at Springfield, in the Fall of 1835. There were present many distinguished men, such as Bishop James O. Andrew, Henry B. Bascom, James B. Finley, William B. Christie, John H. Power, Adam Poe, and others of equal fame; but few attracted more attention than the eloquent young Thomson, who was then so full of promise for the Church. I remember well how a large audience was wonderfully impressed by his burning words, as he preached from the text, 'Finally, my brethren, be strong in the Lord, and in the power of his might.' (Eph. vi, 10.) The next time I heard him was in Wooster, when, after earnest pleading on my part, he occupied my pulpit, and gave a searching sermon from the words, 'They profess that they know God; but in works they deny him, being abominable and disobedient, and unto every good work reprobate.' (Titus i, 16.) Frequently after this, when he was principal of Norwalk Seminary and president of Ohio Wesleyan University was he with me on special occasions, and delivered some of the most instructive and beautiful sermons I ever heard."

One year, in his early ministry, conference was held at Wooster. Bishop Hamline, regarded as the finest orator of the episcopal board, presided and preached on Sunday morning. Edward R. Ames, then a prominent presiding elder and the ablest orator of the Indiana Conference, was present as a visitor, and preached in the afternoon. Edward Thomson preached at night. He fully realized the demand made upon him. Two of our best preachers had delivered discourses, and he was expected to equal them in grappling the truth and presenting it to his hearers. He was at his old home; his widowed mother and younger brothers and sisters were still at the old homestead; the boys and girls with whom he used to gambol were now grown men and women and anxious to hear their old playmate. It was a great occasion, and he rose gracefully and triumphantly to meet the emergency. All acknowledged the evening discourse to be equal, and some said it was superior, to those of the day.

His printed discourses, however eloquent their style, merely exhibit the language, the thought; they can not give the melting tones of his voice, nor the inspiring expressions of his face.

As a writer, Bishop Thomson's style was a model of clearness, dignity, and condensation. His thoughts were elevated, his language correct, and his sentences picturesque and harmonious. All who have read his writings acknowledge their excellence. A number of his essays were republished in Great Britain, and even in Australia, and they have been more popular there than in the New World.

The New York *Independent*, in an editorial written by Dr. Edward Eggleston, says: "As a writer, he has qualities of the rarest sort. None of our eminent American writers excel him in purity of diction, or in 'the art of putting things.' . . . His books of essays and travels are the classics of American Methodist literature." The same journal in another editorial, published a year later says: "Nothing but the system of denominational publishing could prevent his volumes of essays from taking the rank they deserve with the first writings of the age."

Dr. George Lansing Taylor, a most competent critic, says: "The English tongue was never written in a more classic style. No essays in the language, from Addison to Froude, can be read with greater pleasure or profit by the student than such as his 'Close Thought,' 'Mental Symmetry,' 'The Inner World,' 'The Sublimity of the Bible,' 'Skepticism,' and many others. . . . He was the Paul and Plato of Methodism in one." Rev. Oliver Burgess says: "After he was bishop, I attended a few conferences where he presided, and how he magnified his office by his able defense of Christianity! With what delight also did I listen to his discourses at Delaware on commencement occasions, and afterward read his essays, lectures, and editorials. An Episcopal clergyman once said to me, 'I consider Bishop Thomson the most finished writer in the American Church.' And often as I perused his writings have I exclaimed, 'O, how they sparkle.' I was always impressed with their strength and beauty. What a shock, and what a loss was his death to the Church! But his works follow him, and his influence will be felt in the coming generations; and when the names of thousands have perished from memory, Edward Thomson will shine in the firmanent of the Church as a star of the first magnitude."

In earlier life he did not expect to be the author of any thing more than transient articles for the public press. He wrote much, however, and occasionally contributed to the Church journals. But his ideal was so high that he did not think his productions worthy of preservation in book form. His first printed work was issued in this wise: In 1853, Dr. Edward D. Roe, a superanuated member of the Ohio

Conference, requested the privilege of collecting some of Dr. Thomson's articles which had appeared from time to time in newspapers and magazines, and of giving them to the public in a separate volume. As he assumed the risk of publication, Dr. Thomson granted him permission for this purpose, and gave him the profits of the sales.

The volume met with such a favorable reception that the book agents at Cincinnati in 1856, proposed to Dr. Thomson that he prepare other works. Accordingly he arranged his essays and sketches for this purpose, including those which Dr. Roe had published, and they were issued in three volumes, duodecimo, as follows:

I. BIOGRAPHICAL AND INCIDENTAL SKETCHES.— Of the former there are eleven, and of the latter, twenty-one sketches—making together a volume of 389 pages. Dr. Thomson was a masterly delineator of character, and some of his best writings appear in this collection.

II. MORAL AND RELIGIOUS ESSAYS,—Containing 374 pages, and embracing twenty separate themes. Several of these had been delivered as Sunday afternoon lectures in the College Chapel.

III. EDUCATIONAL ESSAYS, — Containing 412 pages, and nineteen articles, some of which the writer had used as baccalaureate addresses at the university.

In addition to these volumes, he prepared also:

IV. LETTERS FROM EUROPE.—This volume contains 299 pages, duodecimo, and includes the letters which he wrote from the old world during his tour for the purchase of books for the university library, in 1854. They are lively, sketchy, full of interesting detail, and contain a large amount of information. In some respects this is perhaps the most popular of the four volumes here named. The paragraphs on the differences between the English and French character, where we mention his first tour abroad, are quoted from it.

Bishop Thomson's literary remains were varied and extensive. Had his life been spared, the world would doubtless have had richer and better treasures of thought from his practiced pen; but he had prepared for the press nothing except the two works which we next name—the first of which was given to the printers while the bishop was on his way to his last conference, and which was issued after his death.

V. Our Oriental Missions.—This was issued in two volumes, 16mo., containing 267 and 281 pages, respectively, and including in the second volume a brief sketch of the author's life. Bishop Wiley, then editor, calls them "the most critical and analytical essays on modern missions ever written," and they certainly gave a new view of the civilization and resources of the Asiatic continent. The bishop was a keen observer, and his record of observations abroad was an inspiration to the Church at home.

VI. The Evidences of Revelation.—This volume has already been referred to as containing the lectures delivered before the Boston School of Theology, and the Garrett Biblical Institute. It contains 327 pages, duodecimo, and was issued in 1872.

CHAPTER XXII.

EDWARD THOMSON A REPRESENTATIVE MAN.

BY J. W. MENDENHALL, PH. D., D. D.

PLATO'S ideal man, the product of a truth-search-ing genius, was endowed with wisdom, temper-ance, fortitude, and justice, and clothed besides with all collateral virtues. He is not designated as a phil-osopher, merchant, physician, or priest; indeed, his occupation is not assigned him; but he is described by the academician as fitted for rulership in a government distinguished for letters, health, uprightness, and love of truth. In many respects the ideal character is magnetic enough; in some respects it is difficult of attainment; at the same time it is wanting in the graces of a religious life, and is destitute of spiritual functions, adaptations, and powers. Plato's man is not the complete man; the ideal character of the philosopher, like a descending star, soon hides itself beneath the horizon.

Thomas Carlyle, searching with microscopic inge-nuity for the signs of permanent greatness or a fixed factor in historic figures, crowds into one word the conclusion of his findings, and points to it as the prophetical birth-mark of growth, greatness, and his-toric fame. *Sincerity* is the test word, the sign of all excellence, the key to all achievement.

Looking at men from an introspective standpoint, our own Emerson is ready to affirm that he is great who is what he is from nature; that is, greatness is *naturalness* developed to its maximum. Greatness is the man unfolded, not enfolded. "Man is that noble, endogenous plant which grows, like the palm, from within outward."

With these guides to manhood we ought to be able to analyze any character or life presented to us; but, like a botanist who, with only a primer in his hand, starts for the open fields with some hesitation, we should take up our subject at this point with some suspicion of weakness in our tests. We seek, therefore, the final test.

An old book, for translating which William Tyndall lost his life, describes the ideal character in possession of attributes not mentioned by Plato, Carlyle, or Emerson, and sums the whole in the incarnation of the Logos who was made flesh and dwelt among us. To the famous list of attributes framed by the above-mentioned writers are joined others that reflect the possibilities of character under religious conditions and adorn it with a beauty not attainable through the virtues of the poet and philosopher. The idealism of the Bible is of a higher cast than the idealism of the academy, and the model character of the New Testament eclipses the model forms of the English iconoclast and the Concord sage. Without particularizing them now, these moral attributes of the Bible, added to those qualities considered supreme by others, enter into our conception of the great man, and constitute the fiber, temperament, and base of the ideal character.

Before those who knew him Edward Thomson stands out as a representative character; not ideal in the sense of distance or mysterious realization, not Platonic in the limited circle of virtues, not *sincere* alone, not only *natural* in the largest view, but he was the embodiment of the New Testament life, measuring up to the stature of a true man, and fulfilling the prophecies of his own great soul to which he had listened in his early years. He was representative in the accumulated experiences, forces, qualifications, labors, and achievements of a great man; and as such he may be fittingly portrayed here.

It is not ours to introduce him as the representative scholar, or college president, or preacher, or bishop, others having that to do, but to enroll him on the list of the Church's representative characters. Back of his official and public career, its brilliancy somewhat disguised by his innate modesty or aversion to demonstration and pyrotechnic, was the man himself, clean, white, circular, not angular, as back of resplendent sunsets is the sun itself. So no reference will be made to the official career, only so far as it may be needful to throw light upon the character. We deal with *character*, a crystalline nature, others with the *career*, a progressive and impassioned career. In physical stature small like Paul and Napoleon, he yet was a concentration of moral virtues that atoned for any deficiency in the former, and enveloped it with grace and dignity. He was not to be measured, weighed, and assigned by what one could see of him—his avoirdupois was not a hint of what he was. The *without* was not a key to the *within*. As the shekinah was not dependent on the veil that screened it from view, so the character of Thomson could not be determined by the robe of flesh that enshrined it. The door to the inner chambers of the soul was, however, at times ajar, and a glimpse of the life within was not impossible to the friendly and sympathetic searcher.

In this day of internationalism it is not worth much to inquire into the nationality of a man, save to learn a new lesson touching the doctrine of the unity of the race; for the emblems of humanity are conspicuous in all nationalities. We are learning, too, the great truth that among all nations he is accepted of God who is a man in his impulses, aspirations, and religious unfoldings and breathings.

Ethnically, Thomson was of English ancestry, and was brought to the United States by his parents when about nine years old—not old enough to have developed an English predisposition, but young enough to absorb American life, and conform to the dream of an original manhood in a new hemisphere. In this international transition he yielded with surprising facility to the manipulating forces of the adopted country, becoming an American in patriotic instinct, and was devoted in after life to the growth of the resources and the extinction of the evils that impeded the progress and threatened the life of the nation. He was as much an American as if he had been born on its soil. This is mentioned more because of its psychological bearing than its value as a fact; it reveals his wonderful or unequaled power of assimilation and adaptation, whereby he made circumstance his servant, and dictated to his conditions, and rode upon them, as Jupiter upon the clouds. Discerning situations,

his intuitions went out like so many tentacula, drawing in the materials to which his nature was susceptible, and converting them into food for his being.
He was master of place, therefore; and of country,
climate, people. Possibly he could not as easily have
become a Frenchman, or German, or Spaniard, or
Italian, as an American; and yet he was large enough
in his sympathies, broad enough in his tendencies,
and strong enough in his purposes to have exchanged
his national inheritance, however royal, for any other,
however humble, that Providence might have conferred
upon him. He was in no sense a cast-iron man, but
had the elasticity of a cosmopolitan or race-spirit,
which subordinated social, and even patriotic, ends to
the larger philanthropy of a race.

We deem these general statements worthy of record in order to indicate the broad-gauge feature in
the character of Thomson; to establish that he was
incapable of narrowness of view or feeling; to show
that he was not possessed of an exclusiveness or
clannishness of spirit arising from birth or nationality;
but that he regarded the race in its unity, and
seemed to broaden with advancing years in capacity,
disposition, and power. His kinship to the race was
a conscious possession, and made him fraternal with
men, and stamped him as a representative character.
On this broad, generous, ecumenical foundation was
erected a superstructure of humanity, whose architecture was Gothic in proportion and beauty, and
whose graces and ornamentation, so far as they can
be phrased, were pre-Raphaelite. In all the points
of a man he was true to nature; he was not artificial; he did not wear a borrowed costume, nor did

he masquerade before men; he was a genuine man, sincere and original, as Carlyle says, the very exhibition of frankness and ease. Because thus natural and open-hearted, let it not be supposed that he was shallow or superficial, or that he may be analyzed without study, for he was as mysterious in certain forces, and as profound for the depths of his character as any man that ever lived; and our task is not an easy one. On the whole, men would not have pronounced him an enigma; but he was a combination of qualities that disadvantages the reviewer and perplexes the biographer.

With confessed difficulties in our way, we shall attempt to examine and describe the moral and mental furniture of the man, confining our observations to the most conspicuous features of his character. Whether we press into service the terms of Plato, Carlyle, Emerson, or the Bible, we shall see that he is the counterpart of their ideal, and answers almost perfectly the reflections of their images.

In a distinguished sense, Thomson was, from the inclination of his nature, a *truth-seeker*, a lover of truth by instinct, and as sensitive to error 'as mercury to the atmosphere. Truth relates to the harmony of parts, or the discovery of things in their right relations. Discord, as in music; deformity or want of proportion, as in architecture; and unfitness, as a large statue for a small niche, are painful to the lover of pure sounds, proportion, and harmony. The lover of truth has an eye to the eternal fitness of things. Error he detects in a flash; falsehood, sham, delusion, mental and moral, supported by sophistry or explained by rationalism, he at once abjures. The errorist walks on stilts; the truth-man on his own feet, and yet is tall enough to embrace the stars. The truth-loving nature, seeking its own in the meshes of error, and struggling against the currents of mad opinion, is often subject to temptation, sometimes to abandon its search, occasionally to indulge in the promised pleasures of skepticism. Young Thomson, heroic in devotion to truth, was inveigled temporarily into skepticism touching the foundations of Christianity. But he was not skeptical like Montaigne, he was not an interrogation point or head-shaker at every proposition, or creed, or moral sentiment. Doubt was foreign to his constitution; love of truth was a natural force to be worked out, not through the channels of doubt, but through a close and devout study of the works and words of God. This love of seeing things in their right relations, of probing error and making it explain itself, in default of which it was driven dumb from his presence, dignified his pursuits and led him to acquisitions that astonished his friends. It dignified his character and won the confidence of all who knew him. Treachery, hypocrisy, sham—these had no place in his nature, in his theology, in his religion.

Error is controversial; truth is modest, calm because conscious of its power, and self-possessed and full of faith as to victory. Inborn, molding and restraining him, the love of truth lifted Thomson above the controversial arena, and made him the quiet, graceful student, eager to know, but not anxious to contest with antagonists. To antagonism he preferred the quiet forward movement in his spiritual researches until he had pressed with his feet the borders of the infinite.　What cared he for the bugles of men calling to war, when he heard the trumpets of angels bidding him to enter the open door of the temple of truth?　In strictness he was not a debater; the dust of conflict produced in him a mental influenza; but he could be aroused, and when truth was at stake his sword gleamed in the sunshine and left its mark upon the form of error at his feet.

Closely allied to this feature was another which is conspicuous only in rare and jeweled men.　Thomson was the personification of the *æsthetic element* in our humanity.　His love of the beautiful was as marked, and it had as decisive an influence on his character as his love of truth.　Philosophers debate over the question whether beauty is in the object or in the person, leaving us in doubt as to its location; and they tell us that one may discern and appreciate the beautiful without being able to define it or understand its essence.　In their hands the subject is as beautiful as a floating cloud, but it is a *cloud* nevertheless.　Our representative helps to a solution of the mystery by demonstrating the subjective character of beauty, for his character was an incarnation of the beautiful.　It had the attractive force and illuminating propensity of beauty, for it flashed its light on all things around it just as a rose window illuminates the cathedral within and throws light on external things.　If objective in things, beauty was subjective in him.　Dr. Merrick pronounces the character of Thomson "beautiful, but unique;" a rare combination of colors, bright, harmonious, and intense in their loveliness.

This must be taken in no narrow sense.　He was as broad and deep in his love of the beautiful, as was Humboldt in his love of science. It broke out or had its manifestation in a circumspect choice of things beautiful in literature, perhaps the highest type and the truest test of the æsthetic element of the character. To the poets, and especially to classical writers, he was attached by a golden chain, weaving their fabled threads into the truth-forms that the Gospel precipitated at his feet, and so presented truth clothed in the matchless garb of classic elegance and religion. Of Latin authors he was fond, and to their study he was largely indebted for that grace of diction and polish of expression that placed him in the front rank of American writers. By this ductile taste he was fitted for the editorships he occupied in the Church. To the beautiful in nature he was drawn by the same law of affinity.

Neither Rousseau nor Bryant had a more acute sense of the divine beauty of creation, which in Thomson often rose to a celestial appreciation of the sublime. From the small to the great, or from the magnitude of the planets to invisible forms of matter, his eye swept over the vast fields of creation's wonders, detecting the order that reigned everywhere, delighting in the harmony of God's works, and ever musing on the proof of the invisible God in the things which he has made. Nature was the storehouse of God's wisdom, and every thing in it was an autograph of the Deity. Thus the beauty of nature was the express image of divine truth.

Notwithstanding this loyalty to nature, she never made a confidant of him—a companionship allotted to the fewest—revealing to him her laws as she had done to Newton and Kepler; but she responded to his search for the sublime, and he could paint a flower, or frame a star, or see the heavens in flame as readily as poet or seer. If he had not the scientist's grip on nature, he had the poet's vision of her beauties, which was far better. Deeper, more striking still, was his discovery of the beautiful in character. Here he was supreme. Moth-eaten character was an offense in his eyes, righteous living his delight. He could portray the one in such livid colors that the wicked trembled as they listened, and so describe the charms of the other that the angels must have rejoiced in hearing it. He could talk of God, angels, the patriarchs, the apostles, the Son of man, the martyrs, and the long line of worthies in the Church with an appreciation of heroism, integrity, fidelity, and honor, that made these virtues stand out like granite pillars in the temple of God. It was as if he ate constantly of the honey of Hymettus and drank daily of the nectar of the gods, so godlike was his vision of things beauti-ful, both in God and man.

The strength of his life was the *elasticity of his sympathies.* Sympathy, as a necessity of circumstance, or the result of a cool calculating judgment, is not always refreshing, and rarely ·inspiring. Still, even in that form it may have a *bona fide* value. Cold men have their uses, just as the stalagmite has its place in the economy of nature. System that quenches all sympathy; iron-cladism that drives ahead regard-less of the rights of others; and the despotism of in-dependence, secured by wealth or social position, may defend itself if assailed; but altars of pity are needed in this world, and men who share the reproaches of our humanity and sacrifice to improve its condition, are in demand. There are vocations in life that can not be prosecuted by a system of red-tapeism, or by an iron-clad spirit, since their own spirit is that of good-will to men, and their greatest reward the elevation of man.

Of these the ministry is first, requiring sympathy as a vital force and as a *sine qua non* condition of efficiency and success. Nor must it be an artificial or simulated feature, but inborn and divinely quickened, otherwise its hollowness will be detected and its effect be powerless. Thomson was sympathetic, not by discipline, but by nature; tender, pitiful, helpful, not for strategic ends, but from the soul's impulses. No quality was more prominent in his preaching than this; it was the key to his oratory. Invariably, and on whatever theme he addressed an audience, they were captured by the subtile force of sympathy, and followed him whithersoever he went. He touched the heart, being touched himself. This was also his peculiar qualification for the college presidency—he sympathized with young men in their struggles to a marvelous degree, so that there was no distance between them, except the distance of acknowledged superiority that nothing could bridge but equal attainment. He was on a level with babes, or he could drive the steeds of Apollo's chariot. With equal facility he could interpret the significance of a tear, discern the virtue of a smile, detect the groan of the soul on the pallid lips of want, and hear the echo of an angel in the trembling voice of a patriarch.

As preacher or educator he was moved by man's necessities, difficulties, mental struggles, and spiritual vicissitudes, for he had felt the same, and nothing was

human that was foreign to him, as was anciently said
of another. It was this kind of sympathy that gave him
strength with people and students who recognized in
him a faithful counselor and a judicious friend.
No maudlin sympathy with errors and weaknesses
was his. He believed in retribution for wrong, repentance and reformation the duty of the wrong-doer,
and redemption the possible heritage of every man.
In discipline, therefore, he was exact without being
harsh, and punitive without being capital. His pun-
ishments were redemptions.

To his penetrating and apocalyptic gaze, human
nature opened its vast possibilities under gracious
evolution; and he saw that every young man was the
father of his own manhood, and the executive of his
own destiny. As the botanist foresees the future of
flower or tree, so he saw the possible unfoldings of
manhood in all who came under his administration,
and was won at once in their interest. He believed in
the kingship and priesthood of every man. With
him there was no caste, save the caste of the soul.
Every man is branded with immortality, and that
made all sacred in his presence. In the dome of every
brain he saw a divine light burning; he would not
extinguish the light. Every man is clothed with a
divine right to existence, and may engage in the pursuit of happiness on the highest highway. With such
lofty appreciation of the worth of man, he could not
be a tyrant or lord; he could not even experiment
with a coat-of-mail; rather he was the open-hearted
soul knit to the soul of the world by threads woven
by divine hands. Do any wonder at his power over
men? The secret is, they had power over him. In

the growth of years he became a magnet, drawing rather than repelling; and while he multiplied friends, he had the rare faculty of winning those who had been his enemies.

His *intellectual endowment,* vast and superior as it was, signally fitted him for a representative position. How one intellect surpasses another, either in the perceptive or reflective faculties ; why one takes to poetry, another to mathematics, another to science, physiologists have essayed to explain, but with little success. On natural principles alone, an explanation must be superficial; and in these days the Platonic principle of pre-existence of souls is quite unsatisfactory. It is sufficient for our purpose to say that it is God's will that there shall be grades in intellectual capacity and power; the method by which grades are established is his own. For the development of his mind, Thomson was not indebted to a collegiate training; nor to early advantages; but the intellectual root being in him, it grew like a tree planted by a river, becoming marvelously great and generously fruitful in a short time.

He was a student by nature; more, he was a thinker, an inquirer, endowed with the philosophic spirit, and was under a kind of Diomedean necessity to think—thought driving him forward, and opening gates and even unhinging them that he might enter new fields of exploration. He was of a sanguine temperament, which, according to psychologists, is considered a sign of affection for belles-lettres ; and the melancholy temperament, considered by Aristotle as indicative of a tendency to close and speculative thinking, was also predominant in his make-up. He could handle the real and play with the ideal at will; he could tear the veil from the solid face of truth, or speculate on the *differentia* between· being and becoming; he was concrete and abstract, descending to the alphabet or ascending into mysteries profound enough for the angels. By the sanguineo-melancholic temperament he could travel around the zodiac of truth, and be on his feet all the while.

Let us not be misunderstood here. We do not claim that he was in such sympathy with the secrets of the universe, or held such confidential relations with Deity, that he could reveal new truths or new principles; he was not an inspired man; he was not called to originate any new system of theology or philosophy; he made known no laws either of matter or mind; but he was on high terms of intimacy with God, so that the great truths of God ever welcomed his approach, and his soul swelled as they entered and abode with him. His it was not to be founder of laws and systems and schools, but it was his to receive with the soul's hospitality the old truths that had been tested by the centuries and had survived the martyrdom of their friends. He was a receiver, not a revealer.

His peculiar mental characteristics indicate a versatility and adaptation and fitness for any station in life. More noted than all was his *power of concentration*—the first quality of genius. While at home in the universe of thought, he could shut himself up in a small cell, and there weave the truth into as fine and delicate threads as the spider the cables of his bridge. The power to isolate himself from surroundings, to enter into a transcendental state, to forget all things save the one in pursuit, was very strong, and accounts for several, and perhaps curious, things in his life. His absent-mindedness, of which many incidents might be given, was a logical result of his concentration, and was an element of power. While it sometimes proved an embarrassment in the social circle, it was understood, and so was not condemned. But this quality, however inconvenient for society, is all-potent in the study, and absolutely a condition of the greatest mental productiveness. Plato insists that every man shall attend to one thing, which is concentration. Thomson obeyed this rule, plunging into a subject as a whale into the deeps, and he did not appear again until he had secured the pearls at the bottom. In this seclusion he made thoughts as bees make honey, exploring flowers for their sweetness, and catching light from shining stars. He was a heroic, joyful, painstaking worker, sifting theories for the truth as the miner does the sand for the gold. On the wall of the cell of Jerome in Bethlehem-Judah is an oil painting, representing Jerome at work with an angel pouring music into his ear. Thomson worked as if an angel were chanting in his presence the strains of the upper sphere; and it is not surprising that his writings are bedewed with a heavenly spirit, and when he spoke that his face often shone as did that of Moses.

Such seclusion or self-forgetfulness in preparation accounts for the fullness of his essays or discourses, which were usually free from side discussions, and contained very little foreign or unnecessary matter. He wrote what ought to be written. He riveted his thought upon a single point. He hammered the gold into leaves and passed them around like a goddess her jewels, or drew them into wires that connected sometimes with the poles of the earth, but oftener with the throne in heaven. The thinking power of Thomson was exceedingly acute and fine, and was ever devoted to the elucidation of the highest themes. That fable of Mohammed that angels whispered to him when trained pigeons were picking peas out of his ears has nothing in Thomson's life to match it; nor is the marvelous the object of our analysis. In common with men of his class, he received from God his furniture of faculties which he made use of in acquisition, adornment of character, efficiency of action, and reaped the reward of success. In this power to concentrate thought upon a subject was the secret of his supposed versatility of talent. When he converged he showed the power of divergence. Centripetal force meant centrifugal influence. Center signified circumference. He was both a point and a sphere. With such contractile and expansive forces, it is not surprising that he seemed to be fitted for one station as well as another, and succeeded equally well in all. As pastor, preacher, editor, educator, president, author, bishop, he was not a whit behind the "chiefest" in these departments, and was at ease in all of them. After a scientific fashion of speech, we may say these were correlated positions, one merging into the other; but rare is the man who can fill one as efficiently as another, and seem competent for something beyond. In these positions, the highest in the gift of the Church, he never quite attained his maximum, apparently because the limitations of his environment were prejudicial to the fullest activity. For some positions he was entirely too large, working with a consciousness of reserve power that pointed to a higher level of life; and when he passed into the bishopric, if any judged it was a misfit, it was because of the greatness of the man rather than the office. The secret of this greatness was not the symmetry of his character, of which more has been made than is necessary, so much as the development of its natural resources, of which the power to think was the strongest.

In conjunction with this developed power was his acquisitive faculty, or thirst for knowledge. He was avaricious for facts, truths, principles, laws. To be ignorant is to be base. An unopened intellect is a reproach. "Wise men lay up knowledge," says Solomon. Early in life Thomson caught the contagion of the student, and began questioning the universe and God. No subject was misunderstood by him; at least its relations, if discoverable at all, were soon revealed. He was not an encyclopedia, a mere storehouse of facts; but his mind was a laboratory, analyzing, digesting, assimilating, and establishing. Not a founder of any system, he was systematic, and hence achieved while others dreamed. He walked in the light of no Heraclitean sun, but was sun-like himself, illuminating others with the orient light of his own soul. But this was not the end of his being, the object of existence. He imbibed not the idea of Goethe, that man exists for culture; or that Platonic conception, that education is the remedy for the world's evils. None saw more clearly the healthful influence of educated mind in the world; he emphasized its necessity in discourse and by sacrifice; he believed in colleges; his reputation is largely that of a successful president and

educator; but culture is not religion, and education is
not redemption. He discerned the weakness of the
intellect in its moral processes; he detected the direction of the intellectual drift of the age toward mate-
rialism; he announced the break-down of the will;
he pointed out the helplessness of the creature in his
best estate, and demonstrated the need of religion.
This is a dividing line in character. Both culture and
religion are essential to the complete man, but the
latter is indispensable to man's eternity; hence it must
be first, it is supreme. .

In a very natural order we are brought to put an
estimate upon Thomson's *moral character* and life, to
separate it from the intellectual and æsthetic, and ap-
praise it on its own merits. However developed the
intellectual, or refined and exquisite the æsthetic sense,
he must be weak who gazes not frequently upon the
Divine likeness, and strives not after the Divine model.
Wanted, gymnastics, geometry, and music, as Plato
says; wanted, education and idealism, as Emerson
says; wanted still more, a divine impulse in the heart
of humanity to lift it to divine heights of beauty and
righteousness. The invocation of religion is as im-
perative as the regimen of the schools. The moral
tone of a man, as readily determined as the intellectual, is the sign of the highest or lowest moral suscep-
tibilities, and proof of manliness, or the want of it.

In this respect Thomson was conspicuous, his
moral character was supreme. The charm of his life
was the artless simplicity and natural transparency of
his character. Conceding his greatness, as men are
called great, he disproves the current theory that such
must be obscure, enigmatical, distant as an asteroid,

and really as unknown as if made of other clay than that that enters into the composition of men. To lofty acquisitions he joined a simple unostentatious manner, that disarmed criticism while it won admiration. Simplicity of character is not inconsistent with complexity of force, or versatility of talent, or the magnitude of achievement. Nor was this a dissembled virtue; rather was it indigenous, and, therefore, spontaneous. On his part there was no desire to be otherwise—there was no secret study to be simple or transparent. Like the crystal, he shone with the light that streamed through him. Simplicity characterized his whole life. On the platform, in the pulpit, and when he used the pen, simplicity of speech beautified every thought and elevated every utterance. He was understood when he spoke or wrote. To attain this end he did not descend into commonplace thought or employ trite expression, for his eloquence of speech equaled that of Addison, and his thoughts were Baconian in strength and coherency. If he did not indulge in what Herbert Spencer calls "compound quantitative reasoning," he did sparkle with the thoughts of the seers and sages, and hurled truth at its enemies as a god would throw clods from Olympus. Thus simple, he was sublime in speech, thought, and action. In the moral arena the same spirit was on exhibition, making him as gentle as a woman; but it did not mean stagnation of the moral life, or indifference while the world was sinning. He was not a god napping. He was gentle because grace is gentle; simple-hearted, because love reduces all things to simple elements. Through this simplicity, as through a lens, we catch glimpses of the deep and unsearchable sincerity of the man. There was no reason for sham or show, for parade or masquerade of his powers, he was the great man; and speech, action, thought voiced his high-born origin more eloquently than fustian or proclamation. He stood like a sunbeam, and blazed into fire when focused.

Joined to this characteristic—in fact, a twin virtue of his simplicity—was that of comparative *transparency*. We mean he was transparent just so far as it was possible. Human nature is its own great mystery, eluding the gaze of its possessor, and refuses to be interviewed by a stranger. The soul silently but effectually closes its doors to sight-seers. In this highest aspect he, like all others, was mysterious; but in spite of the reserve of the soul, he revealed himself or came to the surface just as often as he could, speaking forth the secret of being in a psalm of devotion to his Maker, or in acts of love to his fellow-man. Modest withal, he preferred to be known in his trueness rather than be concealed behind an image of clay. Perhaps the great struggle of life after all is to pass from concealment into light, from obscurity into revelation. Pascal held *semi-obscurity* in perfect horror; total obscurity or full revelation is much to be preferred. The flesh often hinders the revelation of the man; the spirit is in chains, and goes no farther than the length of its tether; but Thomson crept out of the chrysalis at least once in a while, and tried his wings in the sight of men. We attribute to him transparency of intention; men knew his aim, and that it was upright. He was not a dark-lantern character; he was not a spy in the universe of God. We likewise credit him with transparency of effort; men knew what he was doing, and how well he was doing it. He was not a moonshiner in society, armed against his fellows, disloyal to humanity; but blazed out like a sun, and proposed to let his light shine. What more could be asked? What more could he accomplish?

In Thomson we discover the regnancy of a lofty aim, the supremacy of a royal purpose—that of being a man and serving his generation with fidelity, and contributing something to posterity. The measure of life's success is in proportion to its aim. As has been said, he who aims at the stars shoots higher than he who aims at the house-top. However wise, one can not plan his whole life from the beginning, marking out its transitions, shaping its directions, and assign himself at different periods to different positions, or foresee the successes and failures that may fall to him. Nor is so wide and extensive a foreknowledge necessary. What he can do, what he should do, is to purpose on a royal line of conduct, behaving himself wisely in all things, as did David, and resolve upon self-development, the acquisition of knowledge, the fruits of discipline, and the spiritulization of the nature, as God permits and aids. He can aim at the mark set before him in the Gospel, and command conscience, judgment, and will to be friendly to his pursuit, and at last secure the prize. Definiteness and superiority of aim on the one hand, and listlessness and vacancy on the other, indicate the difference between men, explaining success and failure. Greatness or great achievement is not an accident, or the result of a dream, or the favor of friendship, or the compassion of Providence. Rather is it the fruit of an

inborn purpose to be something or to do something
worthy of recognition, a defiant wrestling with ob-
stacles, and a going forward until victory is wrenched
even from the hands of defeat. Purpose, not pedi-
gree, is the basis of performance. Aimless living is
the curse of modern society. Groveling desires, whetted to intensity by earthly conditions and worldly pursuits, the chief end of which is animal gratification or
luxurious living, engage too much the thought of immortal men. The boundary of their vision, which
ought to stretch away into the infinities, is the horizon
of this world. Diamonds may lie at our feet, but it
is better to cast the eye beyond the stars. Happily,
Thomson was delivered from a low aim, and rescued
entirely from the wild state of aimlessness, which is
non-productive, except of degradation. He did not
spend his time, like Diocletian, in catching flies, nor,
like Alcibiades, did he furnish material for gossips.
He rose to the height of a purpose. His bow was
bent, and his arrow sped to the mark as surely as
David's pebble reached the giant's forehead.

Let it not be inferred that he calculated on official
position as the end of life, for he had learned from
Bacon that a man in great place is a servant, without any special liberty of person or action. Thomson aimed at intellectual development and moral
beauty of character—position was incidental, and
came as the result of his fitness for it. The crown he
wore was not placed on his brow by external hands,
but, like the foliage of the palm, grew from within,
and was a natural and not an artificial ornament. In
aiming at personal excellence he secured a twice-fold
reward, excellence itself and corresponding position.

Like Solomon asking for wisdom and obtaining the surplus products of riches and honor, Thomson, seeking only the normal development of his powers, obtained the honors of place, and made others the sharers of his presence.

This gives us the opportunity to answer the question, often raised with respect to men of character, was he *ambitious?* In truth, he was not, as men are, ambitious. Honors, positions, were not his by self-seeking, by the legerdemain of a caucus, by the cohesive power of promises, but as the fruit of superior excellence and acknowledged fitness. The fact is public that when elected to the presidency of the Ohio Wesleyan University he hesitated to accept it on the ground that the General Conference had elected him to the editorship of the *Ladies' Repository,* and he was not at liberty to surrender his trust. By persuasion of friends he yielded his convictions and accepted. His reputation is not that of a place-seeker. He is remembered rather as an unselfish and generous man, aiding others instead of himself; and his record in this regard in the North Ohio Conference, of which he was so long a member, and which honored him by several successive elections to the General Conference, is without stain or reproach. We have taken the pains to inquire of those who would know the facts if he ever became solicitous concerning his election, or entered into close combinations, or formed questionable cliques to accomplish it, and the testimony is universal that he was free from these things. Moreover, it is affirmed that he did not shake hands with his brethren a little more cordially on the eve of an election, or pursue them months prior with small favors the object of which was to secure votes; but trusted in his merits, and was not forsaken. These things establish that a man can be whole-souled, generous, honest, appealing to his fitness for place, and the Providence over him, and win along that line. Place-seeking through suspicious methods and by art, in ecclesiastical bodies, is the sign of decay in religion, and the nervous expression of a dangerous selfishness.

We present Thomson as the representative of a *self-governed man,* a model character in balance. He was a vindication of Solomon's statement that "he that ruleth his own spirit is better than he that taketh a city." Man is a disorganized, revolutionary creature, always in conflict with himself until subdued by righteousness; out of harmony with the kingdom of God. Men are burning up and wasting away through the consuming power of internal conflict. The red-hot fires of passion irradiate their fearful glare over the temple of the soul and reduce it to ruins. Thomson belonged not to this class; he lived not on fire, nor on "bread alone;" he ruled his spirit by the plumb-line of truth, and walked in the light of the divine countenance. His body, designed to be the instrument of the soul, he kept in perfect order for the soul's uses, and disciplined it by the higher law. It lost not its sinew by passion or unchaste indulgence, by intemperance or hygienic violations. Delicately framed, and organized as flowers are organized, it was sensitive to physical surroundings, and was really too small for the great soul it had to carry. Hence, long too soon it gave way to the fatal stroke of disease. But the body was not a runaway

horse, not a steed that would not obey. Thomson
was master. In the realm of the soul there was the
same domination, and thought, affection, and purpose
had to respect the executive on the throne. He was
a calm spirit in full possession of power; noiseless,
but effective. He was not a whirlwind that wrecked
as it went on its errand, but a ray of light, soft, gentle, that painted all things with its own colors. He
was not, therefore, a nervous, fretful, peevish, or agitated man, either alone or in the presence of emer-
gencies, or with great duties resting upon him. He
did not dread the tax of a great problem, he did
not shrink from the performance of an imposing
duty. Without boasting, he felt himself conqueror,
and in the sweet consciousness of power he rested,
fearless of men, afraid only of God. By this quality
he was ordained for leadership, but leadership in the
highest sphere. With strife for leadership he had
no sympathy, nor for common magistracy had he
any taste; nor yet was he disposed to engage in conflict for its own sake, but only for the sake of truth.
He was non-combative in spirit, preferring quietness
to demonstration, peaceful arbitration of differences
to Chinese threatenings; which was interpreted as the
sign of conservatism, or a predisposition to weakness,
but it was misunderstood. He had a genius for ap-
prehending issues, but was slow in outward movement and aggression. This was owing to his caution
and habit of carefulness in preparation before he
assumed a position, and when the moment came for
action he was ready to strike with a Thor's hammer,
and the fragments indicated the completeness of his
execution. Conservatism of manner and radicalism

of faith joined in all his efforts. He disliked mere controversy, and avoided it. , Thersites was not on his list of friends. He was not an experimenter, or innovator, or iconoclast, but clung closely to well tried and efficient instruments, and was ever loyal to the truth, as he conceived it. Patience, therefore, was one of his graces. Charity bloomed in his garden, for he was not easily provoked, and suffered long, and was kind. Humility dignified his conduct and love enshrined his being. Possessing such virtues he was a very proper choice for the editorship of the *Ladies' Repository*, but some of his friends feared that sterner qualities were necessary for the stormy career in New York. The sequel proved that it was the mild-mannered editor rather than a Hotspur who was needed for that crisis, and he so conducted it that the general opinion prevailed that a wiser selection could not have been made. Like John, Thomson could write in the spirit of the Gospel of Christ, winning all hearts, but there were times when the Apocalypse burned in his soul, and he rained out thunderings and lightnings, opening seals, and producing earthquakes in the midst of his enemies. This was rare, but it was possible, and the lamb-like editor was let alone when he turned lion. Success under the trying ordeal in New York pointed him out as a suitable person for the higher office of the episcopacy.

But these qualities of which we have spoken were the satellites of the planet itself. His central spirit, the solid framework of his life, was *holiness*. He was pre-eminently a religious man, devout and reverent by instinct, worshipful and spiritual by regeneration and a love of duty, a Christian in the high art of practice, a saint in the memory of his friends. He was the subject of the one perfection of which Paul speaks in his Epistle to the Philippians, and was hoping to attain unto the other also. This it was that gave a glow to his character. He shone like Moses because he had been with God. Art would have painted him with a nimbus; the Roman Catholic Church would have canonized him along with Loyola and Sebastian. As to truth, he was absorptive; as to holiness, he was diffusive. He sent himself out, and others felt the power. Not that he was primarily, intuitively, or regeneratively faultless; for he was a man, and only at his best estate a redeemed man. But why tarry over weakness in the presence of greatness? Why criticise a masterpiece of art, a statue of Phidias, by pointing to a heel chipped off? Why speak of one feeble note in Mozart's symphonies and requiems? Why shout over a fly-speck on Raphael's canvas? Others may play hyena with the dead—we shall not.

Religion is the chief excellence of man. It is his power; it is his wealth. To stand in the likeness of God is man's noblest heritage; to be an ambassador for God a greater privilege than to be a minister to the court of kings. Such high positions, with their attendant responsibilities, Thomson appreciated, and never wavered in his allegiance to the Master who sent him. He was a rare spirit, an eschewer of evil, a hater of sin, a lover of righteousness, a jewel in the Master's crown. He had all the excellences of Plato's ideal man, the sincerity of Carlyle's original man, the naturalness of Emerson's great man; and, besides and above these, he measured up to the

Bible's standard of the good man, shining with virtues that did not grow dim with the years, and, dying, bequeathed to his race, country, and Church the priceless legacy of the memory of a character as bright as it was beautiful, as influential as it is imperishable.

THE END.